● **WINNER 2023 INDIEREADER DISCOVERY AWARDS**
FOR HISTORICAL FICTION

"The author's command of the mythology is magisterial—she deftly weaves together a tale that revolves around the commerce between gods and humans as well as a brewing civil war among the immortals."

—Kirkus Reviews

"This is a brilliantly written work. The descriptions, the style, and the depth of the characterizations are nothing short of amazing."
—Sublime Book Review

"The author delights with a meaty, gritty, mostly aromatic, wanton and undeniably intoxicating portrayal of the times."
—IndieReader

"Brillhart's beautifully rendered prose and measured, meticulously detailed narrative keep the reader turning pages nonstop."
—The Prairies Book Review

"A fascinating synthesis of traditional and contemporary storytelling in this reimagined tale of lust, power, and grief—one that will resonate just as readily with modern readers as it did millennia past in the agora."
—BookLife

"This beguiling novel is sure to appeal to fans of Homer's poem, who will enjoy the modern twist on familiar characters. But even those new to the story will be utterly charmed by Brillhart's novel—and eagerly await the sequels."
—BlueInk Review

A MOTHER'S
NATURE

The Rape of Persephone Series
Book 2

MONICA BRILLHART

First edition.

While all attempts have been made to verify the information provided in this publication, neither the author nor the publisher assumes any responsibility for errors, omissions, or contrary interpretations of the subject matter herein.

Quotations from the *Homeric Hymn to Demeter* (public domain) translated by Gregory Nagy. Full text available at https://uh.edu/~cldue/texts/demeter.html

Ferryman Press hardback edition ISBN: 978-1-7377991-8-4
Ferryman Press Amazon paperback edition ISBN: 978-1-7377991-5-3
Ferryman Press Ingram paperback edition ISBN: 978-1-7377991-7-7
Ferryman Press electronic edition ISBN: 978-1-7377991-6-0

Library of Congress Control Number: 2023908017

Cover photo © by IMG Stock Studio
Demeter sculpture located at estate of G. Galagan. Sokyryntsi village, Ukraine

This is a work of fiction. References to real people, events, and locales are intended only to provide a sense of authenticity and are used fictitiously. All other names, characters, places, and incidents either are the product of mythology, the author's imagination, or are used fictitiously. Any resemblance to persons living or dead is coincidental.

Ferryman Press, LLC

For Rowan,
my *kore*

CONTENTS

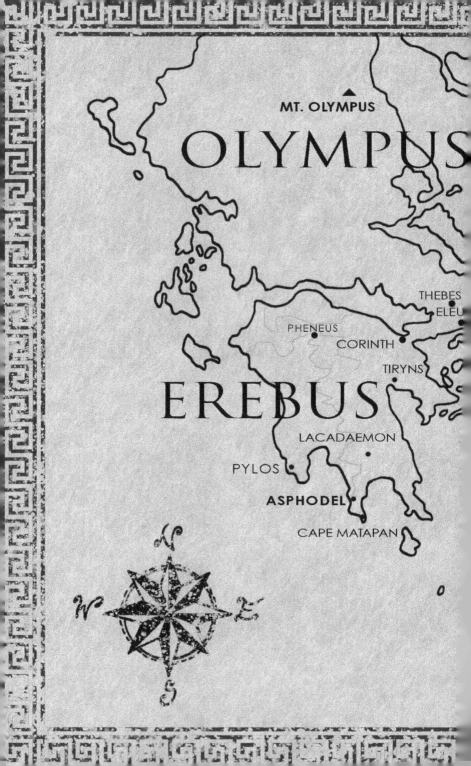

CYCLADES

CRETE

KNOSSOS

▲ MT. DIKTE

Foreword
by Robert Paxton

Until I began my own research into ancient Greece, I entertained very simplistic ideas about the gods of Greek mythology.

As a child in school, I had learned that Zeus was a fickle, philandering tyrant. Hera was a nag. Heracles was a thoughtless brute gifted only with incredible strength. Poseidon was a temperamental sea god. And so on.

And these mythical, static characters were backed up by rudimentary gods such as Hestia, the goddess of the hearth, Demeter the goddess of the harvest, or Hermes the messenger god. Deities who merely possessed names and domains over which they were responsible. Like cogs on some divine wheel, they were typically without personality in my conception of them.

In her developing trilogy, Monica Brillhart has reimagined one of the core myths of ancient Greece and brought these cookie-cutter gods to life. They have become more than chiseled icons of distant, past imaginations. They possess emotions, motives, regrets, desires.

Her work is based on *The Homeric Hymn to Demeter*. The source is perhaps unfamiliar to modern readers but the story behind it may ring a bell. This ancient text tells of Hades' abduction of Persephone, her mother's desperate search and the young goddess' return from the underworld.

In Brillhart's hands, the characters have become more than gods. They are living, breathing humans caught up in a tragedy of divine proportions.

Zeus is still a philanderer, but he is more politician than tyrant. Hades is a glowering overlord empowered with an unusually piercing insight into the human soul. Demeter is a proud priestess who fears for her child like any mother. And her daughter, Persephone, is a teenager like any you might know: naive, virginal, energetic, painfully ingenuous.

The author has accomplished this revivification of dead gods through more than just a sentimentalization of the received narrative. As a student of Greek history and pre-history myself, I am most impressed by the deep amount of research that she has done into these myths. As soon as I picked up the book and began reading, I knew that the writer had put in the hard work of learning about the setting of her story.

Here is bronze-age Crete and ancient Mycenae brought to life. It was the Minoan civilization on Crete and the Proto-Greeks on the mainland, some three or four thousand years ago, which probably generated much of the elementary material that constitutes the Greek myths which we remember today.

But just how greatly these civilizations influenced the later Greeks is hard to say: Much of what we have left of these cultures are a lot of unintelligible texts written with an indecipherable alphabet and a few figurines and pieces of colorful pottery. There is a stark statuette of a bare-breasted, snake-handling woman. And also a huge labyrinthine palace.

Brillhart has taken these mute relics and made them speak. She has translated the silent glyphs of an otherwise voiceless past.

But this is not a dry research text. Here the fragments and artifacts of the past speak in human voices, motivated by all the same emotions, passions and vices that have steered our lives since time immemorial: The heart-wrenching sorrow of a mother seeking her lost daughter, the fury and lust of the man who abducts that daughter before he becomes enamored of her, and the teenage Persephone, who braves the darkest hell while discovering her own soul and her sexuality.

Once upon a time, every myth was a good story for the people that heard it. Good stories speak to us in a way that academic texts cannot. In Brillhart's books, this myth has become a good story again. Like those silent relics of ancient Crete, this book in your hands has come to life, it speaks and tells a story both dark and inspiring, about a mother's nature.

Robert Paxton
The Western Traditions Podcast
June 9, 2023

A MOTHER'S
NATURE

CHARACTER REFERENCE

KORE (PERSEPHONE): the maiden

DEMETER: the mother

HECATE: the crone

HADES (THE UNSEEN, *THEÍOS*): High King of Erebus

ZEUS (THE LOUD THUNDERER): High King of Olympus

POSEIDON: High King of the Cyclades

MINOS: exiled king of Knossos, one of three judges for Hades

AEACUS: former mentor of Hades, one of three judges for Hades

RHADAMANTHUS: brother of Minos, one of three judges for Hades

HERACLES (ALCIDES): bastard son of Zeus

HERMES: messenger son of Zeus

CHARON: captain of the *Narcissus*

KING EURYSTHEUS: king of Tiryns who assigns the twelve feats to Heracles

HELIUS: titan turned god of the sun

OCEANUS: titan turned god of the earth-encircling river

GAIA: titan turned goddess of the earth

URANUS: titan turned god of the sky

CRONUS: titan turned god of destructive time and father of Zeus, Hades, and Poseidon

POTNIA: ancient Cretan goddess of nature

IASION: Pylosian captain

CERBERUS: collective name of Hades's three dogs, individually named Proí, Mesméri, and Nýchta

PART ONE
HIGH QUEEN OF EREBUS

So long as the earth and the star-filled sky
were still within the goddess's [Persephone's] view . . .
she still had hope that she would yet see
her dear mother . . .

—Homeric Hymn to Demeter

PROAULIA

1

Light falls upon the prison bed.

If not for the cold, Kore might mistake the cell for the womb. There has been no need to open her eyes. The world was just as black with them open.

He shut her away in this room beneath the ground. Hades, ruler of Erebus, beloved uncle, and captor.

Kore has not been here long. Not long enough to grow hungry or thirsty. She wept her lungs into spasms, and now the cries have stopped, the spasms stilled.

A male voice punctuates the silence.

"Persephone?"

This name means nothing to her. Kore replies with a voice worn ragged from screaming.

"Who calls me this?"

The rumpled man in the doorway is older than her uncle, but younger than two of the judges who counsel him: Judges Minos and Aeacus, the elderly purveyors of wisdom. He holds a torch above the level of his eye. She has never seen him before, yet he knows her somehow.

A look of horror hangs on his crinkled, raised-brow face.

With an unexpectedly youthful voice, he answers, "Persephone is the name given to you by your father."

Until now, she has not known this name existed. Mother called her Kore.

Young lady. This is all her "name" has ever meant, and the name-lack spared her that vain identity belonging to humans. She would not be a girl with willpower and desire, but a selfless gift for the gods, a virgin priestess. A *kore* is simply a girl of adolescent age, too young to know anything. Too trusting and innocent to run away.

A name brands her a Someone. A youth of sixteen with willpower and desires and purpose, qualities that make a person trouble for the gods.

Persephone likes it.

"I am Rhadamanthus, second judge of Erebus." His elegant himation, dyed the verdant green of forests, implies esteem and wealth, but the cloak is askew, disheveled hair a calico of orange and white and black.

"I am a friend." Judge Rhadamanthus extends his hand. "Let me help you."

Beastly shapes emerge on either side of him. The tops of their ears make the mastiffs as tall as the judge's shoulders. Her heart warms as the three dogs draw to the bedside. With large heads, they nudge her legs and hands so she will pet them. They want love. Love—now! Their need for it makes her suffering lost to them, and Persephone strokes them with steady hands that appear ghostly against dark haunches.

"Tch," the judge scolds the dogs. "Leave her."

"They love me so." Lazy tongued, she drifts beyond physical pain. In the aftermath of violence, her spirit seemed to detach from her body.

"The High King sends his dogs, Cerberus."

A gentle squeeze in the chest. The swelling in her sex returns.

Each beat of the heart pulsates there, shoving one memory to the forefront. Words whispered by the one who will soon be husband:

"Who claims you?"

"Which of these is Cerberus?"

"They answer as one."

She blinks slowly. "Is he angry?"

"Who?"

"My *theíos*."

Rhadamanthus creases his caterpillar brows.

"Is he still angry?" she asks with the honeyed lilt of a child. "With me?"

What Rhadamanthus sees when he looks at her, Persephone knows without seeing for herself. Mussed and knotted milk-and-honey hair. The gown sticks to the scabbed flesh on her back. Bruised fingerprints taint her shoulders. Toothmarks arch across the slope of her neck. She senses bruises under the buttocks and between the thighs. A guilty patch of blood and seed crusts the underside of a torn gown. Persephone tries not to wince.

So sorrowful his face! The kindly judge may even cry. She cannot stand it. She lies to him, sad-smiling and dreamy, saying:

"I am fine."

"Not true." Rhadamanthus advances with two slaves at his heels. They help her up. High in the groin stings a reminder of what was taken from her last night. The stalactite ceiling tilts from side to side. The sensation of twirling in place.

She turns her head and vomits water. The judge thrusts the torch into the hands of a slave. He scoops her up. When the open flesh on her back meets his arms, she flinches.

"I am sorry. Forgive me, young one."

Her mother used to warn her about the dangers of men, had spent her life trying to shield her from them.

"Keep to me, Kore. I will not let them hurt you."

The damos, citizens of Knossos, considered it a waste of a good bloodline to deprive Kore the chance at motherhood. But a life given to the gods is not wasted. Demeter, High Priestess, would not allow her child to be wasted or harmed. She protected her child until the child rose up, fled, and evaded the custody of the gods.

"Mother," Persephone whispers, an invocation.

Once inside her chamber, Rhadamanthus turns her over to an austere but grandmotherly slave. "Tomorrow, you will be High Queen of Erebus."

"This is the day of *proaulia*?" she asks, quivery in the knees.

Proaulia, a ceremonial day of matriarchs. An initiation into womanhood, conducted by one's mother and aunts and cousins and friends and neighbors, women brimming with loving tenderness. In Knossos, Persephone attended *proaulia* many times: day of nurturing ritual. Joyful day.

"Perhaps being without family has its virtues today." Rhadamanthus clears his throat and looks at the floor like a person caught in a lie. "You are in no condition for it. Look, instead, to your slaves. They will help you feel whole again."

Whole again.

She blushes deep into the belly. Her ears are hot.

It has happened. The thing from which her mother shielded her. *It.* The mysterious *it*, the forbidden *it*, the hurtful *it*. The *it* belonging to lovers. Is that what they are—lovers? For whatever happened, it felt uninspired by love. More so, like a slap.

A slap can be gratifying too, if you are the one who dealt it.

One slave drizzles jasmine oil into the bath while another fusses, motioning from Persephone's bled-through gown to the hot water. In answer, the oil-drizzler puts aside the fragrance and pours cool water into the bath so as not to scald her wounds.

"May I do anything else for you, dear Persephone?"

The judge tests the water with one hand and flicks it away. He checks that the three dogs have settled in and searches for another way to be of service.

"Find my mother for *proaulia*," she hears herself say.

"Where can my little ghost be?"

"I am here. Your little ghost is here."

The judge looks at his hands. "I will leave you to rest now."

As he hurries off, Persephone starts to ask again—*Please, is* Theíos *still mad at me? Will he love me now?*—and finds herself too listless to speak above a mew.

The slave drizzling oil looks to be about her age, with a weak chin and unusually long neck and brows that unite above a hawkish nose. The fussier one is as old as Judge Minos, round and squat as the goddess Gaia. Although Persephone has seen them from time to time, neither speaks her tongue and recoil fearfully when she asks them the simplest questions. Slaves cycle in and out of the palace. Faces, ever changing.

Persephone accepts these detached women who are supposed to replace her mother. Replace friends.

So as not to cause further skin-tearing, the slaves lower her into the bath with her gown adhering to the scabs on her back. They grimace in sympathy as if their own backs are tender.

The water stings her broken skin. The women lift the gown over her head, raining pink on her face and shoulders.

They bathe her. Perfume her. Her hair is washed clean, tangles picked with a comb made of polished bone. They tend to the abrasions on the backs of her arms and shoulder blades.

Today: *proaulia*, the day before marriage.

In Knossos, the women would feast. Persephone would collect relics of her childhood: the doll of muslin stuffed with hay, the marbles, the tunic from her first procession. Together with the women of the family, she would burn away her childhood.

They would honor the end of her maidenhood in ceremony, as all lifetime passages should be honored.

Here, the slaves do their best. They bring food, which she devours with hunger that sparks as soon as she smells the salt of the olives, the sharpness of cheese, the savory meat. She chokes on undiluted wine. Persephone drinks more, faster. Her stomach heats as the wine trickles from the corner of a lip made puffy from a man's biting and suckling.

"Who claims you?"

She shudders. No. Think instead:

Proaulia. A day that demands ritual—glorified habits that focus the mind. She must focus hers, lest fear consume her.

"I need a blade," she tells the slaves and gestures as if to cut. She takes a candle and points at a clay pot under the bedside table. The younger slave fetches it and places it on the floor while Persephone rips at the muslin on the mattress and yanks out hay and leaves. Dry. Good for kindling.

The older slave returns. With upturned palms, she presents a dagger.

Persephone takes it.

Most of the rituals, she cannot complete. There is no Mother here. No toys to burn. Only one ritual remains.

Persephone sits cross-legged on the floor and lines the pot with leaves and hay. The slaves stand, hands folded in front of them. Do they show respect only because slaves must? Do they revere holy practices?

Persephone bites the inside of her jaw to keep from crying in want for her mother.

Before *proaulia*, girls go their lives without cutting their hair. She pulls it over one shoulder, twists, and saws at sun-bright locks.

Childhood is stubborn. It fights to stay around. She urges the blade back and forth. Steel rips through each strand. The hair on her head tumbles over her shoulders and brushes the nipple. She raises the severed rope to drop her sacrifice into the flames.

The coil darkens to bronze inside her hand.

The younger slave steps back. The other whispers foreign words—a prayer to gods unknown to Persephone—but prayers for certain.

Persephone supposes she has noticed the change. But subtle changes happen, as when a girl's body changes from a child's body into a woman's body. It is natural, this change.

The hair inside her grip looks as she remembers it in Crete. Not as it looks now with this golden goddess sheen.

Mother once told her:

"For weeks after your birth, people thought you were such an ugly baby—you! Ha! Pure white, no hue in your skin or hair. A little fluff of dandelion with arms and legs. My little ghost."

With a chill, Persephone drops the hair into the flames. The flames spark and smoke. The odor of burnt hair fills the space.

Her heart flutters wildly.

As she stares at her fingers, her hands shake. Yes, her skin too. She has not imagined the pallor—skin once bronze now glows a pretty gold. Sun lack, surely. Fire darkens meat. The god Helius darkens flesh. Too much time now, spent in darkness.

It is all quite natural.

Persephone raises the blade to her face. It feels heavy all of the sudden.

Her eyes should be brown because they have always been brown. The eyes of Kore.

A mirror of steel reflects the color hazel.

SAILING SHIPS

2

In the wee hours, the mother recalls words of prophecy. Only yesterday, a priest uttered with dying breath:

"I begin to sing of Demeter, the holy goddess with the beautiful hair.

And her daughter, Persephone, too.

The one with delicate ankles

Whom Hades seized."

To lose a child is the very worst thing. A mother cannot fathom a more terrible thing.

The crone had sworn this prophecy unfolded before her eyes. Ailing from the wreckage, Kore had landed in good hands. Cared for, coaxed from death by a medicine woman with a penchant for plants.

If not for the chariot of Hades, Kore would still be in the arms of her mother. Instead, she was stolen away and handed over to Zeus, who must be smugly scheming a match with whichever husband has the most to offer.

At the southernmost point of the mainland, Cape Matapan stretches into sea. Demeter can see the port from this vantage. Spotted light from torches litters the coastline like fireflies.

Something about those torches makes Demeter uneasy.

It is a cold morning, before the god Helius rides his fiery chariot over the eastern horizon. The sun god acts as his own herald. He announces his arrival through the blue brightening of the eastern sky. Soon, Helius will crest and spill light over mortal land and sea.

The mouth of Hecate's cave flickers orange-yellow. The old woman emerges with two torches soaked in lime and sulfur, keeping their flames alive until sun-up. Deep lines run along the corners of her mouth. One tiny eye glints black, the other is covered with a film of blue-white. Her hair is the color of metal, sheared into wild tufts about her head. Her nose is a falcon's beak.

Demeter looks to the coast. "Is that unusual?"

"Is what unusual?"

Demeter nods toward the port, under construction since the day the earth opened. A tidal wave had devoured the banks, the ships, and the men who sailed them. "So much activity before dawn?"

"Someone plans to sail, gods permitting," Hecate says. "Pray your captain is not among them."

Hecate flings two satchels over her neck, diagonal from each shoulder. Demeter carries the same otter-skin bags around her torso. The skins travel well by sea, water-guarding their supply of lentils, dried figs, honey, and brown bread. Demeter adjusts them, turns, and hoists the skirt of her cloak as she negotiates a shrub and steps onto the path.

"He is not *my* captain," Demeter says.

"He brought you here, did he not?"

"Yes."

"Then?" With a shrug and skip, Hecate quickens the pace. Morning lends the old woman plenty of vigor. No stoop in her spine, no frailty. These days, a constant fatigue slows Demeter down. She has felt this way since Kore vanished.

"Hustle, lady mother, hustle," Hecate calls, leaving Demeter to inhale the smoke from her torch. "Your captain, Iasion, is our guide to Olympus."

"What makes you so sure?" Demeter hustles, but not for the sake of the captain. Every time the crone brings him up, Demeter reminds her: He is the captain of a trade ship, sailing for Pylos today. In fact, one of the torches at port might, indeed, belong to him.

Yet Demeter hustles because Hecate is not a forgetful woman. The crone's mind is whip-sharp.

"He is special," Hecate insists.

"How?"

Hecate ducks to avoid a low-hanging branch, holding her torch away from wayward tree-limbs. "What makes Iasion special," she says, "is that he does not believe he *is* special."

"How do you know that? You have never met him."

Hecate clucks a laugh and glances over her shoulder. "Far too familiar are you with men who *think* they are special. And you have no tolerance for them. I see it in you."

"Is that right?" Demeter says with a half-smile. The Zeuses and Poseidons of the world think men should lick their feet for being exemplary and women should spread their legs without question. These entitlements make a "special" man insufferable.

Iasion is an ordinary man made humble by loss. All the same, he has a duty to deliver goods to Pylos—a duty that Hecate believes is negotiable. Demeter remains doubtful about that.

As the sky brightens, it does so weakly. Clouds roll in, dimming the light of Helius's rays.

Coastal wind can be a brutal thing. Today is no different. The women carry packs with extra blankets and robes. Perhaps they should be more cautious about travel during the onset of winter. Demeter is not blind to this. Neither is she blind to limitations that go along with Hecate's age, or that two women traveling alone, no matter their age, make easy prey. Demeter is not blind, just resolute. Once a woman bears a child, she forgets herself. No past suffering and no future risks are too great.

Her thighs burn from the steepness of the incline. Demeter keeps her head down to guarantee safe footing. Hecate quick-steps around every crater and stone, adapting to a familiar path.

They are a valley away from the shore when the first ship sets sail. Demeter stops, breathing hard. Her cheeks are high with color that rivals the pink dawn.

"It is too late." She peers at the second ship gliding off to sea. At this distance, it is hard to determine which is Iasion's. Disappointment sours her stomach.

"Piddle." Hecate throws a glance over her shoulder at Demeter. "Keep moving."

Demeter has forced herself along by sheer determination. How much willpower and strength remain? Sometimes she feels she could collapse and sleep forever. Finding Hecate is beyond a blessing. Hecate will spur her along like a tired horse. She will be the voice of wisdom in times of hopelessness. Although the hope Demeter feels now is more hope than she has felt thus far, it is a frail hope.

For months, Kore has been in her father's custody. Much can happen in that time.

Coming upon a narrow creek, Hecate lowers her torch into the water. It hisses, extinguished, but the crone refuses to slow. She slides the dry end of the torch into one of her satchels and hops across a line of stones that provide dryer footing. Demeter follows.

A grassy field divides them from the hill. Wind rustles between blades of yellow and green, grass so sharp it thinly slices her arms and ankles. Hecate finds a trampled path, formed by the tread of

man and beast. At the top of their climb, land juts to sea. A third
ship sails. The first ship catches wind inside two billowing sails
and becomes a distant, westward blot. Judging by the bulbous
underbelly, it holds cargo. Two other ships follow, neither relying
solely upon wind. The triremes are designed to go fast, manned by
fifty oarsmen. They gain upon the cargo ship.

One ship remains. Black sails, blanched by the sun. It also
holds cargo. Demeter knows because that is how she got here.
With Iasion, on that ship.

"Is that his ship?"

Demeter cannot believe her eyes. Hecate was right—one ship
remains, and it belongs to Iasion.

"Yes," Demeter answers. They come to a wide clearing.
Rocks give way to sand. The road to the east leads to another hill
where the polis of Matapan clusters into a series of clay buildings.
The temple is there, as is the agora, the merchants. But they are
not going that way. Today, their mission is at port.

In the months since that day—the day the earth opened, and
Kore vanished—the workers of Matapan have toiled to restore
breakwaters so the ships can bank safely. Rubble and ashlar
blocks, adhered with lime and clay mortar, comprise walls that
stretch their arms out to sea, until the ships are protected from the
strong body of Oceanus. The women hurry there.

Demeter had not considered how to ask for Iasion's help
again. "Wait," she pants, fingers pressed into the stitch in her side.

"Wait?" Hecate asks, nowhere near as winded.

She needs to think. Just a moment to think.

"Speak from here," Hecate tells her, beating one gnarled hand
to her breast.

Iasion's ship is not far. The tattered threads of the rear sail
catching in the wind. A ramp ascends from shore to deck. Several
oarsmen approach it, placing calloused hands on each side.

Aboard deck, a bald head catches light from the sun. Iasion's body resembles a brown egg. Demeter is surprised to find him bare-chested on such a cold morning.

He spots her, waves, and comes to the edge of the ship.

The oarsmen prepare to remove the ramp. If they remove it, the vessel will sail and, with it, her chance of a faster and easier journey to Olympus.

Demeter waves urgently. Iasion hollers something, but she cannot hear him.

Seeing them approach, Iasion bellows to the oarsmen, and they stop dismantling the ramp so he can disembark.

"I said, 'You found the one you were looking for.'" Iasion nods at Hecate, who cranes her neck to a man three heads taller than she. The cleft lip distorts one side of his nose, pulling it flat. The hair on his back is as thick and tightly curled as the hair on his chest. As he nears them, he pulls a tunic over his head.

"By the gods, you are as big as an ox," Hecate blurts.

Elders find freedom in blurting. It is a privilege paid by burden of living so long. Demeter shoots her a look of consternation. Hecate pretends not to notice, and when Iasion laughs his belly rises and falls beneath linen.

"And what news of your *kore*?"

Demeter looks at her feet and gives her head a shake. "She is not here. But I know where she is."

"Where is that?" he asks.

"Mount Olympus."

Iasion would never help her locate a child of Zeus. This is the part Hecate does not understand. One of Zeus's sons ravaged his city, and Iasion lost his wife and seven children in the invasion. Why would he help some strange woman find yet another menace-making spawn?

"Why," he says, narrowing eyes that shift from mother to

crone, "would your daughter be in Mount Olympus?"

Before Demeter can mince words, Hecate blurts again:

"Because she is the daughter of Zeus! The Unseen knew it when he took her and aimed to send her north."

His deep olive complexion turns a lighter shade. "What is this she says?"

"Y-yes." She understands how Kore might have developed her stutter—unsure of herself, afraid of saying the wrong thing. Demeter peers off at the rising sun, squinting one eye and shielding the other. Her face burns scarlet. "I bore a daughter by Zeus. He abandoned me without ever laying eyes on her. She is mine and mine alone. And I will have her back."

Iasion takes in a contemplative breath and plants his hands on his hips. On that ship, he had confided in her about the massacre of his family, and she had not been equally forthcoming.

"Well," he says, turning his attention back to the ship, "may the gods grant your wish. Blessings to you, Priestess. My men await."

He turns to go.

Hecate says, "Perhaps you can save the gods the effort."

"What?"

"Why wait for the gods to bless us? We have already been blessed—with *you*."

"Me?"

"No," Demeter whispers, taking the old woman by the arm. "Come let us go—"

"—Go?" blurts Hecate. "What for? We need a boat, and the captain has one. Why would we go?"

"You want me to take you to Mount Olympus," Iasion states, incredulous.

"Ah, many thanks," Hecate grins. "We accept."

"Ladies," Iasion says, gesturing to the northeast, "*that* is the way to Olympus." Next, he points to the three boats that grow smaller as they sail westward. "*That* is where I sail."

Hecate shrugs, "We can wait. If we sail with you to Pylos and make our way to Olympus afterward, we will still arrive sooner than without the aid of your fine ship."

Iasion manages a weak, disbelieving laugh and shakes his head. "My orders changed as of last night. We no longer sail to Pylos."

"Orders?" Hecate says, "But who orders a captain?"

"This ship does not belong to me," he explains. "It is the property of King Nestor of Pylos, and I've been instructed to provide passage for all available nobility here in Matapan."

"Passage to where?" Demeter asks.

"Asphodel."

"Asphodel?" Hecate frowns. "Why?"

Iasion shakes his head. "I am a captain. If you want news, ask a messenger."

Hecate opens her mouth for rebuttal, and Iasion cuts her off. "My orders are to deliver Matapan nobility to Asphodel and return them home after seven days' time. Then we sail for Pylos. I would like to help you, but this ship will dock at Pylos, and it will stay there until King Nestor has other business for it. It is not my ship to take."

Demeter swallows and gives a false smile to show she is not as disappointed as she feels. "Iasion, of course we understand."

Hecate issues a "hmph" under her breath.

"Hecate is my travel companion," Demeter offers, as if this explains the old woman's investment in the matter.

Iasion's face registers doubt—a tiny flash of the eye—but Demeter catches it. So does Hecate.

"*You* are?" he says. "With respect, how old are you?"

Secretly, Demeter has wondered the same. Travel takes a toll on even the most able-bodied person.

Bundled in her cloak, Hecate lifts a fuzzy chin. Waggling a crooked finger, she tells Iasion, "I have kept myself alive for more years than anyone else I know. Likely twice the number you will, Captain. Come climb the hill to my cave and see which of us loses our breath first."

An oarsman calls out from the ship. Iasion waves in his direction.

"Iasion, you have been a tremendous service by taking me this far," Demeter says. "For this, you will always have my gratitude."

Iasion's full mouth tightens. He starts to speak, rethinks his words, and finally turns to leave.

"Farewell, Priestess," he hollers as he walks away. "I wish you well."

Demeter's stomach sours. As Iasion disappears aboard, the oarsman slide the ramp away.

"No matter." Heading to the road leading to the polis of Matapan, Hecate's sandals crunch against sand and stone. "Come. There is another who will help."

Demeter follows in silence.

The distant vessels disappear over the horizon, bound for the land of the Unseen.

The Mastiffs Tattle

3

Cerberus whines.

The mastiffs must sense her panic rising—or so Persephone thinks, at first. She has been pacing the afternoon away, wearing a smudged path on an otherwise high-polished floor. Watching as the light shifts outside.

Closer and closer, nightfall.

It is impossible to sit still on the evening before *gamos*.

When the three mastiffs of Hades whine, they also begin to pace. In strange circles, they weave around each other, as if braiding their anxiety. Golden eyes aglow, they waggle stubby tails and watch her, expectant.

"What is it?"

The one with the white patch shifts from leg to leg.

There, in the corner behind them, a pair of eyes. Larger, more slitted than mortal eyes, they beam down from high in the corner shadow.

Persephone nearly feels her bladder release. Her skin washes cold, hairs standing on gooseflesh.

She knows this thing.

Down in the darkness of Tartarus, it appeared to her. When the last of the candles fizzled out, the thing stayed with her throughout the night, the touch of its hand like static, tingly and soft, almost mortal; yet she knew it was not mortal, nor was it a shade, as Sisyphus had been a shade.

In some peculiar way, it seemed there to comfort her.

The eyes pull forward, out of shadow. The shoulders of the figure emerge, body glinting with distant stars.

"Wh-what do you want?"

It looms closer, extending a hand to her face. The hair on her arms rises.

Persephone does not budge. There is neither warmth nor coldness in this touch, but rather a fuzzy prickling to her cheek. She blushes at the intimacy.

The dogs let out another throaty whine. Their voices mingle like a song.

The figure dissolves into a fluid-like shape that aims for the doorway and flies out as would a crow.

Cerberus follows it. Persephone trails on bare feet. In single file, the mastiffs trot along. Torches pop and crackle, throwing rays across the corridor.

The entrance to the staircase yawns its square yellow mouth. How narrow, these stairs, these walls. During the night, they seemed to close in like a vice.

From here, she hears men shouting.

A smooth, precision-squared banister runs along her right side. It overlooks a wide space with limestone floors. On her left are a series of windows which start at waist level and go to the ceiling.

The cries of men louden. Cerberus pauses at the window.

On snow-powdered grass, naked men fill the courtyard. The cold turns their flesh a mean-looking red. Bloody tracks run toward the steep decline at the north side.

Two men crest the hill. An animal carcass weighs upon each

of their shoulders. They trudge into the courtyard, dropping their carcasses, and collapse with chests heaving. Blood oozes from their knees from where they have tripped along the way.

Others follow suit. They stagger up the hill. A limp calf drapes over each of their shoulders. Their necks strain against the pressure. Their knees threaten to buckle, and one succumbs to the pressure. He falls to his knees and hollers in pain.

Persephone puts a hand over her mouth. "The guards—"

This morning, the slaves hobbled as they bathed her. They winced with every twist and turn.

"Oh no." She turns to Cerberus. Pink tongues loll between incisors.

One thing she knows: every guard in Asphodel is assigned a mastiff. Yet, there are no mastiffs in the courtyard, and there are no mastiffs inside except the three staring at her.

"Where are the rest of the dogs?"

At this, the white-patched mastiff throws back his head and half-growls, half-barks. On his flat-muzzled face, jowls work as though forming words.

Urging her to follow.

The last time Hades stood beneath these vined arches, the monument of Sisyphus perched upon its pedestal. The marble likeness immortalized Hades's first ruling as High King of Erebus.

Today, red dirt shows in its place.

One might say it had sentimental value: a man-sized statue of the tyrant king, eternally striving to prevent a boulder from crushing him to death.

Evidence of the crime remains. The slaves got most of the rubble, but marble grit sifts between frozen yellow grass and collects there. The slaves had a flogging for their part in it. A worse punishment, Hades decided against. There is no utility in an incapacitated slave.

Grass crunches under his boots. Black lashes collect droplets, and the dead-leafed garden shimmers. Wind burns his nose and brings moisture to his eyes.

Since morning, the sky has opened in intervals. Clouds come and go, carrying mist that freezes as the temperature plummets. The cold white sun withholds affection from the earth.

Familiar footsteps stagger nearby.

"Every time a mastiff is bred," says his old mentor, "a trainer encounters the same set of problems."

Hades keeps his eyes on the barren square where the monument used to be.

Judge Aeacus limps beneath the arch. "A mastiff is born wild and aimless. It is hungry to be led. It needs training in order to live in union with the pack. A firm hand, not out of cruelty, but out of natural law. We all must learn to thrive wherever we happen to end up."

Hades bristles. "Not all creatures thrive this way."

The first bride of Hades, Leuce, was bound to him by marriage days before the start of the Titan War. Could he remember her face today, a face he saw a handful of times, a lifetime ago? He conjures her image through a haze of non-definition. Black hair, blurry-faced, body a pear-shaped silhouette.

She slipped over the cliff's edge and brought about her own death. A sickness of the mind, they had said. The news reached Hades almost a full year after the act itself.

He shed no tears over it. By then, countless brothers-in-arms had died in battle. He knew them better. Mourned them better.

The lustrous face of Persephone burns clear in his mind.

"Rhadamanthus has retrieved the girl, as you ordered," Aeacus says. "You can stop pitying her."

The bare ground is a reminder that he has done nothing wrong. There is no reason for him to feel this way. For every action, there is a consequence. Hades must stand by the punishments he gives.

"She is Persephone, as named by Zeus," says Hades. "You know what happens tomorrow."

"*Gamos*," Aeacus scoffs.

Tomorrow, Zeus, the self-proclaimed King of Kings, cannot complete the traditional task of ushering a reluctant bride from his fatherly home to the home of the groom. From Olympus to Erebus? That is quite a walk. And Hades, a groom at this age? Younger men have been grandfathers. This juvenile role is one

Hades prefers to carry out in seclusion. He thinks about the embroidered silk set for wear the day of *gamos* tomorrow, white on white, as if beginning holy-anew. When the slaves presented his robes, he had wanted to toss them into the fire.

All of it—pageantry.

Despite the untraditional circumstances, Judge Rhadamanthus believes in humoring the Cretan girl's homespun ways and adhering to tradition "to make her feel at home." Rhad is normally right about these things.

"No respectable king takes a soiled prisoner into the day of *gamos*," Hades says. "He takes with him a powdered, adorned nymph."

"I suppose we will see if your Persephone learned her lesson," Aeacus grumbles, "or if she will have us mauled to death by enchanted dogs."

Under a heavy brow, Hades studies the glow surrounding the man who once raised him like a son.

Every man has a glow. Every woman and child. Beasts glow in simpler shades, but still they glow.

With no effort, Hades can detect the sickly glow of green surrounding a man and interpret the emotion of guilt.

Yet none of the judges experience guilt.

Judge Aeacus has not considered himself deserving of punishment. Why would the boy Aeacus once fostered have the gall to punish him? It would denote a lack of respect; however, the judges did watch as the girl, a mere *kore,* ordered the mastiffs to uproot the statue. They did nothing as slaves and guards demolished it with mallets.

Nevertheless, it was the *kore* who, in his absence, took liberties that were not hers to take. One night in the caves will correct the chance of future transgressions. He was right to do it.

Except.

As soon as he jailed his broken child-bride within Tartarus and retreated to the buzzing silence of his room, the *feeling* crept in.

Hades is unacquainted with this feeling, struggles to stamp it out with reasoning.

The girl did not fight him. Cried and screamed, but did not fight.

She clung to him as he took her.

Now Hades remembers the damning words he hurled at Sisyphus all those years ago:

"A man prone to violence finds it easier to kill than show mercy. A thief finds more ease in stealing than in giving. It is a burden to reject your nature. To starve it into submission and to be, instead, a man of honor."

"What about the guards?" Aeacus asks. "Have they endured enough or are you waiting for their toes to chip off?"

As the weather sours, it becomes increasingly miserable outside. Hades knew this when he ordered the guards to strip off their clothes, gather in the courtyard, and line up in front of the carcasses of slaughtered calves.

"They are from Lacedaemon," Hades says. "They have suffered this before."

As babies, the boys of Lacedaemon were washed in wine and examined for health. Their worth was appraised early. The puny ones were abandoned at the foot of Mount Taygetos. Left to the elements, the weak would die. The strong were sorted by the age of seven, herded off in groups to be trained and supervised. They grew up underfed, naked.

But war and hunger go hand-in-hand—they must get used to it. Their mentor would starve them a while, rile them up, and throw scraps to see which boy would fight hardest for survival. Food thieves endured lashes from whips made of leather and jagged lead.

Over time, their naked feet developed callouses and numbed to sharp things underfoot. Their bodies became sensitized to the cold. Pain was part of enjoying the privilege of food.

All this, before *agoge*, their formal training as soldiers.

"One of them took a tumble while lugging that beast downhill. Says he cannot feel his legs." Aeacus adds, "And his gut is turning purple."

With Aeacus, these statements can be a test, to remind Hades that mercy and weakness are bedfellows.

This is a different sort of test. "*She* is no more deserving of your pity," Aeacus says.

There is truth in the statement, but it strikes a discordant note all the same.

Hades is oddly attached to the notion of a young woman belonging to him. Not just any woman, but the beautiful, blossoming, sunny child of Zeus.

His.

Zeus bled his child away with a swift cut of a knife against the palm and then shook on it; it was as easy as that. Then, Persephone became both Hades's possession and responsibility, and when he awoke this morning, it was with a lusty sense of satisfaction, followed by the dreamlike memory of what had happened the night before.

He had come home after the cycle of a moon and found the caves of Tartarus empty of prisoners. Empty because *she* had freed them.

Hades found chaos and acted in response. He had not planned for it to end that way.

"Needs training in order to live in union with the pack."

Training. Just like dogs and slaves. Like the guards.

In the past, joys of the flesh included the vibrations of the soul housed within that flesh. In Persephone, there was no contamination of bliss. When he forced his way inside of her, he felt a hum of euphoria, tipsy delirium from an innocent who offered release alone and nothing else to wreck it.

Without the bad, he could hardly bear the good. When the jagged wall scraped his knuckles, pain distracted him from falling too drunk. The wall tore knees that divided Kore's parted legs. His forearms, bearing some of the impact, stung and bled and pulled him back to the familiar world of pain.

Hades supposes the guards have atoned. Soon, the light of Helius will disappear beyond a watery horizon. They were dragged from their beds before the sun rose and have been in the open courtyard, naked in the freezing wind ever since.

"We should discuss the fate of Tartarus," Aeacus says.

Hades shoulders past the judge. "Guard it better."

Aeacus is short, sturdy like the trunk of a tree. His hair hangs past the shoulders, silver and thinly coarse. As he squints at the rush of sleet, his face folds into hound-like creases.

If Hades cannot avoid the nagging, perhaps he can leave the man too winded to form a sentence. Aeacus struggles to keep the pace.

"Your severity sets you apart from other kings," Aeacus says. "*Tartarus* sets you apart from other kings. Or it used to."

This tactic is aimed to stop him. Hades keeps walking. The judge's words are loaded with an agenda that Hades has no patience for today.

He makes his way alongside a long rectangular pool frozen over in patches. It is unsettling to walk around without the company of Cerberus. His three-headed shadow, missing.

The mastiffs act as an offering of peace. Rhad's idea. The tender-hearted ways of Judge Rhadamanthus sometimes wear at Hades's nerves, but he needs a man like this. The colors of

Rhadamanthus show proudly and honorably and, thus, secure the judge's advisory position.

As they zig and zag their way through the narrow walls, Aeacus says, "We must approach the Erinyes."

"The Erinyes?"

"Yes."

"What for?"

"Because—" Minos appears from the entrance of the central courtyard. "Judge Aeacus fears Tartarus may not hold the terror it once did, and the Erinyes can restore it."

"Tartarus lacks no terror."

The monoliths of Cerberus divide Asphodel from the tribe of the Erinyes. Though they perch in riverside trees while hunting for food and have been spotted on occasion, the tribe keeps their distance well beyond the river. A savage group, they dwell in relative isolation and lash out at trespassers. Segregation acts as an effective peacekeeping measure.

Those who have defied this boundary seldom escape. The ones who have escaped attest to the same thing:

The Erinyes are ruthless torturers.

Judge Minos cocks his chin and takes in a cleansing breath through his nose, as a man might do when seeing the light of day after being confined indoors. His mushroom nose glows from the cold, hair as white-gray as the clouds above.

"The day of the ceremony," says Minos, "the grounds were sanctified."

It rings true. Upon Hades's return, there was a lightness in Asphodel where none existed before. Hades finds an excuse anyway. "She prayed, brandished her arms, and burned incense. Throw in an animal sacrifice and the destruction of a sacred monument, and it must have been impressive."

"Our Persephone is child to a High Priestess," says Minos.

"The gods are her lifeblood."

"She is a child of Zeus," Hades says. "Creating spectacles is also her lifeblood."

An ethereal light flares around Aeacus. As Hades catches it, the same light flares around Minos.

This quality of light surrounds Persephone and makes her irresistible to man and dog.

"What is this spark I see around you?"

"I have no suitable description," Minos says. "See it yourself."

Hades creases his brow. There must be a reason for Minos to accede to this. After all, it hurts a man to be inspected by the Unseen. Their eyes bleed. It is certainly not an affliction a man asks for. Despite the urge to peek from time to time, Hades has never intruded upon their minds without consent.

"Are you sure?"

With a grim smile, Minos extends both palms in a gesture of service.

To avoid inflicting too much injury, Hades opts to look quickly. He is quicker than he intends. Within moments, his own eyes begin to sting and water. Even when viewed through someone else's lens, the light pains him.

He sees enough. Kore at the altar, the sacrificial animal cooking on the fire. He sees her spilling ceremonial wine into the flames, the dogs pulling on the chains affixed to them and the monument of Sisyphus.

When the flash comes, Hades squeezes his eyes closed to ease the sting. Vessels rupture regardless.

"Majesty?" Aeacus frowns.

The judges stand before him, but Hades does not see the judges. Does not hear the judges.

He hears, instead, a screech. He hears the boulder crunching its way down the hill and crushing the condemned tyrant. The downfall of Sisyphus seems to magnify in space and this ceaseless motion unfastens from this world and vanishes.

Shadows and light fly from the palace. Hardened soldiers drop to the ground in terror. Slaves cry out and wrap their arms over their heads, shielding themselves from the magnificence.

A red droplet fattens in the corner of Hades's eye and runs down his cheek. He has only ever experienced this pain when examining the daughter of Zeus.

Now it happens when examining someone who has simply beheld her.

Minos lowers his chin, squeezing the bridge of his nose with two fingers. He dabs at the blood beneath his eyes.

Before Hades releases him from scrutiny, the voice of a nameless god proclaims to his future bride:

"And while you are here, you shall rule all that lives and moves and shall have the greatest rights among the deathless gods."

"Zeus's girl is not as powerless as you hoped," Aeacus says. "You must rein her in."

Persephone sees the dead. He has known it for some time. This is her burden, just as he has a burden.

Hades is not shocked by her powerlessness.

He is shocked by her fearlessness. Shocked that these tortured spirits bent to her will.

Persephone is no little girl running from ghosts in the night and begging for protection.

Hades rubs sweaty palms against the sides of his black himation and shakes his head.

"Majesty?" Minos inquires.

"You saw it then," Aeacus hisses. "How is Tartarus now, eh? Freshly purged cells, done up nicely with beds and food and blankets—"

Hades slips around Aeacus, saying to Minos, "Go lie down. Your head will ache a while."

His heart trips in his chest. Seared into his mind is the golden image of his new pet and plaything. For that is all she is—a plaything, not a weepy love or prophesied goddess.

From the mouth of the corridor running the length of the palace echo the nearby cries of men pushed to their breaking point.

Hades storms into an open courtyard where the guards atone for their sins. In his ears, the giant whoosh-beat of his heart. Open-mouthed, he clouds the air with heavy breath and squints through sleet.

The men are too preoccupied to notice him.

There are a few shy of one hundred, with ten dead calves among them. Not all were present when Persephone made mischief, but if one suffers, they all suffer. There is no greater social recourse than the wrath of a fellow guard who was punished for no good reason.

The collective glow of these guards is that of suffering. Any other emotion was exhausted long ago.

Blue, black, red, the colors of suffering.

A guard bends at the waist and unburdens a dead calf that hits the ground with a thump.

When he spots Hades, his face drains. He falls to his knees, panting. The others do the same, pressing their noses to the ground in supplication. Hades walks between them and toward the farthest end of the yard.

A man lies between the pillars. His head rests on a sack of grain, arm draped across his stomach. Violet beneath wiry strands of hair, his gut distends.

The physician brings a reed pipe to the fallen man's lips. An offering of opium poppy from Sumerian trade.

Hades approaches. The dying guard glows gray-black. Death

is certain, but the glow is bright, and, thus, he will linger a while. His pupils are so small they nearly disappear into the brown of his half-closed eyes.

Hades regards the sea of bowed heads.

"I understand while I was away the gods came to call. As pious men, you responded to the gods in supplication. There is virtue in this."

An involuntary moan comes from the fallen guard. The joy plant sends him into a stupor.

"You believe in death, but there is none."

Hades presses into the black glow, allowing the man's dilated eyes to seep blood while his short, mundane life rushes by in a matter of moments. The stuff streams from his nose and ears. He convulses, then ceases.

"Your life is eternal," Hades says, "as mine is eternal. As my judgment is eternal. You answer to me in life, and you will answer to me in death."

When Hades turns, the sea of faces are raised to him. Their jaws are slack, eyes to the ground in fear of scrutiny.

"Remember who I am."

At the mouth of the corridor, Judge Aeacus stands in shadow, arms folded, smirking.

And dismissing the men, Hades uses the opposite corridor to depart.

SEEING HIM
5

They lead her out of the palace and into the cold. Barefoot and uncloaked, Persephone clutches her arms. Sleet flies into her eyes, stinging her cheeks. Her hair is frosted with it.

The open corridor hugs the side of the palace, lined by grooved, shafted columns with square bases crafted of red jasper. They buffer some of the weather, but Persephone shakes, and her teeth rattle from the cold.

At the southwest corner, Cerberus steps away from the portico and onto the earth. Their paws imprint the dusted, rocky clearing. The air smells cleanly of the sea.

To the south nearest the stables, stands a windowless rectangular structure with double doors made of bronze.

Again, Cerberus whines. Their flat faces point toward the building.

"There?"

The white-patched dog emits a gruff noise from his throat. Affirmation.

The rest of the mastiffs are inside, jailed as she had been jailed in Tartarus. Kept away from her. Their punishment is deprivation, with no access to the light of day or the light of a Cretan girl.

Persephone is about to step onto the icy ground when she sees the figure storming into the yard from the north. She freezes.

Alone, Hades cuts across the yard.

She swallows and glances at Cerberus. Their ears are pricked, heads perked in recognition. If they bolt to greet him, they will reach him in seconds. Give her away.

Persephone hot-whispers, "Stay," and tucks half her body behind the column, peering out like a small child.

Hades flings open the bronze door and disappears inside the pen.

The Unseen. That is what they call him.

Always disappearing. It is a tease, she thinks now. The tease leaves her wanting and just when she thinks she will never see him again, he appears to remind her of how she feels when in his presence.

Hands splayed against the column, Persephone breathes fast, the moisture freezing inside her nostrils and her dress soaking through as the sleet comes in a continuous gust. Violently, she shivers, but as much as her inner alarm tells her to run away, she cannot. Her feet are affixed.

Soul on tiptoe, she observes him, yearning to catch a peek of a man seldom espied.

But only from here.

Safe at a distance.

Persephone fights the urge to cry. Too often, she cries.

Cerberus huddles around her, bags of living, breathing heat intent on keeping their mistress warm.

Minutes creep by—an eternity.

Finally, Hades steps outside. Single file, the mastiffs centipede from the pen. Black-bodied supplicants surround their master.

Hades begins to speak.

Persephone cannot hear him. She chews her bottom lip, squinting at the dogs who gather and listen to instruction.

To her horror, the white-patched dog of Cerberus issues a sudden bark, almost in a greeting.

She pales, steps from behind the column, and holds out one hand to keep the dogs from running away.

Cerberus darts to the yard to join the other dogs.

She has been unknowingly holding her breath. When Hades looks up, it knocks the wind out of her.

If he comes for her, she will run. She should not run, but Persephone knows that she will, for that is the impulse blaring from every muscle in her body.

Positioned around Hades, the perfectly circular formation breaks apart. A few dogs wander toward the golden figure brightening the portico. The others contemplate.

From across the yard, Hades issues a command she cannot hear.

More break from formation. The pack of stragglers increases.

No, stay. Stay with him. If he loses this battle, she will lose later.

Another command by Hades, this time more forceful. The rogue mastiffs stop in their tracks and return to their circle. Persephone's heart races. She wants to place her hand to it to assure herself that she has not died from fright, but her arms will not budge from her sides. Soon she will have to face him. Soon she will have to face a love she said she wanted and now is not so sure.

Love-me love-me goes the heart.

When all mastiffs surround him, Persephone notices his lips move with another command. Cerberus separates from the pack and joins her beneath the portico.

True to his name, the Unseen disappears once again.

A lock secures the temple doors. Hecate brings a wooden key to the light, closing the milky eye to get an undistorted look. Satisfied the little pegs will align, Hecate fits them into their corresponding holes within the lock. With one knot-knuckled hand, mapped with blue veins, she lifts and removes the bolt.

The inside of the temple is cold and dark. Hecate brings a torch from the wall outside and ignites the other torches along the walls of the cella. The old woman makes her way down the aisles until the entire temple crackles with fiery warmth.

Hecate returns to the altar inside the door. Holy men cleared it the night before, taking offerings of the old day and making space for offerings of the new. The marble table is empty. Hecate places her keys there.

"What are you doing?" Demeter asks.

"Surrendering my keys."

"Surely there is a priest who will mind them while you are gone." Demeter looks around.

Hecate gives a peaceful smile. "I have been *klawiphoros*, key-bearer of these temples, for many years. Zeus made it so. Did I tell you that?"

Demeter thinks. Hecate has made no mention of a history

with Zeus, but had been quick to offer that she is somehow well-acquainted with Hera, Zeus's wife. The one who was not jilted and left with a pregnant belly, but who was properly wed to Zeus before the gods.

"Your captain was not wrong about me," Hecate says. "This journey will wear me down. I have no intention of making it twice."

"Why go?" Demeter says. "You need sacrifice nothing on my behalf."

"What sacrifice? I mentioned nothing of sacrifice."

Two otter skin satchels run diagonally from Hecate's stooped shoulder to thin hip. She shifts them, starts to say more, but something over Demeter's head catches her eye.

"Aha!" Hecate's face lights. "There you are."

"Where better to find a meal in the morning?" says an abrasive voice.

Demeter turns. The filthy man standing behind her is bleary-eyed and smacking his lips as if tasting something foul. In his spindly beard, there are crumbs and dried gunk.

Before, she mistook him for a beggar. He is not. He is a nasty drunkard who only yesterday called this High Priestess a whore and knocked the alms of water from her hand. Drunken actions are genuine actions. Perhaps more genuine than sober ones.

"Greetings, Priestess," the drunkard says, fiddling with an untucked strap of cloth binding the stump of his wrist. The tip has seeped, crusted with yellow.

The crone cannot possibly have plans for someone like this—but as Hecate deals her a nod and a wink, Demeter's stomach sinks.

"Oh no," Demeter groans.

This man took her child. Moons ago, he was the captain who whisked Kore aboard his ship, the *Narcissus*. Had he refused her the journey, Demeter would never have known the agony of losing the only thing that had ever truly been hers.

A woman's child is not to be trifled with. A mother bear will rear up with claws and fangs poised.

"Charon owes me a debt," Hecate announces. "A life, in fact. Did you die of the rot?"

"No, I am alive and as pleasant as ever." Charon eyeballs Demeter, who looks irritably at the ground. "Why are you itching to collect on a debt?"

Before Demeter can interject, Hecate says, "We could use a guide to Olympus."

She cannot believe what she is hearing. None of this will be entertained. Folding her arms, Demeter walks out of the temple doors. Matapan bustles with merchants, wheeling carts of their goods.

Behind her, Hecate's presence.

"I am not traveling with him," Demeter says without turning.

"Because?"

"Because we are not safe with him either."

"I do not recall offering," says Charon. Demeter spins with eyes like blades.

The crone turns to him. "You have a boat."

"At the bottom of the sea."

"Ah-ah-ah," she scolds. "Not the ship. A *boat*. The one you babbled about when I was cutting the rot away from your arm so you would not die."

He says, "I talked about my fishing boat?"

"Your fishing boat," she says, "and your mother. Those were your dying dreams."

"So," Charon says, "what about my boat?"

Hecate deals them a disapproving glare, as a mother might glare at squabbling siblings. "Come back inside, both of you. You will be more sensible with food in your bellies."

"Agreeable, you mean," Charon says.

"Food is why you are here, is it not?" Hecate snaps. "Then, come."

Demeter's feet remain fastened to the stone floor. As Hecate and Charon disappear into the darkness of the temple, Demeter hugs herself for warmth.

This is a mistake. Surely, there is another way. Her mind strains to find a solution, but all Demeter feels is urgency. So much can happen in a season. When last she saw her daughter, a vivacious summer had yielded to the cool winds of autumn. Thriving foliage succumbed to nature's cycle. Leaves aged. Lively petals grew brittle, but in a final showcase to outperform the glory days of summer, they became even more beautiful. A spectacle of golds and reds and oranges, confronting death by pleading their worth.

Now autumn surrenders to the brutality of winter. Trees stretch with barren limbs. Empty.

So much can happen in a season. Such destruction.

Reluctant, Demeter walks inside the temple. Before her eyes adjust to the dim lighting, Hecate passes her a fig. Charon's cheeks bulge with them.

Hecate raises an encouraging brow at Charon. "We need passage up the coast—"

"—I know where Olympus is," Charon says.

"Good," says Hecate. "Then it is settled."

"Settled?" Charon snorts.

"At the end of the journey will be Zeus!" Hecate points out. "The Loud Thunderer!"

Charon gives a one-shouldered shrug. He looks as unimpressed as Demeter feels.

"Olympus," he says. "There is nothing for me there."

"So?" Hecate says. "There is nothing for you here, either."

"During the war," Charon grumbles, "I served under Minos. I sailed among his naval fleet. Even got a peek at Poseidon once or twice. I have met my share of kings. You know what I say? Kings are only men. Men, just like me."

"Not just like you," Hecate says. "They are men who will one day be gods."

"Gods?" With a harsh, humorless laugh, Charon projects mushed fig. "I served the gods, hag. I did my part in the war. My role may not have been as high and mighty, but I served. And look." He lifts the bandaged stump. "For their loyalty, kings are fated to be gods. For my loyalty, I am fated to be lame, without purpose. I am fated to receive charity figs and drink myself to death on the temple stoop."

Demeter looks to Hecate, who remains nonplussed.

"Kings," Charon scoffs, shoving another fig into his mouth. "Do not talk to me of kings. Our lots are not the same."

Hecate emits an uncertain hum. "You lost a hand." Hecate taps her milky eye. "Well, I lost my eye. Do you see me crying? I have another eye. It works. You have another hand."

Hecate studies Charon who stuffs his cheeks to buy himself time for a clever retort. Before he can think further, Hecate says, "If you are looking for promise of a reward, there is none. I have no reason to believe ours will be a welcome visit."

The crone's attention fixes upon Demeter. "What happens after you find your Kore?"

Demeter sighs and rubs her forehead.

"Zeus sent for her. She wanted to go. You said as much. But," Hecate says, "you did not say why."

"Well?" Charon interjects. "Why?"

Demeter weighs the response. "Zeus wants only to use her."

"Use her?" Charon asks.

"Kore believes love comes from a boundless well because

that is how deeply I love her. Naturally, she believes a father would do the same. She is young and naive. Simple, really—I am not the only one who thinks so—many have said it before. Simple!"

Hecate notices the furrow of Charon's brow.

"If Zeus cared for her," Demeter continues, "we would have heard from him sooner. He would have come to see her at the first mention of her existence. When she was a useless child, did he send for her? No. But when he could benefit from her? Of course."

"Is it the worst thing," Charon shrugs, "to be the concubine of the King of Kings?"

"Oh, you lame fool," Hecate waves her hand at him. "Eat your figs."

"You are disgusting," Demeter practically spits, wrinkling her face up. "Not to use her for *that*. For marriage."

"Who was making a bid for her?" Hecate asks.

Demeter shakes her head. "I threw the messenger out before he could say."

"What?" Charon says. "You threw out a messenger from Zeus of Olympus?"

"Hermes," Demeter mutters. "I think that was his name."

"You threw out *Hermes*, son of Zeus?" Charon bellows with laughter.

Demeter blushes. She betrays herself with an accidental smile and frowns to correct it. "Yes. And I would do it again. What he asked was disgraceful."

"Disgraceful to," Hecate asks, ". . . you?"

"To the gods."

"The gods are on the hook for an awful lot these days," says Hecate. "For the sake of argument, let us leave them out of it."

"You cannot," Demeter says, "leave the gods out of anything. They are the essence of all things. At birth, Kore was promised to them."

"That was not your promise to make."

"How can you say that? She is my—?"

"She is your nothing," Hecate corrects. "You promised something that does not belong to you."

"Sounds familiar." Charon snorts. "Whose boat are you wanting to use again?"

Demeter's lips tighten. "If you oppose my intentions, why did you agree to come?"

"You know why."

The mother feigns ignorance by shaking her head. "Zeus's wife, Hera, is dangerous, you say."

"The prophecy," Hecate reminds. She stretches the tight spots in her middle back, bracing her hands at the base of her spine and arching. Bones crack. "Shall I recite it for you?"

"What prophecy?" asks Charon.

"*'There with angry hands she broke the ploughs and sent to death alike the farmer and his laboring ox.'*" In the wavering light, Hecate peers at Demeter. "Am I getting it right, lady mother? Is that what the priest revealed to you yesterday?"

"What is she talking about?" Charon asks Demeter.

Voice even and soft, Demeter says, "I do not know what you mean."

"Have you not heard?" Hecate smiles at Charon, a partially toothless smile. "Unless the *kore* is returned, the earth will meet its doom."

"Says who?"

"Old Vlasis, High Priest of Matapan," says Hecate. "In the days preceding his death, he warned of this."

"There with angry hands she broke the ploughs . . ."

She.

He had said wild things, telling her:

"Where the girl was Demeter knew not, but she reproached

the whole wide world . . . "

"I like to think that prophecy can be changed." The old woman pops a fig into her mouth. "Otherwise, what good would it do to foretell it?"

"How about it?" Hecate grins at Charon and raises her brows. "One hand or two, you can still help us save the world. Or would you rather drink yourself to death on the temple stoop?"

Charon glances at Demeter. Only a coward would admit to preferring the stoop. "Can I still drink myself to death on the boat?"

"If you can drink and row with one hand," Hecate wags a twig-like finger at Demeter. "As for you—would you rather trudge up to Olympus on foot in the winter with an old woman in tow? No doubt we will meet a variety of characters, yes? It should only take us a year or more, doing it that way."

Demeter flushes stubbornly. In Erebus, there is no shortage of two things: soldiers and criminals. They will likely encounter both along the way. Being with Charon in a boat seems wiser. At least he is indebted to the crone.

"All right," Demeter agrees.

This is her quickest recourse.

So much can happen in a season.

GAMOS

7

Persephone never imagined this day without her mother. Never imagined it anything like this at all. Rituals comfort her, though. Rituals remind her of home.

Bath begins the day. The water should come from a sacred well—from where was it drawn? She asks the slaves, but they do not know her tongue. They have, however, learned a singular word. Now they greet her, bowing and reverently whispering:

"*Per-se-phon-e.*"

Her name.

Having a father-given name makes her smile.

She knows the bath protects her during this transformation from girl to woman, and yet as soon as her toes touch the steaming water, she begins to shake. In Knossos on the night of *gamos*, girls sing outside the window of new lovers. They sing for fertility, and inside the home there comes the sound of the bride screaming here and there, and in this way the maidens are taught what to expect when—eventually—the night of *gamos* descends upon *them*. But if the bride screams, from what does the bath protect her? Now Persephone cannot make sense of the ritual. She wishes her mother were here to explain it.

The slaves pat dry her scabbed skin.

On her face, neck, and arms, they apply fucus, a powder of ground chalk and white lead. They would have powdered her anyway, Persephone thinks. Not just to cover the bruises. Painting the bride is part of the ritual.

Around her eyes, charcoal. Irises like dark honey inside black trim.

Along her mouth, beetroot sweetened with berry. It reddens the lips to mirror the lips *down there*.

Everything about this ritual is about *it*.

The grandmotherly slave comes inside with the finest, most extravagant purple fabric Persephone has ever seen. Another slave arrives with the saffron veil, thin and delicate as a web. The colors of purple and red mimic colors of a woman's blood cycle.

Over her shoulders, they drape purple silk thin to show the outline of her nipples. It is intentionally thin enough to reveal the definition of her breasts, their readiness to fill with milk and nurture any children her body creates.

For the first time since Knossos, Persephone is fitted with a girdle. It is adorned with jeweled baubles. She must remove it during the ceremony to signify her willingness to disrobe for her husband.

The slave woman hangs heavy chains of gold around her neck. Her wrists are shackled with jeweled bracelets. Ears cuffed with rubies inlaid in gold. A dowry of treasure that fathers drape over their daughters. Did Zeus send these ornaments? Is that part of the ritual done properly? Yes, of course it is. It is perfect, never mind it not being as she imagined. Never mind the powder-hidden fingerprints on her skin and the constant feeling of horror in her lower belly—horror yes, but sometimes she feels a profane thrill.

"Who claims you?"

The saffron veil descends over her face. She sees the world through a scrim of blood.

A slave places a diadem, fashioned into a golden chaplet of leaves, atop her head.

Her heart thumps violently.

A window, lit by frost, casts light across the gleaming floor.

The girls at home rhapsodize of this day. Since childhood, girls know themselves as valuable objects. Vessels for life. The bridge that joins two houses. Many times she and raven-haired Lyris would lie on their backs in the meadow, surrounded by dandelion and wildflowers and nectar-searching bees, and they would titter about the life-changing union of marriage:

"It hurts! Th-that is why they scream. My mother says so."

"My sister says it only hurts the first time. When I marry, I will tell you everything."

Dear Lyris, friend who grew up alongside the girl who was once called Kore. Lyris, whose marriage had been arranged among fathers. Lyris, who had been great with child and thrilled to fulfill her purpose when Kore left.

Her sweet friend, seen of late only in fevered dreams, never made true on her promise. When Kore had prodded her for details, Lyris had acted bored with the subject.

"You just lie still so he can put a baby in you."

"But i-is Mother right? Does it hurt you?"

Shrug. "It only lasts a little while, and then it is done."

But that was no answer! Her friend was suddenly tight-lipped, scarce most of the time and unable to be bothered by Kore, who was still a child in her eyes.

Mother, often telling her:

"Her life is different from yours. Why concern yourself with something you are not destined for?"

Now Persephone watches the slaves mill about, darkened by the red veil. Cerberus the Three trickle inside. They come for affection. She gives it without hesitation, petting them with cold, trembling fingers.

With every breath, the veil flutters and tickles her nose.

"Persephone," the grandmotherly slave says and opens her arms. Longing for comfort, Persephone nearly reaches out to hug her. But this is no offering of comfort. The open-armed slave motions for Persephone to stand.

She does.

Inside the room, more dogs. Many slaves. Sesame garland loops around bent arms, adjoining a line of green-linked slaves to either side of her, forming an aisle. The slaves on each side of the door hold wreaths.

Tradition dictates that the groom must come to Father's home and retrieve his bride and take her to the home that will become hers. But this is not her father's house, and there is nowhere to go from here.

The first man to enter is Judge Aeacus. Cloaked in red, he walks with a pained hitch in his step.

Bearing the second torch, Judge Rhadamanthus enters. His unkempt hair is combed, short beard trimmed to a fine point.

Last, Judge Minos enters with the final offering of fire.

Then enters a white-clad figure. Her breath lodges in her throat. The veil stops fluttering. Hades, lean and square-shouldered, walks toward her fast. Fast, as if he wishes to hurry. Fast, as if he wants to throw her over his shoulder and abscond with her.

"Who claims you?"

Her knees shake. They want to buckle. She allows them to buckle, but covers the weakness by sinking to her knees in proper prostration.

"Persephone of Knossos, daughter of Zeus the Liberator, High King of Olympus," says Hades in his quiet voice, "rise."

He plucks the veil from her head and flicks it aside. The whites of his eyes shine as brightly as his robes. The shadow of a beard darkens his jaw. Something passes between them—that visceral secret shared between two bodies—and her cheeks flush, and she searches his face with watery-eyed desperation.

Love me, she wants to say but does not.

He drops his eyes in response. Drops his eyes, yes, perhaps as a man guilty of love himself; oh she hopes so. He captures one slender wrist, already bruised.

Claiming her formally, Hades pulls her to the door and out into the corridor. Behind them, the gloomy procession of judges, slaves, and dogs march in file.

In Knossos, the matriarchs would sing marriage-songs. Young men would whirl in dance with flutes and drums continuously sounding. The merry crowd would shout good wishes.

This procession snakes silently through corridors. Hulking mastiff shadows slide up the walls. This, reminding her more of a funeral procession than a wedding.

They enter a wide space shining with black and red stone. Four columns carved into helmeted skeletons divide the room, each holding a spear. A round hearth crackles and smokes in the middle of the floor. This room has only three walls, the fourth of which is missing. The room gapes to display a gray sky and frosty sea. Waves explode against the barren cliff. In this open space, it is freezing. Her teeth chatter. Every muscle in her body tenses.

An elder comes between them. He wears priestly robes—a priest! She looks to Hades, dripping gratitude like sweet sap. What matters is that he loves her, and she sees signs of it in these ritual concessions, token gestures that nod to her own piety and culture.

As the priest begins his blessing, she smiles. When the time comes, Persephone unfastens the girdle and peels it from around her middle. She accepts the significance, but when she tries to meet the groom's stare, she finds herself blushing again and looks to the ground.

With love-purpled arms, she presents Hades with the girdle.

A slave comes with a basket of ripe fruit. Hades takes what sits at the top of the pile. A ruby-red pomegranate cut into one quarter—bulging with seeds inside a hive of rind. Juice runs down his hand, soiling the cuff of a white sleeve. He breaks and lifts it to her lips. She scoops the seeds with her tongue.

The nectar trickles down her dimpled chin. She accepts the seeds into her mouth and down her throat. Sour-sweet like ripe cherries.

Everything in this ritual is about *it*.

The red of her cheeks rivals that of the fruit.

The red of the sun sinks low to the horizon and surrenders the day to night.

There, she is pronounced Persephone, consort of Hades, High Queen of Erebus. Hearing those words, the mastiffs begin to howl their own marriage-song, and slaves whisk her away.

My Whole World

8

If the girl screams, she will rile the dogs. With a snap and point of the finger, Hades instructs them to stay in the corridor.

Outside, wind screeches against the sharp angles of the palace. It is a strange, disconcerting noise much like the screeching owl or cat in heat. Cries that mean one thing and sound like something else.

Hades breathes slowly and evenly from his nose. There is nothing urgent in his stride or desperation in the way he carries himself. No flesh-starved withdrawal makes him move faster than intended. He commands his breath and carriage and heart.

The frenzy in his heart and loins he will deny over and over because—no—there is no such frenzy.

When it is finished, he will leave her bed and retreat to his own.

And if he wants, he will do it again tomorrow.

From the hallway, Cerberus complains with a yawp. Wanting inside. Longing to be near her too.

Hades crosses the threshold and slams the door. His heart beats so furiously that it undulates the fabric draped over his chest.

Persephone sits on the edge of the bed, back rigid and hands clutching the mattress on each side of her lap. She is aglow with soft white, highlighting the gold of her skin. It eases him, this glow.

Since the night he took her, Hades has experienced the disquiet of remorse. Thinking: *what if?*

What if, when he touches her, he experiences the fear-based memory of what his own aggression inflicted? His actions, transforming Persephone's body into a looking glass. He would not enjoy the reflection.

Blue, black, red, the colors of suffering.

Yet holding true, the purest of light surrounds her.

From in between little girl plaits, Persephone peers up with her face scrubbed clean. Her eyes shimmer with unspent tears. The simple effort of standing elicits a deep breath and a swallow.

Still, Persephone rises. Nervous-twisting hands clasp in front of her lower belly. During the marriage ceremony, her eyes were full of childlike adoration. He sees it again now, and the frankness makes him squirm.

Glowering, Hades pulls gold cuffs from his wrists and tosses them onto the table nearest the door, cutting silence with the sound of metal clanging wood. His heartbeat slams against the skin of his hands, neck, and lips. The scrapes on his knuckles and arms throb.

He feels her watching. Turns.

Cheeks shining pink, Persephone rocks on her feet, a young child in terror who wants to run, but wills herself in place. Already breathing fast.

He looks at her gown. All she needs is this look. She brushes the gown from her shoulders. Stunned into stillness, Hades works his jaws, teeth gnashing.

"Training."

"A firm hand, not out of cruelty . . ."

She is wickedly glorious. Plump, taut breasts rise and fall as her panic grows, and erect golden nipples blush pink at the tips. A trench divides her ribs and flows to the tight pit of her belly button, pulling his gaze farther down to a darkly gold triangle of hair. Hips and legs—feline with their long curves. Another wave of victory washes over him, as a man who has won the best prize of all. She is, by far, the finest thing he has ever owned.

She gazes at him in a way that oozes that oft-abused sugary preciousness. Nevertheless, this Persephone is unlike the frail Kore he took from the wreckage of the *Narcissus*. Ever since Minos lent him a glimpse, Hades has struggled to dismiss her as the throwaway brat of Zeus.

"And while you are here, you shall rule—"

Willpower holds him in place. Not awe. Willpower.

Hades beckons with two fingers.

Bobbing on her toes and chewing her lip, she obeys. Closer and closer, her steps. He ogles every contour until his eyes land upon the purple thumbprints on her wrists. On her pretty shoulders and neck: teeth marks.

When he sees the bruises, he sees the bruises of his mother.

When he sees the scrapes, he sees the scrapes of his mother.

So long ago did she pass into the afterworld, Hades thought he had succeeded in forgetting her.

He *had* succeeded.

Without realizing it, he takes one step back.

Never mind there is no wounded glow around Persephone. The pit in his stomach is enough.

"I do love you," she mutters sadly. "Surely you know that."

He frowns, eyes half-closed, and blinks at the marks caused by his mouth and hands. Once it had been easy to identify her tears as manipulation.

"You are my whole world." One hand curls softly around his wrist and the other caresses the length of his forearm.

Sweetly, Persephone's lips press to his, then fuller and with offerings of an open mouth. He shakes, frozen while she does it. The sincerity of her touch collides with his regret, and inside of his chest there roars a skeptic's final protest. He grips her shoulders and pries her away because none of this can *be*: she cannot possibly love him, for no one ever has. His hands dig into bruises already there. She chirps in pain.

He casts her to the bed and she lands hard, hair tumbling to conceal the wounds he wishes not to see. Her eyes widen and the pretense of love is replaced with raw fear, a look with which he is better acquainted and far more comfortable.

With a small cry, his bride crab-scuttles backward. Hades grabs one ankle, yanks her to him, and grunts, "Easy, easy," as he might say to a skittish horse. The insides of her thighs fit snugly around his hips. He is on top of her and her belly meets his and there comes the high euphoric rush, untainted, as clean and stupefying as the largest jug of waterless wine.

As he feels the tears on her face and tastes the salt, she begins to whisper-plead that he not hurt her again.

Telling him he does not need to, for she loves him.

Loves him, loves him: this, she keeps repeating like a spell or a curse, one that permeates his mind and heart and, in that moment, he knows she tells the truth. She loves him, and he believes it with the entirety of his being, and any remaining fury relaxes and dissolves.

Hades shushes into her ear and plants her wrists beside her head, pulling back to see her eyes squeezed shut. Preparing for pain.

"Sh-h-h-h-h," he hushes as she weeps, and he continues with, "Sh-h—sh-h-h—sh-h," no longer certain if the hushing is for Persephone's sake or for his own. He slips into the slick, hot sheath, hardly bearing it. He is flying and drowning simultaneously, but would have it no other way, and though he strives to languish kindly in this pleasure, the excitement turns him rough. She lies limp and sniveling, but will forgive him for it, for by her own admission, he is her whole world, and this thought alone sends him over the edge.

Afterward, there is the cool, floating sensation of someone on the brink of consciousness. His skin tingles. Her arms and legs entwine his, coiled like snakes that bind him to the hum of her flesh.

A delicate finger traces along his chest and shoulder. She fingers the starburst of shining pink flesh. The scar.

"Is this from the war?" she asks, meekly.

All he can muster is, "No."

"How did you get it?"

Get up. Get up. But it is impossible. He inhales. "I was shot by an arrow."

"Oh! What happened?"

"I was shot by an arrow," he repeats. He fights the urge to sleep, summoning the energy to leave but failing.

Persephone runs her lips over the thick tissue. "But not in the Titan War?"

"The Battle of Pylos," he says, "began after the city was sacked. Half the citadel burned, the king and nearly all his kin were murdered."

"And this Pylos is here? In the land of Erebus?"

"Yes."

"So you went there to fight the men who sacked it?"

She treads dangerous ground and does not know it. He tries to peel one lithe arm from around his chest, but only manages to place one hand there before he loses the will to move. "Yes."

In her feathery child's voice, she says, "*Theíos?*"

"Hm."

"Was it my brother who shot you?"

His eyes open. "His name is Heracles."

". . . I know."

"Who told you that?"

"No one exactly," she replies, resting her cheek against the scar. "Judge Aeacus said you want my brother to answer for crimes. Perhaps these are the crimes he meant. Am I right, *Theíos*?"

"Your brother," he starts, "committed these crimes and more. He also murdered his own wife and children. Did Aeacus tell you that?"

"No—"

"—and he has atoned for none of his crimes because of who his father is." *Who* your *father is*, he wants to add. Fresh anger almost gives him the impetus to pry her arm from his chest.

Almost.

"Is that why our father gave me to you? To restore peace?"

He sighs from his nose and rubs his brow. "You ask a lot of questions."

"May I? Only one more?"

"What."

She raises onto one elbow and burrows tighter into his side, playing with the hair on his chest. "If you do not want peace, why did you accept me as your wife?"

Her hand looks golden in this light. All of her, golden in this light. A candlelit illusion. Hades slips his hand over hers. Gilded fingers slide between his.

"I wanted you," he admits.

"You did?"

The words are on his tongue. *I have never wanted anything so much.*

"I said one question," he reminds her, "and I answered it." Hades pulls free and stands. He snatches his tunic from the floor.

"Wait," she says, tucking a stray lock behind her ear. "Stay with me?"

Hades makes the mistake of looking at her. He beholds the flushed, naked girl with sunny hair partly dislodged from braids, legs curled beneath her. One outstretched, delicate wrist wears bruises like bracelets.

"Please, *Theíos*. With me."

"You do not want that."

"I do."

His eyes wander across her body. "If I stay, you will not sleep."

She knows what he means. Considering, she nibbles her bottom lip and then concedes by lying down for him.

Hence, the drunkenness continues, each time savored longer than the last, and in between the stirring and spasms, there are semi-wakeful moments of drifting into the ether where he feels only partially present with her in bed, wrapped in love-hungry arms, and Hades is vaguely aware of agreeing when, at some point, she rhapsodizes:

"Tomorrow is our day of celebration. *Epaulia*, the very last day of ritual, I promise! Are you excited, *Theíos*? Oh, everyone loves a party!"

A tribe of goats litters the hillside. Where Charon leads them, there is no road. The goats move nimbly along rocky terrain. A single dog herds perhaps thirty, trotting along the base of the hillside where patches of brush grow tall.

Trailing, Demeter regards the dairy goats and unburdens the weight of her satchel onto her other shoulder.

Once there was a goat named Amalthea. Pretty, long-legged, with a speckled coat that could have been painted by the gods. Her little nose shone the most delicate pink, standing out against the creamy white patches of fur swirled together with auburn. Tethered to the tree directly beside the path leading to the home Demeter shared with the other priests and priestesses in the Knossian cult, Amalthea wore a gleaming tin bell tied around her neck with thin rope.

Zeus had abandoned her there. Abandoned, just as Demeter had been abandoned.

The goat gave plentiful milk. Zeus told her so, and the goat proved him right over the years.

"This is the goat whose milk made me the strong, magnificent creature I am today."

At the time, she found the man, who would one day be known

as the King of Kings, to be lighthearted and silly. The lifespan of a goat would not run the course of nearly thirty years, the age Zeus had been when he planted his seed inside of her, she a *kore* of only fourteen. Even at fourteen, Demeter had not been so gullible as to believe him. Yet she believed him in other ways—why?

If a man would tease her about something as trivial as a goat's age, why in the world did she believe anything else he said? Things like:

"This is when I carry you off and make you mine."

He had not done so in the way she, a gullible child, had assumed. As is custom, he had tossed an apple that she caught without a second thought. Tossing it meant everything. Catching it meant everything. A proposal of marriage, accepted. Lives, altered.

Zeus had not carried her off, nor did he make her his bride. Instead, he left her with the life-altering secret of a sordid kind, growing inside of her womb.

And Amalthea. With her, Zeus left Amalthea. Goats may not live thirty years, but they can live to be half that if properly cared for.

Kore adored that goat.

"Pretty!" the child would exclaim.

Her first word: *Pretty!*

Any pretty thing, Kore would confiscate for her own. Brilliant pink hyacinths disappeared from gardens and found their way beside their hearth. Purple anemones mysteriously relocated from their stalks to the bedside table. The chipper, yellow narcissus was so favored that Kore's little fingers betrayed her with yellow stains. Often, Demeter caught Kore with her skirts gathered up into a makeshift pouch, carrying picked flowers into their home.

"Little ghost," Demeter would scold, "leave them in the ground. They live longer in the ground."

"No!" Before even forming a complete sentence, Kore's defiant will reared its head. "Pretty!"

Oddly, the flowers lived quite long, even without soil to nurture them. They needed no soil when they had Kore. Her sweetness sustained them, her purity. Of this, Demeter was certain.

So, too, the goat thrived in Kore's care. It accompanied her everywhere she went—Kore at four, at eight, at twelve. Amalthea, her constant companion, showed little signs of age. By the time Kore turned fourteen, the white patches in Amalthea's coat began to yellow. Like a hollering elder who could not hear herself talk, Amalthea would bleat obnoxiously all day long.

"What does she want?" Demeter would ask, irritably.

And Kore would say, "Nothing. She is only talking."

At night, Amalthea slept with a little pink nose pressed to Kore's cheek.

There came the day when age claimed her. In the early morning, Kore's scream startled Demeter awake. Amalthea had already stiffened, round eyes frozen open. Arms fastened around the animal's neck, Kore refused to budge.

"It was her time," Demeter tried to console. "Perhaps past it."

Kore held the goat and wept, and Demeter left the room to whisper conspirator's words to the slave girl. How would they convince Kore to release Amalthea?

When the tin bell jingled, they believed Kore had pried her arms from around the goat's neck, finally agreeing to reason. Yet it was not Kore who crept from the room, but Amalthea. Shaking her head, flapping her ears as if roused from a deep sleep, Amalthea trotted into the courtyard and began to graze.

"Kore? Did you see—?"

Demeter had found her daughter asleep, sweating with fever. The goat lived another day, but Kore had taken too ill to celebrate.

The sound of thirty bells grates at her ears. A flat, tinny

noise issues with every step of the herd. The dog's yap, as harsh as a scream. With Charon leading the way, they wade through the animals, goat hair rubbing and collecting on their robes. The apples in her satchel give off an alluring aroma, drawing muzzles to her bag. Demeter shifts the bag higher, arm cramping. In front of her, Hecate does the same.

"Boy!" Charon bellows.

Making his way around a path concealed by olive trees, a boy of about ten years holds a walking stick the size of a spear. He switches the stick from hand to hand, changing its position and twirling it with a flourish. Practicing, Demeter assumes, for the day when the stick is replaced by a true spear. Practicing for manhood. Children of this age hurry through life, blind to the fact that adulthood is not the lofty destination they believe it to be. Disillusioned when they arrive to a coveted age and find it no better.

The boy scrunches his face into a squint, getting a good look through a blaring sun. "You," he says, recognizing the filthy, bearded man advancing. "We gave you up for dead."

"Did you, now?" Charon issues a gravelly laugh. "No relief to see me alive?"

The shepherd boy scratches at a bite on his knee. "What happened to your hand?"

Charon ignores the question. "Where is your father?"

"In the field." He inspects the women and asks, "Who are they?"

Demeter opens her mouth to respond on her own behalf, but Charon cuts her off. "My wife and her mother."

Demeter resists the urge to kick him.

"Someone married you?" the boy grimaces.

"Mind your herd," Charon growls. "Go on."

The boy shrugs and continues past. The last of the tribe

trickles by, taking the cacophony with them. Demeter quickens her pace.

"Wife?" she asks.

"My story is quicker than yours."

Several minutes into their journey, footfalls echo from behind. They turn to see the boy running in their direction, stick clutched in both fists.

"*Kyrios!*" he loud-whispers the word for *master* to Charon.

"What has you spooked, boy?" Hecate asks.

"There is a man back there. Among the trees. He is trailing you; I know it. You must have something he wants."

He glances sheepishly at Demeter. Anxiety pinches in her gut, old wounds flaring.

"Here, take this." The boy offers his stick to Charon. For the first time, Demeter notices the tip is whittled into a point. Charon inspects their traversed path with their footprints visible. He takes the makeshift spear.

Charon asks, "Did he see you?"

Wetting his lips, the boy says, "Maybe?"

"Give me that." Demeter snatches the stick from Charon's grip. She almost breaks the thing in half over her knee and gives the second half to Hecate. But the old woman moves away and sits on a nearby rock.

Before Charon can object, she says, "You have a blade under your robe. How many weapons can you yield?"

Charon turns red in the face. Glances at the path where their foe supposedly lurks.

"I can fight!" The boy reaches for the stick. "My father taught me how to land a good blow."

Hecate looks on with a look of bemusement. Her lack of concern ruffles Demeter's nerves.

If they hurry, perhaps they can lose him. Demeter crouches

and says, "Go behind us and conceal our tracks."

Charon shakes his head. "Running never helps. We will stand our ground and confront him. Get rid of him for good."

Hecate chuckles. Plucking a sprig of rosemary from a neighboring bush, she twirls it between two fingers and sniffs with a smile.

Charon eyes the old woman. "Besides, how fast can the hag move? We stand no chance of running."

"We need not *run,*" Demeter argues, softening her voice in fear that it may travel "We hide and defend ourselves if need be."

As the boy kicks dirt and rocks over their footprints, Hecate stands. Her sandaled feet sink into red-orange dirt, forming new tracks over the covered ones.

"Hey—" the boy whines.

Hecate keeps walking.

"Where are you going?" Charon hisses.

Demeter says, "Hecate—"

The old woman traipses past the boy, her robe skimming the ground.

"What are you doing?" Charon demands.

"I am going to talk to him," she calls. "Sit tight."

"Hecate, stop!"

"Get back over here, hag!"

Hecate waves, acknowledging that she heard their protests and could not care less. As she disappears around the corner, Charon notices the lack of color in Demeter's face.

"Relax," he tells her. "Most of the boats were washed away or pummeled by Oceanus on the day the earth opened."

"So?"

"So," Charon says, "I have a boat. Someone thinks I will lead them right to it." He studies her, up and down, appraising her in a way that makes Demeter clutch her robe tighter. "Years ago, I saw you at the arena in Knossos. I might have been willing to seek you out and fight a man for you. Back then. But the god of time has shown you an unintended kindness."

"What is that supposed to mean?" Demeter snaps.

"It means," he says, "you are not as chase-worthy as you might once have been."

Unconsciously, Demeter touches her face and catches herself. Over the course of the past season, she has noticed the occasional strand of silver. A tiny brown spot has appeared on the surface of her hand, now creeping slightly when she moves her wrist. Certainly—she finds solace in no longer being "chase-worthy." No need to protest something as inevitable as this, and yet at the base of her gut, there is an odd sadness. Loss. But what, besides her only child, has she lost? She should rejoice at such a change. Rejoice that Cronus, god of time, has waved his hand over her physical form and diminished her as he diminishes the bare trees of winter.

Demeter is about to say so when the shepherd boy points toward the bend in their path.

"There," he says.

Hecate trudges forward, her mouth curved into a smile.

And behind her: Iasion.

The morning of *epaulia*, Persephone finds herself alone again.

Hades is gone from her bed. Cerberus sleeps in a pile on the floor. Beneath her, blood-streaked blankets from reopened wounds. Her skin bears evidence of love—old marks turning green yellow and new ones flushed pink and purple. The whole of her, a sacrifice to this love.

Not until evening does Hades return, coldly handsome, robed in deep crimson. A golden serpent entwined in brambles forms the crown on his head. He comes to lead her to the celebration of *epaulia*.

Anxiety has simmered in her gut all day. Already, she fails him as a wife—she knows it! For instance, she should have woven a blanket for her groom. Stupid of her to not to think of this sooner. The moment she heard of his departure for Olympus and what he had planned, Persephone should have taken to the loom and begun weaving a *chlanis*, which they would use together in their marriage bed. More importantly, it symbolizes her contribution to the household—and instead of spending those long days and nights feeling sorry for herself and crying over her mother, she should have been weaving!

Except, she is terrible at weaving.

Theíos places so much effort and attentiveness in honoring wedding rituals. He is a ruler who punishes those who do not adhere to customs. It is unforgivable that she has made nothing for him with her own hands.

Provoke him again, when he is starting to soften?

Last night she slept very little and, today, it hurts to walk and burns when she urinates. This suffering proves her love. It is as normal as the brightening of her hair.

"But i-is Mother right? Does it hurt you?"

Lyris could not explain. Persephone understands why. Yes, she hurts. But she would not undo the hurt, nor the sensation that runs alongside it, the twin of hurt, making her groan in another way. The last time he was inside of her, she had not wanted to it to end and afterward rocked against his hip bone as one cannot stop the motion of the waving ship even when on solid ground.

When Hades walks through the door, she starts to rush to him. Exclaiming, *"Theíos!"* It is her nature to leap and fling her arms around his neck and cover his face with wet, sloppy kisses.

The sternness of his face freezes her. He is not ready for her sort of love. Persephone approaches him as a person might approach a dangerous, but potentially tamable beast.

As she draws close, he appears fixated on her lips.

She takes another step to him and kisses his cheek.

Hot hands roam to the small of her back and trail lower to squeeze the underpart of her buttocks. Despite the soreness between her legs, her body reacts. It makes her pulse thump in the most sensitive parts—the scrapes on her back, the bruises, and especially where he enters her.

He has a glassy-eyed, hungry look. She creates this hunger within him, perhaps her only real power at all.

If she lingers, he will remove her dress.

He will lay her down and muss her face and hair, and the

slaves will have to fix her up all over again. With a little pang of exhilaration, Persephone wriggles away.

"Promise not to be mad at me?"

"Why? What did you do now?"

"I only started the *chlanis* this morning."

He squints. Shakes his head.

"The marriage blanket."

The sockets of his eyes are shadowed caves. He glances behind him as if he expects someone to be there—as if he should ask one of the judges if her negligence is acceptable. Persephone's throat tightens.

There are no judges present. Only three hounds and a slave girl who appears to tidy up.

Hades inspects Persephone's face. Frowning, he demands a wet cloth.

The cowering slave hands it over, and he wipes away the powder and kohl. Persephone's cheeks shine pink from where he rakes the beetroot off her mouth and across half her face.

When she glows clean, Hades tosses the rag to the slave, who fumbles it and scurries away. He extends his hand and gives Persephone a hard look, up and down.

"Come on then."

Persephone's face falls. She is wrapped in the finest silk dyed pale pink, the fabric thin as a blade of grass. Her brightening hair never cooperates with attempted braids and up-sweeps. It slips like water out of every knot the slaves weave. Instead, it hangs long beneath the diadem, gleaming and combed sleek. Veils of dusty rose and white silk wrap her arms and fountain down her hips.

"But—?"

"But what?"

She poses a little. "Do you like it?"

He narrows his eyes. "Like *what?*"

"Nothing, nevermind," she mumbles and begins to mope away, to this celebratory reception that makes her groom so grouchy.

Hades catches her by the arm and tugs her back. The tops of his ears redden, and his mouth opens. Nothing comes out. He only shakes his head as if to tell her that words are not his specialty and expecting more only sets her up for disappointment. A high king is not beholden to anyone. Persephone should be grateful for the affection he gives, even the gruff kind.

She takes his jaw and delivers a chaste kiss on the corner of his mouth. Hades searches for the full of her lips, but she pulls away with a coy smile and takes his hand. "I think you *do* like it," she winks and says with the same lilt she uses on the dogs, "Come on!"

The room called the *andron* is new to her. At home, the *andron* has a separate entrance so the men do not cross paths with the women on the way in. Women are not allowed in such places. This is where men can speak intelligently with other men and pontificate on things women find boring.

But that is not what Mother used to say.

Demeter, High Priestess of Knossos, would declare that with the women hanging around, the men are not as free to enjoy themselves.

Persephone wishes her mother were here to see it with her. On obsidian platforms, couches press flush against walls painted gold, black, and red. Floors are red-carpeted, and tapestries drape across walls. Firelight comes from a large hearth that overtakes the back wall.

There are so many people, and some are *women*!

With crested helmets and bronzed breastplates removed, the guards appear finely robed with women hanging on their arms, women decorated with baubles and painted up in a way *Theíos* clearly dislikes.

As the herald announces them— (a herald!)—Hades does not stop walking. He grips her high under the armpit and tugs her along. She manages not to wince. At home, the king and queen always stop during the announcement.

Persephone must stop comparing. Stop measuring everything against how it would be at home with her mother and a polis that watched her grow up.

Everyone bows.

A strange thing, to be bowed to. From out of nowhere, the judges surround and lead them to the far corner of the room. A pedestal couch, canopied in red and gold, awaits them. Judge Rhadamanthus smiles a comforting smile and winks at her.

Together, Hades and Persephone sit, both in crowns not usually worn. Between their couch and the rest of the room, Cerberus forms a menacing fence. *Do not cross*, the dogs convey.

Persephone glances at her sullen groom who appears rigid and sweating, and notices his jaw knotting as it does when he is uncomfortable.

Lips to his ear, she sings, "Thank you, *Theíos,*" and hugs his arm.

One of the dogs knocks at her leg with his head. Distracted by the crowd, she pets him. Chatter builds. Two flautists hold pan flutes to their lips, blowing skillfully into cane tubes as their melodies intermix.

A group of maidens whirl in dance. In temple ceremonies, Persephone has danced a hundred times! She leans forward and admires every leap and twirl. She searches for signs of amusement in her husband's face. A smile? Tapping his foot? Nothing. When one dancer with athletic skill flips in mid-air, Persephone checks his reaction with childlike hope, but his eyes are vacant.

Piled against the walls are gifts from nearby kingdoms: pots made of gold and silver, vases carved from alabaster, and polished cypress chests with jeweled latches. Vessels are the token gift of *epaulia*. They symbolize a womb prepared to contain life.

Her womb has been the primary subject for days now.

The more Persephone admires the collection of vessels the more it becomes real to her. Hades's hot palm lands on her knee, and the unwelcome pulse in her sex reminds her of what is going to happen right after *epaulia*, and when Persephone thinks about it she cannot count how many times he filled her last night alone. What if doing it so many times is the reason a woman has more than one baby? So as not to panic, Persephone imagines she is a white cat with a precious litter of black kittens, not a horrified girl writhing in bed and hoping to survive the ordeal, which tends to happen to girls who birth more than one at a time.

She watches the other women, confused. Observing them is the only way to learn the expectations. The others have hair done up in tight curls, spilling from flashy sphendone bands. The colors of their hair run in unnatural shades: red as a raspberry, blue-black as the feathers of a crow, or blanched yellow by lime. Chalky powder conceals their natural swarthy complexions.

"The wives are . . ." She struggles for the best word and comes up with, "colorful."

No one seems to hear.

These Erebusian women drape themselves over the laps of their husbands. Kissing their necks, hands rubbing masculine chests and roving all about their bodies until the men are red-faced and grinning. One woman hops from the lap of her husband and swaggers toward them. Pinched between two fingers, a mint leaf on which she chews lazily. A shock-green veil complements the raven curls high on her head.

Persephone sits straighter, mouth slightly agog. The woman's eyes are blackened with kohl, mouth glossy and red beneath an upturned nose. When she locks eyes with Persephone, a look of appraisal creeps across her face.

No doubt she thinks Persephone, High Queen of Erebus, is nothing but a child, ill-suited for a man destined for godhood. Persephone smooths her hair and moistens her lips.

Before the woman can get closer, Judge Aeacus breaks from his post, grabs the woman, and begins to feast on her neck until she squeals and playfully swats him

Persephone glances at the woman's husband. Any second, he will storm to them and punch Aeacus right in the face, surely! But he does not because he busies himself with another woman altogether—this one with burgundy hair and breasts like melons. Persephone's mind turns somersaults.

"Majesty?"

Cheeks hot, Persephone glances up. Judge Minos extends a bronze cup of wine, a gentle smile lighting his face.

She takes the cup.

Judge Minos bends closer. "Are you well?"

Scanning the crowd again, she nods stupidly. Several of the guards' wives have swapped laps, seemingly in the arms of some other woman's husband.

"Do the guards," she whispers to him, "share wives?"

Judge Minos looks around the room. He finger-combs his beard. "These women are not wives."

"Who are they?" Persephone nods toward the woman with blue-black hair whose arms are fastened around Judge Aeacus's neck. "Who is *that*?"

"I believe," Minos thinks, "her name is Minthe." He regards Hades. The high king accepts wine from a cup-bearer who trembles as Cerberus sniffs him like a chunk of meat.

"Women like Minthe," the judge continues, confidentially,

"are paid to provide a comfort that wives might otherwise provide."

He refers to *hetaera*. Whores. Persephone saw one once in Knossos, years ago when she and Mother frequented the agora where merchants peddled their wares. Mother, distracted by the silversmith, had released her daughter's hand—

This happened before she was Persephone. Then she was Kore, daughter, an innocent.

Kore had followed a cat into an alley. There was a woman with a painted face. How profane she looked, with red smudging her thin lips and the apples of her cheeks. The woman's hair was also red—not the coppery orange seen every so often (the color of Poseidon's hair, claimed Mother)—but a burgundy red, like the color of berries masking the dark brown strands beneath it.

The woman was doing things to a man in the alley. On her knees, suckling him. Mother grabbed her arm so hard it nearly yanked from the socket. After that, Kore was not allowed to leave Demeter's side when they ventured into the agora.

Persephone's skin goes fiery cold. "There are so many."

"There are many men."

Not far away, slipping from Aeacus's clutches, Minthe looks at her.

Then Minthe looks at Hades. The high king is too busy talking to Judge Rhadamanthus to notice.

Something ugly simmers in the space between Persephone's gut and heart.

A boy approaches the line of Cerberus. For a young child, he is brave to face the dogs alone. Brave to face Hades the Unseen alone. What an odd place to find a child. This is no setting for a boy. He must be only nine or ten years old, nowhere near acquainted with manhood. Thick brown hair falls over his ears and frames baby-plump cheeks dusted with freckles.

Hades calls for Cerberus to heel. The dogs settle, resting on forearms, and pant contentedly.

When the boy kneels, he lowers his face to the ground.

"King Nestor of Pylos," Judge Minos says. "We thank you for making the journey."

The word "Pylos" itches her mind.

"The king and nearly all his kin were murdered."

Her brother killed this boy's family. Everyone knows it. The room grows hushed. Eyes and ears, wide open.

Heracles changed the course of this boy king's life, and Persephone bears the cost of this sin. Every time her husband touches her, she pays for it.

When the boy king stands, his chest puffs and chin lifts. His unchanged voice booms with confidence. "Judge Minos, I need no thanks for honoring the Unseen. His Majesty came to the aid of my people. Still today he blesses us with what we need to rebuild. My palace is nearly done now. No enemy can spot us, but when I stand on the roof, I can see the horizon in every direction."

"He is only a child," she whispers.

The way *Theíos* looks at her says everything.

So are you. Yet here you are.

"Whatever you need is yours," Hades declares. "I watch over my own, King Nestor. And I have not forgotten your loss."

Persephone stands. She regrets it immediately, but once she is on her feet, there is no turning back. She glances over her shoulder.

Hades watches darkly.

She negotiates between the fortress of dogs. "I have not forgotten either."

The boy falls to his knees again. He has been king longer than she has claimed the role of High Queen. So Persephone also kneels, tipping her chin to look him in the eye. "It is an honor to know you, King Nestor."

Nestor looks up at her, skeptical until he sees no objection from the judges or the Unseen. "The honor is mi—"

"—I am sorry for what happened to your family," she interrupts. "It is unforgivable. Our High King has vowed that the man who did this will answer for what he did." Persephone looks at her husband. "Believe him, for he is a god among men."

Hades eyes her.

"We are aligned in this," she continues. "I will proudly stand beside him when Heracles is brought to heel."

Her words are strong, but her voice is a sweet breeze.

The tension in Nestor's face melts. "Is it true you summoned the gods?"

Murmurs puncture the silence.

"Who says that?"

Nestor gives a one-shouldered shrug. "Everyone."

She sighs, careful not to inflate her actions. "The gods are with us always. We simply cannot see them all the time."

"But they listen to you," Nestor insists. "They appear for you."

The room looks to the Unseen for signs of approval, but he gives none. He simply leans on his elbow, observing—ever observing.

Careful. She must select her words with gentle precision.

Hands folded behind his back, Rhadamanthus breaks the quiet. "Our High Queen is most humble."

Persephone gives the child a savvy smile. "Why do you want to appeal to the gods?"

"Will you ask the gods to bless me?" Nestor says, then blushes. He says in a private voice, "Sometimes I think I am in too deep."

"You are alive while your family is not. The gods must watch over you."

"Yes," Nestor considers. "I suppose."

Persephone places her hand on the crown of his head. Closing her eyes, she feels a deep sense of peace, and while this feeling is just a feeling—and what do the feelings of a girl matter? — she knows that King Nestor will be fine. Fine, despite watching his family die by spear and arrow, fleeing from a city ablaze and smoking.

"You will live to be an old man and a wise ruler." Persephone's heart races from all the eyes fixed upon her, especially *his* eyes. "The gods assure you this blessing."

The boy bows again. Persephone returns to her seat, head down.

"That was very kind, Majesty," Judge Rhadamanthus comments.

Persephone hopes she did well. If she locks eyes with her husband, she will find out. The pressure of his stare pulls her eyes to his.

He is almost smiling. An uplifted corner of the mouth, a twinkle within black, unblinking lashes.

The ultimate victory. An earned one. Her heart pounds, and she watches the crowd return to their merriment and (as Mother would say) debauchery.

The flautists rest their lips and fingers. In their place, a young man with red-gold curls hanging over his brow appears. His skin is the color of a peach and his arms look different from the arms of the men around here, most of whom are soldiers or used to be soldiers. The man's bones are roped with underdeveloped muscle, like that of a boy her age, and his face is pretty, instead of handsome. From a sling on his back, the young man removes a stringed instrument of highly polished wood. Not a harp, but something else.

She perks up. "What is that?"

"A lyre," Hades replies.

Judge Rhadamanthus tips to her. "Your brother Hermes taught him how to play it." He must want her to know that not all her brothers are bad and that she has reason to be proud of her family too—not just ashamed.

With his head decorated with a laurel wreath chaplet and his unruly locks tamed and oiled, Rhadamanthus motions to the lyre player. "*That,*" he says, "is Orpheus, son of King Oeagrus of Thrace."

"He is far from home," Hades says.

Rhad's cheeks glow from wine and excitement. "He arrived with King Nestor."

"Nestor?" Hades peers across the room to this princely lyre player named Orpheus. "Why?"

Orpheus's hands look soft like a woman's hands. Delicate fingertips pick at the strings of the lyre in rapid flow. The music trips from finger to string. It vibrates with a deep twang, a denser sound than a flute. Persephone cannot tell if it is the instrument that commands attention or the person who plays it.

"Before he died, Nestor's father took Orpheus as his ward. Orpheus has been in Pylos ever since."

The man named Orpheus strums his tune. A glorious, beautiful one! She is whisked away on the wings of a song.

So enraptured, she nearly overlooks the most marvelous thing of all. Orpheus lifts his head and glances at the door.

A girl of Persephone's age leans inside the doorway. Persephone has never been so happy to see another *kore* of sixteen.

When Orpheus plays, he gazes at the pretty girl inside the squared entryway. The girl gazes back.

Torchlight casts bronze against walnut-colored hair, big and fluffy and full of curls. She sways in place and twirls the skirt of a blue chiton back and forth in time with her lover's song. Yes, lover—this, Persephone knows without question. Unlike the stone exterior of Hades, Persephone reads their faces easily.

"One guess why Orpheus does not want to go back to Thrace?" Rhadamanthus whispers.

Hades breathes a little laugh. Both of Persephone's arms slither around his bicep. She presses her cheek against his shoulder. Her heart beats in agreement with the music:

Love-me love-me

That is what this song is about. Wanting.

As Orpheus plays, the merrymaking falls to a whisper. When something serious happens, people find stillness. This love song, Persephone knows, is serious. It demands to be honored

Across the room, Minthe points to Cerberus. The mastiffs are asleep. When the song ends, applause startles them awake. They return to upright positions, pretending they never shirked their post for sleep.

The young woman springs from the door and into the arms of Orpheus, who nearly drops his lyre. She smothers him with kisses, and Orpheus returns them happily.

These young lovers seem untouched by darkness. Perhaps their joy will rub off on her and ease the constant churning she feels in her gut. She needs to see youth again. Persephone starts to get up, and her husband's hand closes over her wrist.

"Where are you going?"

"To say hello to—"

"Sit down."

"All I—"

"Sit," he repeats, "down."

Persephone's throat runs dry. Unsteady knees lower her back to Hades's side, and she lifts the cup of wine to her lips. To steady the cup, she uses two hands.

Hades tips his head at Rhadamanthus, and the judge sweeps across the room and interrupts the young couple mid-embrace.

Hades leans in. "You do not approach them," he explains in a voice much softer. "They are mortals. With approval, they may approach *you*."

He pushes the cascade of flaxen hair behind her shoulder, traces his hand over her ear, and fingers the jewels affixed to her lobes. She shivers.

With a wan smile, she nods. "Yes . . . but *Theíos*?"

"Hm."

"Am I not mortal?"

Two young faces approach the mastiff guards. With a hand on each of their backs, Judge Rhadamanthus gently spurs them forward. Orpheus and his lover drag their feet. The whites of their eyes are as clear and wide as the moon. There is a fleshy, youthful fullness to their cheeks, and Orpheus's jaw is without the shadow of a beard.

Neither is smiling. Though Rhadamanthus beams and urges them to approach the High King and Queen of Erebus, the two young lovers look like children caught doing something terrible. The judge may as well have been tugging them along by their ears.

"Majesties," Rhadamanthus introduces, "Prince Orpheus of Thrace and his beloved, Eurydice of Pylos."

They practically throw themselves to the floor.

Hades commands them to arise, and they do. Rhadamanthus delivers a cheerful smack on their backs and returns to his place beside Persephone. Through the hulking heads of Cerberus, the lovers tremble. Eurydice hesitantly reaches for Orpheus's hand. He accepts it with a comforting squeeze.

"Relax," Hades tells them. "You are here to be commended, not condemned."

Neither Orpheus nor Eurydice acts consoled. Persephone senses their terror. She feels sorry for them, and at the same time, a stab of envy she does not quite understand.

She flashes a dazzling smile that dimples both cheeks and gives a little wave. "Hello."

Hades slips her a look of consternation. She drops the smile.

"Your music has piqued the High Queen's interest," Hades says in that quiet way of his.

Orpheus and Eurydice glance at each other. Orpheus lowers his head and stammers, "Oh. Th-thank you for—"

"It sounds just like love," Persephone gushes, unable to contain her smile. Hades straightens as if to tell her to stop talking, but her enthusiasm bubbles up regardless. To show him she is not ashamed to speak of it, Persephone slides her hand over his and clutches.

"It sounds like love," Orpheus grins, "because it is inspired by love." He blushes at the girl next to him with wild ringlets of hair.

"Will you be married?" Persephone asks brightly.

The lovers exchange sideways glances.

Eurydice's voice is soft with affection. "We would like to be married, Majesty."

"But you will not?" Any other outcome is unfathomable to Persephone.

"My father has other plans for me," Orpheus says. He rubs his eye, blinking to clear a particle away.

"Marriage is a contract among kingdoms," Hades says. "And you are contracted to another."

Orpheus looks at Eurydice, their hands fastened. "The contract just happened. By the time I found out, I was already smitten with another."

Eurydice glances at Orpheus, who rubs at the irritation in his eyes. "In spirit," she says, "we are already married—"

"—and in flesh," Hades interjects.

Eurydice turns scarlet and nods in admission. "I will win his father."

"I know his father," Hades says. "He will not be swayed by young love."

The corners of Eurydice's lips turn downward, and she drops her chin. Orpheus puts his arm around her shoulders, squinting and blinking. Where they shone so white before, now his eyes grow bleary and pink. He touches the inner corner of his eye to find a speck of blood on his finger. Eurydice places a hand on the small of his back.

"May I ask the gods to bless their union?" Persephone offers and searches her husband's face. Hades gives her a bemused, but not unpleasant stare. He nods.

The lovers kneel when she approaches. Persephone closes her eyes and breathes slowly and evenly. As she did with King Nestor, she places a hand on each of their heads.

A horrible feeling washes over her, and her stomach roils at the enormity of it. She feels groundless, as if someone snatched the earth away under her feet and any moment she will fall to her death. Persephone falters.

With Nestor, she experienced peace. Not this.

More than anything, Orpheus and Eurydice need the blessing of the gods.

Persephone summons soft words of invocation, speaking slowly as not to stammer, wishing that this wretched sensation would go away. The awfulness lingers like a fading odor.

She has nothing else to say to the young couple. With a faint smile, Persephone returns to her husband's side, inexplicably desperate to cling to him and never let go.

"Blessings are useful," Hades says, "but so is land. Your father will be better won by practical matters. Judge Rhadamanthus will see that Eurydice is given land and a title in our district of Elysium. She will be a bride who comes with something to gain. Tell him the dissolution of your present contract comes with the blessing of the High King and Queen of Erebus."

Astonished, Orpheus and Eurydice blubber words of thanks.

Hades gives Persephone a sly wink. She has never adored him more and whispers the words he has wanted to hear all along:

"Take me upstairs."

Tears of Blood
11

All afternoon, he told himself: *Tonight, sleep.* An abandoned pledge.

Hades uses most of his fading energy to urge her back to his bed chamber. Once there, he sits hard on the bed and removes his sandals, golden cuffs, and crown. This is the last time he will be dressed up for leisure and shoved in front of a crowd. People drain him. The occasion drains him. He endures his role during days spent in court and longs for solitude at night. The crown of rubies and gold irritates him more than a soldier's helmet ever did. Inside the helmet, he can hide. Under the crown, he is on display.

Persephone twirls a sunny lock. Since his return, everything about her appears brighter. Yet this is what he sees in her, rather than the colors. Light. Perhaps the light is playing tricks on him.

"Is something wrong with Orpheus?" she asks, widening heavy-lidded eyes.

"Wrong how?"

Persephone hesitates. "What illness causes tears of blood?"

"Come over here."

She obeys, leading with hips that sway back and forth. Before he can reach for her, Persephone drops to the floor, drapes her arm over his lap, and rests her head there.

He warms to the pressure of her cheek on his thigh. "Why do you think there is illness in him?"

She gives a one-shouldered shrug.

"*Kore*?" He uses this name on purpose, a reminder that his authority comes threefold—as king, as husband, and as an elder.

"Well." She swallows. "I have a feeling that bad things will happen to Orpheus and Eurydice."

"A *feeling*," he says, "or a *knowing*?"

"A knowing." Two slender fingers walk up his thigh. "I thought perhaps an illness might explain it."

Simple child. How could she understand? Helping her would only provoke chatter. He has no interest in chatter.

But he says, "There is no illness."

"Once when you looked upon me, your eyes bled too."

He indulges her by saying, "Yes."

She sits up straight and cocks her pretty head. Staring at him, somehow with a shrewd knowing. "Why?"

"Put your head back where it was."

She places her head on his lap and toys with his hardness as she would a toy newly discovered. The hairs on the back of his neck rise. The muscles in his stomach tighten in effort not to writhe at her touch.

Sometimes he watches himself act in certain ways— uncharacteristic ways he wants to punch himself for. Now he finds himself stroking the back of her silken hair. A beautiful new pet, his alone.

"You knew things. Private things about them." She considers. "And . . ."

Each caress is wind-soft, torture he bears gladly. "Hm?"

"I remember you knew things about me too."

He could stay under her hand forever. Hades and his new pet—who yearns to please him and succeeds. He will reward her in the same way one rewards a pet.

"I have seen it."

She glances up, but knows better than to stop.

"*Seen,*" he repeats. "With my own eyes. Through the eyes of men."

When she speaks, all she says is: "Eyes."

He gives a slow nod. "Yes."

Silence roars in his ears.

"Does it hurt the person when you . . . *see*?"

"Yes."

She considers. "But when you looked upon me, your eyes bled, not mine."

"Yes."

"Why?"

"I do not know why."

"What do you see in me?"

Dumbly, Hades shakes his head. "Light."

This little allowance, a glimpse at who he is, proves to be enough for her.

His nymph bride runs her lips over a bulging lap. "I will be a good wife to you, *Theíos.*"

"Show me."

She pushes the tunic up.

PART TWO
QUESTS

Helios! Show me respect [aidōs], god to goddess, if ever
   I have pleased your heart and thūmos in word or deed.
It is about the girl born to me, a sweet young seedling, renowned for
                                her beauty,
whose piercing cry I heard resounding through the boundless aether,
as if she were being forced, though I did not see it with my eyes . . .
   Tell me which one of the gods or mortal humans did it.

                  —*Homeric Hymn to Demeter*

INKLINGS

1

Hecate is no oracle. But she has heard the word *witch* thrown around enough to know there must be a reason for it, aside from her knack for mending people with things grown from the dirt. Unlike the old priest Vlasis, and his poetic prophecy from a god's-eye view, Hecate simply listens. She prays and listens and, in turn, receives an "inkling" here and there.

Praise the gods for the captain's change of heart. Hecate did not think she was wrong about him. She knew he was important, and here he is. Beneath the evergreen, Hecate eyes him.

At Iasion's instruction, the women wait, seated, as Charon, Iasion, and the farmer unearth the boat from concealment. The boat is bigger than Hecate expected. Nets are wound near the prow. Spears hang against black-pitched cypress.

Pulled ashore and past the embankment of rock and sand, the boat rests beneath muslin weighted by stone and piled high with olive branches. Iasion works expeditiously, while Charon struggles to keep up, tossing branches aside with one hand and panting. Recovering from a lost appendage is hard work, the kind that leaves a man depleted. Hecate sees this truth in the hardiest of men, and Charon is less than hardy these days. From lost muscle and fat, sagging flesh hangs from his bones like limp flags.

"I had to remove the sail," says the farmer, a cousin of Charon's. Their height and stench are all they have in common. The farmer is soft spoken, well-mannered, and has all his teeth.

Charon curses at him for daring to lay a finger on his precious boat, but the farmer explains, "Cousin, I cannot hide a boat with a sail. Such a vessel is hard to come by, and if you hoped to keep it, I had to—"

"I am not an imbecile," Charon growls. "I know why you did it." With the covering removed, Charon steps on the pile of branches and eases himself over the side of the boat. He inspects the wood to see if his cousin caused any damage.

"I think what Charon means is 'thank you,'" Demeter calls.

Iasion throws her a crooked smile. The mother returns it and quickly averts her eyes.

"We can have the mast up by the morning," Iasion tells him.

Under his breath, Charon mutters something about the boards being loose. Hecate suspects his mood soured the moment Iasion showed up, saying he felt guilty that two women should make this journey without escort. Yet they had an escort in Charon, who felt important for the first time in a good while. Important enough to help save the world from doom, as Hecate promised.

Ah, but Charon *is* important. Hecate intuits this. Perhaps more important than the captain.

Iasion must sense the resentment because he slaps a giant hand upon Charon's shoulder. "You keep a fine boat—one of the sturdiest I have seen. The gods must favor you. Sparing it when so many others were lost."

Charon snorts, but his face relaxes.

"We have no room at our hearth," says the farmer. "But please have the barn for the night. My wife would curse if I crammed our home with one more body."

"Eight children will crowd your hearth all right," Charon

says.

"Yes." The farmer chuckles. "Even so, the barn is warm." He raises an arm to the west. "Just beyond the field there. Later, my son will bring you something to eat."

Of the eight children, only one male. The farmer makes good on his promise. Later, after the men erect the mast, the sun disappears to the west. The odor of the barn is more than any of them cares to stomach for longer than necessary. A few shy of a hundred sheep on one side, who-knows-how-many goats on the other. One thing is for certain. For the sake of good sleep, it will be warm in there.

The shepherd boy finds them—not in the barn as the farmer suggested—but huddled beside a bright fire amid a field. Hecate had started it herself with the bow drill and board she yanked from her satchel.

Filling the silence, Demeter prattles on about the timing and importance of three furrowings in a field such as this one. The first plowing should happen soon, in late winter, taking advantage of the rainy season, she says. Hecate tries hard not to nod off.

Charon neglects his bread and stew in favor of something the boy delivered inside a jug. He tips it to his mouth frequently. Only the captain pays attention—undeserved attention—to what Demeter is saying.

Sifting dirt between her fingers, she says, "Three plowings break the ground into fine soil. The weed roots cannot grab hold this way. It should create a bountiful harvest of . . ." she rolls the dirt between her fingers, smells of it, "lentils, I think."

Charon belches. "*Lentils*?" he mocks. "Remarkable!"

With a roll of the eyes, Demeter drops the soil and dusts her hands together.

"You speak like a farmer," Iasion smiles.

"The child of farmers."

"Fascinating," Charon continues. "You know what is equally fascinating?" He brings his jug to the air and waves it in Iasion's direction. "Your sudden appearance."

"Charon," the mother hisses.

"Why are you here?" Charon insists, drunkenly. "I am no fool. A crippled man is not the first choice for a guide." He shoots Hecate a shrewd look. "Am I right?"

Hecate chuckles.

"I thought so," Charon says. "They approached you first, did they not? And you turned them away."

Demeter puts a hand to her scarlet face.

"And yet here you are. Why?"

It is a valid question. Hecate has wondered herself. But it makes no difference to wonder because she had known in her gut the captain would reappear. She has known and not questioned, as it ultimately does not matter why. What matters is that he arrived, playing his part, doing as the gods intended.

Firelight reflects from Iasion's slick head. He looks to Demeter, holding his tongue for her sake.

"Come now, Captain," Hecate says, "What harm is there in answering?"

Before Charon can lower his jug, Iasion snatches it, drinks, and hands it back. With her yammering about soil, Demeter has managed to fake that she is not curious until now.

Iasion says, "I have business there."

"Since when?" Charon says.

"Since the Battle at Pylos."

Charon raises his brows. "You were in the Battle at Pylos?"

"No," Iasion admits. "But I should have been. Had I arrived as scheduled, I would have been. I had been at sea for months. We were late coming to port. My ship should have docked at Pylos weeks before, but the wind was not in our favor. Do you know what it feels like to approach the banks and see black smoke billowing from the hills? I knew as soon as I laid eyes on it. The worst had happened. We walked through the lion gate to find the entire polis sacked. Aflame. The army of the Unseen had come to the aid of Pylos. The Unseen himself had taken off in pursuit of the murderer who brought about the havoc."

Charon lifts the drink again, pointing at Iasion with sudden familiarity. "Yes-yes, I know of him. Zeus's bastard. What is he called again?"

"Alcides," Iasion says.

"No," Charon says, "that is not it."

Demeter snaps. "Iasion should know the name of the man who—"

Iasion finishes her sentence. "—who set fire to my home? Who burned it to the ground and my family along with it?"

"But have you not heard?" Hecate asks. "The news is far-reaching."

"Heard what?" says Iasion.

"The bastard's name is no longer Alcides," Hecate says. "Charon is right."

"'Charon is right,'" the drunkard gloats. "My favorite words."

Iasion shifts. "I did not know there was truth in it."

"Truth in what?" Demeter asks.

"Zeus," Charon slurs, taking a gulp. "He renamed the bastard. Trying to rub away the stain of his sins, as if the *name* is what tarnished him."

"He is Heracles now," Hecate says. "And he has been given feats of strength to atone."

"There are not enough feats in the world to atone for what he did," Iasion says.

"I hate to disappoint you," Hecate says, "but he is not atoning for Pylos. He atones for something else. From what I hear told, yours is not the only family dead by his hands. He killed his own. His wife, his sons."

Iasion stands. Paces. Charon hands him the jug, and he stops pacing long enough to drink.

"If I return to Pylos," Iasion says, "I will never have peace."

"Because?" prods Hecate.

"Because Pylos is a place this monster will never return."

Hecate smiles without humor. "But the monster is likely to return to his father's land. Is that it?"

Iasion looks to Demeter, who cannot feign a lack of interest any longer. "I may not know where *Heracles* is now. But I know he will one day return to Olympus where his father resides. If that is where you are going, then I must go with you."

"And do what?" Charon says. Swaying, he shoots to his feet and catches himself before falling. "Are you telling me that you want to *kill* a child of Zeus the Loud Thunderer?"

"I will succeed where the Unseen failed. I will bring him to justice."

Laughter flies from his throat. "Zeus will strike you for it!"

"Maybe he will," Iasion says. "But I will have my peace."

"If you succeed in killing Heracles," Charon points out, staggering off to piss in the dirt. "If."

"What Charon says is true—" Hecate begins.

"Say it again, crone! 'Charon is right!'" Charon shakes the remaining droplets of urine.

"Heracles has the strength of a god," Hecate continues.

Iasion shrugs, eyes calm with acceptance, "Perhaps a god can fall too."

At this, Charon's foot catches on a root. He topples forward, forgetting that he only one hand with which to catch himself. He extends two and bellows when the nub of his wrist hits the ground. Everyone jumps to their feet. Charon rolls over, cradling his stump and cursing.

As Iasion helps Charon up, Hecate sighs. "I will patch him up," she says. "Then it is time to sleep, Charon. You have had your fill tonight."

Hecate has no intention of returning to the fire. She will settle into the hay alongside the sheep, leaving the mother and the captain to privacy.

After all, it is just an inkling—but her gut proves right once again. The two of them do not seek shelter inside the barn that night.

Hecate is no oracle, but neither is she blind.

THE FIRE

2

"Vengeance is not the only reason I came along with you."

"No?" Demeter grows warmer beneath the cloak.

A moonless sky displays a thousand stars. The fire provides plenty of heat, and the wind shows mercy by seldom disturbing them. Wool cloaks wrapped around them, Demeter and Iasion huddle beside the fire.

Firelight casts little shadow across Iasion's face. A flattened nose provides no contour for shadow. Demeter adjusts her position to face him.

"I know what it is like to lose everything," he tells her. "I do not wish that on you."

"Ah," she nods with a weak smile.

"You deserve a fair life." Picking up a twig, Iasion scratches absently at the dirt, not looking at her. "And I meant what I said. You and the old woman should not be traveling alone."

"We had Charon."

"Charon is a capable sailor, one-handed or not," Iasion says. "But a crippled man is no defender."

"And you will defend us?"

"If I need to," he says. "Having me here already makes you less vulnerable."

"Vulnerable to what?" In her voice, a stiffness. "Thieves? We have nothing to steal except the boat."

As Iasion furrows his brow, his small, close-set eyes shrink into black pearls. "There are worse men than thieves. You should know."

She flinches.

"You should know."

This trauma, invisible as a thumbprint in the dark, has hidden away—and now the light casts upon it and reveals that it has been there all along.

"There are worse men than thieves."

"You should know."

But how can he know what happened to her? With Poseidon, how the High King of the Cyclades had taken what he wanted from her on more than one of his visits to Crete. He sees her as weak, easily targeted. To be viewed this way shames the blush into her cheeks.

Strong. Pious. Lovely. Demeter wants to inspire these impressions in him.

"You are an islander," Iasion explains. "You should know about the Tyrrhenians."

"Oh!" she exclaims and laughs simultaneously, face scalding.

"*Oh*," he nods. "The Sea People are scarcer this time of year, but a man has to eat. The slavers love a strong, healthy woman. They value nearly double a man. A one-handed captain can sail only so fast and fight so many." Flustered, Iasion continues. Hesitant to interrupt the passion, Demeter says nothing. "So yes, you are vulnerable. Strong as you may seem. I did not bring you this far to have you murdered, sold, or molested."

"Molested? I once feared such a thing—"

"You should fear it," he snaps. "It is a reality for a woman like you."

She laughs bitterly. "Like me?"

"Yes!"

"What is *a woman like me*?"

Iasion's face grows pink, and he laughs incredulously. "You." He waves his hand from her crown to her feet.

Why is her heart racing? Why a sudden tingling in her nipples, a heat coursing through her lower belly? She is embarrassed, not by these physical sensations, but by the emotion of hope. Demeter smothers a smile and shakes her head.

Iasion raises hairless brows, forehead rippling into folds. "What?"

"Charon says there is nothing to worry about. I am not 'chase-worthy.'"

"Charon plays his game," Iasion says. "I know his sort. Make a woman feel like dirt, and she will be grateful to bed you later."

Seldom does she feel naive.

"'*Chase-worthy,*'" he snorts. "Ha! The lecherous sneak."

Embarassed, she considers his words. The night settles around them, quiet and nearly windless. For the first time in a long while, Kore falls second in her thoughts. Is it a betrayal to dismiss, however briefly, the sorrow and despair? Somehow, she feels guilty for it. And, simultaneously, grateful.

"Truth is," Iasion says, clearing his throat, "it hardly matters how you look. The pair of you make easy prey. I will not allow it."

"Will it take long," she asks, "to sail to Olympus?"

"Wind permitting?" He looks to the sky. "We should be ashore before Selene shows full face."

Selene, sister to Uranus, god of the sky. Tonight, the goddess of the moon leaves them in peace. Perhaps they have earned it.

"You are stuck with me for a while, then," she says.

"I am not stuck. I willingly abandoned ship for you."

She gives her head a shake. "You mean for Heracles."

At this, he chuckles. "Him too."

Demeter catches him looking at her. When she returns his stare, he does not look away—and yet, it is welcome. To experience an opening of the heart rather than a withering. Lately, there has been only withering.

"Iasion."

"Priestess."

She contemplates, turning scarlet. ". . . nothing."

"Nothing?"

His disappointment emboldens her.

Demeter gathers courage, feeling a strange power in her words. "If I offered myself to you, would you take me?"

When a blush arises to his cheeks, his cheeks swell and eyes water. He glances down.

"That is not why I—" Iasion censors himself, hearing an unintended objection in his own voice. Though she is a fraction his size, Iasion has only ever given her a feeling of sameness. "I would never ask you to—"

"—Of course."

"I want no thanks of that kind."

Demeter gives a half smile. Scoots closer. "That is not how I thank people."

"No?" Watching her draw near, he grows still. Unsure of her intention until now. "You likely give them fruit or such."

"Fruit," she nods, "and sometimes a hen."

Demeter rests her head on the thick of his shoulder.

"Priestess," he says, folding her hand inside his massive palm. "It would be a privilege to love you."

Iasion removes his cloak and spreads it wide upon unbroken soil.

Gladly, she goes to him and rests her hand on the mountain of his drumming chest. Gladly, she allows herself to become someone she has not been in a long while.

Someone besides Mother.

Minos braces his hand against the wall and follows the winding staircase to his quarters. His ankles pop as he takes the last few steps. Brittle bones, deteriorating year after year. He needs food and a nap, and then he can continue with the day. Later, perhaps, he should poke his head in on the queen and lend a kind word. It never hurts to be in the good graces of a queen. He finds himself worrying about her more than he should. He knows the history of the woman who came before her. A short history.

The moon has cycled nearly twice since the day of *gamos*.

At the end of the corridor, the glowing rectangle of his doorway offers the promise of comfort. He makes his way to the end, walks inside, and nearly shouts.

A child stands before him. He cannot be older than six.

Minos's heart jolts and beats wildly.

The boy says, "Come!" and holds out a tiny hand.

Minos places one hand to his chest. Ah! —this is a slave boy he sees from time to time, the one who replaces splintered weapons with fresh ones when the guards train in the courtyard. In his hand, the boy displays a gold coin.

Minos reaches for it. The boy's fingers snap closed, and he brings his treasure close to his body in fear of it being stolen.

"Mine," he says.

For a moment, Minos could have sworn that the head of an eagle was embossed upon it.

Zeus's seal. Such riches will sustain the boy and his family for perhaps a lifetime.

"Where did you get that?" he asks, pleasant.

The boy stashes his gold treasure in his tunic and beckons. "Come."

Tiny bare feet slap against the floor as the boy races down the hall. Minos walks at his own pace. Once he approaches the staircase, he finds the child waiting, impatient, bobbing up and down on his feet as if his youthful body cannot contain its own vigor. Torture to wait for an old man!

"Where are we going?"

"Outside."

Slaves and nobility do not touch. Minos finds himself reaching out regardless and taking the boy's hot sticky hand. He feels a stab of remorse for everything that came before his service here in Asphodel. After the atrocities, no child dares touch him.

Even his *own* children were afraid of him in the end. Of what the madness had done to him.

The child pulls him along. Through the candlelit staircases. Through the narrow corridors.

Minos assumes he will be taken to the central courtyard to find Persephone waiting there in tears. Despite his sullied reputation, she is comfortable with him, the former king who both ruled and became exiled from Knossos during her childhood. His is the most familiar face she has seen in many moons.

The boy steers him past the door to the courtyard and toward the entrance to the palace.

On each side of the doors stand a guard and a mastiff. Torches cast firelight against bronze breastplates. The mastiff's yellow eyes twinkle.

Each guard wrenches an iron handle, and the doors part, spilling winter light inside. Together with the boy, Minos walks through a stone passageway, open to the sky. Flakes land and melt into beads of water.

The boy's eagerness revitalizes him. He finds himself walking faster now, very curious.

Minos knows he should be more cautious. Perhaps he should be concerned about what might await him as the end of their journey. Yet somehow, he is not.

Finally, they are at the farthest end of the lion gate. Overhead, two marble lions roar open-mouthed. The stonemason had carved their fangs to be long and pointed, ribs visible upon emaciated bodies.

Minos can hardly see beyond the nearby pines as the flurries come faster.

The boy releases his hand and scampers away.

From between the pines, a man strides forward. He is enormous. Minos has never seen bigger arms or a broader chest. His hair is tousled with gold-brown curls. He is beardless, and as Minos squints at him, he takes note of handsome features given to him by kingly parentage.

Until now, Zeus's son was only a changing name.

Minos crinkles his brow. So as to feign hospitality, he pastes a smile on his lips and laces his fingers before him.

"Heracles, I presume," Minos says.

To this, Heracles deals a gentle smile. "What gave me away?"

"Your chin."

Heracles touches the cleft beneath a plump bottom lip. "I have my father's chin."

And your sister's, Minos thinks.

Hades has been on the hunt for this man for nearly a year.

Now, here he stands at their doorstep. When Hades went to the battle of Pylos, he had every intention of bringing Heracles back with him. The "brat of Zeus" is what Hades calls him.

Parentage exempts no man from judgment—Hades condemns high ranking men all of the time.

"You should know," Heracles says, fishing inside of his cloak, "I am armed."

How did he get past the Monoliths of Cerberus? Whether arriving by land or river, a stone mastiff skull disrupts the entry roads, each containing guards and their mastiffs. Minos will send a scout to determine if there was bloodshed or if Heracles slipped past them somehow.

Heracles pulls out a gleaming sword, handled elaborately in gold, inlaid with sapphire as blue as the sea. His moves are slow and without threat. Heracles places the sword at Minos's feet.

"Now I am no longer armed."

To be dangerous, Heracles needs no weapon. But Minos will play along.

"I accept your gesture of good will."

"In return, I trust you can lay down your judgment of me, King Minos."

"I am no king."

Against a collar made from a lion's golden pelt, Heracles's cheeks flush.

Minos laughs a little. Is Heracles embarrassed for him? Embarrassed that a king was rightly punished and does not protest his fate? Yes, Heracles is embarrassed because he, himself, could never stomach this act of submission.

"As you know," says Heracles, "I have immunity under my father, King of Kings."

Searching the face of Heracles for any sign of hostility, Minos sees none. Has Heracles come for Cerberus already—his twelfth-assigned feat, covertly plotted by Minos himself?

"Why have you come, son of Zeus?" Minos continues. "What makes you draw me out?"

The man, nearly two heads taller than Minos himself, glances around. Snow dissolves against his skin and collects upon the extraordinarily beautiful fur of his collar. His neck is as big around as his head.

"I suppose you heard about—" Heracles swallows, looking away again. "—about what I did."

"Yes."

Sorrow lifts his brows and makes his eyes glassy. No, he is not here for Cerberus already.

"I murdered my wife." Heracles admits and blinks away tears. "I murdered my sons." His perfect aquiline nose glows red.

"For this, any other man would stand before Hades."

Heracles nods and forces the sorrow from his voice. "I intend to atone for it. I never would have done it, but my father's bitch poisoned me. I did not know what I was doing. I was asleep. Deranged and asleep. I remember nothing—"

"I know all of that," Minos says, holding up a hand.

"I woke up and saw them. I wanted to kill the man who did it." Staring into space, Heracles shakes his head to clear it. "Judge Minos, you have murdered children. Do you recall how it felt when your madness faded away? When you finally knew within your soul what you had done? Did it not strip you to the core? What if those children had been your own?"

No man had ever phrased it so personally. Compassion frightens Minos. His loyalty is to Hades.

"I never longed for pardon," Minos says. "I deserved punishment, far more than what I received. You may avoid Hades in this lifetime, but you cannot avoid the gods. And you cannot avoid the shame."

"Nevertheless," Heracles says, shaking his head, "I have a chance to appeal to the gods."

"To prove you are not evil, you mean."

"So you say."

Minos folds his arms. It is getting colder. Snow mounts, covering dead grass. "King Eurystheus of Tiryns has given you the opportunity to atone for your crimes."

Heracles gives a cocky half-smile. "So it was King Eury who told you about my crime? He answers to Hades?"

"We all answer to Hades."

Heracles stiffens, dimpled chin lifting in defiance, and clenches his teeth. "I answer to no one except Zeus."

"So you say."

"Had someone given you the chance at redemption," Heracles says, "would you not have taken it?"

"I was given that chance," Minos opens his arms wide, like Atlas holding the world. "I am a Judge of Erebus. Service to Hades is my atonement."

"Then help *me* atone."

"According to King Eury," Minos says, "you were given feats of strength. How can an old man help with that?"

Heracles nods once. "I was given ten labors."

Ten? Ah, so Heracles does not yet know that King Eury will soon be penalizing him with two more. Heracles earned the penalty of two additional labors because he asked for help with one and a reward for another. Of course, he is unaware. Otherwise, he would not be requesting help with this one.

"Do you know them?"

"In summary," Minos admits. He thinks back, recalling the few details that King Eury imparted to the throne.

"To slay or capture notorious beasts."

Heracles removes the cloak from his shoulders. "Take this."

With a twirl of the cloak, he winds it around Minos's back and drapes the thing around him. Minos is encased with skin-tingling warmth. The fur tickles his chin. The muscles in his neck relax.

"This cloak," says Heracles, "is lined with the pelt of the Nemean lion. My arrows could not slay him. His pelt was too thick. I clubbed him and strangled him with my bare hands."

Heracles holds up one enormous hand. Minos notices the pointer finger is strangely short in comparison to the others. The skin of the fleshy pink tip looks newer than the rest. "I lost part of a finger. So I used his own claws to skin him. My slaves made for me this fine cloak."

"I see."

"He was my first labor," Heracles says. "It is my gift to you."

"Yes," Minos says, "and what would you have in return?"

Before Heracles can respond, Minos knows. His gut falls. A shiver runs down his spine. He suddenly longs to shrug the pelt from his shoulders.

"To slay or capture notorious beasts."

"My sixth feat," says Heracles, "is to capture the Cretan bull."

Minos looks away.

"Legend has it," Heracles says, "you know where it is."

"I freed him before I fled," Minos says. "Why would I know where he is?"

"You have my word he will not be harmed. Only detained and moved."

This time, Minos does laugh. "Your word?"

"For laughing at the son of Zeus," Heracles warns, "I would kill any other man."

"But any other man cannot tell you where to locate my bull, or you would not be here."

Heracles clenches his fists and takes a step back. Minos removes the cloak from around his shoulders, missing the warmth.

He drapes the heavy thing over his arm and extends it to Heracles.

"You believe I will help you," Minos says as Heracles takes his cloak. "Do not use your father's title to explain why. My allegiance is to the Unseen."

Minos turns. Snow comes faster. He hopes the aggression in Heracles truly is spurred by poison, as Minos is hardly a match for a man of such breadth and strength.

The brat of Zeus calls out. "I think you *want* to help me."

Minos turns. "Why?"

"I believe a man is defined by the sum of his deeds. So do you."

"I never took you for a philosopher."

And Heracles is not wrong when he answers: "Loss will turn you into a philosopher."

Mother never groomed her for this. Marriage was not supposed to be in Persephone's future. Those normal, preparative talks that girls have as their bodies change, as young men begin to appraise them rather than tease them—they never happened.

Persephone does not know how to be a wife. But, then again, nor did Mother. Mother knew only the priesthood.

Except, Persephone hardly sees her husband, really. Only at night, when he seeks her out to delight in her body, like a starved man yearning for food.

Already, the sun has set, but there is no sign of Hades. Perhaps he is angry with her. She can think of no other reason for his absence, and the terror of his anger forces her to pace the floor and tug at her lip and wonder what she did.

Had she not pleased him the night before?

This cannot be—for Persephone has been good. All she thinks is how to please him. In return, he indulges her in conversation. He is not much of a talker, not for someone like Persephone who seeks out conversation like a starved *woman* yearning for food.

For instance, he has indulged her with secrets. Persephone loves a secret! It makes her feel special to know things others do not. He told her of his "insight," which perhaps is not a secret if the judges know—and yet, Hades treats her as one of them now. Part of the fold.

And she knows the names of Cerberus! She had begged to know, tired of calling them One, Two, and Three.

Body glistening with sweat, limbs tangled in the blankets and chest draped in the fabric of her naked arms, Hades had relented, winded from the exertion of spending himself inside of her.

"They are called Proí, Mesméri, and Nýchta."

When he confided these names, he had pointed to each sleeping beast upon the floor. Pleased, she had called out each of their names—clever names as she imagined! *Morning. Noon. Night*. Their ears had pricked, and stubby tails shimmied happily.

"You may call them by name here, but never in front of others. They are Cerberus, guards to the Unseen. To be viewed as sentient will diminish them."

"Not even the judges?"

"Not even the judges."

How wonderful! To know a thing that even the judges do not!

So, if she is treasured in this way, to be indulged with secrets, why would her husband deprive her of his presence now? Why, when this is the best time of her lonesome day?

With each passing moment, Persephone wrings her hands and checks outside the door. Outside the window, the occasional howl of a wolf.

The fifth time she goes to the door, she spots a figure standing at the end of the hall.

She has seen it plenty. Regardless, her breath catches in her throat and stays there, unable to escape. As if breathing might cause the thing to attack.

Although it has never attacked.

The Unholy stretches as tall as the ceiling. She has called it Unholy, for what else can she call a Being that cannot be purged by the gods, cannot be released from these walls?

Persephone stands motionless outside the doorway. Staring at the Unholy. The hairs on her arms and legs stand straight up.

"Wh-what do you want?"

She intends it as a demand. *What do you want!* Yet, words flung at the Unholy can only be whimpered.

With voice and words, It cannot reply. She hears the breathy answer inside her ears, the response like a long sigh or a great wind:

"No."

"N-no?"

If Cerberus were by her side, would they snarl and lunge? Might they chase away the Unholy, as protectors should?

Cerberus is absent. During the day, the dogs sit with her husband in court, providing a fearsome barrier between the Unseen and those who are subjugated at the foot of his throne.

The giant shadow whooshes the sound of:

"No."

Cold tears spill from her unblinking eyes. "Leave me alone."

In reply, the Unholy lifts serpentine arms, saying, *"Obey."*

Then, It is gone. Its disappearance emboldens her, powers her lungs with the defiance to cry out, "Obey what? I do not understand you!"

Fresh anger springs to the surface, from seemingly nowhere, and she stamps her foot. "I never understand you! Stop pestering me!"

Persephone storms from the safety of her quarters. As she stomps, wondering what could possibly be detaining her husband, a curious memory surfaces. The memory of the celebration of *epaulia,* when the men seemed all-too-familiar with the painted women later identified to her as *hetaera.*

"I believe her name is Minthe."

The whore with blue-black hair had no problem glaring at her with a snide upturn of a glossy-red mouth. How familiar is her husband with this Minthe? What else should a man do at night besides take refuge inside the arms of a devoted bride?

Perhaps she has spent too much time with dogs—for she hears an inner growl. Fists doubled, nails cutting into her palms, Persephone takes the stairs quickly, passing guards and mastiffs along the way, and once she finds herself looking down into the wide entry-way just within the palace doors, she spots a young woman standing alone in the center of the floor.

This young woman with dark curls stands with her feet disappearing into the floor mosaic. Aside from the young woman, the large representation of three dog heads is the only visible thing in the room.

"Eurydice?"

Eurydice turns her face toward the inquiry. Her pale face points upward to where Persephone stands at the top of the stairs.

Scarlet and purple fabric decorate Eurydice's lovely form. Familiar colors. Persephone recognizes them from when she was a bride herself.

Flying down the staircase, Persephone glances away for a moment, long enough to lift the bottom of her skirt to keep from tripping. Only a moment. When she reaches the bottom of the staircase, the entry-way is empty.

The inanimate mosaic of the three heads of Cerberus snarls in three directions. With a racing heart, Persephone spins in every direction, searching.

"Eu-eurydice?"

At the west entrance, a strange looking object lies on the ground, as if dropped. Persephone goes to it. She picks the handled instrument from off the floor and plucks one of the strings. The twang vibrates against her finger.

A lyre.

There is only one lyre Persephone has ever seen. This one, played weeks ago, so beautifully that it lulled even Cerberus to sleep.

"It sounds like love because it is inspired by love."

From out of the darkness of the west corridor, the shade of young Eurydice emerges with her eyes unblinking and voice full of sorrow.

"He will never say farewell."

No Special Terror

5

Confession fresh on his mouth, the lyre player goes willingly into Tartarus.

"Eagerly," the judge had said. "He requests the High Queen."

Yes, the accusations are true. Orpheus's bride is dead, her body stolen. Hidden by the distraught groom, who had refused to proceed with funeral rites and sneaked away with Eurydice in tow.

No, Orpheus will not return her. And so he came, by choice, to confess: He has defied Hades's law of sacred burial.

Intercepted on the way to his marriage bed, Hades nearly lets the matter wait until the morning. Let Orpheus of Thrace kneel at the foot of his throne. Hades can have a look at him tomorrow. Now belongs to Persephone, who shines like a beacon at the end of a cave.

"I have a feeling that bad things will happen to Orpheus and Eurydice."

Each step becomes slower until he stops at the final one.

"A feeling or a knowing?"

The mastiffs shift from foot to foot, gazing up for direction. Something about this strikes Hades the wrong way.

"The dissolution of your present contract comes with the blessing of the High King and Queen of Erebus."

Why would the lyre player violate burial law, a law enacted by Hades himself, when Hades had done the pair a favor?

It can wait. He will sift through it in the morning. But Hades finds himself abandoning the staircase leading to paradise and, instead, making his way to the entrance of Tartarus.

Cerberus trails. They detest being taken into Tartarus. But at the entry, the anticipated mastiff whine fails to come. The dogs remain at peace.

A helmeted soldier, standing guard with his dog, takes a knee.

"Orpheus," Hades commands.

The corridor ends at what might be mistaken for a hole in the floor, surrounded by chain-linked iron poles. Inside the hole, crude stairs descend steeply. A halo of yellow light reflects off jagged walls, revealing stalactites above. As they draw nearer to the bottom, torchlight reflects in the shallow water below, puddles mirroring the cave's overhead fangs.

At the base of the pit, the guard casts light toward a tunnel. They step into it and toward the bolted doors on either side.

When the guard escorts him to Orpheus, Hades's spirit recoils. This differs from the old sort of dread within the belly of Tartarus.

This disgust is new. Unexpected.

It is the same cell where Persephone spent the night before *proaulia*. Here, he laid claim to her in a way that elicited a familiar response:

Fear. Obedience.

Since, the nights with Persephone have tired him. Slowed him. Yet desire roars as loudly as before, and he is so mesmerized by it that he becomes a drunkard of sorts. Now, once the initial derangement is spent, he cannot stop from touching her naked flesh until he rouses again. Stroking, petting, immersing himself in his new treasure. Discovering places and rhythms that cause her to purr like a cat, to wriggle and writhe and shudder in pleasure as would a man.

This, a far better response to command than fear.

Hades shoves the thought aside and notices he feels nothing but this singular remorse. Otherwise, the cell is merely a dank pit with all the comforts of a guiltless man's quarters.

"Tartarus sets you apart from other kings. Or it used to."

The moment Hades crosses the threshold, Orpheus looks up from where he sits on the pallet. Quite unusual, to be visited by the High King himself.

Orpheus collapses to the ground, resting his forehead there, palms splayed next to his coppery head. He babbles over and over, "Mercy . . . Please, mercy."

Hades walks to the lyre player. Presses into the light.

Curls hanging over his eyes and cheeks, Orpheus keeps his eyes to the floor. Droplets of blood fall from between the curtains of hair and pool upon stone.

Within the yellow glow surrounding the lyre player, Hades spies a stiff, lifeless form, wrapped in gauze. The form lies upon a slab of rock inside of a high-roofed cave. The path leading to this cave rings familiar. It should. During the Titan War, Hades navigated the Erebusian cave systems. He knows the land well.

Even so, one cave can resemble another. One tree or rock, like the next.

Where Eurydice's body is tucked away, Hades has only a vague notion.

"Give me a reason to keep you alive."

Orpheus does a peculiar thing. He closes his eyes and shakes his head. "I cannot."

As if there is relief in it.

"Do you want me to kill you, Orpheus of Thrace?"

Orpheus peers up. His eyes blaze a ruddy hue. "In this life and in the life thereafter, I will be with her."

Compulsive, unstoppable—this love.

Orpheus catches sight of the doorway. Hades turns.

It has been nearly a full sun since laying eyes on his own bride. The sight of Persephone makes his blood run hotter. Hotter because, while the spectacle of her is always welcome, her location is not.

Their eyes lock. Persephone gasps and takes a step back. Caught. He has warned—and punished— her for intruding Tartarus before.

As he approaches, she drops her chin.

"Kore—"

"—I kn-know, but *Theios*—"

"Why have you come for Orpheus?"

"Orpheus?" She shakes her head. "I-I followed . . ."

"Followed?"

"Eurydice." She looks him hesitantly in the eye. "I followed Eurydice."

For the first time, she notices the lyre player. Blood crusts the waterlines of his eyes. Persephone's mouth hinges open. "What has happened?"

He does not like being questioned this way. "Ask him."

She pauses, thinking it a trap.

"R-really?" she asks, skittish.

Fear is what he said he wanted. Says he *wants*. Yet, at this moment, his stomach turns at her fear. Hades motions to the Orpheus. As Persephone edges away, she looks at him, scared he will pounce. Already, she starts to cry.

To assure her, Hades retreats a step.

Persephone rushes to Orpheus, but stops herself before dropping to the ground. "Orpheus, what have you done?"

"I have committed a crime, Majesty."

She shakes her head. "What crime?"

"I admit it. I am guilty."

"Why has the shade of your bride come to me?" Persephone wails.

When Orpheus swallows, Hades hears the click of his throat, the nervous sound of no moisture going down.

"Majesty," he cries, eyes spilling pink tears. "I cannot let her go. And she cannot let me go."

"What happened?" she says. "Why do I see her shade, Orpheus?"

"She has died."

Persephone sobs. "How?"

He wets his lips, scanning the air for answers. "The day of *gamos,* we walked together, in procession, down the streets. I took her hand, and she was smiling, I am sure of it. I saw no sign of pain. Otherwise, I would have tended to it." His desperate face pleads for an answer. "Does love erase pain?"

Quickly, Persephone answers, "No."

Hades shifts in place.

"Eurydice was my beautiful bride," Orpheus says. "The farther we progressed, the more ill she appeared. But she smiled at me and giggled. How could a sick person be cheerful? I lied to myself that she was fine. She was simply weakened by happiness, the same happiness that made my own hands shake. It was a long walk through the city. She started breathing harder. Breathless from the excitement and the long walk uphill! Would you not think this the cause? Then at once, she paled. All the color in her lips, gone. And she bore harder into my hand, as if giving me more of her weight, needing *help.* She limped and fell, moaning and . . . she started to cry and lifted her skirt. Her ankle was black, bubbled, and eaten away."

Eyes fixed in space, Orpheus mutters, "'What happened?' I asked her. Just as you asked me. 'What happened?'"

Persephone presses both hands over her mouth and nose.

"'A viper bite,' she told me. The night before. She knew she would die. She said . . . if she must die, she wanted to die my wife."

Tearful Orpheus. Around him, the colors of love and grief. Plaguing him, binding him in a death grip.

How grave it is for Orpheus to be without the woman he claimed. How essential this woman became to his very well-being. Had his life been terrible before, and Orpheus did not even know it? Had he been missing something critical to joy? His whole life spent thinking the void was normal?

Yet the void was for love. Love, having become his norm, now tortures Orpheus. Its absence promises nothing but the void.

A lifetime of it.

"Death takes us all," Hades thinks aloud, eying the cave walls, anxious to leave. He needs to be alone.

"Then," Orpheus asks, "why would death begrudge me this small lifetime with Eurydice, when it gets eternity with us in the end?"

"I want to help you," Persephone says.

"You do?" Orpheus sighs, knowing she would.

Hades recalls what Aeacus had told him about Orpheus:

"He requests the High Queen."

"Mine is a woman's heart," Persephone declares, confident of her newfound maturity. "I know the depths of your longing. When longing binds you, you will never be without sadness."

"Yes," says the lyre player.

"And," she adds, "it is also true that your wife stands at your side now."

Orpheus glances to his left and right.

Nothing.

"This world is no longer hers," Persephone says. "She suffers for it, and so do you."

Suddenly, it is hot down here—so why is Hades shivering? His pulse races, breath coming quicker.

"Majesty," Orpheus nods. "Then you understand."

"Understand?"

Now Persephone turns to Hades for answers. *Now* she wants his help. Where is the newfound maturity in which she prides herself? The hardness of his stare conveys that she will get no help from him. Her eyes bounce away as if touching hot coal.

She chose to insert herself into this. She must see it through.

"You hold favor among the gods," Orpheus explains. "Everyone knows it. King Nestor himself said so." He stops, cowering under the scrutiny of Hades. "It is no secret what Her Majesty did for the soldier who died of rot. They say when you blessed him, his body sat upright and spoke words of prophecy."

A guilty blush rises to Persephone's cheeks. As soon as she glances at her husband, she looks away, afraid that her gaze will invite questions.

But Hades knows. Of course, he knows.

He would wager his godhood that these "words of prophecy" were the same words that boomed from the heavens the day Persephone called upon the gods to cleanse Asphodel.

"And while you are here, you shall rule all that lives and moves and shall have the greatest rights among the deathless gods."

Orpheus says, "They call Her Majesty the 'Divine Priestess of Erebus.'"

"Ask what you came to ask," Hades deadpans.

"I need my wife. I cannot continue without her."

Persephone throws Hades a helpless glance. "B-but, Orpheus, there is nothing to gain by releasing Eurydice to the gods until you release her from your heart."

Inside of Hades, something warms and then breaks.

Orpheus draws a breath of courage. "I do not want my wife to be released to the gods."

"Then," asks Persephone, "how can I help you?"

"I—" Orpheus tries to formulate the outrageous words.

Hades looks upon him without a hint of surprise. "Orpheus does not want his bride released. He wants her *raised*."

Silence blankets the room. The pop of torch fire interrupts the quiet.

"I—I," Persephone stammers and resorts to Hades again. "*Theíos?*"

Hades squints. "Why do you believe that this can be done?"

"Faith."

"Faith in a girl of sixteen? For this, you commit a crime that condemns you to Tartarus?"

Before Persephone can speak, Hades cuts her off. "This is not a question of whether or not Persephone is *able* to help you." He seizes her wrist, not enough to hurt, but enough to make a point. Pulling her close, he tells her, "There is always someone wanting help. This is a matter of *discernment*. We do not always get things just because we want them. Do you understand?"

Trembling, she nods.

"What you want," Hades tells Orpheus, "is a reversal of the natural order. There are two things that we do only once. We are born, and we die."

Like a disappointed child, Orpheus buries his head in his hands. Persephone whimpers a little, pulling on the wrist he now crushes in his grip. Before letting go, Hades deals a stern look.

"If the High Queen wants to help you, I will allow it. She may free your bride into the hands of the gods. This will bring Eurydice peace." He pauses and peers down at the young man. "Orpheus of Thrace, the peace of *your* soul rests in your hands alone. Move forward and do not look back. Your faith must be in *me*. This is my command."

"Oh, husband," she moans. "This does not feel like helping."

"Go to your bed." Incredulous, he turns to her. "Take Cerberus with you."

Hades watches her go. Running an unsteady hand over his jaw, he takes one final look at Orpheus. He may be a pitiful sight, but at least the boy is not weeping.

"Your bride will never return to you," Hades tells him. "You can let her go or you can follow her by your own hand. Only one of these choices holds virtue with the gods. But, Orpheus, I will retrieve what you stole. Eurydice's body will be returned to her family for rites and burial. Even if it brings you further pain."

"There is no pain as great as losing her."

And to this, Hades responds, "We will see."

"Bring me the Erinyes."

This is the last thing the judge expects to hear before going to sleep.

Bleary-eyed, Aeacus steps beyond the doorway of his quarters and into the corridor. He had been napping before bed, as one might nibble on pinches of bread before a full meal.

At his door, Hades the Unseen, ruler of Erebus.

To Aeacus, Hades looks as fragile as a child. Similar to the one Aeacus once pulled from the caves of Tartarus, where the boy's *father* would often punish him.

Under a dark fringe of lashes, Hades's black eyes swell from lack of sleep. Aeacus cannot read a man's colors as Hades can, but he knows distress when he sees it.

He catches himself before reverting to the past and calling the High King *boy*.

"What made you change your mind?" he asks.

"I never ruled on it," he says. "Now I have."

"Good. It will be done."

Hades gives a tired nod. He mopes away in a daze with no sign of Cerberus. Aeacus had seen the dogs earlier, following Persephone to the bed chamber she has not occupied in a while.

Since they wed, Hades has kept her in his own quarters, available to him. Down a different exit.

In his stupor, Hades turns right. Persephone had gone left with Cerberus.

"Your new pet went the other way," Aeacus quips.

Hades stops where the hall divides. He knows exactly where she is and elects to go elsewhere. The High King looks at his old mentor as if he has something to say, but he does not say it. Something holds him back.

Pride.

I told you so, Aeacus smirks. *A nuisance.*

Hades says nothing and continues his original path.

Away.

Away from *her*.

Even after he falls asleep, Aeacus is still smirking.

"*Your new pet went the other way.*"

Sweet isolation. Tonight, Hades will sleep alone. He needs to collect his thoughts without a woman distracting him. He strips off formal robes and throws on an older tunic that he forbids the slaves to discard. The older the fabric, the more comfortable it is. He presses the palm of his hand against a column near the window and forces his weight forward, stretching the shoulder wound that stiffens while he sits all day.

It will fluster Persephone to withhold attention. She will question herself and everything that happened with Orpheus. A questioning mind is a dog chasing its own tail. Let her worry her husband is angry. He is not, but she can think so.

In bed, the girl is eager and willing and gives herself like a human sacrifice. If Hades wants violence, she bears it with little protest. It is not violence she fears. It is being ignored.

Isolation is a difficult consequence for a girl with no family and only one person upon whom to rely for affection. The promise of love dangles as a treat.

Within an hour of peaceful solitude, the knocking starts. Quiet, hesitant knocking.

"*Theíos?*"

He considers.

The voice is muffled, broken. He goes to the door and opens it. There stands the pretty child bride, puffy-eyed and runny-nosed. Her lip quivers as she tips a dimpled chin and wipes at each cheek. Pale gold plaits run down each shoulder. She wears the thin bedclothes that make him crazy.

"Are you mad at me?"

Behind her, the dogs whine, wanting their mistress to be happy. He scowls at them and shields the opening of the door with his body.

"Go to sleep," he tells her.

"Not without you . . ."

The daughter of Zeus manipulates with tears and should know that it does not work on him. She will not play at his heartstrings. He starts to shut the door and finds resistance. With a little thump, she presses against the ornately carved wood.

"No!" she bawls. He studies her face for a moment to know if this histrionic display is real. Her cheeks are splotched pink. She sputters and huffs between sobs.

"You do not get to do that!" she wails and pounds at the door once. "You *took* me! You took me, and now you must take care of me! Y-y-y-ou are not allowed to leave me alone in this place ever—!"

"I am not allowed," he seethes, "by *whom*?"

"BY ME!" she shrieks, striking the door again. She gags on her own tears. Long flyaway hairs dust her upraised brow. Around her silhouette, the light burns brighter than he has ever seen, kindled by tantrum. "I SAY SO! You will not leave me alone!"

Behind her, Cerberus growls. The rumble begins in the throat of the first dog, then catches into the throat of the second and third dogs. Proí lets out a perfunctory bark, ordering them both to get along.

He flings the door open so fast she practically falls inside. He shoves her into the hall. "*Kore*, get back to your room. I will say it only once."

The maudlin contortions in her face stop. She sniffs wetly and wipes at her nose again. As she straightens where she stands, crystal tears brim.

"Fine."

He creases his brow, boiling under the tunic. "Fine?"

"I *will* go." Braids flipping, she stomps away. "I will! —and you will not see me EVER!"

"*Kore*."

At first, he trails her slowly. Seeing him follow, Persephone begins to move faster, like a spooked deer in the woods.

"You got your deal with my father and that is all you care about! I know you hate me! From the start, you hated me!"

"Stop!"

"NO!" She keeps babbling. "No, I will not! You ordered me to go away! Well, I do not want to be here anyway!"

When he grabs her, he knows she will yield. It is her game. She will break and shower him with kisses, which he will ward off (of course he can) and send her on her way.

Instead, the sweet nubile beauty throws a punch. It lands squarely across the jaw, surprisingly sharp and strong for a willowy arm. It flies like the dainty tail of a whip. He snatches her wrist, and she screams and flails and swings wildly with one free arm. She wallops him on the shoulder and kicks him in the leg. Blows land on his arms, chest, against the side of his head, until the furious whirlwind of limbs pesters like a swarm of biting flies.

Even after restraint, she bursts into tears once again, squirming in his arms, wailing:

"I will never win you! It will always be! Why do I bother?"

She fights, and he tightens his grip, hoping to silence her, but the words continue to pour. What began as a trickle of hysteria breaks into flood.

"You will not love me," she sobs, "Why did you take me if you do not love me?! It is not fair! You are mean, mean, MEAN, and I hate you!"

Her soft curves create friction against his chest and stomach and groin. The harder she pulls, the tighter he clutches. She will tire herself out. If he squeezes hard enough, she will not be able to catch her breath and gather the next deluge of ridiculous words.

But as the words continue, something within him stirs. Skin to skin, he senses genuine despair.

"M-m-mother!" she cries, "h-help me!" Her bent arms are trapped between her chest and his. "Wh-what h-have I done? I a-am sorry I-I did n-not listen. I am s-sorry. Gods f-forgive me, p-please, I wa-want my m-mother, I want my m-mother—"

He never wants to feel such despair.

He has *caused* such despair.

On and on, she calls for the mother. In his mind's eye, Hades recalls the woman called Demeter who riddles Persephone's past so thoroughly that it is impossible to separate the two. They loved and fought fiercely, and now Persephone begins to speak aloud to the memory of this lean, broad-hipped priestess with a lovely face and cornsilk hair.

"M-mother. I n-need you, I am s-sorry."

He places a hand against the back of her head. His other arm loosens, holding without possessing.

Were the mother to appear, Persephone would escape with her—or try. The thought of it makes him bend, scoop, and carry her off.

All the while, she cries.

Hits him.

Hates him.

Once inside his quarters, he deposits Persephone onto the bed. She curls onto her side and wets the blankets with tears.

"I do love you. Surely you know that."

Reluctant, Hades sits on the bed and lies down beside her. Rolling onto his side, he pulls her into him and strokes her hair. Persephone continues to murmur pleas and apologies to a mother who is not present.

A male would not carry on like this, even if his mother has died, but Hades shares the wound in secrecy. He knows sadness, and there is nothing to say.

In time, she drifts off, but Persephone's cries continue in sleep. The grief oozes like blood not stanched.

When morning comes, Hades leaves the room before she wakes. The corridors are freshly lit, and winter light filters into the window at the end of the hall. Next to the window stands Minos.

With Cerberus at his side, Hades approaches the judge. His bad shoulder aches from where he was lying on it all night, unwilling to let go of the girl. Trying to wipe the events from his head, he stares ahead.

"Good morning." Minos falls in beside him, and they walk together to the assembly room.

He thinks of Persephone sleeping in his bed, and feels a sharp longing to turn around.

Minos says, "I have news of Heracles."

Hades rubs his temple. "Who?"

The judge cracks a smile, flashing colors of bemusement along with it. What had he just said?

Heracles.

He clears his throat. "Until he completes the labors," Hades corrects him, "his name is Alcides."

"My mistake," Minos humors. "I mean Alcides."

Hades knows from what he suffers. So do Minos and the rest

of the judges. Hades rolls his eyes at himself.

When will he be cured of the fog in his mind and pressure in his chest? It is strangely addictive, this feeling.

"I do love you. Surely you know that."

This is fine. Good, even. Intoxication is a short-term state. One day it will wear off, and Hades will no longer be distracted. He will not find himself half-smiling and lost in reverie while some criminal pleads for his life at the foot of the throne. Most of all, he will not forget the name of the man he has been itching to kill for nearly a year. He will be present and in full possession of himself again.

When the drunkenness has run its course.

This should be a comfort. But projecting life into the future makes his gut sink.

Immediately, he releases all such hopes for a time when he no longer aches to be near her.

For now, Hades elects to forget the future. For now, he will enjoy the good.

Minos tells him the truth. There is no keeping the truth from the Unseen.

It has been years since Minos has seen the bull that cost him his throne. Years since he has *seen* the bull—but it has not been years since thinking of it.

Hades knows this and says, "You want to help him."

Minos blinks to make sure there is no burning or blood there. His eyes feel fine. He can see fine.

And yet Hades still knows.

"I do," Minos says, "yes."

Hades pauses. "Can you?"

Minos lifts his brows and blows out in contemplation. The breath rustles his whiskers. "I am one of few who know where the bull is."

"You and your cohorts."

"Of which there are few," Minos agrees.

"How did he get through Cerberus?"

"There was no violence," Minos says. "Likely, bribes."

"Replace every guard posted at Cerberus."

"Yes, of course."

From outside the doorway to the assembly room, Minos

catches a glimpse of Rhadamanthus, already inside and gazing out the window with a strangely somber look. To Minos's surprise, Hades stops before entering.

The Unseen remains silent. Unnerving, this silence. Minos feigns patience.

"Heracles chanced being caught on my land for a reason," says Hades. "He thought the risk was worth it."

"He seemed confident."

"Confident that you would go along with it."

Minos nods. "I was surprised as well."

"If you, with such a grisly past, were able to atone for what you did," Hades speculates, "you must support his efforts to do the same. Is that it?"

"Yes."

On purpose, Minos chooses to be still and do nothing to defend the "brat of Zeus." Before approaching Hades, he decided to be factual, forthright, and to answer all questions honestly. This is the best way to get along with the High King. If one answers in truth and respect, Hades will respond in kind.

"That is what *Heracles* believes," he says. "Now what is the truth? Why do you want to help him?"

"The longer it takes him to complete the feats," Minos says, "the longer it will be before Heracles comes for Cerberus. And the longer it will be before we capture him."

"What is the truth?" Hades repeats, patient as he can sometimes be when a person does not actually know the truth.

"I suppose," Minos says, "I do believe in redemption."

"Try again."

It irks him when Hades pushes like this.

What is the truth?

The ousted king searches every dark corner, every nook and cranny of his heart.

What is the truth?

At once, the pure white bull of years ago appears clearly in his mind. The creature that aided in his downfall. Heat surges from Minos's neck to his cheeks

"Because if I travel with Heracles on this journey," he tells Hades, "I will be able to see the bull again before I die. I *need* to see it again."

"Why?"

Minos shakes his head and says, as honestly as he knows how to be, "I am not sure yet."

At this, the Unseen says, "Go then. Aeacus has his own task. Leave me with Rhadamanthus."

A LAWFUL MAN
9

The first words out of the High King's mouth are not about Orpheus. This, Rhadamanthus assumed, would be at the front of everyone's mind. It certainly is on his.

Ever since the lyre player turned himself in, Rhadamanthus has scarcely thought of anything else. What desperation would drive an otherwise virtuous man to land at the throne of Hades?

Instead, Hades announces there will be no court. That his brother and Aeacus will attend to other matters.

Hades mentions nothing about Orpheus. Slamming the door behind him, the High King plants his fists on his hips and says:

"You had a wife."

He looks terrible. Exhausted.

"Yes," Rhad answers. "Alcmene of Boeotia."

"What was it like?"

"What was she like?" Rhad muses. "*Loud.* Loud, but always in the best humor. Loving. Rotund. Smart as a whip. But mostly . . . loud."

"What was *it* like?" Hades interrupts. "When the day was done. When you were with her."

For a moment, Rhad wonders if Hades is asking him for sexual advice. It would not be the first time a man has, for he considers himself adept in that regard. Already, though, Hades is irritable and frustrated. Rhad will not make it worse by assuming. "Is there a specific situation that is troubling Your Majesty?"

"I am a lawful man."

"You are the most lawful of men."

"I have committed no crimes. Why do I feel remorse?"

Rhad has hoped for this revelation, that it would not need to be coerced or suggested. Sometimes, he forgets: what wisdom may come during that final ascent into godhood, Hades has not yet attained. He is a man. Thankfully, a man with the capacity for regret.

"Is it possible that being lawful and being righteous are not the same?"

This query fails to land well. Law is the Unseen's specialty. Hades laughs a humorless, dead-eyed laugh. "My laws are righteous."

"Once," Rhad says, "there was no law of Hades. No law of Zeus or Poseidon. What goodness was there during the reign of the Titans?"

"We sought to change it."

"Did you seek to change what was righteous," Rhad asks, "or to change what was lawful?"

Hades grunts.

Rhadamanthus attempts to select the best words. Tricky to know what might incite a stubborn response. To say the High King is mercurial would be an understatement.

All Rhad can think to say is, "Sisyphus."

Hades narrows his eyes.

"His sentence was brutal, but lawful."

Hades listens, saying nothing.

"You wished to set the tone for your reign," Rhad continues, "by punishing him as you did."

By now, Hades recognizes that the judge minces his words. He can see the intention in the field of color that surrounds Rhad. How this ability manifests to the High King is lost to someone like Rhadamanthus, whose humanity keeps him tethered to the limitations of this world, while Hades keeps one foot in the god realm. Rhad cannot fathom the depths of Hades's insight, nor the burden that goes along with it. Nevertheless, the Unseen does not stop him from continuing.

"You did set a tone," Rhad nods. "Yet you sought me out because you were searching for a better way. Why?"

"I did not seek you out," Hades objects. "I happened across you during the war, and I thought you would do me good."

"Why did you want for good?"

"Aeacus was my sole council. There was no balance in my ruling. He and I are too alike."

"Perhaps. But if you knew to seek balance, how alike could you truly be? Is Aeacus a man of balance?"

"No."

"Tell me, what is your goal?" Rhad prods. "With Persephone."

He thinks, but not for long. "To keep her," he says, then adds, "exactly as I want her to be."

"You married a child. Children grow."

Again, no response from the Unseen.

"They can grow into flowers or weeds," Rhad says. "You cultivate the garden, Majesty."

"Men and dogs. These two, I know."

"During the time of Sisyphus, you set the tone for your reign," says Rhad, "and you found it regrettable. Yet Sisyphus was an *enemy*."

Should he risk saying the truth? Risk the anger of Hades?

"Be careful the tone you set with the ones you love."

Rhad gives a wan smile. For a while, he has held his tongue.

He has not betrayed his queen—and yet, certain duties fall to him as counsel to the Unseen. Rhadamanthus is a man well-versed in the various customs of the land. He prides himself on advising on these matters, enjoys learning the proclivities of each land, each leader. And Hades strictly adheres to customs—for what are customs if not tribal law?

Certain breaches in custom can be overlooked, especially on behalf of a skittish new bride. Now, however, the gods goad Rhadamanthus with the perfect moment. A stealthy chance to help the High King understand.

"It is in your best interest to have a healthy, happy queen. It is in your interest to multiply."

"What do you mean?"

"Your contract to Persephone is beneficial in keeping peace with Zeus. But when you capture his son as you plan, the Loud Thunderer will, indeed, boom. The law states that a father can renege on a marriage contract if there is no heir within a year."

With a nearly imperceptible roll of the eyes, Hades says, "She has never kept to her own bed. It will happen."

Rhadamanthus feels a twinge of regret for betraying his queen even to this degree, but the matter is too precarious to risk.

"We take wonderful care of the mastiffs. They are fed the finest of meat. Such a steady regimen of food produces healthy, very consistent results in their behavior, their countenance—" Rhadamanthus gives a laugh, "Even their shit, the same healthy plop each day."

By the furrow of the brow and stiffness of his sharp jaw, Hades looks genuinely perplexed.

"However," Rhadamanthus says, "lately, three dogs have had unusually runny plop with flecks of rind."

"Rind," Hades repeats.

Rhadamanthus smiles a sad smile. "The queen has been

ravenous in her consumption of pomegranate seeds in the morning. I have never known the hungriest man to wolf down an entire cup."

Silence overtakes the High King. Almost, he seems incapable of speech, so lost in thought that Rhadamanthus could probably leave unnoticed.

Of course, Rhad delivers a bow and a kindly request for dismissal.

For one cannot leave a king without approval.

Drifting along crystalline waters, Demeter gazes at the reflection of sunlight against sea.

Impossible—she thinks—to detach herself from the role of Mother.

When a child springs from your womb, the child is always part of you. Part of *her*—the best part. Even with distraction, thoughts of the child are never far away.

The wind is calm, rendering the waters steady and hypnotic. Waves slap wood, foam sloshing around Charon's boat. Scarcely has he spoken, but he has nonchalantly vomited over the side of the boat more than once. They hug the coast, keeping distance from rocks and land. Always, land in sight, promising safety.

Demeter and Hecate huddle together beneath the sail. Charon's boat does not look as she expected: perhaps a narrow container of wood capable of floating with four people, five before it starts to let in water on the sides. Instead, the boat is as large as Hecate's cave, with sturdy boards of cypress keeping water out and at least ten people in. There are racks along the side fitted with nets and spears. It is no wonder Charon spoke protectively of this treasure.

Lap, lap, lap goes water against wood. Demeter's eyelids

droop.

She squints against the wind and looks up at Iasion who busies himself with the sail. He looks back, then to Charon who pays them no mind, and back again to issue a cautious wink. Blushing, Demeter stirs against the sleeping crone, who had discovered them by the fire the day they set sail. Hecate had said nothing besides:

"Charon is not far behind."

Letting them know that the drunkard would stagger from the barn soon. In case the lovers wanted to take separate pallets.

They had. It would be risky to jeopardize loss of the boat. Charon's pride was wounded enough by Iasion's appearance. Still, Iasion accepts Charon's captain commands without the slightest perturbation.

"I willingly abandoned ship for you."

Once, she might have been naive enough to hope for a future in a declaration such as that. But there is no keeping a man away from his mission, and this mission is seldom a woman. The woman is merely a welcome respite from it.

Overhead, the sail billows. With the shore a long mass of brown to the left, the day shines bright, cloudless, and mercilessly cold. Charon adjusts the rope to move the sail to and fro. When it requires more than one hand, Iasion comes to his aid.

The sweet arms of Oceanus, rocking them in their cradle, have already sent Hecate into a loud-breathing, snort-filled sleep.

Demeter also feels sleep trying to grab hold. The biting wind is not all that prevents it.

Wind and mind. The dreaded mind, the thing that separates man from gods. Surely gods do not torture themselves like this, with the dreads and fears that feed the mortal mind. The gods are certain, precise, unerring. Every famine or plague, every meager harvest a move of stratagem. Unlike a mortal woman and her mind.

Since stepping foot on board, Demeter has not stopped fearing the future.

This one thought, she never considered until now:

What will she say to the celebrated King of Kings?

Demeter last saw him a lifetime ago. A young mother, she stupidly humored herself with dreams of reunion. As years elapsed, so did hope. Even when she resolved to approach him about Kore, the prospect had not seemed real. It was fantasy. A *what if?*

The veil parting fantasy and reality, as thin as the veil between this life and the afterlife. It inched upward when Hecate agreed to help her. Inched more with the arrival of Charon and his boat. With Iasion by her side, the prospect of getting to Olympus is a near certainty.

Fantasy rarely spurs trepidation like this.

The chariot of Helius sails high overhead. Tiny compared to the blue closeness of Oceanus. Around the sun, the halo widens. Her eyes water from the brilliance.

Only a moment ago a tiny speck, the sun grows larger in halo, rounder, wider, and somehow more solid.

Entrancing, this light.

The brilliance darkens to gold. In the center of the sun, two radiant eyes beam down at her. Mouth of the sun, opening for her.

She gazes, the soft tissue of her irises burning painfully, and yet she must not look away from a god who has chosen to show his face to her.

Truly, he must favor Demeter, for she has not called upon him—but he upon *her.* Demeter raises her arms to the sky, opening for the god's call, ready to receive.

"Helius, if ever I have pleased you, tell me. It is about my Kore . . ."

A sizzling reply:

"Demeter! You shall know the answer for I greatly respect you and feel sorry for you as you grieve over your child—"

The face of Helius turns to the west.

"—No one else among all the immortals is responsible except the cloud-gatherer Zeus himself . . ."

When she turns her head, the sea vanishes. Her bare feet plant firmly upon grass, a wide-stretching meadow speckled with wildflowers.

In the distance: Kore.

Demeter exclaims. Her child shows no reaction. Instead, Kore bends to pick a large yellow flower.

Beneath Demeter's feet, the earth splinters. Grass and root pull apart. The earth breaks, spilling dirt and rock into a cavernous, glowing pit. Demeter tries to cry out:

Kore!

The girl's ankles part with the ground. A great whinny pierces the sky as horses the size of behemoths spring from inside the fiery chasm.

Demeter screams a soundless scream. Paralyzed in legs and in voice.

From inside the chariot, one massive arm extends, skin like the night sky twinkling with stars. Demeter sees only this motion before Kore's body transforms to pure light and vanishes inside a chariot of flames and black smoke. In mid-air, the horses loop like slithering snakes, changing direction, for they no longer gallop for the sky. They turn, eyes blazing red, strangely skeletal in their bodies, snorting hot air through their nostrils as a bull might.

She tries again:

Kore!

"Priestess?"

Demeter turns around. She stands at the edge of the boat that undulates beneath her feet. Her hands clutch the wet cypress.

No longer preoccupied with the sail, the men stare. Hecate has roused and peers curiously at Demeter.

Iasion comes to her.

"What?" Her face is wet with tears and sea.

"You were shouting." Iasion places a concerned hand on her shoulder and steers her back to her seat.

"I was?"

"Cried out twice," Charon adds, "for that girl of yours."

Hecate studies her, removing the blanket from her own shoulders and placing it around the mother. Demeter blinks at it as though wrapped in something she has never seen before nor knows its purpose.

"You are shaking, lady mother," Hecate tells her. "Warm up."

Charon reluctantly extends his jug. "This will make you warmer."

The idea of putting her mouth where the drunkard's has been makes Demeter shake her head. The sizzling voice of Helius is branded inside her ears.

Now more than ever, a sense of urgency overtakes her.

"No one else among all the immortals is responsible except the cloud-gatherer Zeus himself . . ."

What has he done? For what is he responsible?

Iasion stoops, prying in a soft voice. "Are you all right?"

She nearly shakes her head *no*. "Of course. Yes, I—I fell asleep."

"You heard the mother," Hecate snaps. "Go back to your sail."

Iasion obeys. Hecate leans in and whispers, "What is it? What have you seen?"

In the sky, the sun is but a small white force.

"Helius," Demeter murmurs.

"He gave you a message?" Hecate presses.

"I-I think so."

"Can you make sense of it?"

"We are on the right path. I must speak with Zeus."

Hecate nods and pats Demeter's trembling hands with one of her own.

The boat is silent until they dock for the night.

Days pass. Nights. They stop often, for Iasion makes a practical captain and forces them to dock if he sees anything on the horizon he does not like. True to his word, they travel safely, without incident, as if smiled upon by Helius and Oceanus alike.

Their stops to avoid slavers, the periodical delays to accede to the wind or the weather, compound her anxiety.

With each stroke of the oar, the reality of Olympus draws closer. And she thinks, again and again:

What will she say to the one who fathered her child?

Who conquered Titans and channels lightning?

What will she say to the man who left her?

The simmer of anxiety turns into a boil.

Oh, but for the safety of fantasy.

PART THREE
THE TURNING

He [Hādēs] gave her, stealthily, the honey-sweet berry of the
pomegranate to eat,
peering around him. He did not want her to stay for all time over there,
at the side of her honorable mother, the one with the dark robe.

—*Homeric Hymn to Demeter*

At Bay

1

An official Olympian ship would draw attention. The news of it would mimic a flash of lightning: a bolt from shore to the throne of Hades.

This is why Judge Minos finds an old cargo ship at bay in Kambos. Nothing about it draws a fuss. Minos should know; when he ruled Knossos, he developed the finest naval fleet ever seen. If he is to leave behind anything good in his legacy, Minos hopes it will *remain* one of the finest naval fleets ever seen.

The man preparing the ship for departure, however, is as conspicuous as a man can be.

Built like a monolith, Heracles tightens the rope to the mast-crutch. His shoulders appear stone-carved, chest padded with thickly veined muscle and brown-gold hair. Heracles dresses modestly enough in a blue tunic, but Minos notices the glint of gold-cuffed wrists catching the sun. Despite the briny water threatening to tarnish the gold, this makes no difference to the young man. A son of Zeus can easily replace them.

Above the sea's roar, Heracles calls out, surprised: "You came."

Minos lifts a hand, squinting against the mist. The day is new and the water, biting cold. Moisture dangles from his whiskers.

He tastes salt on the tip of his tongue. Beneath his feet, shells and stone are fixed in mud-sand. A few steps out, the water laps at the hull. The wings of gulls sound like blankets being shaken free of dust. One bird emits a joyful squawk.

Heracles balances his weight against the railing and hoists his feet over the side. Hurling himself over, he lands sure-footed, thumping against wet sand, and wipes his hands on the front of his tunic as he makes his way to greet the old judge.

At least, Minos certainly feels old. Admiring Heracles's agile movements, Minos feels a pang of fear. He is nowhere near that spry and has not journeyed in years.

"I am surprised you escaped unnoticed," Heracles says.

"Do not mistake me as disloyal. The Unseen is aware of our business."

Heracles's mouth slackens. He peers into the distance, expecting an army, and seeing none.

"He allows you to go?"

"Yes."

A grin lifts the corners of his full lips. "This sister of mine turns out to be a run of good fortune for me. Hades grants me his trusted adviser? Not only am I safe from him, apparently, I am *family*."

His laugh is robust and charismatic like his father's.

Something whizzes by Minos's ear. The object gives an airy whistle as it flashes by in a strategic line.

The arrow misses Heracles by a hair.

The arrow pierces sand, angled until a wave pulls it free.

Heracles examines his newly torn sleeve. A rip in the tunic is the only physical evidence that the arrow had come near him.

Before Minos can react, Heracles rakes him aside with one powerful arm.

Minos braces himself. His wrists bear the impact of the fall, reminding him that he is too fat to take a spill like this. Luckily, the sand provides cushion. His teeth mash together, and he rolls over onto his side, cloak swaddling tight around him.

Heracles stares at the attacker. A wiry young fellow with straight black hair. Half his face, a melted ruin of scarred, ruddy flesh. He raises the bow again.

There is no question now. He aims at Heracles. His capable arm is straight, hand drawing the string and elbow jutting at a severe angle. One eye clamps shut as the other measures the aim.

The young assassin charges forward. He is a short man with short legs taking short steps; however, his pace is furiously quick.

He screams, "For Pylos!"

Pylos.

The tide comes in. Minos flips over, propped on his elbows, and sea water soaks through his cloak and chills his buttocks and thighs.

Cloudy-faced, Heracles creases his brow. The dimple in his chin deepens as he purses his lips and sprints to the boat. Two more arrows sail. Barely missing him. Heracles throws himself over the hull and disappears over the side. An arrow lodges into the cypress.

Minos watches as the assassin marches ahead, bow lowered now that the target has vanished.

From inside the boat, Heracles reappears. He holds the top of a crate by its leather straps. As he jumps from the ledge, he keeps the makeshift shield in front of his chest.

The assassin slides the arrow from its pouch. Arrows fly as fast as the assassin can manage. Reaching back, loading the arrow, letting it sail—this takes time and solid nerves. Realizing this, the assassin stops. Heracles storms closer, the arrows half-through the wood, their pointed noses not far from Heracles's flesh.

The assassin is doomed. He understands this. He cannot load

quickly enough, and his steps reverse, backtracking so he can make one last futile attempt at the target. His ankles cross, and he falls smack on his ass.

The bow fractures against rock and sand, still lodged in the assassin's hand—the assassin whose face pales from the certainty of death.

Heracles drops on top of the young man and grinds his knee into his diaphragm.

The assassin struggles to breathe. When Heracles grips his neck high beneath the jaw, the man's face grows scarlet, sweating and trembling beneath the pressure. Instinctively, he pushes against Heracles to escape the crushing weight.

Heracles captures the assassin's drawing hand in one fist.

"When I let up, you are going to tell me who you are," Heracles seethes. "And if you do anything other than tell me the truth, I will move both hands to your eye sockets. Ready?"

Heracles relaxes his grip on the assassin's neck, but does not release entirely. He eases his weight back, allowing the man to draw a breath.

"I come in honor of King Nestor of Pylos," the assassin half-croaks.

King Nestor lost his entire family. The boy king wants revenge. At nine! Who is this misguided assassin? He is just a boy himself, one who must either be stupidly optimistic or suicidal.

"'In honor of?'" Heracles mocks. "You mean *by order of.*"

"I did not train to avenge the royal family," says the assassin. "I trained to avenge my own. You burned our great city. Our sisters, our mothers—Look at me! Look at my face! It was you who did this."

"Hades sent you," Heracles accuses. "Do you deny it?"

"He does not need to deny it." Minos stands, winded. "As Judge of Erebus, I deny it. You have my word."

Heracles looks from assassin to judge. At some point during these past years, he has gained the ability to think before acting.

Minos could fill his head with affirmations, assuring him that Hades maintains peace between their houses, but no amount of sunshine will convince Heracles.

"Frankly," Minos says, "an arrow flung by the Unseen would not have missed. He would not send a clumsy boy to do his bidding."

Heracles considers. He glances from Minos to the assassin, whose hand is still locked inside Heracles's fist.

"You know it to be true," Minos says.

"I come of my own accord," the assassin says, "and I am not the only 'clumsy boy' who wants you dead. There are hundreds like me. Men left without their wives and children." He struggles not to cry, but tears betray him. "You took them from us, and you have not answered for it."

Heracles quiets. The undulation in his chest slows its pace. Behind his blue-gray eyes, there remains fire, but one that dwindles. To the assassin, he says, "Surely you have heard by now. I am a man who kills often. I murdered my own wife and sons."

"I have heard."

"What makes you think I will not kill you too?"

Pinned and defenseless, the assassin closes his eyes.

With one swift push, Heracles snaps the man's wrist. His weight only allows the assassin enough air to yelp weakly.

"No more arrows for you. Now run back to your boy king."

The "brat of Zeus" stands up and looks Minos in the eye.

"I am not that man," he says. "I never was."

Heracles begins to walk back to the ship.

Minos follows. "Where are the oarsmen?"

"What oarsmen?"

"The ones for making the ship go across the sea."

"Oh. You think I came here in this thing? No son of Zeus should be seen in this. This is for the bull. I must bring the creature back to King Eury. For proof."

"You have no oarsmen?"

Heracles throws a handsome grin over his shoulder. "I was hoping you could help me with that."

PRISONER OF WAR
2

A dozen guards surround Aeacus as they make their way beyond the courtyard. This morning, he is tasked with finding an Erinyes tribal elder. Feral creatures, concealed by trees and secret caves.

Here in the courtyard, lumps of black litter the grounds. There are dogs everywhere.

Where the monument to Sisyphus once perched—a rectangular patch of dirt. Upon the dirt, the delicate child queen has laid out several blankets. She reclines with a pale, downcast face.

Queen—ha!

They should call her what she is: *pallake*. A prisoner of war, used as a concubine.

Judge Aeacus tells himself this often. Persephone is an unwitting prisoner of war, and she will not last long. Just as Leuce, the first bride, did not last long.

"Let me help you inside." Judge Aeacus steps around the dogs. "You will freeze to death out here."

To prove him right, a biting wind whips into the yard. Her locks catch the breeze, and she pulls the hood of her cloak overhead to shield her small ears.

"No thank you," she says, wistful. "I am happy where I am."

"You do not look happy to me."

"Oh."

"Go inside."

"What for?"

Aeacus slumps, irritated and not in the mood to be nice. Turning a pet into a queen leads to things like this. It gives her courage to speak freely. To feel entitlement. To disagree. Hades should have retained her as a genuine *pallake*. There would be no confusion then, and no need for pleasantry.

"Do not be selfish," he says. "I can see by the marks on your neck how your nights are spent. By now, you must be brimming with seed. A sickly vessel is no good to a husband."

Her dimpled cheeks flush. She shifts uncomfortably and hugs her cloak tighter. Snuggling into the dog at her side, she stares into space and mumbles something that Aeacus cannot hear.

Aeacus cups his ear. "What is that you say?"

"Nothing."

"Take my hand. You stirred things up with the lyre player. You felt the need to meddle. Well, now you are under a direct command from the Unseen. He has given you instruction, has he not?"

Pursing her plump mouth, she nods and looks to the ground.

"Then come along."

"I am happy where I am," she insists hotly.

"Until you do as you are told, the lyre player will remain in Tartarus." Aeacus hurls his words. "Is that what you want?"

She shrugs. "Tartarus is not so bad now."

Were it not for the dogs, he would pull her up by the scruff of her cloak.

"It *was*," says Aeacus, "until you cleaned it out. And it will be again. Soon."

She stares at him through frank eyes that burn like the sun.

Persephone stands and dusts dead leaves from her cloak. "How do you mean?"

The pest loves to question.

"Tell me, sweetness—"

"Where I am from," she says, "a queen is called Majesty or Highness. Is it not the same in Asphodel?"

Her question drifts from her lips with a dim-witted lilt. He narrows his sagging eyelids and peers around at the dogs, alert and ready to defend. Unlike the first wife of Hades, she has their protection. With the first one, Aeacus needed only to coax her close enough to the edge. A single shove—and she vanished from the affairs of the king before she became a problem.

"What you want," he says, "is *respect*."

Persephone blinks at him, face blank, and yet Aeacus senses she is wilier than they all give her credit for. A daughter of Zeus would be.

"True queens command respect," he tells her. "They do not snivel and cry all the time, and they do not pout when things fail to go their way. True queens know they reflect their king."

Chin up, Persephone cocks her head and pulls a strand of hair from her lips. "Once, I thought you might be kind. You are not."

Aeacus laughs low in the throat. The brat is almost cute.

"I think you are a bully," she spouts. "So is my husband."

"Your husband is also your king."

"Well, you can tell the king that I refuse."

"Say that again? My hearing, you know."

She takes a step back. The dogs encircle her, keenly attuned to the scent of need on the girl's pretty flesh. "Orpheus *wants* his wife with him. I cannot deliver her unto the gods. It would be robbing him of a *true* love."

The way she says it implies that, by now, Persephone knows she is neither wanted nor true. Perhaps Hades has risen to the occasion and set her straight. Prisoner of war. A scorned one at that! Aeacus begins to laugh again.

"I will not free her spirit unless Orpheus wants me to." She scratches her nose, face flickering with uncertainty. "Do not try to talk me into it."

"I would not dream of talking you into anything," he says. She hardly needs his help with sabotage. "Certainly. I will relay the message to Hades that you *refuse* the command."

The girl scowls prettily and chews on the inside of her lip. "True queens command respect."

"Oh yes. This will show him."

"Good," she says and glances toward the palace.

"You talk of respect," Aeacus prods. "For what should Hades respect you? Right now, there is only one thing you are good for. And I think we both know what that is."

"You may go now."

He smiles a slick smile. "What else might command respect?"

"What do you mean?"

Beyond the courtyard, the guards wait, unable to hear their discourse. "If you know what is best for Orpheus, prove yourself. Make it so, *Highness*."

"You try to get me into trouble." Persephone frowns. "I know this now."

"I am a servant to the throne of Asphodel. I only want what is best. The same as you."

Her eyes roll, and Persephone gives her head a shake.

"There is no better way to earn respect than by demonstration. Think of it this way. You purged Tartarus. Ruined it, in my opinion—but what does my opinion matter compared to your sovereign will?"

Her mouth clouds the air with a big sigh, and Persephone starts to leave. He is losing her. Losing an opportunity.

"If I have been tasked with restoring its severity," Aeacus adds, "obviously, you wield the power of the gods."

Persephone stops.

"I have misjudged you," he lies. "I found you weak. Unworthy of a High King."

He measures his words. Too many compliments will arouse suspicion. "You have already refused the High King's orders. If you have a better resolution, show him. Or shut up about it, and do what he says."

With that, Aeacus lets her be.

THE LARK
3

Persephone assumes there will be no shortage of dead things here, but she is wrong.

The slaves must clean up often. She scours the courtyard for a dead lizard or mouse. Perhaps a rabbit, who could not outrun the mastiffs and paid a bloody price. Better, though, to find an animal whole. Less for the gods to do.

Among leaves and shrubs, she finds not a single dead creature. The gods challenge her today. But, if this is the will of the gods, they will make her successful even if she struggles. That is the nature of the gods, to reward those who please them.

Her mind drowns in the old man's words.

"By now, you must be brimming with seed."

Every morning, slaves bring her a *mastos* cup filled with pomegranate seeds. The cup is intentionally molded into the shape of a breast, the appropriate symbol of fertility. Dripping, sour-sweet pomegranate seeds pile from the deep to the rim. They will help ripen the womb so a child can be planted there.

She has not eaten them. Not yet. In shame, she tells no one.

Cerberus eats the seeds, three muzzles fighting over one gulp. No one is the wiser.

Persephone does not know why she does this.

Is this life not what she fought for? The thing for which she forsook her own mother?

"What else might command respect?"

During her childhood, Persephone witnessed what had happened when Mother had been reduced to the function of growing the sewn seed. Everyone had known that Zeus gifted her the role of High Priestess. It was not earned by anything but her womb.

How sullen it made Mother to think about it. Moreover, Demeter had grown silent to learn that her own daughter had heard this truth. A mother wants to look capable, strong, and purposeful—especially to her child.

"What else might command respect?"

Obedience does not command respect. It does not even seem to command attention. Unlike when she disobeys. That certainly draws attention.

A crested lark lands upon a low tree limb. Bold move for a bird surrounded by mastiffs.

The bird sings its liquid, warbling song in welcome.

Pale brown wings expand, displaying red underwings. The lark descends and hops to Persephone's feet.

Blind to the bird at her feet, the dogs seem not to notice.

When she stoops, the young lark remains still. The downy young feathers have more speckles than the older feathers do.

The gods have provided everything but faith.

Once, a mangled soldier was attacked by his own mastiff. When she blessed him, he sat upright. For a moment, he lived! She had no priestly tools then. No wine or ribbon or incense. No sacrifice, such as this.

Despite the furious hammering of her heart, her mind reasons. A whirlwind of reasoning.

Persephone reaches down and wraps her fingers around the

soft plumage, around the tufted head. When the lark shimmies, she holds tighter.

No-no-no.

She is not killing the bird—not really! This sacrifice will prove her faith, and the gods will reward her for it.

With panting breath and drooping tongues, dogs gather around.

Tighter now, the curl of slender fingers. The lark struggles. Gently, she compresses—only hard enough to cut the breath—and yet the beak pierces her fingers.

"True queens command respect."

Mastiffs whine.

Smothered inside the soft flesh of her palm, the bird twitches. Stops. Shudders.

The creature goes limp.

She looks down, horrified and uncertain.

"Right now, there is only one thing you are good for."

Prayers tumble from her lips. Her eyes squeeze tight in concentration. She blows the life of the gods into her cupped hands.

Come back. Come back.

The veil is thin between this world and the next. There is no death. She sees this in men, sees it when their mortal bodies fail and something else remains. The essence of them remains, like a footprint on sand.

The bird is dead weight, soaked in her sweat. Bloodied from where it had picked at her flesh in a desperation to break free.

Yes, she has witnessed souls depart from their vessels and linger. Human souls.

Not animal souls.

Animal blood is let in ceremonies in spring and also for the harvest. In her short lifetime, Persephone has seen plenty of sacrifices.

But she has never seen the essence of a creature like this—not as she does with man. With the human *self*.

Her body goes cold, light, and porous. She feels faint.

Never has she seen the essence of a bird because the bird has no *self* to shed.

The bird is only a spark from the gods.

No-no-no.

The lark remains still. Lifeless. Un-revived.

With a sudden rush of panic, she deposits the bird on a nearby stump so she can wipe the guilt off her hands and think.

She has killed this innocent.

What was she thinking?

The nature of a woman is to give life, not take it. Her nature is to create, to grow. So much lovelier the earth in the spring!

Not like now, with so many dead things.

Tears spilling down her cheeks, Persephone backs away. The dogs whimper, wanting to console her. Her smile can make their stubby tails wag. Her distress, however, is unacceptable.

"Right now, there is only one thing you are good for."

Her body careens, ground rocking underfoot. The sky, the palace, and the mastiffs spin in place.

She might be sick.

In chorus, the dogs let out a howl—and then she sees the beating wings, speckled with youth, rise from the stump.

The bloody lark takes flight, singing its liquid song.

UNWILLING

4

"You are chipper," says the wife, wry-toned. After sixteen years of marriage, Zeus's favorite thing about the queen is still her voice. The voice of Hera—a furry blanket. She tries to sour it with cynicism like this. It does not work.

Surprised to see her in his quarters tonight, Zeus agrees. "I am!" For weeks, Zeus has not quit beaming. And because of his *brother*! Hilarious! A visit with Hades makes no man happy.

After the agreement, Zeus's old brother-in-arms had disappeared fast. Hot to get home and claim his prize! Good for him! Good for all of them.

The dowry has been selected and now travels by sea, around the capes and into the land of Asphodel. With these ships come jewels and livestock and precious stone slabs for monuments, all of which Zeus would send a hundred times over and still consider it worth the cost.

"Fine," Hera says. "You shook Hades off your back for now. Do you think it will last?"

"I am a god who arises to any challenge."

Since boyhood, Zeus has loved winning over tough adversaries. Doing so is a welcome feat. One he never loses. Everyone likes Zeus of Olympus. Even the ones who do not want to. On his part, this is not an eagerness to please, but the understanding that a friend is preferable to a foe, unless inevitable. Wars are costly. Not just in soldiers. Citadels are sacked. Male citizens die first. Women are raped and murdered or taken as slaves along with the children.

Now, Zeus admires the bulbous round eyes of Hera. They remind him of long-lashed cows grazing in the field. And her legs! Under the robe, they stretch long and slender like a prized mare. These are the things he likes about his wife. When he sees her, he always lists them in his head. Reminders that it could be worse.

"Are you here for a quick roll before bed?" Winking, he cracks his knuckles.

She ignores him. "The Unseen agrees to keep peace now. What happens when Alcides commits another atrocity? Is he immune to punishment forever?"

No. Not here for sex.

She is here to make sure nobody *else* provides him with it. Hera will not kill his good spirits. She sits away from the windows, beside a crackling hearth. She stitches a pile of cloth on her lap. Her tall lean body is covered by layer upon layer of thick fabric. Her purple robe is hooded, covering the crown of mahogany hair that trails down her shoulder in a thick braid.

"I know no one named Alcides," Zeus reminds her. He moves away and strips off his himation in front of the window, which he opens despite the frost. Outside, ankle-deep snow blankets Mount Olympus. The damned fire keeps the room piping hot. Hera and her cold nature. A man could cook meat in here.

Silence. No matter. She can go ahead and hate him for now, but she must give up in the end. As part of rebirth, one is renamed. With Alcides's atonement with the feats of strength, the world will now know him as Heracles. What more perfect a punishment for the woman who drove Alcides to madness? Let the world forever know him by her name. Bind them forever! Like it or not, mother and son they shall be. They already share one thing in common: guilt. She who delivered the potion of madness must also atone.

"Enjoy your namesake," he had told her. "Hera-cles.

"It is cold," Hera says. "I thought I might sleep here tonight."

"Is your hearth broken?"

"We can huddle for warmth. But do not touch me. I am having my blood."

"You still get that?" he teases.

She swings her arm overhead and flings the wad of cloth at him. Zeus laughs.

Ordinarily, women retire to private quarters during their bloody time. He never enforces the practice in his own house. He grew up in a cave with a nymph and her two little nymphet children. They bled and never made a fuss over it. He learned of the blood early. How old would he have been? Six perhaps? Five? As far back as Zeus could recall, he frequently walked in on one of them yanking a wad of red-soaked rags from under her skirt. He thought them wounded! Is that not what they said?

"I have a wound."

Until one day his young self pointedly asked the youngest nymphet. "What wound?"

"From the hole."

"What hole?"

And she had taken his hand and stuck it high under her tunic and he felt the hot, fleshy, sticky, down-covered slit, and Zeus has not stopped trying to get back to that awe-inspiring place since.

Someone raps on the door.

"Enter at once!" he cries dramatically. "Save me from the harpy!"

Hermes pokes his head inside. "Sorry to knock. You have a visitor. I know it is late."

"Tell whoever it is that if it cannot wait one night, it is too late for me to help them solve whatever needs solving."

Hermes shakes a curl from his eye. "Not you." He tips his head to the queen. "Her Majesty. If it pleases Her Majesty, of course."

Hera straightens in her seat. "Who is it?"

"A hag who claims to be the midwife who pulled you from your mother's womb."

The wife springs to her feet. A smile sizzles across her face. Ah, lovely smile. Zeus will add it to the list.

She clasps her hands. "Tee? Hecate?"

Hermes nods. "That is her name."

"Ha!" Hera rushes to the door. "Awfully late! When did she arrive?"

"Just now."

On the way out the door, Hera barks orders. "Make sure Hecate has food, a room, a bath drawn for later."

Zeus vaguely remembers the crone. At Hera's request, he rewarded her allegiance to him during the war. Made her a keybearer somewhere. He glances around for the wine. Does this mean Hera will leave him alone for the night? How long does he have? Women love to talk. He imagines the two will be drinking wine by the fire for hours. Does he have time to send for Semele? No, it would take too long. He considers the slave girls.

"I need to speak with you."

Zeus turns.

At the door, a cloaked woman takes to her knees to show humility. The top half does not betray the truth. She stares at him unblinking, pursing her chapped mouth. Her cheeks are leaf-dry and burning pink as the skin threatens to crack and bleed. The woman's hair, an uncommon yellow, hangs dirty and clumped from what Zeus assumes is sea wind.

"Let me guess," he says. "You are not here for sex either."

The woman flinches as if smacked and clutches the cinch on her cloak. "I am *not*," she says, still kneeling, showing the obligatory deference, and meaning none of it.

Zeus walks away from the window and pours a cup of wine. Damn it all. "Here, drink this." He sighs. "Mother of my child, how may I be of service to you?"

It takes effort for her to stand. Demeter trembles, but not from fear. She is bone-thin with dark hollows beneath otherwise big blue little-girl eyes.

"You look terrible," he complains. "Why would a perfectly beautiful woman let herself shrivel up like this? It is an injustice! A betrayal to the god of beauty, who was generous to you. This is your problem. You never appreciate a gift."

Demeter drinks from the cup. Beside his chair, a platter of grapes and bread and cheese. He pushes it at her. "Sit down. What have you done to yourself?" Zeus remembers her as a fourteen-year-old girl with wide, welcoming hips and perky nipples on small breasts. Who is this now in front of him?

He motions irritably to the seat across from him. He was in such a good mood until women got involved.

The mother sits. She eats. Her dirty-nailed fingers shake. Zeus rubs at the burning sensation in his gut.

"Does my appearance offend you?"

"It should offend me!" he bellows. "It should offend *you*!"

"I made a fast, cold journey. The King of Kings will forgive me for not preening."

"I will not forgive you," he says. "I should toss you out—just as you tossed out my son Hermes."

Why Hermes returned so readily from Knossos, Zeus will never understand. He sent the boy to retrieve his daughter, Persephone, and trusted it would be done. When Hermes came back fruitless, Zeus could hardly believe it. Heracles would never have failed Zeus in this way. That boy has persistence. No obstacle is too treacherous, especially the obstacle of a clingy mother. Let the shrew curse and throw dishes and toss him out. Zeus had been clear:

She may have her conniption.

But bring back the girl.

Hermes had not. They had argued:

"You have other daughters who would kill to take Persephone's place."

"Get back on that ship, and do not return without her."

"Since when do we snatch girls from their homes and drag them off unwilling?"

"Since the dawn of time, son."

"Father, Hades will not be fooled by your offering."

"He is no different from one of his dogs. Throw a steak at one and he is less likely to maul you."

Zeus does not mind a good debate. He always has his way in the end and enjoys debating his doubting, altruistic son.

In fact, Zeus did have his way in the end. The gods saw to it.

Now, the quarrel between him and his brother is resolved. Zeus has seen that good fortune came to both children involved. Heracles enjoys safety. Persephone enjoys the title of High Queen of Erebus and her children will inherit kingdoms.

One may even suggest that Persephone got the best deal of all.

"I could strike you down for refusing my order," he tells the mother, tearing off a piece of bread to soothe his stomach ache. "What do you want? How are you sitting before me now? Remind me to flog the guards."

"I arrived with Hecate."

His son made no mention of a woman accompanying the

crone. Quite an omission. "Hermes is complicit in this, eh? Clever. Ha-ha. Remind me to flog him too."

"I know you have my Kore."

"What makes you say that?"

"She was seized from Hecate's care. By the soldiers of Hades, your ally. He would have delivered her to you."

"Why do you think so?" Zeus lifts his brows. He chews a wad of bread, waiting for an answer that does not come. "Because once Persephone learned I sent for her, she could think of nothing except seeing her father?"

Her cheeks redden. The crazy woman wants to yell at him. Demeter contains herself and swallows the chewed clump in her own mouth. "Is she well?"

"She is fine!"

When the relief washes over her face, Demeter softens and brightens, resembling the girl she used to be years ago. "Praise the gods." She buries her face in her hands.

"There," he says. "See, all is well. You can be assured that our child lives more highly than any of my other children. She does not want for anything."

"Oh," she breathes, cheeks shining and eyes closed. To calm it, she places one hand to her heart. "Thank you."

But She says it to the gods. Not to him.

To him, she asks, "Will you take me to my Kore?"

He chuckles. "What for?"

She hesitates.

"Not so you can whisk her back to Crete?"

He laughs again at the expression on her face. "Do you know the penalty for stealing from Zeus the Loud Thunderer? I will give you a hint. The punishment is part of my name."

"Please," she moans, at last with true humility. "Allow me to see her."

It is hard to stop chuckling, but Zeus manages. "Ah, my Demeter, I might allow it if she were under this roof. But she is not."

The bloodshot cheeks wash free of color. "Do not say it."

"Persephone married well."

Observing Demeter's face is like watching a great tower fall. His heart softens, for he is not a callous man and wants only good things for the people he loves. Sometimes those people simply do not know what is good for them. To look at the mother, one might think Zeus murdered the child instead of elevating her to an entirely different spiritual realm.

"I give generously to my children," he says. "With my seed, I gave life for your womb to nurture and grow as a mother must. As she is now, in youth, I give Persephone kingdoms and the opportunity for glory. Remember this: Your role as nurturer has been served. My role continues even after I die; with the blood of Zeus in her veins, she is born one step from immortality. In making her the bride of Hades, I give her almost certain godhood."

He says the name, and Demeter blanches.

Hades.

Hands flying to her mouth, Demeter stands and bumps the tray of food. It crashes to the floor. Grapes roll.

"The Unseen is no unfitting husband," he says with eyes that harden and a tone that softens, more fearsome than his thunderous boom.

"How could you do this?" She rakes at her hair.

"Careful. Do not be too proud in your anger."

Demeter widens her eyes again, beautiful sea-blue gems surrounded by white. She reaches for the arm of the chair and lowers herself back down into it.

"We talked of the gods once," he reminds her fondly. "Do you remember?"

She stares, claws pressed to her mouth in horror.

He continues, "I deferred to your expertise on the subject, of course. Do you remember what you told me? You told me that at the moment of birth, the gods breathe a spark into the womb and infuse every single one of us with an element of holiness. In us, you said, the spark exists and waits to be fully ignited by the gods. And if that spark ignites, it is because you have pleased the gods beyond measure. You are part of them eternally then. Do you remember any of this? Nod if yes. Yes? Good. And you also said this is why good kings and queens are revered as gods, as their servitude unto mankind is a sure way to please the gods so they will ignite that holy fire and never let it burn out, even in death."

Demeter continues to stare, so he continues to speak.

"Within us all—you said it yourself, by your own philosophy. You gave birth to her. You allowed the spark to be given. Now you must surrender to the rest of it. Let her find favor from the gods so that her spirit is ignited."

"She had favor with the gods! I saw to it!"

"Is that so?"

Demeter cries. "I did it without your help."

"Demeter."

"You were never there. You were gone. Her life was mine to mold."

"You did mold it."

She continues to cry, babbling, not making any sense to Zeus, who contains his desire to shake his head and roll his eyes. There is love in her tears.

"You devoted your life to motherhood and to the gods. Rejoice that our child will do the same."

Nose puffy and shining, eyes swollen and glowing blue, Demeter asks, "There is no changing it?"

"It is done."

"She cannot want this," Demeter insists with a feverish shake of the head. "She forsakes my promise of dedication. This union is cursed. Surely there is a way to—"

"Let me be clear." With a level glare, Zeus leans forward. He is sick of this woman's ingratitude. "Persephone is no longer in your charge. Leave her. Go home. If I hear you have been making trouble in Asphodel, I will not hesitate to take action."

"But I am her mother. I have a right to see—"

"You have no right," he hisses. "No right to the life of Persephone. No right to meddle in contracts between High Kings. And no right to speak to me as if I am a neglectful lover from days past. I am the King of Kings."

She fumes but does not open her stupid mouth again.

"Now," he says, getting up and stepping back so that she can do the same. "Is that all?"

Darkness shadows her face. "No."

"What else?"

"Why did you toss that apple?" she asks.

He blinks, thinking perhaps this is a riddle of some sort. "What?"

"That day in the market, you tossed the apple, and I caught it. Yet you knew you would not have me as your wife. So why did you do it?"

Did he toss an apple? She seems to think so. "Maybe you looked hungry."

Demeter looks at him for a moment. The sadness in her face! Zeus wishes he could recall an event that seems to have meant so much to her. She stands up and walks away.

At the door, she turns and says, "You ruined me."

The mother departs.

He had not thought of it. A man's greatest assets are his children. Once she became a vessel for the child of Zeus, Demeter was no longer an asset. She had been claimed by a High King. Claimed but left alone. His dark brows meet. The corners of his mouth droop, and he finger-combs his beard.

Apple? Did he throw an apple?

Zeus clears his throat and reaches for Demeter's unfinished cup of wine.

Demeter rushes into the open air. Wind seizes her cloak, flapping it hard. Pregnant clouds flare with blue light while thunder rumbles among the hills and valleys.

Is the Loud Thunderer angry?

Certainly, the sky is angry. Does that mean *he* is angry? Why? As it is with kings, he got everything he wanted. None of the responsibility but all the reward. Zeus and his threats, his petulance, his selfishness.

She has heard things about Zeus. Never has she seen a demonstration of his famed power over the weather, his divine collaboration with Uranus, god of the heavens. So favored, Zeus controls the lightning in the sky.

No man is more powerful than this.

"Persephone married well."

She will be sick.

"The Unseen is no unfitting husband."

Demeter does not make it past the portico before retching over the side. Clouds whip across the sky as gusts siphon through the colonnades and pierce her eardrums. Jutting diagonally an arm's length overhead, lit torches crackle and whoosh.

"Remember what you told me?"

Yes, she does. She remembers every word she ever spoke to him, every interlacing of fingers, every silly joke exchanged as they lay on the grass beneath the rain tree.

"The gods breathe a spark—"

Shut up. Shut up, shut up. Zeus has no right to speak of the gods after what he did! None of his actions came from a place of godliness. He acted out of greed and acts that way still.

At night, the guards continue to man their posts. A high king must be protected.

Oh, but for a moment, he was unprotected. There in her presence, Zeus found himself vulnerable. She might have poisoned his wine. She might have found something sharp and stabbed him with it. As the rage swells, Demeter fantasizes grabbing the bread knife and sticking it through his eye.

He would deserve it!

Zeus defies the gods. He gave their child away to the one whose name is seldom spoken, often called the Unseen or Dark Zeus. If someone as abhorrent as Zeus represents light, then how much darker is his counterpart in the south? Demeter rends her hands together, yearning to strangle the father of her child.

Oh gods, help me. Hear me.

The spark, divine and righteous, rises into her throat.

"They will ignite that holy fire and never burn out, even in death—"

In the hills, an overhead flash ignites an evergreen, as tiny as an ant at this distance. Now, it is only a spark. With wind like this, soon it will blaze.

She braces herself on the cold stone wall of the palace exterior and rests her cheek there as she tries to gain control. Her throat hisses fast and thin, like the labored breathing of birth.

"You," calls one of the guards. He steps in her direction and waves his hand as if shooing away an insect. "Get out of here. No beggars on the palace grounds."

Before she can respond, Iasion appears from the staircase.

"This is Demeter, High Priestess of Knossos. And mother to a child of Zeus."

Hot tears pool in her eyes. Demeter, High Priestess of Knossos, wrecks her own life, so why would anyone trust her holy counsel?

The soldier laughs. He looks her up and down. She knows how she looks. Broken and dirty and haggard. But it is Zeus's fault she looks like this. Had he left them in peace, she and Kore would be sitting in front of their own hearth, plump and smiling.

"This one, an old concubine? Only one of those words sounds fitting." The guard talks to Iasion as if she were not there. With the tip of his spear, he lifts the bottom of her cloak to inspect the shape of her ankles and calves.

Iasion steps between them. He is a head taller than the guard and stands close enough to appear threatening. "I said she is favored by your High King."

"Zeus is your king as well as mine," the guard says. "Stand back."

She mutters, "Zeus may dwell with the gods one day, but right now he is a man—and one who steals an offering from beings far superior."

From behind, hands clasp her by the arm as another guard pulls her away. Her heels drag against marble. To gain a better hold, the guard grabs her by the hair.

Iasion lunges. A spear crosses him, in warning. Iasion shoves it aside and delivers a blow to the shoulder of the man who seizes her hair.

The gods animate her. Demeter jerks free.

She is no longer sea-weary or exhausted. With animal claws upraised, she hurls her body onto the guard and pounds on his plated chest. Her knuckles burst open and streak armor as the thin bones of her fingers ring loud upon bronze. Her screams and curses vibrate against the metal.

Shocked, the guard falls flat on his back. She straddles him, pounding with bloody fists. Her hair is darkened with grit from weeks of travel. It falls in front of her face. The guard brings both hands up to shove her off him when Iasion grabs her from behind. Their bodies collide.

Demeter screams. "Let go of me!"

The fallen guard rolls onto his side. "Whore!"

Iasion's arms are like pythons, but her legs flail and arms thrash. Her boot catches the guard directly below the eye socket where the helmet gapes open.

Iasion drags her from the portico. Between kicks and screams, Demeter can hear the jangling of armor. Breastplates and spears hurry toward them. The guards swarm.

"Demeter," Iasion says, "stop now!"

Held tight in nonthreatening arms, she relaxes. Once Iasion believes she has come to her senses, he tells her, "Go."

Iasion turns in time to see the spear aimed at his shoulder blade. On reflex, his arm extends.

Demeter screams, throwing herself between him and the blade.

She staggers.

Only for a split second.

Yet it is enough.

As the spear rises into the flickering sky, Iasion thrusts his arm forward and grabs it with one sure-handed swipe.

The sky fills with white light.

There rings out the loudest noise she has ever heard—nothing less than the cracking of a god's whip. Her ears pop and ring from such a sound.

Sparks fly from the upraised spear. The guard holding it goes rigid.

Iasion flies backward, back hitting the sky-drenched earth. Smoke swirls around one shoulder.

The other guards take to the ground, averting their eyes from the blinding wrath from above. "Zeus!" their mouths imply. Their voices are muted inside Demeter's clogged ears.

People say he controls the bolts. That is what they say.

Demeter has not believed it until now. Not believed it, for he is only a man. A man who seeks to win.

Dots of light flash in her eyes. She shakes her head, rain soaking her hair. She screams for Iasion. When he does not move, Demeter drops to the ground beside him.

As cold rain plunks against the stricken guard's breastplate, steam rises with a sizzling hiss. The others cannot touch him without burning their fingers.

Iasion's hand is black, crisp like charred game. From wrist to shoulder, burns zag like tree branches.

"Iasion!"

His eyes are closed. Body running cold, Demeter slaps at Iasion's wet cheek. Stunned, she sits back on her heels.

Zeus.

Surely the gods do not favor a man like Zeus—and yet where she suffers, he prospers.

The guards totter to their feet.

Freezing rain bites at Demeter's skin. Her eyes dart from man to man. Helmets streaming with rain, they advance.

Demeter looks, again, to Iasion.

Her skin burns with fury. Her spirit seems to rip from flesh.

From ceremonies and invocation, Demeter knows this feeling well. Ordinarily, the potion of kykeon induces this state. Tonight, there is no need for this tool.

Demeter feels the quickening in her breath. From a mysterious place inside the chest, something ignites.

"The gods breathe a spark—"

Brighter, the god flame burns inside. She cannot contain the eruption that follows, like the mighty volcano of Thera not far from where Poseidon resides—rushing up and gushing outward.

Heart roaring in her ears, Demeter opens her mouth and shrieks. Overhead, bony-winged silhouettes burst from treetops and into the night sky. Bats.

Her shrill cry echoes against columns that gleam in the torchlight.

She heaves and shrieks again. Her face glows red, shining with tears.

The screams catch between the columns of the palace of Mount Olympus and for every cry she gives it seems as if ten more cries echo against marble walls. The shrieks haunt the entrance of the palace, and yet she continues to suck in chestful after chestful of air, each time erupting from within the throat and heart and some blazing chasm deep within where the wrath of the gods still flames.

Heave.

Shriek.

The guards recoil.

When her voice fails, Demeter pants and hunches over to catch her breath. Her throat is raw. Breathing makes a wet scraping sound from the base of her vocal cords.

The guards stand with arms dangling at their sides. No man reaches for a weapon. No man moves at all. Their faces hang. The last of her screams die within the chamber of echoes.

With these brazen screams, the gods have stilled her attackers. They have given her the gift of escape.

Demeter runs into the darkness. Rain stings her cheeks. The

path, no longer lit.

Her legs pump beneath her. Mud slings against her ankles. She runs, surefooted despite her blindness. The gods spur her.

Tonight they will have vengeance for what was taken from them. Taken from *her*.

Everything she loves: both man and child. Without her child, a mother does not know who she is. Before Kore, there was nothing, for Demeter had been a child-mother herself. Mother is all she has ever been.

The name seldom spoken bubbles up.

Hades.

She must be dreaming. This cannot be real.

Where can my little ghost be?

The freezing night air presses into every pore, but the fire from her veins makes the coldness feel scalding.

Where are you, little ghost?

Keep to me Keep to me Keep to me

She rounds a bend in the road. Her swollen throat burns from screaming.

Keep to me . . .

Where are you, little . . .

". . . bride of Hades."

The rain slows. She sinks into cold mud.

Lost in the night, Demeter senses the expanse of a field. Peeking from behind the clouds, starlight offers little illumination. Against a blue-black sky, skeletal trees meet the horizon. She turns. In the distance, she sees the spotty golden lights from the palace of Olympus.

The stars dim.

Demeter stands inside a void of darkness where not even the gods can see her. Can they?

All around, darkness. Emptiness. Like an empty womb after

the catastrophe of birth.

To the gods, she begs, "See me," but the sound is like a croak.

She will accept no weakness. She raises her head higher and gives every breath as she shrieks:

"See me!"

Mud squishes between her toes.

She spies the beastly outline of a lone ox, tied to the yoke of the plough tail. The horns catch the starlight.

Demeter drops onto the sodden ground. Her tears are hot, the rain cold.

"Do not forsake me." She can hardly hear the croak of her own voice. "Help me."

Red eyes blaze before her. Fog thins.

The ox is monstrous. Four times the size of a normal ox. He lifts his neck to the sky and wails.

Demeter prays aloud. Her words are seized, transmuted into the language of the gods.

Demeter digs her fingers into the mud. How horrible a feeling, giving life only to lose it.

Her hand closes around a jagged rock. She pulls it from the earth. Squeezes hard. Into the stone, she pours her emptiness. Into the stone, she releases her hatred. Squeezing until her fingers ache, until the skin splits.

Zeus shall not steal from the gods and still prosper.

He shall not reap for his own gain.

Zeus shall not reap anything ever again.

The curse drifts from her lips and into the stone.

Demeter thrusts her hand deep inside the mud and buries it. Somewhere in the distant hills, rain tries to extinguish flames ignited by thunderbolt. All around, a foul stench:

Of death and smoke.

"*Right now, there is only one thing you are good for.*"

This one thing, she will not provide. Persephone cannot provide it, as she has never been so sick. Not even in the days following the ceremony when she invoked the gods to cleanse this place.

Those days, spent asleep with fevered dreams.

Today, atop discarded sweat-soaked fabric, she whimpers. Deep within the belly, a nauseating cramp racks her with moans and leaves her shaking. Her heart flutters like a trapped moth.

A slave presses a wet cloth to her cheek. Several rustle about the room, busied by her sickness. They do not know what causes it. No one does, except for Persephone.

The god-power makes her sick. To a *kore* of sixteen, their divine fire acts as poison.

Yet she gave life! To the little lark, praising her with its resurrection song as it flew away . . .

This illness will burn out, but the lark will continue to live, and that is enough for her. The convulsive shakes, cold sweating, and the stricture in her belly are worth the exchange. Her agony for the bird's life.

The bodies of the slaves are a blur, like figures moving

through oily water, shimmering in her tearful eyes. A slave places a bowl beside her head just in time. She dry heaves once, then twice, and finally empties her stomach of bile.

All she can think is:

Mother.

Between her legs, a trickle, followed by a hot gush. The pain dulls. The slave discards red-soaked cloth.

Persephone's womb has bled many times before. This time is different, as if all the blood expels at once. She cannot remember the last time she bled.

"By now, you must be brimming with seed."

Her ears ring. Despite her closed eyes, the room tilts and rocks.

Fresh in her mind, the words of the mean old judge assault her.

"There is only one thing you are good for."

"Mother." Even lying down, Persephone feels faint. Yellowed by torch and candle, stinking of iron, the room seems to constrict like the serpent swallowing a field mouse.

The slave consoles her. Chilled water soothes her forehead. Her hair, darkened by sweat, hangs in clumps over the bed.

Despite the comforting slave, words of slander land upon her, falling like rain from the sky.

Words like:

Sickly vessel.

Whining, arrogant pest.

And:

Selfish child.

Wings flutter from the open window. With a warbling tweet, the lark descends onto the rim of the basin beside her head.

"I-I gave life."

Three pomegranates are scattered upon the table. Had they

been there before?

Eyes watering through slits, she watches as the three pomegranates multiply. Six. Twelve. They mount—more than she can possibly eat.

The lark pecks at the tough-skinned fruit. Skin and rind burst apart with each jab of the beak. Drops of red juice stain its feathers.

Feverishly, beak stabs fruit, demanding seeds. Pomegranates tumble to the ground and crack with ripeness.

"A sickly vessel is no good to a husband."

Useless. She is useless to him in every way.

The gods kiss her with sleep. She slips into the comforting dark of nothingness. Time ceases.

Opening her eyes, Persephone squints at the figure sitting beside her on the bed. Fear spurs the rhythm of her heart.

Unholy.

A mortal hand descends upon her forehead.

Hades sighs. There is a tightness in his voice when he says, "I have heard a hundred suggestions today. By slave, physician, and judge."

Persephone stirs. She looks for the bird, for signs of fruit. The bedside table is empty, save for the cleaned basin.

"Theíos?" She shivers. What racked her body has gone, leaving an ache in her head and abdomen.

Hades sighs. "Let me see . . . I spared you the vapor bath of cow dung. Others suggested sticking cantharid beetle and bile into your rectum."

Slowly, reality assimilates. The bleeding of the womb, the pain.

"I see how none of those remedies will help," he says, gazing down at the bronze cup he holds.

Is it anger she hears in his voice? Something else like anger— like the tone her mother would take when she was worried and mad at the same time.

The gods must be punishing her for what she did to her poor mother.

Persephone looks to the window, seeing nothing but stark gray sky, devoid of birds and song.

"The child must be honored with a name," he says. "It is in our interest to do it. So I named him Zagreus."

She knows of the custom he speaks. If they withhold the name, the gods will withhold blessing them again in the future.

Hades extends the cup. "I want you to drink this."

The way he says it implies regret, but leaves no room for refusal. She gazes at the proffered cup, firelight glinting against the red contents.

The wine burns sweetly on her tongue. It is good. Better than before. Sugary tart wine, easy to drink.

A speck of thin yellow rind drifts atop.

Hades stands. "All of it."

Persephone brings the liquid to her top lip, gazing up at him. She takes another sip. Seemingly satisfied, Hades starts for the door. He glances back before leaving. She drinks again.

When he leaves, Persephone places the cup aside and burrows deep beneath the blankets, body and hair unexposed, buried safe inside the private void of her bed.

The cavalry approaches with gifts. Offerings. Two black sheep and two dairy cows trudge along, tethered.

The path requires single-file travel. A few riders precede Aeacus, cresting the hill toward a clearing of grazed pasture where they will not risk setting the trees ablaze. For their task, they bring along bundles of wood. No use in wasting time by searching for kindling.

This is the agreed-upon meeting place between court and tribe—and these, the agreed-upon offerings.

Almost comedy—Aeacus thinks—that they should make a ritual out of summoning the Erinyes.

For there is never a need to *seek out* the Erinyes. Traverse the face of the canyon for more than a moment, and they will find you.

"Halt." Aeacus steers his horse to the front.

The tribe can only be summoned after nightfall, and it has fallen. The judge hates being this far beyond the citadel without sunlight. They must camp until dawn. Impossible to make the journey back to Asphodel the same day they set out. Judge Aeacus is no longer cut out for day-long riding and sleeping in tents, without the luxury of stone walls trapping valuable heat inside.

In the clearing, Aeacus watches the soldier assemble the three fires.

"Ignite them."

The center lights first. The other two catch moments later.

"Well?" says the soldier to his left.

"Unload."

A white flag whips from Judge Aeacus's spear. Strips of white muslin hang from bronze spears, and helmets reflect torchlight. The gales are terrible in the canyon. With the steep terrain and siphoned wind, the journey is bad enough. But the land and its conditions are not what prevent a man from escaping the monoliths of Cerberus and entering by canyon wall instead.

No mortal can breach the tribe of the Erinyes. This is the tribe's purpose, their manner of thanks-giving.

To these barbarians who live among the hills, Hades is avenger, savior, and god. He restored their home, their sacred nest.

The Erinyes will answer the call of the Unseen.

Before Hades took the throne, King Nonius had detested these savages. To drive them out, the cuckold king burned the forests. Destroyed his very own Erebusian land, just to eliminate the pests inside.

Tyranny and tolerance never go together. Hades had won them over with promises to restore their native homeland. The tribe became a fearsome legion to rival that of Hades's father. Since the Titans fell, there has been peace for all, but most importantly, for the Erinyes who make far better allies than enemies.

The tribe has enjoyed years of lush forest and solitude in reward for their service. Allowing them to "keep" any man who avoids entering Asphodel through the monoliths, the High King humors their most primitive of amusements.

The soldiers unburden their horses: jugs of wine, milk, and honey. These allotments are placed several paces out. They hammer wooden pegs into the dirt and affix the ropes that are attached to the livestock.

Offerings placed, they wait no more than a moment.

Three hunched figures immortalize from the thicket across the clearing.

Aeacus suspected as much. For a while, they have been followed. Stalked by blood-shot eyes hidden among the trees.

Flesh painted black with mud, they advance. Their eyes shine. Each wears a tribal headdress, a skull helmet with a ratlike snout and fangs. Amazing what a little muscle and fur will do to transform the shape of the canine head. Snake skins coil from the top of the mastiff skulls, four springing from each headdress

The crones are naked. Muscle ropes over their bones. Erect nipples show above their ribs. There is no fat where the breasts should be. Springing from between their legs, thickly triangular tufts of black and silver hair.

For the sake of warmth, the Erinyes don a singular article of clothing—cloaks forged from the severed wings of bats.

The sheep bleat nervously. The horses remain still, but their riders shift and tighten their grip around their spears.

It has been years since Aeacus has communicated with the Erinyes. His tongue feels dry and limp in his mouth.

The words coming from the center crone are croaked, garbled, and mispronounced, as speaking is an action rarely performed.

"Ehre wanax?"

Wanax. King.

For the first time, Aeacus notices red-cast specks upon her cloak, how the splatter of tacky gloss glimmers against firelight. Her claws are marred with dried gore and mud.

"Erinyes," he says, "I am Judge Aeacus, counsel to Hades the Unseen—"

On each side of the central crone, the two others mimic:

"Un-seen." They test how the word feels in their mouths. One drifts to the sheep, examining the texture of wool. The other pulls the ropes free from their pegs.

Head tilted, the middle crone progresses a step.

"What are you called?" Aeacus says. "Your names."

"Nah-yme," echoes the woman in the blood-spattered cloak. When she smiles, pink gums cut against the darkness of her painted skin. Her canine teeth remain, short and worn to points. "Nah-yme."

She squints and studies him, studies the six additional soldiers frozen atop their horses. The other two crones size them up as well. When they draw closer, his horse back-steps and whinnies.

"Your High King sends for the one called Allecto. It is an honor to be called upon by Hades, the Unseen."

Reverent to his name, they hiss:

"Eh-dhees."

"Eh-dhees."

"Wanax Eh-dhees."

Aeacus shivers. They are perfect.

With each distorted word they speak, the soldiers grow increasingly uneasy. Aeacus notices the riders prod their horses, encircling the harpies. Their cloaked shadows flicker against the ground. There are six men in their group, and all seem ready to seize the barbarians and drag them back to Asphodel.

"Stand back," Aeacus mutters, diffusing. After all, these are not just three old uncivilized women. Not at all.

His soldiers have no memory of the Titan War—they are too young.

These words of caution, however, arrive late.

A raw cry—a battle-cry—erupts from the central crone. Aeacus's pulse gallops harder, quicker.

Hundreds of torches light in rapid procession. The blazes overtake the forest, illuminating crowns of snake and mastiff skull.

Aeacus knows—knows so well—there are beings of every size, age, and sex among those trees.

Dry-clicking laughter trips from the throats of harpies.

The central crone steps to Aeacus. "Ah-llecto, I."

When she speaks, the insides of her mouth show redly against mud-blackened skin.

They have both aged since their last interaction, over a decade ago. Caked with oil and grime, a metallic patch of hair disappears into the headdress. Her full, silvery brows connect at the top. A bulbous nose droops over her upper lip.

"Allecto of the Erinyes, you have been summoned by your High King."

Though the forests are lit with threatening torches, Aeacus relaxes as the elder leader concedes. She raises her sinewy arm and says:

"Un-seen."

From the trees comes a rush of sound much like wind against leaves. Hundreds lift—however poorly—the name of their god to the heavens.

"Un-seen."

FURY

8

Hades has not seen his bride in days. The longer the duration, the more tenacious the thoughts.

As he awaits the tribal elders, guarded by Cerberus with Aeacus and Rhadamanthus on each side of the throne, Hades still thinks compulsively of *her.*

Rhadamanthus had told him:

"You cultivate the garden, Majesty."

Yes. He needs this garden to be fruitful. Failure will mean war. He will never relinquish his prize, fruitless or otherwise.

Persephone must be healthier. Her *womb* must be healthier.

She has avoided the fruit for a reason—but, for her own good, something needed to be done. She should have been eating those seeds all along—and clearly was *not*—or this suffering would never have happened.

When her womb failed and the blood came, the counsel of men came with it.

"I have heard a hundred suggestions today. By slave, physician, and judge."

Suggestions and blame. They had blamed her age by saying a girl is best impregnated around fourteen, following the first blood. The child's mother had clung to Persephone years past her time, so her womb stagnated. A fertile womb requires that it be used often. Sex keeps a woman healthy.

The physician recommended cures to prevent future failure. Everything from eating pomegranate seeds to bathing in cow dung to burning myrrh, wormwood, and garlic between her legs so as to keep the garden soft and wet.

They interrogated the sullen husband too. Their method of helping involved much suspicion.

Had he noticed her eating strange herbs?

Felt ointments at the slit where he enters her?

Nothing unusual—a poultice of silphium, perhaps?

Hades had glowered. Of course he noticed no such things. If he had, Hades would not have known what they were for.

Yet hearing the word *silphium* brought to mind the singular time he had encountered it. As a boy, he observed a slave grinding a plant and taking the dish into his mother's quarters. The slave did not tell him what it was. Hades simply caught the word when he peeked into the nervous orange hue surrounding her.

Silphium.

He remembers because, in the days after, his mother had fallen sick. The slave who ground the herb had exited her quarters with blood-soaked cloth.

This is the last thing Hades needs on his mind.

Within the throne room, the opening doors throw light upon the aisle. The herald comes inside and begins to announce:

"Allecto, elder of the tribal—"

When the herald feels movement behind him, he glances over his shoulder to discover that the Erinyes have not waited for introduction.

Three crones drift into the room, faces lit with awe, necks craning from floor to ceiling to columns.

"—e-elder of the tribal Erinyes of Erebus, land of the Unseen."

Their hunched bodies shine distinctively.

Like flames, colors arise from them. Seldom do people emit only on color. Shades mingle and swirl, dependent on matters of spirit. In a cloud-like pattern, these colors fluctuate continuously.

Not with the tribal elders. This fascinates Hades the most. So single-minded and righteous, they always radiate but one assertion.

Red light twirls around Allecto, holding true, showing him the burn of endless anger. Hades has seen inside this anger before. The steady emanation promises layer upon layer of nothing but rouge. An affliction rooted this deep can mean only that it formed early. Born of anger. Raised in anger, stoked by anger.

"*Philoi*," he welcomes, using the word for *friends* despite Aeacus's warnings against it. *Friend* is not a word the Unseen uses often, and he does not take it for granted. Nor do the Erinyes.

When he greets them with honor, there comes a perceptible flicker surrounding the one called Allecto—from red to white and back to red again.

Peace.

This brief flicker assures Hades that their bond remains. They are the daughters of Uranus who ruled before Cronus, Zeus's father. Hades's father.

Hades should not forget his father had castrated theirs. Hades struggles to see Cronus, the ousted ruler of Olympus, as *father.* He was the seed, but no father.

Fatherless rage is a woeful thing.

Allecto came into the world, doomed to a life of outrage.

Once, Hades had made her bleed from the eyes. He had tracked her anger back to the womb. The day of her birth, a pregnant tribal woman had received news of her lover's castration and death. As the grief had morphed to outrage, it sent her womb into premature spasms.

Thus, Allecto, bastard of Uranus, was born.

Hades stands. The dogs stand with him. Both judges flash dismay when the High King descends from the throne.

He greets his ally with warm familiarity. "Allecto."

The crone begins to cry. The spark of gratitude interrupts the red surrounding her.

Hades is unacquainted with the other two elders.

Where Allecto emits the fury of anger, the second crone shines her own sort of fury.

Eagerly shoving her way past Allecto, the slighter crone kneels before him with her eyes clear and wide. Her necklace appears made of pebbles. Closer inspection reveals them to be human teeth. With her arms extended beyond the supple elastic skin that forms her cloak, she exudes the green of jealousy.

"Megaera," he says without being told.

From legend, the crone knows what to expect from her first encounter with the Unseen.

"See," Megaera grunts and falls to her knees. The language of her shrunken, naked body implies openness, submission. She grips his hand and placing it on her eyes. "See."

Her muddy tears dirty his palms.

See.

To everyone who knows of them, the Erinyes are primordial monsters devoid of human reasoning or compassion—and yet, Hades *sees*.

Skin to skin, he experiences what it means to be housed within the shell of her.

Inside the sizzling green, the jealousy unfurls fueling her righteous heart.

They are called savages. Barbarians. But what is more barbaric than mutilating your own father and throwing his severed genitals into the sea?

Barbaric was Cronus, the one who overthrew their father. Barbaric were his allies. While Titans enjoyed rule over kingdoms for this act of barbarism, her own tribe—many born from the seed of Uranus—had been deemed *primitive*. Their homes had burned for such a crime.

Megaera's jealousy consumes her. Why does she live in trees while the Olympians build castles? Why is she reviled while the truly primitive ones are revered?

Blood mixes with the tears seeping between Hades's fingers. "I understand your rage."

Falling beside her, the third crone turns impatient. She grasps his free hand and places it to her eyes.

"See."

Can a woman to be older than Allecto herself? Indeed. She is sister to Allecto's dead mother.

"Tisiphone."

Tisiphone, older and yellow-eyed.

In Tisiphone, the world could erupt into flames. Hers is a fury bent on destruction. She had scurried to save them as the trees and the bodies of her kin burned, her children among those lost.

Those flames mimic the glow surrounding Tisiphone. Her eyes water pinkly. Before he can injure her further, Hades backs away, and the women cower at his feet.

"Erinyes," Hades says with genuine affinity, "I know the root of your furies, and I answer all your needs. Will you do the same for me?"

There has, of course, never been a question.

"Sah-yme."

Allecto, Megaera, and Tisiphone nod, darkened faces uplifted in grace, rather than humbled to the floor. They will serve him until their dying breaths.

Hades assures himself that everything is as it should be.

Tartarus will be restored.

"Then," says Hades, "each day, witness what the judges witness. Do with my prisoners what you will. You are women of justice and honor. You will deal your furies wisely."

Aeacus says, "Might we tell them of Orpheus?"

Rhadamanthus utters no sound. He exudes a combination of energy that Hades witnesses often: something that appears as blue, yet in shadow.

Hesitation. Strangulated communication, the kind caused by fear of being outnumbered.

Without the presence of Minos, perhaps he is.

Hades tips his head to Rhad, speaking low. "You object to this."

"I—" Rhadamanthus ponders. "I trust your moral authority in all things, Majesty. But we should not kill the prisoners sent to Tartarus. True justice cannot be served by snuffing out a life. The lesson is merely cut short."

Aeacus breathes a laugh, but Hades silences him with one hand.

"Then there is no reason to object to these women," Hades says. "They have no taste for killing."

"They will be just?"

Aeacus smirks.

"They are nothing if not just."

Ash falls upon Olympus. The morning after their arrival, Hecate meets Charon beyond the palace as planned.

The absence of Demeter and Iasion—unplanned.

"Where are they?"

"How would I know?" Charon asks.

The agora bustles with reports of Zeus's ravaged land. Hecate searches for signs of a bald head or of the mother's yellow, sea-frizzed locks. The longer they wait, the more her stomach sinks.

The ground squishes with frozen mud and charred sludge. Each breath tastes of something burnt. All night the wildfire raged, overtaking farmland and field. During the worst of it, Olympus had been lit with a halo of distant fire.

A lightning strike to the trees, the guards had claimed. And also, a strike to a man—one of their own.

Whispers of "Zeus!" echoed through the halls, and Hera rolled her eyes at the insinuation that Zeus had anything to do with it.

For why would Zeus strike his own people?

The darkest time of night turned brilliant with flames. The order came: flee while it was safe.

As the horses and donkeys were gathered, as carts were

loaded with supplies to make camp south, the wind shifted, and with the help of sleet, relieved them from burning to death. The gods showed mercy.

Today, it continues to flurry ash as the clouds spit freezing rain. Farther up the range of Mount Olympus, the flames dwindle in a thin zig zag of orange.

Despite the fire, Charon's shoulders are relaxed, brow less tense.

Hecate eyes him. "Enjoyed yourself in Olympus, did you?"

The drunkard clearly spent the night guzzling wine and doing who-knows-what-else, thus cannot say what happened to Iasion or the mother.

Hecate is at a loss. It never occurred to her that they would not be where they said they would be.

"Seems to me that we all enjoyed ourselves in Olympus." Charon grumbles. "The world burned around us, but we had our fun."

Hecate had not been around to keep watch over anyone either. Her role was diversion, which she completed to task. Now she curses herself for letting the High Queen seduce her with temptations of a softer, warmer bed. Once news of the wildfire came, Hecate could not sleep anyway. The uneasy feeling in her gut had taken hold and stayed.

"Tried to enjoy it," Hecate admits.

"Not just you and me," Charon says. "The missing turtledoves too."

Hecate does not deny the insinuation. What for? He expects her to deny it though. Already has a response formulated.

"You think I am so drunk that it makes me stupid? I have been drinking since I was a boy." Charon shakes his head, "Iasion can have her. She is of no value to me. And my debt to you is paid. You got your passage to Olympus."

Hecate feels deterioration bone deep. From the cold sea wind. From sitting too long. From walking too much. From being around drab spirits, one who lost a daughter and the other who lost a hand. From deception and from the agendas of others who unapologetically misbehave when things do not go to suit them.

Hecate wastes no energy on balking about anything. Complaining is as useless as worry. Neither is a good way to spend the precious little vigor she has.

"Now that I am here," she says, "the High Queen thinks she has to entertain me. Keep track of me."

"She expects you to come back?"

"She assumes I came to stay in her company. A woman my age ventures from Cape Matapan to Mount Olympus? What should she think? I stopped by to say hello?"

Hecate steps past the barren field and onto the dirt pathway leading to Olympus proper. The hills smoke, and yet the merchants were already setting up their carts when she passed by them this morning. Hurrah—the gods favor them; therefore, business continues.

"What did you say to her, anyway?"

"That I am old," Hecate says. "Dying and whatnot. Told her she is the closest thing to a daughter I ever had. Now she has me tended by nosy slaves. In case I suddenly keel over."

Charon wheezes laughter. "You, dying? Nobody was ever so alive."

"I said it to explain the journey. Do what you can to find the turtledoves," Hecate says, leaving no room for question. "I will do the same."

She is quick to return to the quarters set aside for her by Hera. Eager to squirm her way out of these soggy boots and wiggle her bare toes by a fire.

To think.

By the time she passes through the entry hall within palace walls, it is nearly afternoon.

Soldiers hurry from a nearby corridor.

Trailing the entourage, the High Queen strolls forward, long in the face until spotting Hecate. As Hera hitches her skirt, her emerald garments sweep the floor. Hecate is also dressed in finery. Her robes are the color of the sky before it goes from blue to black. Hefty fabric, absurdly stiff for Hecate's taste, but Hera likes to make a fuss.

"Tee!" As a baby, Hera shortened her caregiver's name into something more pronounceable. She uses it to this day. "Where have you been?"

"Gathered a search party, did you?"

Hera takes Hecate's arm and gives her elbow a gentle squeeze. The queen insists on walking arm-in-arm, although Hecate walks just fine by herself.

"Zeus is surveying the damage personally," Hera says. "To put everyone's mind to rest that he did not . . . you know."

"Smite them?"

"Uranus was furious last night. But why? What grudge has he with us?" The ever-pious queen steers Hecate along.

"Good question."

"The fires spared some areas. Or so we thought." On purpose, Hera throws her voice within earshot of the guards. "These 'helpful servants of the throne' have been whispering amongst themselves all morning. I caught on."

"Aha," Hecate says. "We are going to see what the whispering is about?"

"I insisted," Hera says.

Inside, the smell of incense mingles with that of last night's fire. Outside, however, there is only the stench of ash, leaving a film of powder to spit from her tongue.

They stand between columns as big around as tree trunks. Far below them, the grand staircase ends in an immaculately swept courtyard. It fans and splits into two directions—one path towards farmland owned by the crown and one path into a small village.

From where they stand, Hecate can see the village.

The people flow toward the pathway to the fields. The forest obstructs her view of the rest.

Like insects drawn to a cadaver, crowds flock to the road traveling north. The children weave in and out of adult legs. The men stride with purpose. The women trod, hitching their skirts and chattering to one another.

The soldiers trail down the stairs. At the top, Hera cautions, "It is colder and farther than it looks, Tee."

"Oh," Hecate waves, "you can handle the trip. Do not speak so poorly of yourself."

"You want to walk?" Hera challenges through half-closed lids. "Fine, you stubborn goat."

Out of spite, Hecate quickens her trot down the stairs, a pace or two ahead of the guards. She regrets the sharp stabbing in her knees instantly. Like the wheel, legs have momentum. There is no stopping now, and so she concentrates on keeping her footing.

"Tee," the queen scolds.

At the bottom, Hecate nearly collides with a woman wiping her hands on an apron while trailing behind others who make their way to the field. Hecate bends at the stitch in her side and takes in a few whooping breaths.

"As spry as Hermes, are you?" Guards jangling alongside, Hera joins her. "Am I already wearing on your nerves? Well, make peace with it. You cannot tell me you are dying and then expect me not to hover."

Hecate is mother to nobody, but takes a maternal pride in Hera's bossiness. Behind them, the river of citizens dams up.

Those they pass stop to bow. None dare follow Hera closely. They are likely in the presence of a future goddess and treat her as such.

The walk from palace to field takes longer than Hecate imagined. The land itself is a mess of mud, ice, and sprigs of dead grass.

Hecate spies the heaps of fur drawing flies on the ground. Her heart pounds, not from exertion but from dread.

The smell hits them.

They spot a few surviving livestock. Mouths foaming. Open sores oozing pus and blood.

Hera squints, pinching her shawl across her nose. In the distance, a cow collapses. Vultures circle.

Stupefied, Hera struggles to keep from gagging at the stench.

Farmers pace the fields, in groups and on their own. The sky grows slate-gray. Sunlight peeks through and casts shadows against winter-bitten trees in the distance.

Hera points, sleeve billowing in the wind. "Are those . . .?"

The crone squints as far back as the field goes, where royal stables and barns meet the horizon. Massive brown-black lumps speckle the pasture. Horns grow from them.

"Zeus's oxen are dead," says the guard at Hera's side.

"How?" Hera scans the once-thriving livestock.

The guard shrugs. "Disease strikes quickly in beasts."

Hecate wanders forward, hearing the chatter of queen and guards somewhere far back in her head where nothing is truly heard. She hears, instead, words spoken by a dead priest.

"So there with angry hands she broke the ploughs . . ."

What has the mother done?

Hecate looks to the sky again. The sun is no longer in sight. Dark clouds threaten to unleash rainfall, and around her the onlookers begin to scatter to avoid the deluge. Women clutch their veils and men hoist children onto their shoulders to make for a quicker trip back.

Five paces away, Hecate spots a single white mound disturbing an otherwise brown earth. A mound the size of a fist.

Hecate stares down. She wets her finger and touches it.

Fine white powder. She tests it with her tongue.

Salt.

". . . sent to death alike the farmer and his laboring ox."

Hecate specializes in healing, not in harming. But she senses evidence in what she sees.

Twisting her fingers past the salt and into the mud, she feels a solid lump and clasps it. A violent shiver begins in her bones. Hecate pulls the rough stone from the ground.

". . . there with angry hands . . ."

"Tee, we must go," Hera calls. "Heed the sky."

Chunks of hail, as jagged as the curse stone found beneath the soil, begin to fall.

They nick exposed skin, making lumps and bruises that Hecate can already feel, but cannot yet see.

Gone, now, most of the day. A cold, muddy, ashen day.

Hail-fall reminds Zeus of the clang of weapon against shield. It sounds the same. As jagged chunks fall from the sky, the soldiers position their shields above Zeus, despite his gilded helmet. There is no foliage under which to take cover. Wildfire consumed the evergreens overnight.

Beside him, enjoying the protection of his own set of bronze shields, Hermes hugs his arms. With a nod, he raises both brows, clamps his lips together, and hollers above the cacophony, "Nice weather we are having! Thank you!"

Helmets prevent the soldiers from being beaten up too badly. Some use their shields to protect their horses. Hooves stamp in the mud. Necks rear in protest as their riders try to shield them and take control of them simultaneously.

With these Olympian soldiers, Zeus left the palace not long after sunrise. Hardly anyone slept after news of the fire.

Upon surveying the charred damage, Hermes had winced. "We should be thankful it happened now and not before harvest."

Zeus agreed. This was not the *worst* thing. After all, farmers sometimes burn fields before the fallow. The trees and barns (and their contents), a horrible casualty. During the night, Uranus pitched a fit, and nobody knows why, least of all Zeus. The King of Kings has committed no offenses.

From farther down the trail, a young man bursts into sight, clad in the blue and silver of Mount Olympus. Soaked through and freezing, the boy bleeds from the scalp and brow, but does his duty regardless.

"Majesty, you are requested at the fields west of the palace."

"Why?"

"One hundred are dead of plague overnight."

"The cattle?" Hermes draws closer, bringing with him the overhead canopy of shields carried by soldiers. "*My* cattle?"

Technically the cattle belong to his brother, but Hermes had stolen them fair and square.

"Yes, and some of the oxen."

Zeus mutters, "Damn it all."

At first, he had considered explaining it away as lightning he purposely wielded for some greater, wiser lesson. Perhaps he should allow everyone to think so. The truth of it looks bad on him. A leader who claims to control the bolts, but somehow failed to control these?

Still, deceiving them clashes with some internal code of honor. Zeus would never call upon the sky god to smite his own people—unless they deserved it. They do not.

Anyway, lightning can be explained as his own doing. But disease?

Hail reverberates against bronze The runner wipes blood from his eye. Zeus pulls off his helmet, curly graying locks plastered to his head with sweat.

"Here." He throws it to the boy.

The runner fumbles it. Gaining purchase, he cradles the helmet to his stomach to prevent the *helmet* from being struck.

"Put the damn thing on your head," Zeus barks.

He obeys. The helmet is large above his scrawny shoulders.

When the last of the hail rains down, they travel to the fields. Chunks of ice glimmer in the setting sun.

The stench is horrendous. Almost unbearable. A hundred rotting beasts draws an awful lot of flies.

Staring across the field littered with hail and death, Hermes huffs a non-humorous laugh. "People will say we have been cursed."

Zeus grunts, unable to look away from the carcasses being picked clean by vultures.

Of Persephone's marriage, Demeter had said:

"This union is cursed."

Why does she keep returning to his head? He prefers to remember Demeter as she had been before—young, sunny, and ripe. Years cannot erase first impressions, and the image of the young *kore* he met by the apple cart all those moons ago is branded in his mind. A young man eager for the pleasure of reproduction, a young man designed for reproduction, Zeus had seen, in the girl, a glowing fertile nymph, unplucked and ready for seed.

Of course, he remembered her fondly.

Valued her.

"You ruined me."

Crow shit. How could he have ruined this nothing-of-a-girl from Knossos? Zeus had given her offspring, riches, and title.

High Priestess!

There is no greater role except king!

"You ruined me."

Ingrate. Turning up her nose at these blessings.

Zeus spurs the horse and steers the cavalry away from the field. His stomach growls. His ears, nose, and fingers are numb from the cold. While he would love to fling himself into the pampering arms of his slaves, enjoying a hot bath and a meal and a good lay, these things are not in his immediate future. It would not be right. A little compassion and gratitude will go a long way right now.

When they step inside palace walls, night has fallen.

"Where are you going?" Hermes asks when a few of the soldiers hang back to escort him down the opposing corridor.

"Infirmary."

"To visit Georgius?"

"Who?"

"The man who was zapped."

"Yes."

Zeus follows the soldiers, and Hermes catches up.

"What are you going to tell him?"

"I am not sure yet."

"I will go with you," Hermes says. "I am not saying I hope he is dead, but . . . I owe him a pig, so I should know either way."

Inside the infirmary, where the ceiling is not much taller than Zeus himself, the physician freezes in the middle of cleaning a bloody tool with his apron. Dropping the blade, he sinks to his knees. Shaking, horrified.

Zeus furrows his brow. Most react in awe when first setting eyes on the King of Kings—but terror? He scans the room, seeing three of the beds occupied. A muslin cloth covers the entire body of the pallet to the right.

"Stand up," Zeus says with an effort of patience. "Which of these men is—"

He glances at Hermes, who whispers, "Georgi—"

"—Georgius," Zeus finishes.

The physician gestures to the covered pallet. Hermes peeks beneath the muslin, winces, and nods.

This elicits another sigh from Zeus. Today has been a day of many sighs.

"Deliver the message to his family," he tells Hermes. The task suits his son, who is not only personable enough to deliver bad news, but clever enough to dodge any backlash. "See that they are provided for—and, for the love of the gods, son, give them the pig you owe."

The uncanny sense of being ogled draws Zeus's attention. From the bed across the way, someone watches him. The man's head is bald, lip perforated with a cleft that pulls his nose flat. Bandages cover one arm and shoulder, and encircle his neck. His large frame occupies the entire bed, feet spilling off the end.

"They told me two were struck," Zeus says. "Is that the other one?"

The physician's knees are still pressed to the floor. "Y-yes, Your Ma—"

"What is your name, physician?"

"Thouki, Your—"

"Thouki, have you committed some crime?"

"No, Your Ma—"

"Then get off the floor. I did not strike Georgius, and you have no reason to cower."

Uncurling his fists from around his apron, Thouki stands.

Hermes picks up the surgical instrument and hands it back to the physician. Thouki takes it and resumes polishing the blood away with his apron.

"What happened exactly?" Hermes asks. "Who is that?"

"They say a madwoman attacked. Last night during the storm. This man was with her. The bolt came. That is all I know."

Madwoman. Zeus strides to the bed where the man watches.

"Are you companion to the one called Demeter?"

The man gives a slow blink.

Thouki approaches. "Majesty, he has been unconscious most of the day. Was like this when he woke." He pokes at his temple.

"Foggy in the head."

In those glassy eyes, recognition flashes. Recognition at the word *Majesty*.

"King of Kings," slurs the man.

Zeus says, "First the old woman, then Demeter, and now you. Should I expect more surprises?" He turns to Hermes. "Who arrived with Hecate, son?"

Son. Once again, recognition lights the man's eyes.

"I saw only the crone," Hermes says with upraised, guiltless hands. "I saw no madwoman, I swear."

"Nor this one?" Zeus frowns at the man who studies his son. "Whatever your name is."

The bald man breathes hard through his nose.

"Were you two planning something? Big man like you . . . You offered to help the mother take Persephone away. Is that it?"

Zeus might as well be speaking to the wall. The man hears nothing he says. He sees nothing but Hermes. His breathing hisses from his nose in quick bursts, throat beginning a rumble.

"You do not know this man?" Zeus frowns. "He seems to know you."

The man growls the name:

"Heracles."

Lightning scrambles the brain before it kills you. No unscrambled brain would confuse Hermes as Heracles. Hermes has the body of a runner, not a warrior.

Hermes cannot help himself. A laugh escapes his throat. He makes the mistake of flexing his nonexistent bicep and winking. "Sure."

Has his son no capacity for reading the body language of someone who intends to kill? Has this life of abundance robbed him of the primal instincts ingrained in the average man? The instinct of being hunted, for example.

Zeus extends a bejeweled hand to Hermes. "Be caref—"

When the man snatches the blade from the physician's hand, Zeus has little time to react. Hermes stands nearer the man than he. He is an easy target. The man lunges, unsteady on his feet and too altered to know this act alone is suicide.

The soldiers at the door rush to defend the young prince.

The fool staggers, flailing the arm with the knife. "You murdered them!"

Zeus takes him down with one sweep of the leg behind the man's knees. It is easy. The unstable giant falls.

"Ah," Hermes says, unscathed. "I see Heracles is making friends again."

The soldiers seize the man under the armpits, and his legs kick in protest even though he is hardly able to walk.

"Let it be known, I will strike any man or woman who questions my sovereignty." Zeus locks eyes with each man in the room, one by one. "I did not lash out at Georgius. He merely got in the way."

What an abominable day. Zeus cannot recall the last time he felt such woe. The fairer sex is not always so fair. Sometimes, madwomen emerge from pretty packages.

He finds himself envying Hades. He hopes that his brother is enjoying his mountable peace offering right now because Zeus has gotten too much grief over it already.

Right now, Zeus would trade places with his brother in a heartbeat.

PART FOUR
ORPHEUS & EURYDICE

And she [Demeter] was visited by grief [akhos] that was even more
terrifying than before: it makes you think of the Hound of Hādēs.
In her anger at the one who is known for his dark clouds, the son of
Kronos,
she shunned the company of gods and lofty Olympus.
She went away, visiting the cities of humans, with all their fertile
landholdings,
shading over her appearance, for a long time. And not one of men,
looking at her, could recognize her.

—*Homeric Hymn to Demeter*

The Restoration of Tartarus
1

For every creature, there is good use. In matters requiring brawn, Hades utilizes the guards. The dogs, for instinct and ferocity. The judges keep him in balance.

But there are no better torturers than women. They seem almost built for it.

Cocooned by serrated walls that reflect green-black against torchlight, Hades stands at the bottom of the steps as the Erinyes await their mission.

Snuff the life out of a man, and he never learns. One must endure the lessons of life, for the benefits of learning precede death. There is no justice otherwise.

The guards haul Orpheus out of his cell and deposit him in the center of the circular clearing where the staircase meets earth. Judges Aeacus and Rhadamanthus stand to his left, within the clearing and in sight.

The women watch in shadow.

"The High Queen feels sorry for you," Hades begins.

The colors surrounding Aeacus betray his core feelings for Persephone. Resentment shines like fury—the shade of it hot and charged. As for Rhadamanthus, his facial expression never lies and, right now both his face and his light exude uneasiness.

"I am a fair man. You say your offense was done out of love. Most crimes are committed for far worse. For this reason, you earn one chance to atone. Return Eurydice to her family. Allow Persephone to deliver her spirit, and you may leave. If you refuse, I will persist. Tell me now, and spare yourself the grief."

Terror blares from Orpheus's form. He fears for his life.

Regardless, the lyre player tells him: "No."

In shadow, the Erinyes glow brighter, more urgent and eager to strike.

Long ago, Tartarus began with a simple pit for mining. Craters, both deep and shallow, pock the walls. Some had been dug by the hands of slave boys chipping away for silver or iron.

Others were used as crypts thousands of years ago and have not served the same purpose since. They resemble lava tubes, the length of a human body, roomy enough for a man to worm inside.

Hades stares at one, unblinking. His gaze fixes there, as if he has fallen asleep with open eyes. He and the Erinyes are like one mind. They think as he thinks. They discover the poetry in their punishments

"You are not in your right mind. We will restore it for you. Have you never considered the experience of an unrested soul?"

A trembling Orpheus answers, "I imagine the torture is not unlike my own."

Hades laughs fully. "Your imagination is shit."

With the lyre player's head angled to the ground, he has not noticed those who await him in shadow. A nod from the High King signals them.

The Erinyes emerge.

The guards hoist Orpheus from his knees. He gawks as if witnessing nightmares come alive.

One of the dogs lunges for a newly discovered rat skittering between floor and wall. The hairy thing wriggles from between canine teeth. The dog rears his head to drop the rodent deeper into his mouth where molars begin to pulverize it.

Orpheus tries to fight. He flails and strikes out at anyone who touches him. The guards capture him by the arms. Two stalwart men far overpower one genteel youth. Fighting with no chance of triumph—why? Hades has seen it time and time again. The flesh may be doomed to defeat, but the spirit is ever-rebellious.

A subdued Orpheus cries out. For a moment, Hades believes he will relent after all. It no longer matters. The opportunity to atone has come and gone.

"*Philoi*," Hades says to the mud-painted elders, "I leave Orpheus in your hands."

Orpheus pleads as the women, muscled and smiling, lift and carry him to the crater in the wall.

The contrast of Aeacus's pleasure and Rhad's displeasure is sharp. Hades dismisses them and follows with Cerberus close behind.

Allecto's unintelligible words carry upwards.

"Brayd essss trahpd an-so ayoo—"

Her words mean nothing to Orpheus. The Erinyes shove him inside a tubular crevice in the wall where dead men once rotted.

Orpheus may never understand their words. But he will certainly feel their truth.

The bride is trapped and so are you.

Hades is halfway up the staircase when the screams silence.

This is the first time she has been out of her bed chamber since it happened. Since the blood. When, at last, vitality floods back into her veins, her skin buzzes with it.

"A sickly vessel is no good to a husband."

Days now since . . . since the lark, and Persephone feels much better. Practically, she feels as if nothing ever happened that day when the bird came back to life. Nothing at all! She can easily pretend.

From high on the staircase, Persephone spots an entourage of bodies crossing the hall. Soldiers and judges lead the procession.

She crouches, tucked behind the stone rail where she peers between bars, and watches them disappear into a corridor. There are two destinations down that corridor. The infirmary and the entrance to Tartarus.

The pack moves quickly from one end of the hall to the other. She has only an instant to make sense of what she sees. First, she spies serpents. Bobbing serpents, perched atop three inhuman creatures. Does she imagine them? They are gone before she can rub her eyes and check. Cerberus follows close behind them, nonplussed.

Of course, where there is Cerberus, she can also expect to

find *him*.

Persephone does not want to see him—but suddenly there he is, just as she expected. Her body reacts in two opposing ways, starting with a dump of coldness upon her head, as if someone empties a bucket of water over it. At her root comes the antipodal surge, a pulsing heat erupting in the groin, tickling her lower belly, flipping her stomach, and finally setting fire to the center of her breasts. Somewhere at the heart, these senses collide. Cold, hot, at odds, steaming her skin with a fine moisture.

Part of her wants to retreat, to brood. Brooding has been her preferred activity as of late. Persephone has milked the privileges of illness for as long as she can. Hades will expect to see her soon. Him, enjoying the fruits of this union but no responsibility of ownership.

"Your faith must be in me. This is my command."

Hades commanded this of Orpheus. Put faith in the Unseen? Every time his words echo in her head, they seem increasingly stupid.

Today, Persephone moves about in a daze. Observing and curious. Resolved to stay angry with him, she decides to feed that ravenous fire that needs kindling. The best way to do this is to see what he is up to. Something tells her she will find plenty to be upset about—and she is victoriously happy about it! Happy to see him as he is and not as she hopes. Or, rather, *hoped*.

Persephone is not worried about the guards. She is not, in fact, worried about anything. The ground is cool beneath her feet. There is no one around that she can see, and she is downstairs and walking past the hall leading to the infirmary within moments. The infirmary door is closed, quiet from within.

She knows exactly where they are going. Not to the infirmary to pay respects to the wounded—oh no. They are going to Tartarus.

They still have Orpheus down there, trapped, and unrepentant.

Cerberus must not get a whiff of her scent. Otherwise, there will be no sneaking past. She retreats into the main hall and up the staircase where she started. This bird's eye view of the hallway works well enough.

In the beginning, she waits patiently. After a while, she begins to pick at her cuticles and nibble a rough patch inside the bottom of her lip.

The distant patter of feet rouses her.

Rhadamanthus sweeps into view. He takes in a whooshing breath through his nose and exhales with a great sigh. Aeacus joins him, unperturbed, followed by Hades and the dogs.

The dogs slow. As their heads crane around in search, their stubby tails wag.

Persephone tenses.

Hades glances around, finding no evidence of what Cerberus smells. Hades issues an order, and the lagging dogs quicken their pace to follow him.

With guards trailing behind, they cross the mosaic floor and disappear into the corridor leading to the throne room.

Persephone waits. The procession is over.

"Hm." She can imagine only one reason why anyone would go into Tartarus and not come out. She has never witnessed the High King or his council escorting prisoners there. Those serpent things must be evil to deserve a personal escort by the High King and his council.

On the other hand, the lyre player remains in Tartarus. And Orpheus is not evil at all. He is not even *bad*.

The ones who are *bad* are walking to the throne room. Persephone snorts, invigorated by righteousness.

Persephone makes it as far as the entrance to Tartarus when she realizes something is wrong.

There is no guard. No mastiff.

When Eurydice led her down there before, Orpheus was a prisoner. Is he not still?

The steepness makes it hard to descend fast. With every step, the air grows colder, wetter.

Tartarus is eerily quiet. Persephone stands at the base of the stairs, fine hairs on her arms lifting as they once did when she first ventured down there. It seems like a lifetime ago. In those days, when these caves had been tainted by the souls of the unrested, the hair on her arms had risen. Now, there is no such otherworldly fear. There seems to be nothing but the dim light of a torch, leading the way to the corridor of prison cells. She finds the lyre player's room empty. There is neither blood nor overturned items—nor a trace of light.

Her breath steams the air.

The faint drip of water monopolizes her ears.

Door to door, Persephone visits, finding each one wide open. Each room, unoccupied.

She emerges into the circular pit at the bottom of the staircase. The crackle of torchlight mingles with the drip of water against stone.

Beneath that, very faintly, she hears something.

She takes one step toward the noise.

Beside the staircase, white eyes cut through the darkness. Persephone lets out a sharp cry that echoes among the stalactites. On the other side of the stairs, a second pair of eyes.

Unholy.

Persephone stands very still. The eyes watch, immobile.

The hum grows louder, more rhythmic and punctuated.

Screaming. What she hears is the muffled sound of screaming. Yet there is nothing before her except a wall.

Something strokes her hair. Persephone turns. The thing peering back looks like a goblin smeared with the pitch used to seal boats. A sharply angular skull with familiar-looking fangs crowns the head of this creature. Persephone immediately knows—she stands eye-to-eye with the remains of a mastiff. Coils of snake skin sprout from its skull.

As with a punch to the stomach, the wind flies from her lungs.

Despite her horror, the creature in front of her holds fast to the length of her hair, radiant against a hand so dark.

Persephone hears open-mouthed breathing from behind.

Despite the escalating drum of her heart, Persephone turns. The eyes, previously in shadow, have since emerged. They belong to creatures who stand half an arm's length away.

Their words tangle on their tongues, some mutation of the words they must hear others speak. Persephone struggles to understand.

The one holding the lock of her hair says, "Ayr o Eh-leos."

The other two issue stilted laughs that sound percussive, not melodic like a human's.

Persephone is frozen. The inside of the creature's mouth is starkly red, as if she has been sucking on carrion. *She*. All three are naked under layers of mud and fleshy-looking black cloaks. Somehow, there is nothing immodest or shameful about their nakedness, just as there is no shame in the nakedness of the mountain lion or the bear. She has no idea what these creatures are or where they came from. She knows only that her *theíos* brought them here personally.

One wears a necklace of human teeth. Persephone cannot tear her eyes from it.

Because of her sickness, the slaves have cared for her these last few days. Mastiffs only get in the way, and it is not good for the dogs to lie around. Since that day with the lark, Cerberus has been standing guard over the Unseen. No threatening jaws protect her now.

"I am P-Persephone, High Queen of Erebus, wife of Hades the Unseen . . . and daughter of Zeus the Loud Thunderer."

They stare. Somewhere within earshot, Orpheus screams. She swallows and scans the area for any sign of him.

One of the savages comes closer. She removes her toothy necklace. The two other hags gaze at the necklace with unusual fondness as she lowers it over the crown of Persephone's head.

The morbid beads kiss her neck. Persephone touches them and shudders. "Th-this is dear to you."

The woman deals an encouraging bob of the head. "*Wanax* Eh-dees." The words are said with recognition, respect.

Eh-dees.

The reverence comes from mention of the name *Hades*. Not Zeus, but Hades.

They are neither prisoners nor goblins, but servants to the Unseen. Decorated in mud paint and tribal headdress.

They stare at the teeth around her neck with love and sentimentality.

"These are not from prey," she says, mostly to herself. "They are from your lost kin."

They smile, baring their gums and worn-down incisors. Is this how they think of their High King? As family?

An odd family, these women.

From some invisible place, the screaming continues. Before she put an end it, Persephone often heard the grinding of stone against stone. She would hear the eternal lament of Sisyphus from some other realm—and Persephone listens carefully now, hoping that Orpheus's screaming is not the same sort of thing. A protest of the dead.

"Do you hear that?" she asks.

"Of course they hear it."

High upon the stairs and barely visible, the bottom of a man's robes descends into the torchlight.

Aeacus glances at the tribal women.

"You hear it too?" Persephone asks. "Is that Orpheus?"

"Why ask a question when you already know the answer?" Judge Aeacus takes his time coming down to their level. At the bottom step, he advances no farther.

"Take me to him," she says. "Now."

The three tribal women hesitate. They look to Aeacus. Look to her.

"This is an interesting predicament," he says. "Hades the Unseen gave the order to punish the lyre player. Therefore, they cannot free him."

She stamps her foot. "Orpheus has done nothing to deserve this!"

"For as many times as you have been warned," he says, "it continues to surprise me to find you breaching Tartarus. Of course, you are High Queen and our superior. So we cannot exactly restrain you, either. Can we?"

The maiden Kore donned her sweetness like a cloak. The maiden Kore could not stand to be out of favor. Now, impaled by the glare of Judge Aeacus, she finds that she can bear the wound and not want to fall apart. She does not care if he hates her. Because she hates *him*.

One moment, he wears the hatred candidly. The next moment, he draws a mask of his own making over his face. The mask, as simple as a smile, and yet if anyone looks closely, they would see the mask as a mask. Persephone recognizes a thing she wears so well herself.

"You may leave," she dares say. "I am speaking directly to—"

She regards the three figures, unsure how exactly to finish the sentence.

"This is Allecto, Megaera, and Tisiphone of the Erinyes

tribe," Aeacus introduces.

They bristle at the mention of their names. Something tells Persephone they are not altogether ignorant of what is being said.

She has no desire to get them into trouble. If she convinces them to help, they will surely be punished. Her husband likes to do this. Punish.

Aeacus continues, "I can only do so much without breaking any rules. Are you sure you want to start problems, sweetness? You have been unwell. Are you hardy enough to bear the consequences?

"Do not threaten me."

"It is not a threat," he says. "It is a fact. And you know it."

Tears burn her sinuses. She doubles her fists. "Why do you care to get involved? Just go! Leave me alone. Why are you always around?"

"I will leave," Aeacus says. "I will take them with me. That is the best I can do to obey the wishes of both my superiors . . . you being one of them, I mean."

He smiles again.

"You will only leave long enough to return with my *theíos*."

The judge purses his lips and shrugs. "But I am slow. I will give you time to talk to your lyre player."

"I changed my mind." Persephone licks her lips, distracted by the sound of Orpheus screaming. "You stay. Go over there." She points to the clearing where the Erinyes stand, observing.

The judge lifts both hands in surrender and obeys. Victory bursts deep inside her chest.

"Tell me where Orpheus is."

To Persephone's delight, the one called Tisiphone raises her arm and points.

To Persephone's chagrin, Tisiphone points at a wall.

Frowning, she takes a few steps and touches the large stone

wedged there. It is out of place. Odd shaped, poorly fitted. There is a crevice where stone meets stone, wide enough to let in air.

And noise.

She puts her lips to the wall. "Orpheus."

In response, a hushed cry.

"Oh my—" Persephone jabs Aeacus with an accusatory stare. "What have you done?"

The judge crosses his arms.

"Help me get him out," she orders.

"I told you," Aeacus said. "I cannot stand in your way, but neither can I help you. Are you trying to have us punished too? Surely not."

The stone is wedged tight. Four times the size of her head, hefty and fitted inside the wall like a stone in front of a tomb. She presses slender fingers into the crevice, pulling with her fingertips, but they simply slide off the water-worn surface. Her fingernail bends back, and she shakes her hand and shoves her finger in her mouth to get rid of the sting.

Aeacus says, "I know what you are thinking, but we have not left him for dead."

"You buried him!" she cries. "He will die!"

At this proclamation, the one called Allecto hisses and spits to the side.

"He will not die," Aeacus assures. "Go mad? Who can say."

She tries to budge the stone again and fails. The screaming quiets. Is this a hopeful sign, that Orpheus knows she is trying? Or is it a sign that he has no air to breathe, that rats have eaten through his ribcage and into his heart?

"Orpheus?" she yells. Looking frantically around, Persephone blows the hair away from her eye. She grabs a stone and marches to the only torch in the wall, held in place by an iron bracket. Removing the torch, she angles it against the wall so it will not tip over and leave them in darkness. With a swing of the stone overhead, she brings it down upon the iron bracket. The stone splits, but the iron remains attached to the wall. She finds another stone, this one larger, and smashes it against iron. This time, the bar chips away. She smashes it again and again, until the stone in her hand crumbles apart and the iron bracket clangs to the ground at her feet.

"Fine. Do not help me."

As she grabs the iron, her pale hand bleeds. She stomps to the wall, shoving the metal end inside the crevice between the wedged stone and the opening. Pressing her shoulder against the bar, she pushes with all her might. Her feet slip against the wet earth.

Aeacus snickers. Having four sets of eyes staring at her makes this impossible.

She rubs her shoulder and silently curses that Cerberus is not here to intimidate on her behalf. The dogs are always good to have around.

"You say you will not help or hinder."

"Correct."

She motions toward the corridor of cells. "I command you to go in there."

With half-closed lids, Aeacus gives his head a shake and blows through his lips. "Persephone. I advise agains—"

"Do it!"

When Aeacus smiles, Persephone wants to snatch his lips right off his face. He nods to the Erinyes, who look increasingly confused. "We must do as the High Queen says."

Quickly, Persephone escorts them to the first cell. They outnumber her four to one. Their loyalty is all she can rely upon—no comfort.

She stops at the first cell. "Elders," she says to the tribal women, "I am sorry. You have done nothing wrong. But I need you to stay inside here for a little while. Please?"

Gesturing inside, she says again, "Please."

Allecto nods, still enthralled by the color of Persephone's hair, stroking it like fine silk. "*Wanassa*," the old woman calls her, with both reverence and fondness.

"*Wanassa*," Megaera and Tisiphone mimic.

They go inside the cell. Persephone shuts the door and latches it.

"What did they say?"

Aeacus spits the word: "Queen."

Saying it as if the idea is preposterous.

"Go inside," she snaps.

Chuckling, Aeacus does as he is told. Persephone slams the door and smacks the latch into place.

With these prisoners safe inside, unable to leer or gawk, she flies to back to her task.

"Orpheus!" she shouts, "I am here!"

Wrapping both hands around the bar, she urges the thing forward. What taunts her most is that she can feel it budge. If she found it unmoving, it would not drive her so mad. She angles the soft part of her bicep and charges into it. Part of the stone breaks away, freeing the bar. She jumps back before it lands on her foot. Persephone picks it up like a spear and chisels the corner of the rock. The pieces split apart in infuriatingly small chunks—but they do split apart, raining down on her toes and nicking the tops of her feet.

When she has chipped away a sizable mass, Persephone jams the bar back into the crevice and shoves. The entire thing jostles, rubble toppling down. Hair hangs in her face. She wipes at it, smearing blood and grit across her fair cheek.

With one final push, the stone dislodges and explodes against the ground.

"Orpheus!"

The top of his coppery hair crawling with cavern spiders, Orpheus pants. "Help—help me—"

The vault is too high. She can reach inside only up to her elbows, but that is not far enough to get a decent grip. She grabs the tunic at the tops of his shoulders and pulls. He weighs more than the stone.

"Can you turn on your stomach and try to crawl out?"

Panting, Orpheus begins to wiggle. His arms hold instruments, not weapons. Without the necessary leanness, he would not be able to maneuver his shoulder to turn over.

Like a babe sliding from the birth canal, his body flops over the side and hits the floor. Orpheus, face grimy and swollen and wet with tears, rustles his clothes and hair. Wild-eyed, he lets out raspy screams and curls against the wall, rolling himself into a protective ball.

She drops beside him and wraps her arms around his shoulders to remind him he is still alive. He is not dead, not buried. He is here, with her in this pit, and he can rely upon her for compassion. Her embrace assures him of these things until he grows still.

His finery hangs diagonally over his shoulder and under his armpit, exposing half of a slick, hairless chest. Scrapes and scratches bleed on his arms, chest, legs, knuckles. Shallow cuts. He is otherwise unscathed.

"Why will he not kill me?" Orpheus sits back against the wall and hugs his knees. "Or leave me a rope so I can do it myself."

"No, Orpheus."

"This place is not as I imagined." Orpheus scans the lit room. "I have heard of this underworld, that shades curse the grounds and torment prisoners who tremble in their beds."

Persephone says nothing.

"Because of you," he continues, "it is honored by the gods."

"Is it?" She supposes so. But she knows that inside these walls there is a craftier spirit, one who evades the gods and walks this place still. What kind of presence can do such a thing? Is it malevolent? She thinks not. Is it benevolent? No, it is neither of those things. It is something else, something Persephone cannot name.

"Please forgive me."

"For what?"

"You are kind. I came here believing you could help. I never thought beyond that. I thought of nothing else but Eurydice. You must leave me now. Pray to the gods that the Unseen does what is right."

She can hardly believe her ears. "What is right?"

"In time," he says, "he will grow bored with torture. He will see it is futile and put an end to me."

"That is not the way."

His face shines with tears. "Then what is? More than two weeks. That is how long it has been since my Eurydice left this world. Her body was wrapped. It was readied. The day of the funeral pyre, I sat looking at the urn that would soon house the ashes of my bride. I could not allow it to happen. I had to . . . to try. I did try. And I failed."

"If your wife is not in the urn," Persephone says, "where is she?"

Orpheus grins with glistening eyes. "Safe."

"From what is she safe?"

"Anyone who might take her away from me."

Perhaps he is right to cling, as her mother had been right to cling.

"Show me the body of Eurydice," she tells the lyre player, "and I will appeal to the gods."

"But the Unseen has forbidden it."

Persephone breathes a soft laugh. "I will handle the Unseen."

Total darkness. One does not sit in total darkness often. Even partial darkness is tolerated, at best. Understandably so.

Without a scintilla of light, Aeacus sits on the edge of the pallet, arms folded for warmth. Being thrust into darkness, eyes open, jars his nerves. It arouses his sense of mortality, causes the heart to speed and breath to quicken.

He keeps his eyes closed. This darkness exists because of closed lids—and that is all. His mind accepts this explanation. No need to panic.

Judge Aeacus can only imagine what the lyre player must be enduring.

From the commotion on the other side of the door, the hair prickles inside his ears. He hears the groan of the iron latch in the room next to his. Muffled voices.

The lock slides open. Aeacus opens one eye to see the taut silhouette of Hades, encircled by dogs.

"I told you," Aeacus says to the High King.

The room lights as Hades comes inside, with Rhadamanthus trailing behind Cerberus. The dogs have a nose for the girl, but then again, Hades had smelled her too. So had Aeacus. That floral scent does not exactly linger around the guards.

"How long has she been gone?"

"Four hundred and fifteen reasonably slow breaths."

Hades flinches at the acerbity in his tone. He had told Aeacus to give the girl the benefit of the doubt. To make certain the Erinyes do not harm her. If she wanted to talk to the lyre player, fine.

Aeacus stands, and they leave the cell together. The amount of leeway that brat receives boggles his mind.

"The Erinyes will track them," Rhadamanthus says. "Orpheus will lead you to the body, as you wanted. There will be no further cause to torment that boy."

Hades gives Rhad a wry look that makes Aeacus think maybe the High King is not a lost cause. "Fleeing with my wife? I can think of no better cause."

"Their intentions are not sordid."

"She intends to raise Eurydice."

"Slow down," Aeacus says. "You behave as if she can do it."

Hades allows the dogs to pass. "She belongs to me. From now on, I want her fixed to my side. Day and night. She will never have an unsupervised moment. I cannot trust anyone except myself to keep her in check."

"You have court."

"Then Persephone has court."

Hades takes the stairs fast. When—oh when—will he tire of the girl? How long has it been now since they married? Judge Aeacus does not recall, but if it is long enough to impregnate her, it must be long enough for the novelty to wear off.

How can Aeacus steer her into chaos if Hades is always around? At this rate Judge Rhadamanthus will have to poison the little shit and be done with it.

While Rhadamanthus tries to keep up with Hades, Aeacus ascends with the speed of a sloth. Minding his thoughts, minding his emotions, until the Unseen has disappeared.

Aeacus closes his eyes and focuses on the stillness.

He counts each breath. He calms his heart.

Getting rid of Persephone is for the ultimate good of the Unseen. Of that, Aeacus is convinced.

He is convinced.

He is convinced.

Because if Aeacus is not convinced of his righteous intentions, the Unseen will know it. If he feels even a morsel of guilt or insidious delight, Hades will see it in those damnable colors that threaten to betray the judge daily.

The quicker he takes care of her, the better.

The Ninth Sunset

4

Far from the base of Mount Olympus, Demeter beholds the destruction. Here in the valley, she cannot see the palace. They say there are fifty-two peaks, with Zeus overseeing everything from the tip-top. His palace nestles within groves, glorified by clouds and eagles.

Except today, it is marred with smoke. A brown haze travels the length of the mountain range. The nighttime glow of fire held an awe-inspiring beauty, unlike the aftermath viewed by day. By day, the air stinks of ash. It covers her skin and hair, collects upon her lashes.

Wandering. What a disorienting sensation this is.

From where Zeus resides, she is not even a speck. She is nothing.

Never has Demeter been Nothing.

She was Mother.

High Priestess.

Now, she is neither of those things.

Now, she is hysterical. She is the bringer of misfortune.

"Priestess, it would be a privilege to love you."

What happened to Iasion rests solely in her charge. She may as well have hurled the bolt that killed him. If not for her, he would not have been there grabbing for that spear.

Let Hecate have her friend and the palatial opulence she deserves in this oft-unrewarding last cycle of life. Demeter will not tax her any further.

The road away from Mount Olympus had been easier than she expected. Working her way down from the peak, she managed a fast and oddly sure-footed pace. Descent is easier than ascent. It takes less willpower and more surrender.

Mud squishes inside the leather soles of her boots, soaking her feet despite the coverage. Demeter walks until sludge and dead grass give way to sandier terrain, until her mind goes clear. Freezing wind numbs her nose, hands, and feet. She hardly feels the gunk between her toes or the impact of her feet against the ground.

With the coast in sight, Demeter looks to the eastern sky. The heavens are covered by a gray film. In the blackening distance, a flat sheath of cloud lurks its way closer to shore, carrying with it a massive gray deluge that extends from heavens to sea.

Thunder rolls. The cloud sweeps over the land.

"You cling because you fear death."

No, Hecate was wrong to say so. We will die: this, the singular thought that terrifies and turns the non-believer into a pious man. Demeter does not fear death. The promise of it eases her mind like a solace.

The first chunk of ice hits her shoulder.

She stands, face uplifted, hands outstretched. Offering herself as sacrifice for what she has done since that morning Kore disappeared. For who she has become.

The gods will surely take her.

Ice the size of a man's fist pummels the sand. As if hurled directly with the intent to end her, a cold blow of pain hits her square in the face, snapping her nose and knocking her to the ground.

Demeter blacks out.

"Persephone married well."

No, but that was just a dream. What happened, a dream.

"The Unseen is no unfitting husband."

Clarity rears its head for the briefest of moments, but in that moment, the truth rushes in.

"You have no right! No right to the life of Persephone. No right to meddle in contracts between High Kings."

She wakes, surrounded by ice sullied with ash and soot.

Her eyes have already begun to swell. As she struggles to upright herself, the ice glints like diamonds.

Blood pools down the back of her throat, making her gag and spit. Her lip and chin drip red.

Demeter wipes her face on her sleeve, finding her arms bruised and cut. Ocean waves bring chunks of hail, foaming tides bursting against a cliff's edge. She staggers toward a small cave opening. The day grays in and out. Stooping, she braces her hands on her knees until the danger of fainting passes.

"Erebus."

Pray not the name of Erebus, god of death, namesake for the land of the Unseen.

"The Unseen is no unfitting husband."

The dying sometimes call upon Erebus for mercy. Spitting blood, she continues to jabber for the god to hear and answer. Where is the god of death now? Have all the gods gone to do her bidding?

Why would they, when she is Nothing? Why help her when she cannot deliver on a simple promise? The promise of Kore.

Once inside the cave, Demeter presses her hands into the wall. Her eyelids and cheekbones engorge with blood. She uses the wall as a guide, going deeper into the small cavern. The ceiling drops lower, and she stoops, limping into the quiet dark.

She should care about the threat of bears.

She should care about the wolves, the boar. The deadly creatures big and small, ready to kill her.

Sleepiness, warm and tingling, washes over her body with an abrupt seduction that stops her where she stands. She surrenders to the sandy ground.

She could fill her cloak with rocks and step into the deep of the ocean.

But her life is not hers to take. She gave it to the gods long ago. They must be the ones to claim it when they find her service done.

Thus begins the count of sunsets.

Day one concludes without mercy from the god of death.

Day two comes and goes, the weather oddly temperate despite the season, robbing her of the ability to die from the cold.

Day three, she no longer hungers or thirsts. Beetles scamper over her feet. Her body hurts, racked with cramps that seem to rip through her leg muscles like blades. Her head blares with pain.

She lives.

Eight sunsets she observes in total, without food or water or animal hide.

On the ninth dawn, Demeter knows. It is The Day. The Final Day. With her eyes closed, her heartbeat quickens. The organ of love panics when faced with its end.

Light beams into the mouth of the cave. Particles dance there. White orbs float inside, and when Demeter blinks, she sees the fragile image of a child coming forward.

"Where are you, my little ghost?"

The Kore who haunts her is a little waif no older than five—sweet and reliant upon Demeter for everything. This Kore adored her.

With cupped hands, Kore bends to her. Fresh water drips between her tiny fingers.

Kore says, "*Thina, thina!*" and tips her hands to Demeter's mouth.

Fresh water floods her throat, and the desire of her physical body causes a reaction of instant swallowing.

Her sweet child, pale enough to be mistaken as ghostly, flashes the dimples in her cheeks as she smiles. When she speaks again, a man's voice erupts:

"*Thina!*"

Nose swollen shut, Demeter coughs and spews water and blood. Her purple-ringed eyes dart about, unfocused.

A man speaks in a foreign tongue.

Someone yanks her to her feet, binding her wrists behind her back. An innate sense of flight takes hold, and Demeter runs. One last burst of life allows her to run hard, wildly, unsure where her steps will take her. She makes as far as the beach.

The ship banked on shore is small, agile, and designed for speed. It is exactly the sort of ship that Iasion would have avoided, not long ago when she truly understood how it felt when a man showed love.

Cloth descends over her head. The world goes dark. Arms encircle her from behind, hoisting her off the ground.

The ninth sunset, Demeter spends at sea, forced to drink and eat. Forced to devolve into a strong and healthy woman—the kind that the Sea People would gladly sell as a slave.

TRIBULATION
5

In the days that follow Demeter's flight from Mount Olympus, Hecate watches the prophecy unfold.

She had tagged along, hoping to stop it. Hoping to stop the gods.

The old woman swallows her pride, admits to herself she was foolish. Would events have transpired this way, had she not inserted herself into them? She has not considered it until now. The gods are having a laugh at the crone and her hubris. Wisdom is a cunning trickster. How wise is she now, watching the gods have their way despite her efforts? Perhaps even because of them.

Plague incites the death of oxen and cattle from Mount Olympus to Mount Othrys. Blink-of-an-eye deaths that draw flies fast, and the only solution is to burn the carcasses where they lie in their mammoth forms.

Hail ebbs and flows over the course of days, mighty as stones hurled from Uranus. They take shelter and wait.

One evening, the icy assault ceases. The clouds blush pink, parting to reveal the chariot of Helius making its way across the sky. Shining upon them once again. Half a moon of this mess, and everyone can finally open windows and doors to make sure it is safe, including Hecate and the High Queen, Hera.

The women stand at the highest point of the palace. From this vantage, they see the wide valley below with its olive trees planted in beautiful rows. The sky is purple rose. Peaceful.

Stonemasons built this platform high and unadorned, save for a focal point in the flooring, an elaborate mosaic of a half-naked Zeus, concealed by a wrap over one shoulder and covering the groin.

Granted, Hecate never saw the High King in his youth, but she suspects the likeness is a bit optimistic. Their feet are covered in fur to protect them from the cold. They look like animal paws, planted upon the gold-bronze paint of Zeus's face.

"Did Zeus look like this when you met him?"

Hera cocks her head, studying. Laughter bubbles up. She says, mock-serious, "Now now. Everyone wants to be immortalized at their best."

"Imagine when man unearths these relics a thousand years down the line," Hecate says. "They will be ashamed of themselves, looking the way they do. I can hear them now. 'A thousand years ago, every man in town was built like a god!'"

"Are you mocking my father?"

Hecate and Hera turn. Breathing the fresh air, Hermes smiles at them. His royal blue tunic is short despite the cold and lined with silver embroidery.

"Yes," declares Hera.

"Oh joy! May I play along?"

"Get away from here," Hecate swats at the air and pooches her lower lip. "You are just like the rest of them. Soon enough, you will find yourself painted on floors and chiseled into statues. And you have skinny legs and monkey arms, but I would bet my cave that your likeness will not!"

Hera laughs, and Hermes pretends to be offended. He poses, gazing proud into the distance, fists planted to hips.

"I am the finest example of manhood," he booms with a deepened voice intended to sound like Zeus.

Through their laughter, Hecate's ears begin to ring. She sticks her finger in the waxy canal, jiggling to clear it. The ringing grows louder, as piercing as the sound of metal scraping metal.

No one else seems to notice. Perhaps her ears are going as bad as her milky eye.

"I saw a marble likeness of Poseidon when I was in the Cyclades." Hermes strolls to the edge of the platform where a stone wall stands between him and a cliff. "Poseidon showed it off to me. He was prouder than he gets after catching a swordfish."

"And?"

Hermes belts, "Ha!"

"Really?" The High Queen smirks.

"I tried to be kind, but it was so hard."

"Tell the truth," Hera says, looking up at the young man. "You laughed in his face."

"I like to poke at him sometimes." Hermes shrugs. "The last time I visited, he challenged me to spear fishing. Sore loser."

"You caught more, eh?" says Hecate.

"Stole his trident," he says. "Far less work."

The piercing sound grows to a sharp buzz. Maybe she is losing her mind. She has been inside too long. Confined like that—it is unnatural. She cares nothing about gilded walls and fine food and slaves who insist on coddling. She craves the outdoors like any other beast.

"What is that noise?" the High Queen asks. "Do you hear it?"

Hermes concentrates. "I hear it."

An insect swooshes by her face. Hecate feels the vibration of beating wings against her cheek.

The horizon is grungy. Far beyond the valley lies the sea. Hermes cranes to get a better look.

"There with angry hands—"

Something catches against the hood of her cloak. Brown wings struggle for flight. Bent spindly legs.

Hera swipes at her upswept hair. Chestnut locks tumble around her shoulders. Hermes clutches his cloak and flaps it. The creature dislodges and flies away.

The buzzing stimulates the fine hairs on her skin and inside her ears. A shadow casts over the valley. The swarm passes over the land like a great cloud.

"Inside!" calls Hermes. He takes Hecate by the crook of the elbow.

Her legs are stiff. The wings of locusts hiss their sound:

"—she sent to death alike the farmer and his laboring ox."

"Come!" yells Hera. She and Hermes each take one of Hecate's stubborn arms and lift-shuffle her across the mosaic and into the safety of the palace.

Back inside stone walls.

"Something is happening," Hera declares, face deathly serious. "The gods are angry. I want to speak with the High Kin—"

"Actually," Hermes says, "Zeus sent me to find Hecate."

Hecate wraps her gnarled hand around his arm. "Hermes, take me to your father. It is time."

"Time for what?" Hera loves to know things. When she does not know things, she becomes insufferable. As a babe, she had cried nonstop until she had grown strong enough to crawl around and snoop. Then, as is by magic, she was the quietest child around.

"To catch up."

Hermes whisks her away. The High Queen hurries alongside, asking what is happening. What does Hecate know?

The old woman is good at keeping secrets. She does it all the time when people visit her for medicine or concoctions that might help the fates work in their favor. Nobody holds a key to the lock on Hecate's mouth.

The area outside Zeus's bedchamber displays walls with blue, white, and silver paint. Painters have created the sky on these walls, heavens bifurcated by the zig-zagged gold of Zeus's bolts. There are plush cushioned benches around a hearth and a long marble table for refreshments. On it, jeweled kraters for wine and heaping bowls of fruit.

Hermes approaches the guards who stand at each side of Zeus's bedchamber door. He mutters something to them and knocks

"Dear Hera," Hecate says to the queen, "Will you grant me a kindness?"

"Yes?" Hera says, uncertain.

"What I need to discuss with the High King," says Hecate, patting the queen's arm, "is something only he needs to hear."

Hera stares, dumbfounded.

"I must speak with him alone."

"Why?" Hera drones. "What are you keeping to yourself?"

The deep-voiced Zeus says:

"You disrespect your elder. Heed the old woman and leave her with me."

No, Zeus does not resemble the mosaic, but he is handsome and bearlike and reeks of charisma. And the beard! Perfectly curled, and silver shining.

Hera stiffens. The stately queen, handsome in her own right, sticks out her tongue at her husband and strolls away.

"Do I need them?" Zeus hitches his thumb at the two guards.

Hecate knows he is joking. In a moment, neither of them will be capable of joking, so she entertains him while he is still feeling jovial. "Bah. They are no match. You will need to summon a few more to thwart an assassin like me."

Zeus's laugh is pleasant. He dismisses the guards and motions to the table brimming with fruit and wine.

"Hungry?"

"I have eaten more in the past few days than I have in the last ten moons."

"Good. The queen holds you in the highest regard, and anyone who makes the queen happy makes me happy. She is much more pleasant to be around. You have my gratitude, Hecate. You also have my curiosity."

"You want to know about the mother."

His brown and silver eyebrows are level, splintered by the line of a frown. "You brought her to my door."

Hecate looks to the east wall, where a steady tapping meets closed shutters. Zeus must think it is rain.

"Open the window." Hecate smiles as if he is in for a treat and makes her way to a cushioned chair. The High King of Olympus obeys her command. She, an old hag, giving orders to the King of Kings!

Zeus opens the louvered marble shutters.

Locusts pour inside.

"What—?" He fumbles to close the shutters. As the bugs invade, he stamps on them with one foot. He uses his fists for the ones that land on tables and walls. Hecate watches, wishing she could be amused instead of disturbed. Winded, Zeus wipes the splatter from his fists against a purple chiton.

"They appeared as quickly as the fire and plague," she tells him.

"Absurd. There are no crops to—"

"No crops to feed locusts. Yet here they are. They came from across the sea."

Zeus comes to the red-cushioned chair near the hearth and sits on the edge of it, elbows on splayed knees.

"I saw it with my good eye," she says, tapping her finger

beside it. "I know locusts do not come in winter. Hail does not last as long as it did. Oxen and cattle do not drop dead throughout the land overnight. And the bolts. Well, the bolts do not betray the Loud Thunderer."

"I hurled those bolts because I had faith in Uranus to put them out before it reached homes. And he did."

"The guard who died may not feel so spared."

Zeus's lips tighten. He would never harm those loyal to him. That is hardly good for military morale. "You heard about the stricken guard."

"In passing."

"Then hear it directly from me. The man I struck was a traitor, a conspirator. I am King of Kings. He may sail from Crete with Demeter, but all men, women, children, and crones answer to me."

Despite what she feels, Hecate refuses to give him the reaction he seeks: a tearful admittance to being a conspirator right along with Iasion. She conspired about nothing. Her efforts are transparent and available to any man who asks.

"And the mother?"

"I saw her only once and not since."

"Is Iasion dead?"

"What is he to you? What is Demeter to you?"

"The gods are warning you. They are showing you what is to come."

"What is to come?"

"Tribulations."

"How do you know?"

"The mother wanted something from you."

"I refused."

"Clearly." Hecate rends her hands against the warmth of the fire.

"Let me guess. You urge me to reconsider?" Before she can

respond, Zeus snaps, "What is all this about tribulations?"

"Prophecy said as much," she admits. "Fool as I am to believe I could change it, I am not so foolish to believe you would reverse the decision you made about your daughter. Hera told me of your recent dealings with the Unseen."

"Did she?" he says wryly.

"Affairs of kings mean nothing to an aggrieved mother, you know. To her, there is nothing more important than her child."

Zeus breaks into an understanding smile. "You are telling me that Demeter has cursed my land."

Hecate sits back. "She is High Priestess of Knossos."

He holds up a hand, bejeweled with signet rings. "Do you believe the gods favor some crying woman over me? You have forgotten yourself, elder. So has she."

"Beware a mother's nature," she tells him. "Hers is the most ferocious love on the earth, in the sea and sky."

"Persephone stays where she is. Nothing is going to change that. Curses can be undone. The wrath of my brother Hades cannot. It would result in an endless war. You have no idea how many will die."

They have been alone until now. Before Hecate can say anything else, two guards appear.

"Our time is up." Zeus stands. "Worry shortens your life, crone. Let me take care of the gods. Come. Join our table."

Zeus offers her an arm. She accepts it. Never refuse the arm of a king. It is poor diplomacy.

To the guards, he commands, "Bring me every priest and priestess in Olympus."

"We will make things right with the gods," the Loud Thunderer assures. "You have my word."

The journey from Kambos to Cape Matapan takes the lion's share of the first day.

Minos adapts to the sea with rekindled enthusiasm. The oarsmen work hard. Heracles is no sailor and elects to "save his muscles" for the bull instead of rowing. Happily, he allows Minos to take charge as captain.

Minos is delighted to relive the old days when he spent as much time on sea as he did on land. Navigating the coast consumes his focus. Despite winter winds, the rusticism of sea life is exhilarating.

Second day, they sail from the cape to the island of Kythera, a halfway point between the mainland and Crete. At camp, the fire roars, and a clear sky lights with stars and silver moon. Elk meat roasts. Wine flows in abundance.

Starry-eyed as maidens, the oarsmen laugh at every word Heracles says.

"The stables had nothing to do with strength," Heracles explains, regaling his fifth and most pungent feat. "Shovel the shit of more than one thousand cattle? King Eury, that sack of blubber, hoped to see me covered in the stuff."

There is something about excrement that wins a laugh from

old and young alike. Minos also finds himself chuckling. It is no virtue to become drunk, but Minos forgives himself this tonight amongst the hearty laughter of men.

Heracles makes a face, mocking the feat with a roll of his eyes. "Please. I saw more shit after Hera fed me rotten fish."

When the men guffaw, Heracles laughs with them. "The stench was vile. I took one look and walked away. You know what I shoveled instead? Dirt. Ditches that stretched from the rivers to the stables. With one hardy rain, the stables cleaned themselves."

Heracles is more clever than people think. Minos is pondering the events of his recent tale when Heracles decides to direct his drunken merriment in his direction.

"I am glad you are here, Minos." He gives Minos a jovial slap on the back. "Are you sure you would not like my cloak?"

Heracles pulls the lion's pelt from his shoulders. Minos starts to object.

"I insist!" Heracles drops it over Minos's shoulders and sits beside him.

The cloak smells of leather and beast.

"So," Heracles says, drinking the last from his cup. "Is it true?"

"Is what true?"

"The rumors," Heracles asks, half-smiling, chin cocked.

Minos shifts in his seat. "Of?"

With his meaty hands, Heracles mimics a creature-walk. "Did your wife give birth to a deformed bull baby?"

A few oarsmen burst with laughter. Others contain their laughter out of respect. All faces, however, strain to fight the extent of their amusement.

There is detectable good in Heracles somewhere, but his pride gets in the way. From what Minos can tell, the children of Zeus are complicated.

"Queen Pasiphae gave birth to a child with defects," Minos says. "It did not live. But it was not created from bestiality, and the loss was no surprise. A woman of her age rarely conceives."

"That is not what Poseidon tells everyone. He is still angry that you never sacrificed that bull like he told you to."

"What you speak of is a tasteless joke turned into gossip."

Would there ever have been a time, in his youth, when Minos would have dared fight a man like Heracles to defend his wife's honor? Minos would like to believe so.

Surrounded by snickering oarsmen and a vaunter of this physical size, Minos keeps his calm despite the wine loosening his sense of restraint.

Irreverent one second and somber the next, Heracles says, "Would you rather be known for a fantastical lie or a terrible truth?"

"You know the answer to that."

"Maybe Poseidon was nice to start the rumor. "

"I will thank him when I see him next."

"I am serious. When you die, what you are famous for will become your legacy for all time."

"Yes, yes." Minos waves in dismissal. "Hence the imperative for you to succeed at your challenge."

"I do not want to be known for what I did. Do you?" Heracles's brows sit level over his eyes, making him appear fierce by nature. "The 'minotaur' killed those children, not you. This fabled creature can take the fall. Better to be known for the lie. The lie would not harm you. But the truth? It will humiliate you."

"The lie harms my wife, and she has done nothing wrong."

"You have developed great humility, Minos," Heracles says with a drink. "It does not look as good on you as you think it does."

In the beginning, the thing that made the bull special was that it was a gift from Poseidon. Not everyone gets a gift from the high king of the Cyclades. Poseidon did not go around doling them out right and left.

Except there was a condition. Sacrifice the bull to the gods.

An albino bull, exceptional in beauty and in size.

Minos had not liked the sound of it from the start.

With the murder of his son, Minos came to suffer madness.

"Loss will turn you into a philosopher."

A philosopher or a murderer. Minos can attest to this himself.

He envisioned the bull as a vengeful god. Inside the labyrinth, he locked this god away, keeping it close.

Those responsible for his son's death tried to make up for their deed with gifts of children. Sending him *replacement children*. A million could not have replaced his one treasured son.

When his horned god demanded those children, Minos had provided them. Who was that Minos, the one who would lock children into a maze with a panicked bull?

"This fabled creature can take the fall."

Minos stands and dusts the sand from his palms. As he begins to walk to his tent, Heracles calls over his shoulder.

"Minos, I know about the twelfth labor."

Minos stops. His ears attune for menacing tones in his voice.

"If I had told you earlier," Heracles says, "you might not have trusted me enough to come on this little jaunt across the sea."

The brat of Zeus sounds fatigued, heavy-tongued.

"Not trust you," Minos repeats. "Why? Because you might kill me once you got what you needed, and I was no longer of use?"

Facing the fire, Heracles says, "I could, you know."

"But Heracles, you said it yourself." Minos says, apathetic. "You are not that man anymore."

Heracles muses, taking another drink. "The twelfth labor.

Capture Cerberus. Your idea, was it not?"

"It was."

Heracles nods. "Good one."

"Sleep well, son of Zeus."

Without looking away from the fire, Heracles raises his cup. "Enjoy the pelt."

"What do you want?"

"Some welcome." Hecate figured she would find the drunkard here. His prized possession rests in a cove. Charon banked it there to avoid thieves, but would never risk staying away for long.

The sail is punctured with holes. The cypress, dented and splintered by hail. From the looks of it, Charon has managed to assemble wood and pitch since she saw him last. Some damage is patched, but not much.

"Think you can mend it?" she asks, running her hand over a sizable puncture.

"Whenever I see you, you want something," Charon grumbles, adjusting the sail with one hand. The cloth descends, quivering in the wind. "What do you want?" He looks toward the brush and trees for the answer and finds nothing. His voice sounds clearer, eyes less bloated and red. "And how did you get here?"

"I caught a ride on an offal cart."

"I see no cart."

"The owner went along his way. It took half the day to get here."

Charon laughs under his breath and shakes his head. He releases the rope and allows the sail to collapse on deck. Hecate notices his hand shaking. "The answer is no."

"The answer to what?"

"You want me to take you back to Crete."

"Wrong."

"Good."

"I want you to take me to Asphodel."

Charon issues a belly laugh, tossing back his head for effect. "What is funny?"

Wiping a tear of hilarity from his eye, he says, "The Unseen kept the girl, did he? Well done. I would have kept her too."

"Come on down. We will have a talk."

He says, cheerfully, "I am done with you and the mother and that flat-faced giant. The lot of you can go to the crows. Considered my debt to you repaid."

A fire burns on shore, safely away from the ship. Hecate goes to it and warms her hands. From the deck, Charon watches her, expecting her to plead her cause. She does not.

Fish bones and clay pots are strewn around. The jugs are tipped over, collecting sand inside the rims.

After several minutes of silence, Charon joins her beside the fire.

"Iasion is dead," Hecate says, watching the orange flames dance below her palms. "The mother is gone. No sign of her around here, I suppose?"

Charon shakes his head with scorn. "Idiots. Then Iasion caught up to Heracles like he hoped?"

One crooked finger points to the heavens. "Stricken."

Charon's mouth opens in a moment of disbelief. "Fuck off."

"I swear to the gods."

Hecate had checked the infirmary, finding beds occupied by unfamiliar faces. She had combed the polis, looking for signs of the mother. The loss hit her with hopelessness first, then with an odd desperation.

"What happened to your fancy friends up there? They toss you out?"

"Toss me out?"

"For helping the mother."

"I left."

"Do they know you left?"

"I know a good messenger," Hecate says.

Enlisting Hermes seemed the best option. He delivers his share of bad tidings. Guilt curdles her stomach when she thinks of dear Hera receiving the news of her absence. She hopes the High Queen does not take it out on the boy. Hera would never have agreed to let the "dying" old crone leave her care.

Truth told, Hecate nearly asked him for a different sort of help. Hermes, the messenger, has delivered transgressors to Asphodel. He could breach the palace of Hades without fuss. But the boy loves his father, and Hecate has no desire to come in the way of that. If Zeus found out his son was aiding Hecate in this mission, he would want to strike him. Then again, Hermes's loyalty to his father might cause him to refuse her altogether. Might cause him to tell the Loud Thunderer exactly what the old crone was up to.

This.

This is the only way. Charon will have his purpose yet. That is all man needs to keep on going. Purpose. Without a hand, Charon believes he has none. Wallow, wallow. *Oh, woe me.* Hecate has no tolerance for this sort of thinking.

"I can help you with the boat if you tell me what needs doing. My hands work as well as any man's. And I am stronger than I look."

Charon looks to the empty jugs. "Are you deaf? I told you—"

"I know what you told me."

"I am getting rid of the boat."

Hecate looks up, fire burned into her vision, obscuring his face with the phantom of dancing flames. "Because your jugs are empty?"

"Because I cannot sail it!" he yells, voice echoing off the cliff side.

This nonsense again.

"Then why fix it?" she challenges. "Sell it for scrap."

"If I can fix what Uranus broke," he says, "I can trade the junker for some things that will help me get by for a while. A functioning vessel is worth more than scrap."

Hecate nods, glancing around. "And after you 'get by for a while'? Then what?"

"I live spontaneously," he says.

"You could die spontaneously." Kicking up sand, Hecate starts toward the boat. Seaweed spools with the tide, tendrils clutching the earth. "I can help with the sail."

Charon follows. His tattered robe the color of mud hangs from his body. "Help all you want, but that will change nothing. You might as well run back to your plush life, if they will have you."

"I am not made for plush life. Give me something to do. If you want to sell the boat in the end, sell it. I cannot stop you."

Extra hands allow for expedient work. Over the next several days, Hecate enjoys the busy-ness, proving to herself that she needs purpose as much as Charon. These menial activities—holding the boards in place, patching holes, gathering supplies—add up. Charon's jugs run dry, and this gives him focus. His mood is pleasant, but he remains staunch in his resolution.

He will no longer sail.

Until the morning they wake to the early light of dawn and predatory birds calling out with discovery. The stench of decay triumphs over the usual smell of seawater.

Dead fish cover the shoreline. Egrets and storks fight for carrion. A brown eagle emits a dominant call, staking claim.

Hecate might believe that every fish in the cove washed up overnight. Their bodies pile, shining and bobbing as the waves lap. She covers her nose and mouth with the sleeve of her cloak.

"The prophecy," Charon says, surveying the carnage. "How does it end?"

She sniffs. "I know enough to tell you we have to see this through."

One morning, moons ago, she had unsealed the doors of the temple in Matapan. The decrepit priest, Vlasis, had come inside behind her. He said nothing, but Hecate knew that Vlasis had been ailing for days. Finally showing face, he shuffled inside with a faraway gaze fixed straight ahead. With sallow skin and hollow eyes, Vlasis disappeared into the *adyton.* An animal, looking for a place to die. A holy place, as was his right. Hecate had not distracted him. If a man wants to be alone in discourse with the gods when he passes, who is she to get in the way?

While he took refuge, Hecate had gone about her business seeing to the temple chambers where they kept the coffers of food and drink. She decided to look in on the priest.

He had smiled a dreamy smile. His whiskers dripped with kykeon, the brew that thins the veil between the human realm and the god realm.

He began to rhapsodize with words of poesy.

"I begin to sing of Demeter—"

As he prattled, the narrative coalesced.

"And her daughter Persephone too. The one with delicate ankles, whom Hades seized."

Hades.

Soldiers had stolen a girl from her care. Soldiers from Asphodel, the polis of Hades. When Vlasis sang, he sang of this *kore.*

"She cried with a piercing voice, calling upon her father, Zeus . . . But not one of the immortal ones or of human mortals heard her voice. Except—"

Was this intended for her ears? Invocation is a personal and sacred practice. Though fascinated, Hecate had turned for the door.

Vlasis spoke again.

"—except for the one who keeps in mind the vigor of nature. She heard it from her cave."

Her hand had frozen on the handle.

"She is Hecate . . ."

His words painted an ethereal picture, one where those on earth had already ascended into godhood.

"Hecate came to her, holding a light ablaze in her hands. She came with a message, and she spoke up, saying to her: 'Lady Demeter . . . I quickly came to tell you everything, without error.'"

Chills swept through her body. These invoked words dared an old woman to rise to a task that she had no intention of taking on. How could she? Travel is dangerous for a youth, but for a crone?

"Was there anything in that prophecy about me?" Charon asks, and for a twinkling moment Hecate sees hope inside his eyes. Hope that he might be part of something bigger, that the gods deem him worthy of use.

"Why else would I have come to you?" she lies.

"It is amazing you have lived so long. Your schemes are reckless."

"When you follow the gods in faith, they will light your way as best they can."

She had thought that purpose would be enough to spur him on, and maybe she was right. But she underestimated the value of a man who feels *chosen.*

For this, a man would take his chances in the land of the Unseen.

What am I doing?

She is going to get in so much trouble. Persephone clutches the satchel of herbs against her hip.

"They looked dead," Orpheus says, glancing back.

He means the dogs.

"They are not," Persephone says. "They are asleep."

"What did you give them?"

"The same thing we give to sacrificial animals before we offer them to the gods."

"Poison?"

Anxiety shortens her patience, the severing of an otherwise long rope.

"The gods respect the life we give them. So should we. We put them to sleep before we slit their throats. To spare them the suffering. Everyone knows this."

The mastiffs will wake up extra thirsty. This is the most suffering they will endure. Persephone could not let them follow. She and Orpheus are conspicuous enough already, and they need to be careful about the tracks they leave.

"What you gave the dogs," says Orpheus, "is what you give to a sacrificial lamb?"

Within her satchel rests more of it. Enough to render an elephant asleep.

"I gave the dogs more," she says. "They are bigger than lambs."

What am I doing?

This, Persephone thinks but does not heed.

When I know I will be punished . . .

In time, Hades will find her.

She hurries. Persephone needs time to appeal to the gods and reunite the lovers. She needs enough time for the lovers to flee. And for her to—?

—to do what?

Hide?

Run?

Face the Unseen?

With Orpheus at her heels, Persephone speeds through the corridor. If she stops, she will not have the courage to continue. She will lose her nerve.

What you want is respect.

She is stupid, so stupid! How could she have fallen for what Aeacus had said? If she could only pause to think, to pray for guidance.

All she knows for certain is that she cannot let Orpheus be returned to Tartarus.

Persephone points to the top of the stairs. "That is the slaves' entrance. They enter next to the pen where swine are kept and slaughtered. Sometimes I get so bored, there is nothing to do but look around."

As Orpheus swallows, the bony lump in the middle of his throat bobs. His musician's fingers curl around the torch until his knuckles turn white. "Outside there are no dogs and no guards?"

She shakes her head. "Just farm and pasture and forest."

The long-legged Orpheus takes the stairs two at a time and Persephone with the hurried steps of a child.

The crisp smell of winter fills her lungs, and she squints at the the barns and stables in the gray-white day. Four horses graze in the pasture.

Nose to the sky, Orpheus studies the incline to the southeast, how the palace walls seem to grow from the mountain like a glorious anomaly of Gaia. "There is no way to get past the monoliths without cutting through the forest. Once we do, we must go north and inland."

How long will it be before someone begins to wonder what happened to Judge Aeacus? Standing out here in the open makes her feel vulnerable to capture.

She strides into the field. The nearest horses perk their necks. One studies her from a long-lashed eye that blinks to clear flies. The horse chews, contented. Several paces off, the second horse takes a curious step in her direction. A shining brown mare.

"Hurry," she says, placing a comforting hand on its mane. "We have to go."

Orpheus nods, nervously wetting his lips before climbing on.

They flee through the forest, not noticing the treetops swaying back and forth, as if waving to a friend in the distance.

T hey will find her.

"From now on, I want her fixed to my side."

Persephone is coming back.

Hades knows this. Still, he hates how this feels in his gut. Tracking her, uncertain that she will stay put once caught.

"I will go—and you will not see me EVER!"

There had been a trail of sleeping mastiffs on his way out. At least ten, rendered unconscious so his bride could flee without dogs tagging along.

"I do not want to be here anyway!"

His stomach hurts. Heart constricts. This is fear, but why? What is there to fear?

There is certainty in this pursuit. Four guards on horseback follow their High King, hauling a cart for Eurydice's body once Orpheus reveals it.

"You are mean, mean, MEAN, and I hate you!"

Beyond the lion gate, Hades and his men stop to survey the tree lines. Frenetic movement draws their eyes to the north.

The Erinyes conduct the way. With feet balanced upon the limbs, the tribesmen grip overhead branches and shimmy the evergreens. Dusk blackens trees and men alike, human torsos blending with the treetops. Their legs and arms appear as branches.

Direction established, Cerberus locates the scent and leads.

Well into the night, the small cavalry travels northeast by torch. It begins to snow, brightening their path.

Time brings comfort. Time allows the mind to spin stories, for those stories to seep in and be accepted by the heart.

"I do love you. Surely you know that."

The heart slows. Stomach calms.

"I do love you."

Persephone did not leave. She is merely rebelling.

"—and I hate you!"

This must be what it is like to go insane. Sometimes, he feels too many things. To fear and to want, to rage and to hope all in the span of a single breath.

The dogs guide them into a ravine. During the war, he traveled by cave. Many cave systems have more than one entrance, this one included. The path ahead leads to the most visible entrance.

Something like thunder echoes against the canyon walls.

Two horses without riders burst into sight, galloping in a crazed attempt to flee.

Their own horses startle, whinnying and kicking up their front legs. They barely dodge the stampede.

As the unmanned horses race from sight, Hades lifts his torch to a narrow embankment.

Hades parts with his men.

They will block one entrance. He and Cerberus will intercept from the other.

He dismounts his horse and follows Cerberus to a tall, narrow crevice, like a fox den that burrows into the earth and widens into a maze of caverns.

His heart begins to race. His stomach sours.

They will find her. Persephone is coming back.

But does she want to?

His torch reveals a cave ceiling that expands to dizzying heights. Bats hang along the stalactites.

The cave interior arcs like a moon. When they veer left, the phantasmal smell of death hangs in the air, arousing the snouts of the dogs. The stench transforms from faint to solid, as solid as taste.

To the right and left, sliding within the crack where ground and wall convene, snakes slither along their way, as the tide might move in harmony with the moon's pull.

FOR LOVE
10

To keep Eurydice safe, Orpheus had constructed a stone wall to cover the makeshift tomb.

As snow falls, he climbs it, feet hooking into the crevices between stone layers. He reaches the top and pulls stone after stone, casting them to the ground.

The sound of nature grows shrill in the night, as if the land screeches in protest.

The wall is a third of the way dismantled when the smell reaches Orpheus. Heaving, he jumps aside and braces his hands on his knees until the nausea passes.

Why am I doing this?

Persephone shoves aside the doubt. The risk must be worth the consequences. Only one thing will make that so.

Love, of course.

Really, this is about helping Orpheus. That is all.

"Right now, there is only one thing you are good for."

Apprehensive, the young husband turns to her. "Majesty, has my wife visited you again?"

Persephone hates to see him suffer, hates to see anyone suffer. "I have felt eyes."

"Eyes?"

This is not a lie. She has felt eyes, but Persephone doubts they are the eyes of Eurydice. In fact, Eurydice has not shown her face since the day she revealed Orpheus was imprisoned.

"Eurydice watches," she assures the worried husband. "She is with you."

Orpheus resumes his work, pulling stones free until there is nothing left but an ankle-high pile. The mouth of the cave is a black O. Cold air emanates from inside, as does the rancid odor of decay.

Orpheus looks around. "The horses can graze here."

Persephone reaches into her satchel. The mare nuzzles her hip. "She must come inside with us."

From the bag, Persephone unearths a fist of herbs. Red-veined, tipped with frosty green. Their fragrance is as potent as the smell of death, only theirs is a pleasant and earthy-sweet smell.

The mare shuffles in the direction of the hand bearing temptation.

The cave is far bigger than Persephone expected, with a wide clearing perfect for ceremonies and rituals. An ideal place for a priestess to convene with the gods.

Once inside, the mare extends her neck to the herbs.

"Majesty?" Orpheus watches uneasily.

A tear betrays her and freezes against her cheek. She reminds herself as much as she reminds him: "In ceremony, we feed herbs to the one we sacrifice."

"Real queens command respect. They do not sniffle and cry all the time."

"Oh," the lyre player says. Sacrifice had not occurred to the him before now.

The muslin-wrapped body of Eurydice rests on sandstone. At the base of it, the cloth is tacky, dark. The flesh inside already begins to seep and wither. Persephone pulls her cloak over her nose and stands closer to the mare.

"What you want is a reversal of the natural order."

The horse chews the first herbs.

Orpheus begins to cry. He paces and pulls at his hair.

"The gods are with us," he says. "They are with us. They will side with love."

These are not declarations, but questions.

"We need an altar." She is dizzy with nervousness.

They gather wood and stones, a half-successful distraction from the fear.

"Thank you," Orpheus says. "For risking yourself for us."

"I risk myself for love."

It is true.

Except not as she has been saying. Persephone sees it now.

What she is doing would be unforgivable by a man who does not love her.

Sometimes she thinks her husband loves her. Sometimes.

Mostly, she wonders.

They arrange melon-sized rocks into a large circle in front of Eurydice's body. With his torch, Orpheus lights the fire.

Farther back in the cave, black depth.

"What is back there?"

Orpheus shakes his head. "It narrows. Parts of the cave are knee-deep in water. Why?"

Sweat breaks out over her brow. Oh, but this is a terrible thing. Stupid girl.

"There are two things in life that we do only once. We are born, and we die."

The gods will never grant this.

What if she kills this beautiful mare for nothing? Animal blood is hardly equal to this task.

She remembers the lark and how afraid she had been when

she killed it.

She remembers what it cost her to revive it.

Longing comes like a wave—for mother, for husband, for judge. For anyone wiser than she.

Yet from that longing springs a voice:

"And while you are here, you shall rule all that lives and moves and shall have the greatest rights among the deathless gods."

The words proffer their vibrations in her heart, as the vibration of thunder can be felt in the heart.

Persephone looks around for the source. "Did you hear that?"

Deathless gods.

You shall have the greatest rights . . .

On reflex, Persephone snatches the herbs from the horse's mouth. She ignites them by torch and drops them to the ground in flames.

"Go." She pushes the mare towards the open mouth of the cave.

The horse wanders outside, drunk-staring but awake.

"But you needed a sacrifice," Orpheus says.

You shall rule all that lives and moves . . .

"Yes." Persephone draws a blade from the satchel. "There is always a sacrifice."

She drags the blade across one palm.

Orpheus exclaims.

"We will trust the blood of the gods works as well as the life of a horse."

She drags the blade across her other palm.

At first, she feels no pain. As the blood seeps through sliced skin, her palms begin to ache and sting.

A human light passes beside her. The shade of Eurydice works to reform.

Persephone's voice gushes with relief. "She is with us!"

"Eurydice?" When Orpheus smiles, there is a type of madness in it. It is exhilarating when faith reveals itself as truth. Persephone understands.

Eurydice's ghost slips toward the corpse. In her limited years, Persephone has only witnessed the shades at their most bewildered. They die and are confused by death.

And they do not stay long. With the burial laws of Hades, few shades remain on the earth. They move on, as they should.

Persephone has never seen one with a purpose until now.

She watches as the essence of Eurydice falls upon its former mortal form. It fades into the muslin, into the once-living flesh of the young bride.

"Majesty. Look."

From corners and crevices, serpents slither along the ground.

"Do not be afraid," Persephone says. "They come to invoke."

She extends both hands over the fire. The blood hisses, but the serpents do not. They approach the hem of Persephone's cloak in silence.

Black, green, yellow, red. Serpents of many colors, mesmerized by a call to the gods.

They offer their bodies. Writhing, eager to help.

Persephone grasps one in each bleeding palm and raises them above her head.

The cavern blares with light.

The source of it stuns Hades. Serpents brush against his feet. Bats screech and swarm, searching for escape.

A radiant formation of orbs and fractals hangs in the air. It resembles a flower.

Cold shock seems to drive his soul from his body. Hades drops the torch. It extinguishes in a small puddle.

The cavern still blares with light.

Across from him, four soldiers appear at the entrance and halt before going further. They drop to the ground. Without hesitation, as if no part of their nature can deny the Holiness present. So, too, Cerberus drops to the ground, and each mastiff rolling over in submissive succession.

Hades has seen this light before. He sees it any time he lays eyes on Persephone, the brilliance emanating from her pores.

Now Persephone lies prone on the ground beside a bound corpse.

There is no light in her. Suspended overhead, the orbs change shape.

The orbs concoct images.

Flower. Deer. Pomegranate.

The light illuminates the wrapped corpse, oozing darkly through muslin. The figure groans and pants in a panic. It paws at the cloth over its mouth and eyes.

With a garbled, heaving breath, the body cries, "Orpheus!"

But the doting groom cringes at the sight.

Hades draws his sword.

And when Eurydice hears the sound, she turns to him, saying: "*Theíos*."

Mother often spoke of the Spark.

The Spark lives within everything.

This is the secret to summoning the gods. The Spark is the thing that always is and always has been. The gods are All Spark— and everything in existence contains their essence because the gods have breathed everything into being.

The Spark connects all things.

In her hands, snakes lash. Yellow scales reflect firelight.

She closes her eyes and connects to the life force within the snakes. As they writhe inside her grip, they remind her of what dwells within herself—the resistance, the surrender, and the ecstasy.

"Divinities, come." She says it as though they are already by her side, as greeting a person within earshot.

This is not the way of High Priestess Demeter. Mother's invocations brim with emotion and command. Her cries are pleas.

In Persephone's light voice, there is conspiracy.

The joining of sparks seems to begin at the soles of her feet. Her toes scrunch. As if she is hugged by snakes larger than the ones she holds, a constricting sensation slides upward. Persephone writhes inside her shell, a spirit molting its skin.

Orpheus glances at the cave opening.

He whispers, "What is that?"

She sees it.

Persephone knows it well.

There stands the giant shape of a man. His black silhouette cuts against the cave's opening where snow falls in large wet chunks.

For a moment, she is frozen. She hates being afraid! She hates feeling alone and scared and belittled, and now something crazed and feral springs up from her gut. A hunted animal flees. The helpless ones do. But she is the daughter of Zeus and Demeter! She is bride of the High King of Erebus! Neither man, monster, nor god will have dominion over her.

The figure's eyes glow white.

She needs the mother goddess who is charged with fertility. She needs any divinity who will grant her the wisdom of a mother, wisdom superior to her own version, which perhaps is not wisdom at all, but sheer will.

"Mother Gaia, Potnia, Rhea, Givers of Life—"

Orpheus falls to his knees, crying out in fear. "Majesty!"

The being at the entrance of the cave flies forward, glittering with starlight inside its black form.

There comes a flash. The entirety of her body thrums. An invisible force straightens her spine like a pole.

She is vaguely aware of dropping the serpents.

Vaguely aware of her human feet ushering her to Eurydice's dead body.

Of her bleeding hands, pressing against Eurydice's shoulders.

The blood seeps into the cloth and works its way through it, onto decayed flesh.

She breathes fragrant breath into the bound contours of Eurydice's face.

Giver of life.

Giver of life.

The essence of Persephone splits.

She is here, she is there, in this world and beyond it.

She is the snake, the spider, the worm. She is the algae, the clover.

She is without form.

She is all-seeing.

She is light, floating, unanchored by flesh.

She perceives the body of herself—of the young Persephone—standing beside the mummy.

She perceives the gaping mouth of Orpheus, how he marvels at her presence.

And something else. Something hangs directly beside her—

Unholy.

Before, It had seemed inhumanly big. Now, It appears the same size as She.

"You shall have the greatest rights among the deathless gods."

The voice, like a caress to the inside of her thigh.

Persephone is no longer afraid. There is only love.

From deep inside the cave, the part not visible, comes a tiny fragment of light. Firelight.

"What is back there?"

"It narrows. Parts of the cave are knee-deep in water."

The void brightens. The depth of the cave is revealed as a tunnel leading deeper inside the earth.

A mortal appears, three dogs at his side.

Something tugs—like someone pulling urgently at her skirt.

It is the spark of Eurydice, housed within the dead.

Awaiting animation. The spirit pulls like a woman crawling her way out of the dirt.

Persephone's floating euphoria spirals down.

Her light merges with Eurydice's. They are One.

She is dense and heavy. Aching. Tingling.

Giver of life.

From far-off: the cries of men. Her ears provide her only reality, for her eyes have fallen blind.

The faintest impressions of light.

The shouts of men echo all around.

At once, she feels the sensation of her own skin again. It burns like a sore, all over. Every breath is watery and foul.

Something is over her mouth and eyes. Muslin.

She sits upright, thrashing her arms.

She hurts! She hurts in body and in heart!

She is—

She is—

No no no.

Who was she before, if not Eurydice?

What came before this hideous moment of rebirth?

Renewal is the essence of birth. But she finds no renewal here.

Eurydice's voice comes from her mouth.

"Orpheus!"

The spark of Eurydice feeds off her own. In fear, she clings and binds herself with a love that was never meant to bind, thinking that if she can capture it, then she will never be without this love.

Wild panic grips the dwindling essence of Persephone.

Where is my body? Where is my body? Where is my body?

Her hands grope for the wrapping over her face. Her sight restores.

In front of her, Orpheus staggers backward, unable to accept her as the wife he once knew.

Asphodelian soldiers burst into the cave entrance.

A metallic scraping comes from behind, like the drawing of

a sword.

The man standing before her is Hades.

Hades.

The spark of Persephone recognizes this man.

In a voice belonging to Eurydice, she says, "*Theíos*."

Hades rears the sword.

The pain is a punch. Fast and dull.

Thereafter, there is only darkness.

Once the body has what it needs—the basics of water and food—it springs back to life with remarkable resilience.

By shirtless men, seemingly impervious to the cold, Demeter is fed and watered to see if there is life to revive. They inspect her hair, arguing among themselves. Brittle hair, newly and faintly tinged with the metallic sheen of silver.

Kore's disappearance had already taken its toll, leaving her bones without meat to spare. Recent days invited more deterioration, hollowing her cheeks, making her spine and ribs tactile against her fingers.

The watery horizon glimmers in her swollen eyes. Men are deep-skinned blurs, yelling because they must assert their commands over the waves and crying, over the periodic screams and protests of women not battered enough to be left alone.

"You are not as chase-worthy as you might once have been."

And the gods laugh at their manner of kindness.

Demeter had believed they sought to stone her with hail. But they had sent it to save her. With these healthy bodies available, no man bothers with hers.

She is glad to be spared, also, the burden of sight. Bruised and engorged, Demeter's eyes cannot witness what happens around her.

The first captive whom oarsmen drag aside is a *kore*. How old, Demeter cannot say. As the man yanks the girl from the plank upon which they sit, she cries out, voice high-pitched and youthful and holding a type of fright that comes from inexperience.

In full view, the oarsman marches the *kore* to the back of the ship. Through distorted vision, Demeter sees exposed flesh and the pivoting thrust of movement.

And she can hear perfectly. There is no mistaking those screams, those cries.

The man deposits the girl in her seat when finished. Shoulder to shoulder, Demeter feels the girl's violent trembling.

"Keep to me, *kore*," she whispers.

The whimpering softens. Silences. The girl rests her head against Demeter's bony shoulder, finding a mother's solace despite the lack of cushion there.

Within the mother, something breaks. Tears threaten to spill as she presses her cheek against the warmth of the girl's scalp.

The collective heat of bodies keeps her warm. There are eight captives, bound at the wrists and ankles and chained together tightly.

As the swelling abates over the course of days, sharpening the figures on deck, Demeter keeps her eyes to the boards beneath her feet. Nowhere else.

Other slaves are taken aside. Two boys—one not old enough to consider fighting. The other boy, old enough to try and fail.

The days pass, and Demeter's face fades from purple to yellow-green. The puffiness subsides. She manages to breathe from one nostril. Spends less time drifting to and from consciousness.

The oarsmen enjoy inspecting her hair. In their hands, it gleams like the sun. They talk to each other and laugh like men who find a useless stone only to rub away the grime and discover gold.

Once the body has what it needs, it can thrive.

Some innate part of her warns:

Eyes down.

A woman knows when looking at a man is the same as daring a man.

The day comes when the oarsmen spot a vessel far ahead—one worthy of chasing.

On days when they see no other ships at sea or along the horizon, the oarsmen take turns rowing. Today, all arms go to work, and the ship increases its speed.

The oarsmen's busy hands lend Demeter the courage to look up. Her neck aches. Her sight has cleared considerably.

She and the girl lock eyes.

"Asli."

"Sorry?" the girl whispers.

It is not Asli. A blink of the eye tells her as much. The same age, yes. But she is not the slave Demeter had left behind in Crete.

Asli has a voice and a place at the hearth.

To be a servant of the gods is the closest a slave will ever know of freedom. Asli is *favored*. Not tortured. Not raped.

What happened before Asli came to live with them, Demeter has never considered. Or perhaps she hid suspicion away in the guilty recesses of her mind, thinking if she did not ask, she would never have to know, never have to weigh her part in it.

Demeter clutches the girl's knee protectively, startling her.

"Keep to me."

The girl glances at the approaching shore. She nods quickly, understanding. They draw closer to a cove, cliffs high on their right. The anchor splashes.

The butt of the ship is near land. The nose juts to sea.

Four of the oarsmen dive into the water and swim toward

a stone archway that is too narrow for them to breach. At the archway, the swimmers submerse underwater and disappear.

Demeter frowns. The vessel they chased is nowhere in sight. The commotion of docking ensues. Oarsmen lower planks that crash into the sand. Tethered feet hammer against them as the captives descend in a pack.

Tents and spikes land at their feet. The eight captives are to erect four tents. Demeter's legs and back groan with stiffness.

"Your name?" Demeter murmurs to the girl.

"Rhea."

With closed lips, Demeter deals a gentle smile. "For our ascended queen mother, the goddess of—?"

Fertility.

In any other context, Rhea would have blushed with sheepish pride and said yes.

They both pale, realizing, simultaneously, that this name is no blessing for a captive.

Halfway into the process of raising the tents, the four divers return with goods, but no additional prisoners. Whomever they found on that boat must not have been of value to keep. Demeter shudders to think what they do to the ones who are not healthy and whole.

Spike in hand, Demeter sneaks a look at the returning swimmers who dump items upon sand.

A vase for wine. Sheep skin. There are dead fish inside a net, as well as a wide stone plate, unadorned and functional for cooking.

Then she sees the bow drill.

Hecate's bow drill for making fire.

Demeter's eyes widen. Hecate had left it with Charon in the boat when they arrived in Olympus.

Demeter scans the headland where the swimmers had raided.

Handing her the corner of the leather wall flap, Rhea whispers, "Are you well?"

Demeter fumbles the cloth and nods. The moment Rhea turns her back, Demeter eyes the stolen goods.

They had been chasing the drunkard all this time.

Why her heart sinks, Demeter does not know.

Charon is no friend of hers.

Rekindled
14

"There is no pain as great as losing her."

Upon the stone ground, two young brides lie motionless, without their light.

Never has darkness been this terrifying. Not as a boy, locked away inside Tartarus. Not during war when navigating unexplored tunnels, unsure if death awaited him along the way.

What Hades experiences now is the absence of joy and hope as men falter in the darkness.

"I need my wife. I cannot continue without her."

Whatever had been before Persephone's light, Hades can hardly remember. Nor can he fathom existing after the light.

This need not be.

Choppy breath cuts through the darkness. His breath. The breath of soldiers, of Orpheus, and of the dogs.

Hades shakes and runs his hands along the gritty earth until he finds the arm of Persephone.

Then, at once, a spark ignites and brightens like a kindled flame.

PART FIVE
THE NURTERER OF MANY

She [Demeter] made that year the most terrible one for mortals, all over the Earth, the nurturer of many.

—*Homeric Hymn to Demeter*

HOLY LIGHT

1

T hey await the morning light.

Before setting out into calf-deep snow, the people within the cavern wait for the newness of day.

Soon the god Helius will come. He will blaze hope across the sky.

Of the four soldiers, none witnesses the dawn. Sunlight pours into the cave, and their irises reflect no color. The water lines are red, swollen. Without pigment and sight, the soldiers strain to control the tension in their breath, trying not to release the howl of fear that brews inside.

Though rendered blind by a Holy Light, they must not show weakness in the presence of the Unseen.

Hades sees their fear, regardless.

"Orpheus?" he says to the back of the man's red-curled mane. "Can you see?"

The lyre player sits with his arms wrapped around his knees. Face to cave opening, Orpheus lifts his head.

His colors do not betray him. There is only impenetrable blue, a sadness at the depth of his being.

He has not turned to look at Eurydice since she fell.

Hades, however, has looked at his own bride. Compulsively,

he has felt for the movement of Persephone's breathing.

Each time, thinking:

Please, please . . .

Luckily for Orpheus, she lives. Beaming brighter than the sunlight, though cold to the touch.

This morning, Hades sees her with the assistance of Helius.

This is how she must look to the gods.

Hair, once bronze, as flaming as the sun.

Flesh, once bronze, alabaster as the moon.

Against his palm, her hand beams white. Hades sees no veins beneath the delicate skin of her wrist.

Clacking hooves and voices echo in the canyon. Figures appear at the cave's opening.

Orpheus stands to face the cavalry and tells Hades, "I should have obeyed you."

Aeacus and his team of soldiers step inside with torches lit.

"You wanted me to trust you," Orpheus says. "I did not. And I am sorry."

"Will you not face me when you speak?"

As Aeacus and the soldiers draw closer to seize him, Orpheus turns. He kneels before the Unseen.

The water lines of his eyes glisten red around ice blue irises.

"Please," he says, "I deserve to die."

Hades scoops Persephone's limp body in his arms. "Then you will live."

BY SEA

2

In the beginning, the journey southward fares well.

For days they pass down the coast as smoothly as when they came. On the seventh day, another ship appears from behind, barely visible. Given her bad eye, Hecate does not notice it.

Charon's eyes are sharp. He spots it as a speck on the horizon and curses, barking orders so they can take cover before they are seen. The ship transforms from speck to blob too quickly for Hecate's liking.

"There." Charon tips his head toward a cove where waves pound rock with a vehemence that would make the most iron-stomached man sick, at best.

Outstanding headlands tower around the cove. Basalt rock, four times the size of their boat, juts from the sea. They use their oars to push the vessel away from collision. Formed by centuries of water wearing against stone, the inlet leads to a small patch of sand. Sea foam knocks against the hull. Charon's face is pale against a beard sprayed with froth and salt.

"You and I make lousy commodities." Hecate consoles, unsure how true it is.

With no room to spare, the boat slides between an archway of black rock. The sides of the vessel scrape, making Charon grit his teeth until they clear the arch. A generous wave drives them toward sand. Charon hoists himself overboard with one hand. Submerged to his knees in water, he guides them to shore. Once she sees the ocean floor beneath the tide, Hecate joins him.

They lug and anchor the vessel, hiding it from immediate attention. Charon collapses, robes soaked from waist to toe. "We stay here until they pass."

She and Charon huddle together for warmth. Her teeth chatter. They cannot risk making fire or the smoke that goes along with it, not until the slave traders are beyond sight.

They wait in the torturous wet-cold, eyes fixed on the gap between jutting rocks, praying to the gods that the Tyrrhenians zip by in a rush. The wind cuts through skin and muscle and aches her bones. Charon's lips are blue.

"What if they already docked?" she says.

Drawing a U shape in the sand with a stick, Charon taps above the southernmost point and to the right. "Here we are. Thorikos, near the Laurion mines. Lead and silver mines. So they sell plenty of male slaves in this area." He taps the other side of the peninsula. "The women? They usually sell the women here."

Hecate nods. "Which is?"

"Athenai, the biggest polis in Attica." He waves the stick around. "Anyone living around the area travels to Athenai for women slaves. But selling them is the last thing the Tyrrhenians do. First, they use them. For as long as they can. And they let them out to sailors."

He surveys the crone, judging her tolerance for seedy admissions.

Nothing he says surprises her. "Is that so? Personal testimony?"

Laughter pulsates in his throat but Charon knows better than to let it escape his mouth. That might earn him a smack across the head. She starts to smack him anyway, but that is when she hears a distinctive splash interrupting the sound of waves and ocean birds.

Charon leaps to his feet, grabbing her by the cloak. "Get up—come on!"

As he pulls her up, Hecate's legs wobble. "Wha—?"

He tugs her along for the first few steps, but then he lets go and jogs toward the trees.

Hecate surveys the inlet. Charon's boat hardly fit through the arch. A lembus vessel would never be able to pass through. Beyond the opening, a ship bobs upon the sea. She holds her breath, watching the anchored vessel rock with the waves.

From out of turquoise water, the heads of four men emerge. Their black hair shines wetly, knotted high at their crowns. Bronze hoops hang from their ears. Despite the cold, they are bare-chested, hairless as dolphins with dark skin gleaming like beautiful sap. They trudge from water to land.

Two men investigate Charon's boat and its contents.

"*Mur ati nacna*," one of them orders her.

"He says to stay where you are."

Charon has returned. He has not abandoned her. His arms extend along his sides to show the Sea People that he is defenseless and maimed.

The scavengers push them to their knees and rummage through the provisions on the boat.

Two men argue and gesture toward their newfound captives.

Charon speaks up. "*Trinruva, alpan culichna, ulpaia . . .?*"

They stop arguing and eye him for a moment.

One hollers a reply at Charon, who answers in a way that silences them.

The cliff side cups the shore, but from the other side of the cliff wall there comes more ruckus—shouting men, a wooden plank hitting the ground. The Sea People have banked on the other side of the cliff and sent these men over to raid their food and supplies. They had aspired to find able-bodied sailors on Charon's boat. Instead, they found a cripple and an old woman.

Arms loaded, the scavengers take what they want, namely the fish she had caught and the plate to cook it on. They have little else to offer. The men survey the condition of the boat, the hooks and nets to determine if any can be of use. When they leave, they leave with full arms.

But they do leave—all four of them—and Charon and Hecate remain kneeling on shaking knees as the Sea People, not popular for sympathetic hearts, show atypical mercy by disappearing around the cliff wall.

"Are they coming back?"

Charon pulls her up by her armpit. "Possibly. Let us go while we can."

It takes time and struggle to get the boat back out to sea. Nobody docks here for good reason. By the time they triumph over the tide, both are heaving and exhausted, frozen to the point where they consider stopping and wrapping themselves in the sail. But however merciful the Tyrrhenians had been, Charon does not want to risk it. He puts as much distance as he can between them.

Mercy, indeed! The gods appear to be on their side. Look at them go—so very favored are they! This, Hecate assures herself, smugly.

Then, the fishing boat gives out. The thing leaks all the way around the Attican peninsula.

Over and over, they bail saltwater.

Bend, scoop, straighten, hoist.

Bend, scoop, straighten, hoist.

Gnarled hands ache from clasping the bucket. Her spine begs for rest, the connecting muscles tight and strained and on the verge of revolt.

Cheeks high with flush, Charon eyes his precious boat. They are ankle-deep in water. Without two operable hands, his attempt to simultaneously bail water and maneuver the vessel meets with utter failure. He grows more disgruntled by the second, cursing everything he can think of: the gods, the mother, and particularly the disaster many moons ago that left him with a severed hand and indebted to this damned crone who is going to end up costing him a boat.

By the time they reach Corinth, the vessel is a third as impaired as it had been before they patched it. Their feet and legs, previously aching from the cold, are now numb. Hecate can hardly curl her fingers anymore, and the pain in her back will soon cripple her.

"We can seal it again in Corinth." Charon struggles to remain close to the shore in case the boat crumbles around them and they must swim.

"This horse is on its last leg, my friend," Hecate tells him. "Time to let it go."

"There is no faster route than by sea."

"You mean," Hecate corrects, "if we do not wind up on the ocean floor."

Sea spray dotting his beard with salt, Charon glares at her. "What are you getting at?"

"We dump the boat in Corinth," Hecate says.

"Dump the boat?" He sneers. "I would sooner dump *you*."

"It is a lost cause, and you know it."

Snorting, Charon shakes his head. "Flippant hag. This is not your boat to lose."

At the isthmus of Corinth, Charon succumbs to the haranguing. He haggles to offload the remains of the fishing boat. "The boat for a horse" is his request, but the boat is a wreck and only worth its parts. In the end, they leave Corinth with a pungent mule that carries their meager belongings on its back. Hecate is grateful to walk. It allows her to stretch her legs and spine, and moving her body restores some warmth.

"Stubborn old woman," Charon gripes, "get on the donkey. You have nothing to prove to me."

"You get on the donkey," she says. "I like to walk, and I will walk until my feet become as useless as that boat of yours."

In Erebus, bustling towns die away. The land looks almost uninhabited, the occasional herd of goats reminding them that there are people here somewhere, hidden away on their small farms. Living inconspicuous lives, untouched by the lofty expectations of the gods.

Near dark, they stop to make a fire and set up camp. Despite the cold, Charon sweats heavily, half-moons of perspiration under the arms of his tunic and across his chest and back. He smells worse than the donkey.

"What did you say to the Sea People?" she asks. "I know you are sailor. But sailors speak one language—their own—and not very well."

"I called them brethren. I told them to take what they wanted."

"Brethren?"

Their daily catch of fish cooks upon rock.

"I was borne Etruscan."

"You said you served Minos in the war."

"Both things cannot be true?"

"Why did you serve the Cretans in the war if you are not native to Crete?"

He shakes his head at her ignorance, scratching at the lice in his hair. "The Sea People are slave traders. Not slave owners."

She blinks. The gods test her wisdom, test her pride. She hesitates before she asks, "And so?"

"And so," Charon says, "I told you. They sell slaves in

Thorikos. In Athenai. They sell slaves to *you* people. You enable them to do their deeds. Slaves come from everywhere, even their own native land. When someone is captured and sold, it can easily be an Etruscan who is sold. It can just as easily be a Cretan who buys the slave. A Cretan who impregnates that slave. And the slave produces . . . what? More slaves. When I had the choice between my mother's fate and joining ranks with King Minos's naval fleet, I chose the fleet. Either way, my life was bought before I was even born."

"Charon," Hecate declares, resigned to admitting she is not as wise as she thinks. "I had no idea."

"Nobody asks." His voice is hollow, genuine.

The fire crackles.

He changes the subject with a jarring quickness. "What if the mother is dead?"

"Dead?"

"You said she was gone."

"I never said she was dead."

"Where is she then?"

"Time will tell."

"Oh, 'time will tell'," he laughs. "The god of time is all about destruction. We are born to one fate only. Death."

"Why the sudden rancor, Charon?" she says. "Has something made you doubt the gods?"

His frustration gathers momentum. "The *kore* ran away. The day the earth opened. I was there, remember?"

A smile touches the corners of Hecate's mouth. Sparse brows lift. Firelight dances in her milky eye.

"Maybe the daughter of Zeus hates her mother. Ever think of that? Then what? No reunion. More plagues. Death to mankind."

Hecate readjusts the blanket around her shoulders. "Yes. I have thought of that."

"Well?"

"Well, what? You look to me as if age provides me the wisdom of a god. Did I ever claim it to be a god? I am mortal. I am only doing what I think needs to be done, and I see no one else stepping up to take my place. As the world goes to chaos, every man and woman and child will laze about woefully, thinking that someone *else* needs to save them. Someone *else* needs to come along and make things easier. When the plagues run amok, when the crops fail and the earth begins to die, who will save us? The kings? Ha! You said yourself! Kings are just men. No, Charon, it is us. We are responsible for our lots. What better a life have you to live? You have had your drink, your whores, your adventure. These things are empty. You are empty. You hurl suppositions at me right and left, thinking I will relent, thinking I will doubt myself and the gods right along with me. Well, I will not doubt. Sometimes the sun is not shining. Sometimes the path is lit by your *own* torch! Sometimes you can see only the step in front of you. And you know what I think? I will tell you. My life will not be spent in resignation. I will not lie down and watch catastrophe as if I am helpless. I am not. You are not."

Charon grunts. "You do not need to holler."

"Yes, Charon. Sometimes I do."

W hen camp is made, the Sea People force their captives into a single line and lead them, linked to one another by the waist and bound at the wrists, onto a dirt path.

The two young boys are first in line. Then Rhea. They arranged her this way to indicate her worth. A girl of Rhea's age holds value.

Demeter is second to last in line. Her legs, atrophied and scrawny, barely manage to keep up with the others.

Ahead, Rhea steps over stone and root, throwing a look of caution over her shoulder, peering around the arms of other captives to make sure Demeter pays attention to her steps. They care for each other instinctively, as a mother and child might.

Rhea looks nothing like Kore. Her two front teeth protrude, freckles like constellations on apricot skin. Her dark kinky hair holds an undertone of auburn.

How Demeter loves her! Needs her—more than she can express. Without expectation, Demeter targets this love as acutely as with an arrow.

Skulking along with the cliff to their left, Demeter sees the little cove the oarsmen had looted earlier.

In the briefest of fantasies, Demeter had imagined escaping

with Rhea during the night. Stepping over Charon's broken body and onto the boat, sailing off to freedom.

The cove is empty. No evidence of a boat. The Tyrrhenians must have taken pity on the crippled fisherman. Stolen his goods, but left him with his boat and his life.

Thorikos begins at the base of Velatouri Hill. The homes and smithies are built staggered and irregular. At the pinnacle of the hill, a small temple casts its shadow over the polis. Demeter has spent her life in temples. Loss squeezes her heart like a rag. She admires it, recognizable by the covered portico held in place by columns.

Flanked by crude chunks of stone, the road opens into a central courtyard marketplace where goods are peddled.

As the Sea People line them up and offer them to the highest bidder, Demeter wishes she could take the girl by the hand and tell her what she used to tell Kore.

"I will not let them hurt you."

But her hands are bound, and Demeter can make no promises.

Atop the hill, the temple glows inside a single ray of sun.

Again, she thinks of Asli.

Asli is not here. She is at home, with Demeter's uncle in the priesthood.

Serving the priesthood.

This is not coincidence. Demeter perks her chin and surveys the courtyard.

Women barter for fruit and grain.

Mining foreman peruse the two boys on display, finding them ideal for crawling inside constricted places. Demeter watches the children transfer from slaver to miner, as an exchange might take place for anything else: a cow, a bag of apples, or bundles of wood.

As expected, the boys sell first. Beefy men, cloaked in fur, frequent the merchants.

She finds what she is searching for.

In a purple himation, an elderly man wanders through the square, hands linked behind his back as he observes the business of the day. The sacred headband of the priesthood, woven from olive branches and ribbon, hugs the crown of his head.

This holy man is to Thorikos what Demeter had been to Knossos. She, a High Priestess. He, the chief of male priests, the Hierophant.

From the pouch in his hand, he selects an olive and pops it into his mouth. He is not here to buy. He is here to observe, to pass the day. Demeter can tell by his lack of engagement with the ones who pull him aside to show him well-crafted pottery or silver.

From her former life, she knows a slave does not look a priest in the eye. Certainly not one of his stature.

Demeter stares him down. She ogles so fiercely that even the densest man could not deny the sensation.

The Hierophant furrows his brow and saunters her way. His beard hangs below the breastbone. Twice her age, diminutive and non-threatening, the priest stops at arm's length.

He offers an olive.

The Tyrrhenians unleash the two matronly slaves standing beside Rhea. The slaver transfers them to a nobleman, a younger man looking for house maids.

Bound wrists nestle into the concave of Demeter's abdomen. She is filthy, stinking. Her mind races.

The priest stretches his hand out to touch her head. "May the gods find you good service."

The young nobleman glances at Rhea.

"I will not let them hurt you."

Now he lingers, appraising. Looking at Rhea differently than he looked at the matronly slaves.

"Please," Demeter whispers to the Hierophant, "you must

take my daughter."

The nobleman talks with one of the slave traders. Negotiating, motioning toward Rhea as if she is not worth the price, not when he has already purchased two others.

Idiot. These Tyrrhenians do not bargain. The nobleman tries.

"I offer her my blessing." The priest regards Rhea. "I am not in need of any—"

"She can weave the baskets for procession. Clean the temple. Cut ribbon for animal sacrifice."

"Our initiates do that," the priest says, examining her closely. "What you describe, using slaves for menial work, is a luxury afforded to a much larger polis than this one."

She stares him dead in the eye.

Now the Hierophant takes notice in how Rhea shakes, tears landing on the dirt at her feet. He notices the way the nobleman sizes Rhea up, lifting her robe, prying her mouth open wide to examine her teeth and tongue.

In the Cretan priesthood, a newly acquired domestic slave is welcomed as part of the family. When Asli first came to live with Demeter and Persephone, they feasted on nuts and fruit and adorned Asli with garland.

This nobleman will not give Rhea such a homecoming.

One of the slavers, face hard and rectangular, catches them talking.

As he starts toward them, the Hierophant asks Demeter, "And can she also gather fruit and grain?"

Anyone else would say yes. Few would understand what he truly asks, certainly none of the *damos* who have lived apart from temple life.

A priestess would know.

Only a virgin can assist with food preparations. Their purity likewise purifies the food.

The Tyrrhenian approaches, leather strap in hand.

With a quick shake of the head, Demeter answers the priest.

No.

The leather strap snaps smartly against her lower back, stinging beneath her clothes.

With her eyes fixed to her feet, she can hide the tears that redden them, hide the dripping of her nose. Demeter does not want this slave trader to think, for an instant, that he can make her feel a thing.

He gestures to Demeter and says, "Woman?"

"No—" the Hierophant stammers, hand raised in refusal. "No. Thank you."

As the priest steps away, Demeter's back hitches with tears. The Tyrrhenian shows him the other options, ones that have the muscle needed in both chattel slaves and slaves of state.

"No," the Hierophant says, then adds: "But I must take that one for the priesthood."

The priest does not wink or nod conspiratorially. He simply ushers the slave trader to Rhea and nudges the nobleman away.

"Blessings to you, good man," he says to the disgruntled buyer. "This *kore* has been called to serve the temple of Pontus."

A mere nobleman cannot argue with a Hierophant. The Tyrrhenian unleashes the rope tied to Rhea's waist.

The cord between them separates.

The girl glances her way, and Demeter can only nod and smile with her eyes in a way that lets the girl know:

"I will not let them hurt you."

By dusk, only three captives remain. When they return to camp, the Tyrrhenians instruct them to take the net stolen from Charon's boat and gather fish. In the gloaming, Demeter stands ankle deep in sea foam with the last young male captive. He did not sell. On the voyage, he had broken out in large patchy lesions.

His gums are red and bleeding. The Sea People will kill him if he gets any worse.

There are at least twenty Tyrrhenians at camp.

Since the marketplace closed, Demeter has been keenly aware that she is the only woman left among them.

She casts Charon's net into the waves. An elder male slave trudges up the embankment to search for wood. Demeter hands the net to the sick man, who will have an easier time casting a net than hauling wood. Where his health wanes, hers waxes.

Mostly, the Sea People make themselves cozy beside a fire.

Demeter joins her elder, and two of the Tyrrhenians trail along. Keeping watch so their remaining commodities do not run.

Thick, brittle vines grow along the ground, creeping upward along the trunk of an evergreen. They would be easy to snap off. Easy to light, to keep an encampment warm.

Red hairs grow from the vine, sticking to tree bark. The ivy itself shriveled and dispersed long ago.

The elder slave avoids it.

But the gods have given Demeter something to do.

Keeping her hands busy, Demeter gathers the kindling. The slavers pay attention to two things. They make sure Demeter and the elder gather wood, and they prevent them from fleeing. Apart from these two things, they make terrible guardians.

Demeter reaches for the vines, jutting out around the base of the tree, climbing high in an explosion of dry kindling.

The elder sees. He opens his mouth to tell her: *Be careful. Step away from that.*

As fiercely as she had eyed the Hierophant, Demeter stares the old man in the face. He is a head shorter than she, small-boned with silver hair sprouting from inside his ears.

He stops himself before speaking. When Demeter nods with deliberation, the old man halfway grins, showing long yellowed teeth.

They gather wood and vine, clutching bundles tightly in their arms, despite the sap oozing from the freshly cut branches. They join the encampment and place the kindling next to an already raging fire.

When the blaze dwindles, the elder captive adds kindling, stoking the charred wood with a stick. Sparks and fumes plume upward, smoking the fish the Tyrrhenians eat, keeping their exposed skin warm despite the coastal wind. They breathe the toasted air in between chugs of wine.

To reduce the risk of conspiracy, the Sea People separate the captives into three separate tents.

"Sit," the Tyrrhenian says, pointing at the wool on the ground. The tent holds nothing but blankets, not a sharp or hefty object in sight.

Demeter obeys.

In the frigid darkness, he watches.

Her heart maintains an oddly steady beat.

Eyes down.

He picks up a length of her hair, admiring it.

Her hands remain still and steady on her lap.

Outside, the Sea People call to him, voices exuberant and raucous, baiting him to join them in their feast by fire.

He exits the tent.

Already, Demeter's arms and neck have begun to itch and erupt in blisters.

CONSPIRACY

4

"Have you seen her?"

"Of course I have."

The long trudge through snow stole the daylight from them. To give Persephone warmth and rest, they stopped once the sun began to set.

The Erinyes shelter the girl tonight. They keep her warm with piles of animal skin and a well-stoked fire.

Aeacus and Hades stand outside the straw hut. One could easily mistake it for a jumbled mess of sticks and bamboo. It is not a kept home, but a hive assembled specifically for any of the tribe's infirm. In their garish headdresses, the tribal elders come and go from the hive.

To call it a hut is an insult to huts. But Hades had not liked the girl's "color" and insisted they stop, still several more hours from home in this snow.

Feeling sorry for her again.

Aeacus denies himself the luxury of fuming. He must appear concerned, and so Aeacus recreates his concerns in his mind, which produce the colors one would expect. They incite the emotions that Hades will accept and not suspect conspiracy.

Aeacus thinks of how it would result for him if Hades were to die, leaving the child of Zeus to inherit his lot. How his own life would change if she ever assumed control of things.

An infection, that girl.

Thinking this, Aeacus speaks with real concern beneath words that are not the true source of his concern. "They say she may not recover from this."

"She will."

"Judge Rhadamanthus is correct about the law," he shrugs with regret. "Zeus can renege on his agreement if the girl produces no child. But you can renege as well."

As the night life sings around them, Hades shakes his head. "Why would I want to do that?"

"There is absolutely no good that comes of her presence."

"She is the only good thing here."

Those words stagger Aeacus for a moment, partly because he cannot believe the sincerity with which Hades spoke them and partly because he never thought he would need a retort for such a sincerity in Hades. He recovers by saying, "I understand the need to have some pleasure at the end of the day, but that can be delivered by a hundred other women."

"What difference does it make to you?" Torchlight glitters in Hades's black eyes. They shift, no longer looking Aeacus in the face, but looking beyond Aeacus.

At the *colors*.

"For some time now, I have seen tones in you that I have not seen before," Hades says. "And I have honored our agreement. I have left you to your own sins. But I am going to ask that you be transparent with me now. Lately, I see more frustration around you. More anger. Mostly, I see fear."

"Have you seen conspiracy?"

Hades considers. "No."

Aeacus does not know how to kill her and get away with it.

His sins will radiate from his pores, and Hades will see that one act that does him in. Poisoning. Pushing her off a cliff like he did with the other one.

Back then, Hades had been away for a long time and, by the time he returned, any lingering guilt about Leuce had long since expired, if Aeacus had felt it in the first place.

Aeacus blinks away the thoughts like a man shoveling dirt over a pile of shit. To mask them further, he summons the next strongest emotion that comes to mind.

"I must be blunt." Aeacus crosses his arms.

"Blunt about what?"

"How could you allow Orpheus to go unpunished?"

"He did not go unpunished," Hades says. "I banished him to Thrace."

"There are few offenses worse than the ones he committed."

"Trust me. I dealt the worst of consequences."

"Really?" Aeacus says. "Tomorrow Orpheus will wake up to the sun on his face and plenty of maidens swooning over his fingers on that lyre. That sounds pleasant to me."

Swinging his torch away, Hades issues a cynical laugh. "You are as faithless as Orpheus. And you speak of things you know nothing about."

Aeacus lets him go. The cavalry sets camp upwind where the smoke of their fire will not contaminate the queen's precious air.

The judge waits until Hades is out of sight and then makes his way to the little hut where Persephone sleeps.

With mortal lips, Persephone smiles at the dark intruder.

Once, Persephone had been afraid of Him.

Unholy, she had accused.

Back then, she was merely a girl. It was normal for her to fear Him.

The shimmering silhouette stands at the foot of her bed. In the beginning, she had perceived the figure gaunt—skeletal even—and yet it must have been fear that made Him so. Now Persephone sees Him for what He is. His shoulders bear a strong, muscled shape. The entirety of Him, black with twinkling flares that fill the void like stars in the night sky.

Her body is racked with fever and chills. The gown she wears sticks wetly to her back. The blankets beneath her are drenched with sweat.

He tells her:

"Rebuke this sickness. Your body is an illusion."

Between her eyes, the sensation of pressure. It prickles and tingles its way up her forehead, into her scalp and through the crown of her head, taking the fever with it.

Her palms stitch themselves whole inside the bandages.

The One she had called Unholy slips his hand around her

ankle.

Warmth creeps from her calf to her groin and finally to her heart.

Then He is gone.

Persephone opens her eyes. The air is thick with herbal fumes, tingling her nose and chest with each soothing breath.

She sits upright in a state of perfect health.

Judge Aeacus stands over the pallet of fur and hide, steely hair hanging limp around bearded cheeks.

He drops something that Persephone cannot see.

"What has happened to you? Your eyes." He shakes his head in disapproval.

Persephone does not bother to answer. "Are you my enemy?"

"What?"

She remains still, neither fidgeting nor fiddling with her hair. Only her eyes move—to the floor and the cushion Aeacus had dropped when she awoke. "You hoped to find me sicker. Less likely to fight back."

Aeacus shakes his head. "My only aim is to check on your welfare. I will leave you to rest."

And he leaves.

Or starts to leave.

Cerberus lurks inside, sent to guard her.

Aeacus stops.

"You are not so good for my husband, I think."

He turns. "I am not your enemy. You are. You make your own trouble."

Persephone showers the dogs with affection and stands. Her pale-yellow gown is streaked with dirt and blood.

"I have never had an enemy before." Unwrapping the gauze from her perfect hands, Persephone continues, light-voiced. "I do not think I would like it. Not at all."

"What god or goddess has made you whole again?" Implying that any god or goddess willing to help her must be bad.

Fear looks especially sad on a nasty old man like this. Persephone takes no pleasure in it.

With a deep breath, she casts her eyes upward, searching for an answer and saying, simply: "The goddess of myself."

The face he makes! Persephone erupts into giggles, finding his gaping mouth and buggy eyes to be toad-like, and toads have always made her laugh.

"My husband loves you. You are like a father to him. Is this so?"

"Yes."

"Could you ever love me as you love him?" she asks with genuine hope. "As a father?"

Judge Aeacus spits out her kindness. "A loving father would save his son from a menace like you."

She nods, buzzing with a sweet, calm peace. "Okay, Judge."

With Cerberus distracted by belly rubs and ear scratches, Aeacus disappears into the night.

Persephone pays him no attention. Aeacus is nothing. In the world of gods, he is but a mortal.

Her attention pricks.

At her feet, the dogs roll, bellies up, writhing and whimpering in the presence of the otherworldly shape in front of her.

Persephone likes that He is with her. It makes her feel less alone. More purposeful. Protected.

Again, she is told:

"And while you are here, you shall rule all that lives and moves and shall have the greatest rights among the deathless gods . . ."

Persephone asks him, sweetly, "Husband, what will you have me do?"

"Those who defraud you and do not appease your power . . .
shall be punished forevermore."

Persephone smiles. Oh, how she adores Him.

Gifts

6

"*Y*ou *are my whole world.*"

Hades is alone in the tent until the mastiffs enter.

He gives a hard snap. "Cerberus. Back to your post."

They ignore him, yawning and plopping down beside his pallet.

These days, it feels as though he is losing control of his whole life.

"*My whole world.*"

"Cerberus," he fumes.

An explosion swells within. He starts to lash out, but it will not help. It will not be enough to yell at dogs; he will need to rip the tent apart and burn the forest to the ground to release what threatens to rise.

"*They say she may not recover . . .*"

Persephone parts the flap and comes inside.

His breath fastens to the inside of his throat and releases in a great rush. He flies to her and touches her cheeks to prove that she is real, the soft-shining creamy skin without a freckle or blemish or pore.

"*Have you seen her?*"

Something has happened to her here in Erebus. Hades has not

imagined it.

The first time he saw her, her eyes were dark. Now, the irises are ringed with orange-brown and twinkle with amber flecks. In the light of a candle, they look themselves like flames. She gives him a dimpled, bright-beaming smile that surprises him as much as her presence, as much as the changes that have been occurring in her over time.

He takes her hands and turns them over in his. No gashes.

The way she gazes at him, Hades might think this is the first time they have met.

Maybe it is.

With dry, unblinking eyes, he says, "How do you feel?"

She radiates pure joy.

"Alive."

"I was sure . . ." His flesh burns hot-cold. A deep tremor begins in his muscles. ". . . you died."

"Oh no!" The wide-eyed Persephone blushes, shaking her head at the false accusation. "Never."

"There is nothing funny about this."

"I know, *Theíos*," she says. "Most everything about it was wrong. Except for my intention."

"What *was* your intention?" He has never needed to ask this question of anyone.

With a child's simplicity, Persephone says, "To see if you love me." Finger to lips, she speculates. "I should have just asked you. Right, *Theíos*?"

He shakes his head, dumbfounded.

"Would you have told me the truth?"

Any other offender would throw themselves at his feet, quivering with apology and a certainty of punishment.

Persephone acts like someone who is already forgiven.

She also acts like there is nothing to forgive in *him*.

Perhaps he should yell. Shake her. Some men might even strike.

But he finds he does not want to. He is giddy with the relief of having her back, not angry with him, happy and whole. Seeing the newness in the way she looks at him, Hades is tempted to believe he never aggrieved her. If she has the grace to see him anew, then he can certainly *become* anew.

"You cultivate the garden, Majesty."

He hugs her, distracted by the pleasurable humming friction of her body.

"Listen to me," he fumbles. "What you did was—"

"Regrettable."

Sighing, he grasps her by the arms and pulls back. "My orders, to you or to anyone, might seem like punishment, but they are not. When I give a command, the intention is balance. Do you understand what I mean?"

"You mean whatever you tell people to do is for their own good?"

"It is cause and effect. I am the effect."

She looks down, contemplating. "Hm."

"I have banished Orpheus to Thrace."

"Well . . ." She shrugs, sighing big. "Okay, *Theíos*, if you say so. But it would have been kinder to kill him."

"I am unconcerned with kindness. Tell me. What would happen if I killed him?"

"He could be with her," she answers.

"Death has eternity with us in the end, remember? Orpheus argued this once himself. I told him to have faith and release her. He did not. He cannot go to his grave before learning to do so, the easy way or the hard way. He could have let her go only once. Instead, he forced himself to suffer it twice."

She says, "He has no choice but to let go now."

"Yes, the hard way," he says. "So, I am not 'mean,' as you said. I am evenhanded. You must trust me."

"Oh, I do." Dreamily, she snuggles against him again, forehead resting in the crook of his neck. Saying into his ear, "You make a fearsome god."

She uses it in the present, an occurrence already so. He shivers, liking it despite the peculiarity.

"Did you know," she asks, "I was intended for the gods? My mother made a gift of me at birth."

He knows, but says nothing.

"I want to serve them. Really, I do," she muses. "I am not sure I know how anymore."

"You serve them as I serve them."

"How?" she pleads. "Tell me. I promise to do it."

"Your gift is your purpose. Just as my gift is my purpose."

She pulls back, thinking, studying him for the answer and getting none. "But what is it?"

"To heal."

"Man knows you for punishment."

"I also reward."

"Reward for what?"

"The judges report to me of men and their acts. The bad men and the good. Both stand before me." This pleases her, which pleases him. "When they are good, I commend them for it."

"What do they get?"

"Land. Beautiful fields, crops, pasture."

Persephone thinks about it. "But when you summon them, the kings are afraid."

"Yes."

"Because man knows you for punishment," she repeats.

"Consequences are a balancing. That is how they heal," he says.

Swallowing she asks, "And my purpose. Is it to heal?"

"What do you think?"

"I thought maybe it was to help you remember."

His brow creases. "Remember what?"

"Who you are."

"I know who I am," he says. "I am your keeper, and I have failed you."

It comes out before his pride talks him out of it.

"What else?" She delivers a petal-soft kiss on the corner of his mouth, his cheek. "You can whisper it, if you want. No one will hear except me."

His mouth brushes the soft bend of her ear, stroking the peachy down against his bottom lip.

For her ears only, he says the words—hot, hissing words that have been steaming and building the pressure to crack through.

"You know I love you. I adore you."

She flings her arms around his neck and kicks her feet up behind her in sheer delight.

"I knew it!"

"Your needs and wants are mine." Hand shaking with need, he pulls her gown over her head. "Your friends are my friends, and your enemies—"

Face alight with an unspoken memory, she asks, "—shall be punished forevermore?"

"Yes. That, too."

He cradles her, naked, in his arms and lays her down

"Then, *Theíos*," she says, flipping over and astride him, "you should talk to your council."

Her eyes glitter like dark amber jewels in the lamp light.

 "You mean the judges?"

And she heaves a sigh and begins:

"Well. Just one."

A golden-eyed wolf stands at Hades's right.

Aeacus squints through the smoke. It is early. His eyes have not adjusted to the sun. Despite the daylight, a fire burns high for warmth.

Hades and Cerberus warm themselves beside it, next to the wolf.

Drawing closer, Aeacus recognizes it for hide. The ears of the wolf protect Persephone's head. The fur covers the soiled yellow gown she wears underneath.

It is comically big on her. She wears it like a child.

Aeacus ignores her and greets Hades with, "Lovely day."

A log crumbles inside the flames. Sparks drift upward, and the three mastiffs sit nearby, gnawing on the bones from a morning meal.

Aeacus realizes quickly: the soldiers are gone.

High in the perches of the trees, the nearly imperceptible outlines of the Erinyes shift on their branches. They observe from above and likely from within the thickets.

"Old friend," Hades begins in his too-quiet voice, "I have a problem."

Aeacus clears his throat.

"What sort of problem?"

Hades's eye sockets are pits of darkness. The luminous hands of his bride latch to his arm.

Aeacus never acknowledges the girl. He cannot fixate on her, lest his own hatred taint the charge around his body and betray him.

"Your queen," Hades says, "believes you want to harm her."

"Is that so?" Aeacus laughs, so very shocked by these girlish concerns. "How troubling. May I ask why?"

"Lots of reasons," she says with a lilt that makes her sound witless. "Mainly because you say mean things and try to get me in trouble, and you called me a menace, and that is how you treat an enemy."

Every emotion in his body must be betraying him right now. Every murderous thought, written in his colors. Aeacus tries not to grit his teeth.

"I think we were all more upset last night than we are today. For my words, I apologize. I hope you will forgive me."

"Yes I do!" she says, genuinely pleased. The furred hood sinks farther down her forehead, obscuring her view. She pushes it up and blows a lock of hair from her eye. "Thank you for saying so." She tugs at Hades's sleeve. "May we go now, *Theíos*"

"No, beloved," Hades continues, level-staring. "Not yet."

Beloved.

Goosebumps rise.

Hades says, "To harm the queen would be treasonous."

"I certainly agree."

Hades says, "Good."

More silence. Aeacus struggles to keep his mind blank. Sweat trickles beneath long hair the color of steel.

The dogs lick their snouts and resume chewing on the bare bones of something large.

"Then," Hades says, "you will not mind if I take a look."

His beard hides the color draining from his cheeks. Aeacus cocks his head and sticks out his chin as if he did not hear correctly. "A look?"

"It is all right, judge. You are pure-hearted," Persephone's young face is unflinching, brows upraised with curiosity.

She clearly knows about Hades's gift of insight. And if she knows, then it is because Hades elected to share it with her.

Suddenly, Aeacus recognizes the enormity of his folly. Persephone is no fleeting threat to be replaced by a high-class whore.

"Does our agreement not withstand the test of time?" Aeacus asks.

"If you offer yourself willingly," Hades explains, "the agreement stands."

To prove himself willing, Aeacus takes a leisurely step toward a log and sits. He laughs, hoping to color the light with a jovial charade. "Why is it necessary for me, your oldest and most trusted friend, to endure what a criminal would endure? Is loyalty such a fragile thing?"

"Loyalty is earned first," says Hades, "and nurtured thereafter."

"But you have already judged me as disloyal. You decided it the moment she said it was true. Why?" Aeacus does not feign the hurt in his voice. He supposes it has been there all along, lurking beneath the exterior. "Did I misjudge our bond?"

Hades only stares. He is not as level-headed as Aeacus believed. He is drunk from the cunt.

"Was I sentimental to think our bond like father and son?"

"I overthrew my father. You were all for it, if I remember."

"I encouraged it for *you*," Aeacus says.

"Mm."

"Look at you now," Aeacus urges, arms open to insinuate the prosperity of Erebus. "Is this not the best a man can do? You trusted me, and all of this became yours."

Leaves begin to shake in percussion, their dry sound all-encompassing as the Erinyes encourage justice to come of this spectacle.

His eyes burn.

He has often wondered what it felt like when men fell under the scrutiny of Hades.

The feeling of sand stuck between lid and organ—that is how it begins.

Aeacus springs up, holding a hand over his face like a man shielding the sun from his eyes. However instinctive the reaction, it makes no difference.

Thought pops up, unfettered.

Aeacus is accustomed to thinking wretched things. He is equally accustomed to swatting those reckless thoughts aside before they get him killed. Shove them down. Deep down. But where do those thoughts go?

As the ache overtakes his skull and thoughts fly out into the ether, he realizes: the mind is a closed box. Inside, devilish thoughts hunker in corners. Propriety and self-preservation keep those devils in check, locked tight. Now, an iron bar pries the box open. The top of his skull screams at rising pressure. Teeth grit. Tears stream from the inner corners, turning the world red and watery. Blood trails into his beard.

The box is open, and monsters break free.

Thoughts erupt, ones that have not left his mind since he first had them. The recent ones spring up first. Thinking, just last night:

How do I kill her and get away with it?

While she slept, he studied her. Just a minute or two of cutting off her breath, and the menace would be gone.

His mind purges, one thought triggering another.

They should call her what she is: pallake. That is all she amounts to. A prisoner of war, used as a concubine.

His sins rush by in a series of insults and ill-intentioned encouragements.

A sickly vessel is no good to a husband.

These memories suck from his mind like marrow sucked from a bone. The pain sears from the top of his head down to his ears. He tastes the metal of blood as it floods past the beard and onto the tongue.

Guidance, terrible guidance for the gullible daughter of Zeus—

"Purge the caves, and you will know peace."

Mind flayed, the act of controlling his thoughts seems ludicrous now. How was he ever able to detain them? They are snatched from him as easily as one can snatch a blanket from an infant.

Hades will stop soon. He has discovered what he needs to know. Aeacus prays it will end, leaving him with sight.

The pressure increases.

Aeacus gags. It is not only his eyes that bleed. It floods from inside his nostrils, down his throat. It tickles the insides of his ears. Men sometimes fall victim to a terrible pain in the head, rendering them without speech, without ability to move one side of the body. In a moment of panic, Aeacus considers a life of this kind. Invalid. Useless.

This panic falls secondary to the thoughts foremost in his mind.

He sees the pregnant Leuce standing at the cliff's end.

His hands shove.

"We call this the Vanishing Point."

His blood-tinged sight fades to blindness. Hades's face is

now present only in his picked-clean mind.

Death-thoughts should be of glory, of nostalgia, of pride. Not these.

Opening the deepest kind of shame, Aeacus recalls with crystal clarity the early days when Hades was a boy.

Of teaching the boy to fight and speak for himself, while resenting the task and thinking:

What an odd little brooder.

Treating Hades kindly, knowing it would pay off some day. The child had been traumatized enough by his own father and happily accepted the next-best version of father in Aeacus.

The old man is fleetingly aware of being on his knees in front of the fire.

Aeacus, first judge of Erebus, feels his spirit detach from flesh. His body hits the ground.

The Unseen issues a final command to his bride:

"Deliver him."

"*Did your wife give birth to a deformed bull baby?*"

They walk past Knossos, where his son now reigns. Where Pasiphae, his wife, still lives.

Gods bless her. Bless the ones he left behind.

The palace spans far and wide, encircled by red pilasters upon the hill. Minos stops to admire it.

Though he cannot see it from here, it is easy to imagine the palace fresco of the red bull, set against the blue sky. Easy to imagine the painted walls of his throne room. How his own throne, small and modest in comparison to the throne of Hades, would make his tail bone ache if he sat for long.

As dusk falls, the horizon darkens with rose and purple. Fog collects at the base of the hill.

Heracles pauses. "Do you need a moment?"

"No." Minos picks up the pace. "We can be at the farmhouse by dark if we hurry."

The group travels south where Minos had "hidden" the bull. If one can hide a bull.

These sailors want to see Heracles capture it with only his hands, just as he claimed to kill the Nemean lion with his only his hands.

The oarsmen belong to Hades, and their allegiance lies therein. Even so, curious minds are quick to bend allegiances. And today, they want to see a legend in action.

As far as the citizens of Knossos are concerned, Minos is not supposed to be roaming free in the land he once called home. If he shows his face, they will recoil in terror, for he is exiled. Banished from the land he once defended in war.

Hades allows it because it achieves a goal.

"The longer it takes him to complete the feats, the longer it will be before Heracles comes for Cerberus. And the longer it will be before we capture him."

"Minos," Heracles calls from behind.

"What?"

"We can stop." Heracles lifts an arm in the direction of the palace. "If you want to see your family, we can set up camp while you go."

Minos turns. "My family has spent years rebuilding their lives since the day I was brought to justice. Why would I interrupt their lives now? They deserve peace. They deserve more than what I gave them."

"You gave them the kingdom. What more is there?"

"Dignity. Honor. Two things with which you seem unacquainted."

"If you do not want to be seen, I can help you get inside."

"Why? Do you want to assuage your guilt, son of Zeus? Hm? Give the old man a final moment with his loved ones before you kill him?"

Heracles calls out to the oarsmen, "Stop here! We will camp for the night."

His eyes never leave Minos.

"Minos, you are an old man. I hope you told your family goodbye. I hope you fled to Sicily knowing that there was nothing left unsaid, undone. If not, there they are."

"Stop if you like." Minos says. "In the morning, take the path south and keep an eye to your west. Watch for the settlement of Vathypetro. The farmhouse is around the back."

He had stolen the bull away from the citadel in case Poseidon decided to search for it among the Knossian stables. Minos continues walking. He will not stay the night here, pining over a kingdom lost.

"I believe a man is defined by the sum of his deeds."

In his youth, Minos thought the worst thing a man could do was die with regret in his heart.

"I do not want to be known for what I did. Do you?"

Yet sometimes the worst thing does, indeed, happen.

Seeing his resolution, the oarsmen follow him to Vathypetro. So does Heracles. The path cuts into the forest like a thin blade. When they emerge, acres of pasture spread out around them.

Night falls. They will eat and sleep in the field, where Minos cannot see the palace of Knossos glowing majestically on a hill.

While the oarsmen set up camp, Heracles shrugs a fur bundle from his shoulders. Heracles's pack is wrapped in bear skin. He flings it open, revealing a carefully folded blanket enfolding an array of goods. Heracles proves himself to be methodical and prepared in this way, with four torches and leather flasks for water, dried meat, and flint.

Heracles lights two torches and hands one to Minos.

"What is this for?" Minos asks.

"Are you coming with me?"

"Will you be capturing the bull tonight?"

"No, Minos. I thought it might be nice if I could see the thing charging at me instead of wrestling him half blind."

"I have no interest in reunion. I am a shade, an invisible helper."

"That poor farmer is going to answer my knock and piss himself. It might be easier if he saw a familiar face."

"I have made this easy enough for you already, son of Zeus."

Heracles shakes his head and stomps away. By now, the farmer has spotted them from his window. It is hard to miss fifty men setting up camp and making fires in front of your house.

Heracles's torch bobs from the field toward a hilly area where the modest farmhouse sits. Once he is out of sight, Minos wanders off, feigning the need to empty his bladder in privacy.

Torch in hand, he navigates the terrain.

Anymore, Minos considers his heart as a shriveled piece of fruit. Dead to any form of arousal. At night when he closes his eyes to sleep, he often cannot feel the beating at all. Now he feels the pumping of blood in his veins, like a young man on the brink of battle, filled with vigor.

His torch casts against a structure to the left.

The barn is old, shabbier than Minos recalls. Made of gray wood and stone and clay. There are barrels hugging one side of the barn, with nearby hay bales stacked into a pyramid.

He sniffs. The breeze carries the smell of death.

Minos takes a few steps in the direction of the wind, extending his torch.

There are dead sheep everywhere—one hundred or more, stiff beneath unshorn wool. He has never seen anything like it.

With an unsteady hand, Minos unlatches the barn door. Rusty hinges groan as he pulls it open.

Horses whinny inside their stalls. He hears them, but cannot see them.

The light catches a white form. A monstrous thing emerges from the darkness, moving slow. Light flashes against its horns, reflecting against red irises.

"Hello, old friend." Scalding tears flood Minos's eyes.

On a hill in Knossos, his old palace glows. His family dines. His wife sleeps alone.

He expected a rush of love when he found the bull alive. Hoped for it, perhaps.

But what he sees is an animal and nothing more.

"Minos, you have murdered children."

Fourteen youths, eviscerated by the horns of this bull.

Minos enters the barn. The hooves of the Cretan bull paw at the earth. Hot clouds expel from its nostrils.

"When you die, what you are famous for will become your legacy for all time."

In that instance, the bull charges.

"I deserved punishment, far more than what I received."

He cannot seem to move. Does not want to move.

There is a rightness in it. A balancing of scales, exacted in the blink of an eye.

FLIGHT

From inside the tent, Demeter cannot hear the onset of wheezing.

The coughing, however, begins like raindrops on a hard surface. It starts softly, sporadic. One cough subsides, and two more erupt. Demeter smiles, listening to the lot of them join in chorus. They gasp between uncontrollable bouts of hacking.

She sits back on her heels. Her skin burns and itches from poisonous sap.

There comes a piercing scream. One of the other captives must have acted too quickly. Fled before the toxins had fully overtaken their captors.

Demeter closes her eyes, breathing long and deep through her nose.

Two more screams erupt, each less energetic than the one before.

Swallowing, throat parched, Demeter waits for crescendo. She waits for the sound of thirty chests heaving. For the fitful coughs of an entire ship of men whose throats have mysteriously begun to itch and swell. Whose very insides seem to itch, tongues thickening, having eaten fish cooked and coated with the soot of poison vines.

She scratches at her arms and neck. They bleed, but she sits calmly and listens to the song of their torture.

As soon as the noise reaches its peak, Demeter covers her mouth and nose with a blanket and emerges onto the beach.

In the orange flickering of the fire, the Sea People spit and vomit upon sand. Some have fallen unconscious from swollen airways. They drag their nails over their necks and arms and chests, unable to find relief.

The body of the sick captive lies, motionless, speared through the middle.

Demeter looks to the tent of the elder slave. The leather flap has been thrown open. Footprints lead from the tent to the path they had traversed earlier today.

North, the only path there is. There is sea in every other direction.

Any Tyrrhenian survivor could decide to follow those prints if they bother to chase down an old man.

One of the slavers sits upright, lips blue, gazing at her through puffy, watering eyes. He had lit the camp fire himself, but left the kindling to the slaves. Oily hair hangs over his shoulders.

Demeter approaches. Peering at her, the Tyrrhenian wheezes, *"Un."*

You.

Demeter plucks Hecate's bow drill out of the sand and tucks it beneath her armpit.

Slipping around the tent, she removes a stake from the ground. She unwinds the wool blanket from around her mouth and folds it around the spike and the fire-starting tools until the bundle is secure. At the cliff, Demeter presses her back to the stone and side-steps around it.

Waves crash against her knees. The coldness hurts. She clutches the wool bundle overhead to keep her bundle dry.

The shore widens as Demeter navigates around the headland.

She staggers beyond reach of the waves, but close enough to allow the tide to erase her footprints.

She watches the evidence of herself disappear.

Throughout the night, Demeter heads south, keeping to the coastline and scratching her arms and neck raw. By morning, she has traveled around the tip of Attica.

The sun crests the hills and treetops, glistening against the body of Oceanus. Coastal winds bite through the fibers of her cloak.

Demeter makes her way inland and takes cover in a grove. She can use the shelter, but also the soil.

Groves thrive best in clay soil. Demeter grabs two fists full of loam and squeezes to test the dampness. She navigates among the twisted trunks, itching beneath the open, oozing blisters. When she spots a puddle of mud, Demeter drops beside it and slathers her arms and neck. It soothes her skin, allowing her muscles to relax and lungs to breathe without tension.

Her nose pricks to the stench of decay.

Three paces away, a fly-cloud swarms around the carcass of a goat.

If a thirsty man can see a mirage of water, then perhaps mirages can also evince in morbid forms.

Stretching into the fog, piles of limp fur scatter the earth. Goats. With the toe of her frayed boot, Demeter pokes the mound of brown and white fur. The carcass rocks in place, disturbing the flies.

She had begged the gods for destruction, and they burned Olympus at her entreaty.

"Do not forsake me."

The night that the skies rebelled against Zeus, the gods showed the Loud Thunderer that Kore belongs to them still.

Their divine will be done.

She wants to die. But she will not. She will serve them as faithfully as the gods serve her—until the day they decide it is done.

The clay relieves her skin and adds a layer of warmth. When she has walked the day away, she finds a cave in which to sleep. Shivering, Demeter unleashes the bow drill and spike from inside the folds of the woolen blanket. She throws the blanket over her shoulders, exhaling steam.

Crouched at the mouth of the cave, she presses down hard with a stone the size of her hand and turns the shaft. Powdered charcoal collects inside wooden cavity of the hearth board, and soon embers smoke and glow.

With gnawing hunger, she tracks a rodent like a hungry cat. The thing could be diseased. It is not. The gods would not keep her alive only to allow her to die by mouse.

She sleeps a sound, dreamless sleep. When she wakes, the sun is new and the morning cold.

She rips a thin piece of wool from the blanket, winds it around the spike, and dips it into fire.

Torch lighting the way, Demeter wanders forward and waits to see what the gods will do next.

She wanders north for three days. Close to the road, but not on the road. Subsisting on creek water and berries and the occasional bird egg. Shaking fingers siphon through the meager pickings along the way. Her feet are bleeding and split. Her hair is caked with the grime of days.

"Why would a perfectly beautiful woman let herself shrivel up like this?!"

Those who spot her from the road do not stop. Some men regard her with disdain, but mostly she is invisible in this state. No one disturbs her at all.

"You ruined me."

Demeter squints across the brush and dirt and sees a conglomeration of clay houses in the distance.

A fortification wall encases a city with fertile land and mountain views and evergreens that frame the road.

Olive groves abound. Cattle graze, and there are goats being herded to the east. Although winter seizes the land, the sun shines harshly against the back of her head. For hours, she has been walking without shade.

Not far from the grove, a circular arrangement of clay bricks is stacked to thigh level.

She notices the rope and the handle.

This is the day she finds the well. The day that the gods set Demeter to task, once again.

An inhuman image breaks through the gray scrim of unconsciousness.

Hulking shoulders, lambent red eyes.

It has the body of a man bulging with muscle beneath thick, wooly hair.

It has the head of a bull with ridged horns angled downward.

Air driven from him, Minos tries to gasp and finds nothing for his lungs to grab onto.

"This fabled creature can take the fall."

Minos strains for a breath. His back radiates pain from where he landed flat upon it. His chest aches and his ears ring a shrill sound.

One weak breath encourages another. When his lungs begin to function, Minos gasps and the musty, sweet stench of livestock floods his nostrils.

As consciousness restores, the hallucination recedes.

Both the body and the head belong to Heracles, who looms over him. "Minos! Are you—"

There is more to his words, but Minos hears the ringing in his ears foremost. Sparks dance inside the closed lids of his eyes.

Near his head, hooves disturb the ground. A wild, thrashing

sound.

"I do not want to be known for what I did. Do you?"

Hay sticks to his cheek, jutting out from his beard. Warmth spreads throughout his midsection—strange because he feels nothing but the warmth. Otherwise, the entirety of his core is numb.

The high-beamed ceiling twirls and dives into darkness. Minos focuses. Cobwebs adhere to the beams of the ceiling. The smell of livestock fades under the stench of burning straw. Not far from his outstretched arm, flames cascade from his dropped torch.

Fire rages at his side, scorching the sensitive underparts of his eyes and threatening to singe his beard.

Minos touches his belly. Pulls his hand away. Crimson.

A breeze parts the smoke. Heracles grips the horns of the beast. The bull pushes. Digging his heels in, Heracles shoves back, asserting a god's strength. The bull's head whips in an attempt to free its wide arching horns, shining like bone in the fire.

With a strong cry, Heracles rotates one horn toward the ground. The bull snorts and thrashes until Heracles is hoisted. His flailing feet catch the bull directly in the snout. Foot planted between the eyes, Heracles stomps twice. Dazed, the bull falls. One horn splinters at the tip.

Heracles hurls himself onto the creature and straddles it. "The rope!" He gestures to a peg on the wall.

"What you are known for becomes your legacy for all time."

Minos presses the wound in his gut with the wadded-up hem of his cloak. Nausea strikes.

The screeching animal bucks on its side. Heracles's arms coil around its neck.

Minos grasps the rope and throws it.

As Heracles binds the hind legs, smoke fills the barn. Minos coughs, spraying a fine blood mist. He shivers, teeth chattering.

Heracles ties the bull into submission. He must deliver it to Tiryns alive. One eye on Minos, he drags the beast out of the fire.

"Brother," Heracles says, slack-faced, "keep still."

There is no need to demand this. A floating sensation envelopes him. Pleasant, almost.

When Heracles returns, he pulls Minos into the clean air and props him against the exposed underbelly of the bull. Agitated breath distends and deflates the animal's belly, jostling the the middle of his back.

Horses burst from the barn and scatter across the field and into the night. Drawn by flames, the oarsmen drag troughs of water in vain. It will burn to the ground.

Heracles kneels before him, placing a hand on his shoulder. "Minos—"

"My sacrifice," Minos manages to say.

"I was never going to kill you, Minos."

"I know."

Overhead, the celestial bodies blur. He focuses there. The stars appear to swell brightly. Their brilliance merges, seemingly in formation, taking the shape of a horned creature against the black sky.

The legacy of Minos, already written in the heavens, if not placed there by gods, then by men.

"Talk to me, Charon."

"Do not drop dead on me, old woman, or I swear to the gods—"

"I have no plans of dying and leaving you to deal with my corpse. I just like knowing there is something better ahead soon."

Winter petrifies Hecate's joints. Earlier, her legs groaned, stiffening the farther they walked. With a little haranguing from Charon, Hecate had relented. Now she rides instead of walks, prompting a new ache in her hips.

"I told you. The fastest way to Asphodel is by water. I know a village. In Pheneus, five rivers unite. One of them practically leads to Hades's doorstep."

The promise of the nearest village dangles in front of her like a carrot. She can collect herbs, trade medicine for blankets and food. The pair of them have managed to encounter good charity so far, but she cannot tolerate the cold and hunger much longer. Even an animal needs a den and hibernation.

"They say that men who drink from this river end up dead," he tells her. "Poisonous water. The people of Pheneus know the trick to drinking it. You must sip it. It will make you vomit and cramp, but after a while you can grow invincible to the poison.

Problem is, most travelers have no idea and guzzle from it freely."

"That," she says, "is not the pretty picture I had hoped you would paint."

Charon sighs. "Very well. I was there once in the spring. There are fields, trees, lakes. Maidens frolicking in the flowery meadows, bunny rabbits and sweet berries and all that. Sound better?"

"But this is not spring."

"Death river or no death river, it is where we are now."

Mountains loom darkly, shadowed and barren and frosted at the top. The village nestles snug at the foothill.

"Help me down."

"Careful. It is muddy."

She lowers her foot onto the soggy grass, mindful not to slip and slide. Ruddy brown mud squashes against the soles of her boots. Marshland, she thinks. Their feet will be wet in no time, and as the sun god makes his way to the west, it grows colder.

To their left, a path trails up a forested embankment. A small procession appears with a priest leading the pack. Behind him, two novitiate girls with garland headbands muddy their pretty frocks as they navigate the path. A hooded priestess appears last. She holds the fabric of the hood closed beneath her pointed chin.

The priest regards them with disdain and carries on his way.

The priestess stops. "If you are travel-weary, you can find food and shelter at our temple."

"Thank you, Priestess," Hecate says, casting her eyes up the embankment.

Charon says, "Where can we trade this mule for a ferry?"

The priestess narrows her eyes. "Keep your mule."

Hecate and Charon exchange glances.

"For now, we can still offer you a meal and a pallet. In the morning, turn back. Return from where you came. There is no ferry, not anymore."

The priestess catches up with her company.

Hecate's eyes drift to the donkey trail. One person lingers at the top of the cliff—a woman wearing a dark cloak.

Intuition whispers.

"Come on," Hecate says, taking the mule by the bit. The hill is steep and rocky, in need of clearing.

By the time they reach the top, both are out of breath.

The woman walking toward them, away from the panoramic cliffside view, is clad in a tasseled cloak gaping open to reveal a tight, short-sleeved bodice. Multi-colored braids edge along the hems and seams of her gown. Against the wind, the skirt billows with blue and red and yellow material sewn together and overlapping like roof tile.

Light-brown hair coils down her back into a point, a thick headband of silver preventing it from blowing in her face.

This kind of elaborate garb belongs to no farm woman.

"Who are you?" Her face is oblong with prominent round cheekbones. Straight black brows accentuate the walnuts of her eyes.

Immediately, Charon clasps Hecate by the wrist and yanks her to the ground.

"Kneel," Charon says beneath his breath. "We stand before the daughter of a god."

Hecate does as he says.

"I am Charon, sea-farer and captain of—"

Skirt hitched, the noblewoman eyes the stump where his hand used to be. "Captain, you say?"

Shame flushes his cheeks. She may as well have accused Charon of sexual impotence.

"Indeed, Majesty," Hecate interrupts. "Charon is such a skilled captain, he can do it with one hand."

One corner of the woman's mouth lifts in a smirk. When she speaks, her gentle voice carries a lisp that adds to her charm. "I see. And what about you, crone? Are you a skilled sea-farer, too? After all, the daughter of Oceanus must be particularly fond of sea-farers."

It dawns upon Hecate to whom they speak. Her tendency to think aloud causes her to blurt, "You are Queen Styx, second-born of Oceanus."

Styx levels her chin and studies them.

"I am Hecate, keybearer to the temples of Matapan. I am honored to kneel before you."

"What does Matapan want from me?" Styx asks, looking tired. "Before you request anything, think carefully. These days, I have little to give."

"We request sleep, food, and ferry," Hecate says. "We have traveled from Olympus."

"Stand." Impatiently, she waves them up. "Tell me of Olympus. There is rumor of pestilence there."

"It is no rumor," says Hecate. "The fields of Zeus himself, no less."

Styx glances at Hecate's cloak, a garment as fine as her own. It gleams with gold piping along the hood. "You have been sent by Zeus the Loud Thunderer?"

Before Charon can speak, Hecate interjects, "We act in the interest of the King of Kings."

"You might say," Charon says, "we are on a diplomatic mission."

"What kind of mission?"

"We seek an audience with Zeus's daughter," Hecate answers, "the new bride of Hades the Unseen."

Queen Styx laughs, eyes pooling with moisture, and gives her head a shake. The tip of her nose is rosy from the chill. "You want to use my river."

Charon gestures to the mule. "We have this animal to offer in exchange for a boat. Nothing big, just something that will carry us safely to Asphodel—"

Queen Styx, ruler of Pheneus, has not stopped shaking her head. "My river is not fit for travel. It is unholy."

"Why do you say that, Majesty?" Hecate asks.

The woman motions for them to follow. She guides Hecate and Charon to the cliff's edge and motions below with a grand sweeping of one arm.

"Behold."

Hecate's knees weaken. Before she sinks to the ground, Charon grabs hold of her arm and steadies her.

What Charon had claimed is true.

Here, five rivers converge. From these heights, they glisten red in the setting sun.

All five rivers flow with blood.

Styx says, "My father, Oceanus, is punishing me for something. I wish I knew what."

"Abomination," Charon says.

"So I ask again," Styx says. "Do you still want to brave my river?"

Hecate swallows. Her companion remains silent.

With a little huff, Styx turns her back to the scene and walks away. "So I thought."

For once in her life, Hecate cannot speak.

Charon's palm is still wrapped around her bicep to prevent her from collapsing. Through the sleeve of her cloak, she feels his hand shake.

Dipping below the horizon, the sun god blazes orange. The mountain collects fog like a blanket drawn over the eyes, refusing to see what lay at its feet.

"Come then, 'diplomats of Zeus,'" mutters Styx. "My house will gladly receive you for a night or two."

Inside the central monolith, Rhadamanthus clutches the window sill with sweating hands.

From here, Asphodelian guards oversee the river. Two windows, each almond shaped, form the blazing eyes of a mastiff. Torch-lit calcite glows from within.

At noon, the sun positions itself perfectly between the valley walls and onto the surface of the water. Rhad hoped to be the first to greet the returning party, hoped that everyone in the party would, in fact, return. He did not know what Hades would do to Orpheus.

The snow blares with daylight. From inside the monolith's right eye, Rhadamanthus gawks in disbelief.

The river runs the color of fresh-drawn blood. The rapids spatter the snow alongside the riverbank.

Guards pace the banks with their mastiffs, ogling the flow.

A soldier ascends from the stairwell. "The Unseen is back."

"Thank the gods. Does he know?"

"Not yet."

Rhad nods, twisting his hands.

The Erinyes must have ushered them home through the forests.

Hades has been gone a day now. All of them, gone.

Underfoot, the wooden floor vibrates with river flow. The monolith's open mouth accepts the river and any riverine vessels along with it.

Today, there is not a boat in sight.

Rhadamanthus takes the stairway two steps at a time and trips over the bottom of his robe. He catches himself on the wall and slows down.

Exiting from the south side of the station, he stomps through bloody sludge, into the snow and onto the path where his horse is tied.

The mastiffs posted around the area have scarcely stopped barking and growling at the river. The high stink of dead fish rises in the air. Rhad covers his nose with his sleeve. The banks are foul, but along the road, the snow radiates a pristine white.

His feet taint the ground with ruddy tracks.

In this snow, it takes the afternoon to navigate the switchbacks and find his way to the lion gate. He is cold, wet, and filled with dread.

"The Unseen is back."

There had been no mention of Orpheus or Persephone.

On the way inside, Rhad instructs the slaves to gather buckets of snow and to dump them inside of urns for storage. The gods may show wrath, but they have a way of showing mercy to those who can redeem themselves.

Out of breath, he stops under the portico near the central courtyard. A few soldiers train. Guards linger. Their demeanor is casual, unperturbed. News of the river has not made it this far.

Rhad relishes this last moment of peace before panic erupts.

His brother's timing is terrible. Minos should be here. But he is not. He is across the sea, doing this crazy thing with Heracles—

Rhad ventures past the courtyard and to the cliff's edge.

Oceanus reflects an undisturbed blue.

His heart calms a bit.

Mercy, once again. Whatever they did to offend the gods, there is still hope of appeasing them.

He retreats to the warmth of the palace. The doorway to the assembly room is open and lit from within by the hearth's lively fire.

Rhad pauses in the doorway.

Hades sits beside the hearth, tipped forward, hands on Persephone's hips. She stands in front of him, stroking the back of his hair as he rests his forehead against her stomach.

"Are you sad, *Theios?*"

"No."

The High King's head is lowered, betraying no expression. This is the closest thing to vulnerability Rhad has ever witnessed in Hades.

The entirety of Persephone appears to shine with an essence of the sun. She runs her nails through the back of his hair.

"There is no shame in mourning," she consoles, "even if the person was bad."

"I mourn no man." Hades looks up at his bride. "I mourn the loss of trust."

Movement pulls Hades's attention to the doorway. A slave breezes by Rhad with a basin of water and a rag for washing feet.

Rhadamanthus looks down at his boots, dirtying the floor with slush.

As the slave positions the basin in front of a chair near the hearth, Hades motions to Rhad with two fingers.

Come in.

"Hello, Judge!" Persephone appears beside Rhadamanthus and pulls his cloak from his shoulders. "Here, let me take this wet thing. You sit."

Her eyes, skin, and hair beam white gold, as if Helius himself lights her from within. To get a better look at her, Rhad squints and cranes his neck. She nudges him toward the hearth.

There is both strength and lightness in her touch. Her eyes, both uncanny and innocent.

Rhad stops short of sitting.

The slave awaits. Hades awaits.

Inside the basin, the water is clear.

"Well?" Hades says.

"Majesty," Rhad says, "I have something to tell you."

"Yes. I know."

"You know?" Rhad sits, but when the slave starts to reach for his boots, he says, "No. Save the water."

Eyes cratered with exhaustion and sorrow, Hades dismisses the slave.

Persephone positions herself on the arm of Hades's chair, crossing her ankles prettily.

Rhad's mouth opens, but Hades interrupts.

"I gave the three of you more autonomy than you realize."

Rhadamanthus frowns. "What do you—"

"You had the autonomy of your own thoughts."

Gave. Had. Hades says this as if those times have passed. "Tell me the worst thing you have ever done."

Thoroughly dumbstruck. Rhad looks to Persephone and thinks:

Where is Aeacus?

What happened to Orpheus?

His eyes burn. He rubs them. The sensation passes.

"Aeacus was found guilty of treason," Hades says. "Orpheus is being escorted back to Thrace."

"Treason for what?"

Aeacus was certainly a challenge to work with, but treason?

Perhaps Rhadamanthus is more naive than he thought.

"For more sins than I can allow, even for someone who—"

Hades cannot finish the sentence.

Persephone slips her arm around his shoulders. "Someone who was very close."

Rhadamanthus's hands are freezing. His knees tremble. Despite the fire, he cannot warm up.

"Tell me the worst thing you have ever done," Hades says. "The worst of your sins."

The mere suggestion is enough to entice those sins to the surface.

"Has there ever been a time you conspired against those who offended you?"

Judge Rhadamanthus has sat through this questioning before. It is not intended to generate honest answers. It generates, instead, honest emotions that a man can ordinarily hide. But if the sinful memory emits the smallest hint of guilt or malice, the Unseen will latch on and bleed the truth right out of a man.

"Tell me what you think of me, the one you supposedly serve."

During this, Rhadamanthus says nothing. He does not need to.

Hades stares. His eyes focus just beyond the line of Rhadamanthus's body.

Rhad braces himself. He expects the sting in his eyes to resume, to worsen.

Persephone leans into Hades and loud-whispers, "I do not think he is bad, *Theíos*."

The Unseen must see the sadness that Rhadamanthus feels about being questioned in this way.

There are no ill-intentions to conjure.

Hades knows this.

He sees this.

Even Persephone, in her own naivety, is wise enough to recognize friend from foe.

"You have earned your privacy then," Hades says, weary. "I am glad."

"Majesty," says Judge Rhadamanthus, "I have no need for privacy. I will tell you everything you asked and more. Soon, I will. But if I launch into a lifelong story of my pure intentions right now, the sun will set before I finish. And you will not forgive me for letting this wait."

"Why is there blood on your boots?" Persephone notices, pointing to the leather.

Hades looks down at Rhad's boots. "What has you so afraid?"

"The gods."

Demeter peers inside the well, smelling fresh water and relishing the faint mist on her cheeks.

Footsteps shuffle within the grove. Soft-colored chitons ripple between the olive trees. Youthful voices ring pure.

One by one, girls traipse into the clearing where Demeter sits beside the well.

The littlest girl leads the pack. She races to the water, unflinching.

The other three girls slow from their buoyant jog into complete stop.

Cherubic faces stare at her with alarm. Demeter returns their stares with adoration.

"Hello!" chirps the smallest. Braids hang over each shoulder. This sweet little child, only five or six years old, runs to the well. The myrtle garland on her head shakes askew. With a proud chin and natural uplift to the corners of her mouth, her face rests in a smile. She leaps up, grabbing hold of the crank, and hangs there with her legs bent at the knees. The handle sinks from her weight. At the bottom, the taut rope jostles the bucket.

Demeter answers, "Hello." The cadence in her voice softens an otherwise frightening appearance. So as not to scare the little girl, she hides her scabbed arms inside the cloak.

"My name is Demo!" The child beams the introduction, swinging from the crank and poking her tongue through the gummy gap of her missing front teeth.

"Demo, you say?"

"Ye-es," Demo sings.

In the field between well and grove, the two other girls budge. Apart from the mole differentiating them, they are identical in appearance and a few years older than Demo.

The twins approach and study this emaciated stranger with a rash creeping from under her cloak and up the exposed part of her neck, face scarred by hail.

"Demo?" Demeter says, playfully because a playful stranger might not alarm them as much as a suffering one. "Demo is almost my name, too."

"Nuh-uh," the little girl giggles.

The twins draw nearer.

The fourth and final girl—a *kore* on the cusp of womanhood—finally realizes that she is doing a terrible job of protecting her younger sisters by allowing them to chatter with such an unsightly, haggard stranger. Built stout like a boy, she carries a bronze water jar and quickens her pace to join her sisters at the well. A golden clip shines in her upswept hair. All the girls are immaculately clean. Their sandals appear newly made of fine leather.

Little Demo simply asks, "Who are *you*?"

The four sisters have the same square shoulders and hips, the same swarthy skin. They look at Demeter expectantly.

"My name is D—"

How can she stamp this withered flesh with the once-mighty name of De-meter?

The Mother.

The name feels wrong on her lips.

"My name is Doso."

Her name was Doso once, until she became the mother of Zeus's child, the mother who fed an entire polis with bounty from her family's farmland. The mother of novitiate priestesses who had looked to her for spiritual nurturing.

The Mother of many.

Before that, there was only Doso.

"Oh I see! Do-so!" The girl taps Demeter's shoulder and then points to herself. "De-mo!" She giggles at the simplicity in this comparison.

The twins are less jovial, but innocence still allows them to smile with curiosity.

"I am Kleisi, and this is Kalli."

Of the four maidens, Kalli strikes her as the shy one. The mole on her cheek could be the reason. Insecurities have a way of quieting a girl. She does not even open her mouth to breathe, as if doing so would only encourage speech.

The chattier Kleisi squints at Demeter's exposed rash. "What happened to your neck?"

"Poison vines."

"You should be more careful, Lady Doso," little Demo says with a wag of her finger.

"Yes, it was silly of me."

Now the eldest girl interrupts. "Kalli, help Demo or this will take all day."

A silent Kalli goes to the crank and gently swats Demo away.

"You do not live in Eleusis." The eldest places the water jar onto the bricks and folds her arms.

Demeter admires her. "What is your name, *kore*?"

"Thoe."

"Thoe, you are correct. I do not live in Eleusis."

The crank groans and squeaks. Demeter watches the bucket

ascend, dripping fresh water.

Little Demo plops down next to her and grins with envy. "You are dirty."

"Demo!" snaps Kleisi. "You are so rude."

"We are the daughters of Kleos," Thoe tells her.

"Your father is a blessed man."

Wiggling a loose tooth with her tongue, Demo laughs. Her chuckles ricochet down the well. "Yes! Because he is the king of all Eleusis!"

"Ah, is that so?"

"What happened to you?" asks Demo, patting the top of Demeter's hand consolingly.

Pulling the sloshing bucket against her chest, Kalli transfers it to Thoe, who pours water into the bronze jar. The hooked handle of a ladle swirls inside. Once the jar is full, Thoe hands the ladle to Demeter.

"Please drink."

She has forgotten this simple pleasure, of water cooling the tongue and coursing down a dry throat. Her hands shake as she drinks. Breathless, Demeter thanks them.

The bashful twin speaks up. As softly as a kitten's mew, Kalli asks, "Do you need help?"

"Girls," Demeter says, "you are very kind to me. Your father must be a fine ruler."

"He is!" agrees Kalli.

"And your mother," Demeter says, "should thank the gods for you every day."

"She does!" the little one cheers.

There is something confident and savvy about Thoe, the eldest. Kore lacked this type of maturity. Kore had the body of a woman, the mind of a child.

A weak girl is doomed as a bride to Hades.

"Lady Doso," Thoe says. "You look unwell."

Lately, Demeter doubts everything. Every reprimand and correction, every indulgence she allowed her child, every sentence she completed on Kore's behalf, thinking she was helping. Protecting her, sparing her from suffering.

Perhaps Kore retained a child's mind because Demeter wanted it that way. She knew what she was doing—did she not? Making Kore so timid, so controllable?

Demeter smooths the grimy hair poking from the hood of her cloak, unconsciously tucking it behind her ear to appear less pathetic somehow.

No mother is perfect enough to churn out children like these. Compassionate, strong children ready to take on the world. They must be a sweet mirage. The well, a mirage.

"Are you sick?" asks Demo.

Demeter takes another drink, this one longer than the last.

"Why are you wandering around by yourself?" Kleisi adds, since the other girls are already asking questions.

"I am not from your beautiful polis. I am from Crete."

"What is Crete?" says Demo.

"Stupid," Kleisi says. "Crete is an island far far far down past Erebus and across the sea."

"I am not stupid, STUPID," Demo whines, shoving her sister who laughs.

"Why have you come to Eleusis?" Thoe asks.

"I found myself here by chance."

Kleisi scrunches up her nose. "Chance?"

"Do you know of the Sea People?"

The stoic display of maturity flies from the eldest girl's face. "Sea People?"

"What Sea People?" Demo asks. "Do people live under the sea?"

"Sea People are bandits on ships," answers Thoe.

"Oh."

"They burn down cities and steal things."

"Oh!"

"Not only things," Demeter points out. "They also steal people."

Demo rolls her eyes. "How can you steal a person?"

"Did the Sea People steal *you*, Lady Doso?" Kalli whispers, hands cupped over her face in horror.

Demeter's mind whirls. Perhaps their mother does not protect her children from the horrors of life. Perhaps she scares them with the truth.

Any more, Demeter does not know what is right or even if there is such a thing as right in motherhood. She only knows the gods have given her a well. They have placed her with these girls.

"Yes, the Sea People captured me," she begins. "We docked in Thorikos—"

Four innocent faces gaze at her. This is hardly a story for children.

"—but I escaped while they sat by the fire. I am fine, girls. Aside from an encounter with some poison vines."

Fearing herself to be the only doubter, the youngest child looks to the older ones to see if Lady Doso is truly fine or pretending.

"The Sea People are dangerous," Thoe says. "Our city wall keeps them out, though. My father says whenever a pirate is captured, he is sent straight to Hades."

The replenished water in her body now flows from Demeter's eyes.

"The Unseen is no unfitting husband."

"You have suffered an awful lot," Thoe says, placing her hand on Demeter's shoulder. "Let us help."

Lowering the bucket, Kleisi shrugs. "Come with us."

"Yes!" squeals Demo. "Come with us!"

 The eldest nods. "There is food at the temple."

"I would never take without giving."

"But," says Thoe, "what have you to give?"

"Only myself."

What is she saying? And why is she saying it to these girls, who clearly have a mother who loves them? Some queen of Eleusis has four beautiful daughters all to herself, while Demeter has nothing.

"The Sea People took me to be a slave. I am no slave. But I am a servant. Perhaps the gods will it."

She is no one unless she is Mother.

She can roam the earth, she can beg the god Erebus for death, she can hide under the guise of another name. But she is Mother. Without this role, she is Naught. Her life belongs to the gods. They keep her alive. In Thorikos, they had showed her why.

"Perhaps," she babbles, "there is a house in need of someone to care for their children. That kind of work would be good for me, I think. I could see to the tasks of any man or woman in need of help."

Demeter's cheeks burn with shame. Crying in front of these girls. Begging for work. She is too hungry and depleted to control her own tongue.

She shakes her head. "Forgive me for being so—"

The sun dips farther east, kissing the tops of olive trees. Demeter stares at the blinding light. The rays of Helius are like a reminder.

"I greatly respect you and feel sorry for you as you grieve over your child—"

Kalli, the quietest, reaches out for the haggard stranger's hand. Touched by the rays of Helius, her silhouette appears to beam with divine authority.

"Lady Mother," she says, "the gods want us to help those who suffer. Our family will take one look at you and give you whatever you need. You can wait here, if you want us to ask permission first."

"Or," Kleisi snickers, "you can argue about it with the gods."

The girls laugh at this, the most ridiculous notion in the world for a mere mortal.

Demeter laughs too.

Taking the bronze water jar from Thoe, Demeter balances it atop her head. She follows the children beyond the field, past the grove, and through the walls of Eleusis.

The following day, the well no longer holds fresh water.

Persephone has never been inside a throne room before.

The space is interesting, she supposes. Dark . . . severe. But, otherwise, nice.

This morning, Hades shows her his throne before anyone else turns up, even the herald.

She is to spend the day here with him and Cerberus.

"Every day," he had told her. "From now on."

Persephone grips his hand inside both of hers, hugging his arm and strolling beside him, pleading.

"But I think I can fix it, *Theíos*, I really do."

He says nothing in response, so she corrects herself:

"I *know* I can. I should. I am supposed to!"

Cerberus pounds up the stairs to the throne. Hades nudges her lower back, urging her to go.

Something changed in him when he saw the river. He questions himself now.

"*Theíos*, you have not offended the gods. It is impossible."

"I never claimed to think so."

His silence says it. Throughout the night, he had wanted her body often. His desire, unchanged. Yet, in between, he kept silent or grumbled one-word responses.

Persephone should allow him his sadness. He regrets what happened because he is sad, not because what he did was wrong.

"You are not so good for my husband, I think."

When he apologized, she had forgiven Aeacus. Everyone deserves forgiveness if they are sorry—but Hades, in his wisdom, had seen unforgivable things. He must trust his judgment.

She hates that her husband doubts himself because of a river.

Anyway, Persephone knows a test when she sees one. Mother told her all about the gods and how they test.

"I could hold ceremony and appeal to the gods for cle—"

"I said no."

"But why not?"

"Because," he says, and she hears the old irritation in his voice, "something happens to you when you summon the gods."

"A bad something?"

"It makes you sick."

"But I am well!"

He takes her face in his hands. "Do you remember what you promised?"

"That I would listen to you?"

"Then listen to me."

At the top of the stairs, the golden helmet of Hades gleams on its pedestal—an ornate, disembodied skull with hollow eyes. She inspects it, awe-stricken that anyone would wear it on their head all day. It is exceptional and precious, a piece of art.

Hades watches her. Always watching.

"You wore that in battle?" She marvels, hands hovering around it but not touching. "Is it really gold?"

"Yes."

"May I touch it?"

"You may wear it." He approaches from behind, reaches around her head, and lifts the helmet from its perch. As she turns, she slides her buttocks along the front of him. She can feel his sex through the fabric. On purpose, she grinds into him. It makes him happy, like petting a dog.

The golden skull descends onto her head. Once he releases it, she squawks and clutches the sides. Her laughter and words echo inside the gold. "It is so heavy!"

Hades removes it. The faint smile on his mouth makes her heart squeeze. She wants to keep the smile there always, so she kisses him full on the lips. She cannot stand his unhappiness.

Here, Persephone stays the day with him. She is pleased to do it!

At first.

Standing beside him at the throne is not as glamorous as she expected. Most of the kingly business consists of men arguing with each other over landholdings or goats. The rest of the business is about men murdering each other over landholdings or goats.

Interrupting these encounters, farmers beg for aid. A plague, they say. Overnight, disease mysteriously claimed entire herds of cattle. Pigs and sheep too.

A day of this, then two. Then three and four.

"Every day. From now on."

By the fifth day, she is ready to pull her hair from the roots.

When the night comes, she folds her arms and returns his silence to see how he likes it. Persephone strips quickly, as if it were a chore, and then falls back onto the bed with her arms and her hair splayed. She sighs loudly.

Hades undresses slowly. Watching watching watching.

The silence is maddening. How can he stand it? How can he say *nothing?*

He kneels between her legs. She turns her head to the side.

"Why are you pouting?"

She bolts upright. Her hair flies wildly around her face and shoulders. "Because, *Theíos*, look at everything that has happened. The river and all those animals dying—"

He sighs, distracted by her nakedness, gripping beneath her knee and roughly stroking her thighs.

"—and even though I should not have done what I did for Orpheus, I still *did* it. And I purged Tartarus, too! You had to bring in the tribal women to make Tartarus seem bad again!"

"I will think about it."

She blows a strand of hair from her eye. "Any time my mother used to say that, it meant no."

He kisses her before she can say anything else, continues kissing as he pushes her down and crawls on top.

Further attempts at talking result in more kissing, making it impossible to talk.

The next day is much the same. Landholdings and goats.

Runners from distant lands approach the throne to petition for aid.

They all say the same thing:

"The earth is failing."

Any man declaring the end of the world is hit with the sobering wisdom of the Unseen:

"The goddess, Gaia, will live eternally, long after your mortal body turns to dust."

But there are others who say:

"The gods are angry."

This only spurs Hades's silent doubts.

Finally, during court one day, something interesting happens—except, it is a very bad something.

The herald announces an official-looking guard. He appears like the others appear: shaking and panting. Being in the presence of her husband brings out a fear in men that she has never witnessed before. They quiver and sometimes faint.

The guard stops at the bottom of the steps, kneeling with his helmet to his chest, greasy hair plastered against his head.

This one is dressed in Knossian colors.

"Oh!" she exclaims. "You are from my home!"

Hades tightens his grip on her wrist.

"Savas of Knossos," Rhadamanthus says, "why do you approach the Unseen?"

Persephone's heart soars. "Savas? It is me, Kore!"

Savas tips his head for a better view. She is positioned high at the top of the staircase at her husband's left.

Hades dislikes her speaking out like this, but only because he does not understand her elation.

Mother!

Probably by now, her mother has heard about the new High Queen of Erebus. Perhaps Demeter sends forgiveness for what Kore did, leaving like that.

Hades springs to his feet.

She and the judge jump at the abruptness of it. The dogs also leap up, ears pricked and heads craning with bared teeth.

Hades stands very still.

At the bottom of the stairs, Savas of Knossos rubs his eyes.

The Unseen holds out his hands, calming Cerberus before it is too late.

"Savas of Knossos," says Hades, "you may go. Thank you for your message."

Rhadamanthus furrows his brow. "Message?"

No! He cannot! Not before she asks about Mother.

"Wait, *Theíos*—"

"Take him out." The guards escort Savas from the throne room. The man looks both confused and relieved, throwing a curious look over his shoulder in Persephone's direction on his way out.

Hope of seeing her mother is also on its way out. The panic turns her livid. She is about to tell him so when Hades grabs her arm and says to the judge, "Follow me."

Inside the assembly room, Hades motions to the chair beside the hearth.

He instructs Rhadamanthus to sit down.

Rhadamanthus sits, as perplexed as she.

"Rhadamanthus," Hades says, sitting opposite the judge, elbows on his knees as he leans in. "Minos has fallen."

Persephone's face must look like Rhadamanthus's right now—drained of color.

"The Cretan bull is on its way to Tiryns, in Heracles's custody."

Poor Rhadamanthus! His eyes moisten, and she places a hand on his shoulder.

Rhadamanthus stammers, "H-how?"

Persephone goes to the table to pour him a cup of wine.

Behind her, Hades says, "He was gored."

The door to the assembly room is ajar. In the gathering hall, she notices Savas recovering while the slaves offer him refreshment and wait for his nerves to calm.

"Gored?" Rhad's voice is wet with emotion, but Persephone cannot see his face because she is preoccupied.

Savas recuperates, just steps away.

For once, Hades is not paying attention. "The bull got him—"

"—but it was not his job to interfere with the bull," Rhad says. "Heracles was to do it—"

In the hall, Savas drinks from his cup and says something to one of the guards standing nearby.

With one fluid movement, Persephone slips into the hall and hurries to Savas.

"Highness?" His bloodshot eyes widen as she draws near.

"*Kore*?"

"Savas!" She drops to the ground beside his chair. "Is my mother well?"

"Demeter is well." He inspects her strangely. "I mean she was well when I last saw her." Savas regards her, the corner of his mouth cocked in a smile. "You look so different."

"Please," she whispers, "I need to know if she forgives me."

"She would forgive you anything."

"Really?" She nearly cries.

"I have not seen her in a season. She left the temple, the *damos,* even her servant."

"Left where? What do you mean she left?"

"To look for you."

With a glower and clenched fists, Hades emerges from the assembly room. It does not phase her. She is delirious with gratitude.

Savas falls to the floor in supplication.

"*Theíos*!"

Hades's grip fastens around her arm.

He clings because he adores her—that is all. Why else would he cling so tightly?

"My mother is looking for me!" she says. "Savas told me himself!"

Now that she thinks back on it, Persephone no longer knows why she thought her mother was so bad. Demeter only wanted the best for her. A child could not ask for a more attentive, loving mother.

Sometimes Persephone wonders about Orpheus. Curious if he moved beyond his clinging.

Hades considers the desperation in her face.

"Where is the mother now?" he asks Savas, whose forehead touches the floor.

Savas tells them, "No one knows."

Hades sees the enormity of her longing, and so he must also see the enormity of her disappointment.

Persephone is sure of this, for Hades sees everything.

But there is no mistaking the noise from her husband's throat.

A faint sigh.

The sigh of relief.

ACKNOWLEDGEMENTS

So many helping hands go into the final stage of the book-writing process. I want to thank my editor and grammar guru, Ron Butler, for working tirelessly to get these edits back to me in a short period of time. Thank you to Robert Paxton from *The Western Traditions Podcast* for his support of *The Rape of Persephone* and *A Mother's Nature*. I am extremely thankful to my beta readers for their feedback.

I'll never stop thanking Terry Wolverton for the ten years I spent at *Writer's at Work* in Los Angeles. And I'll never stop thanking my family for cheering me on. *Especially* my husband, Aaron, who is my biggest cheerleader, only without the pom-poms.

Above all, I thank you, Courageous Reader, for shaking off the past trauma you endured during high school English class when the teacher assigned you Homer and then quizzed you afterward. I appreciate your willingness to give mythology another try. This time, no quiz!

GLOSSARY OF TERMS

Agora: a public space in ancient Greek city-states
Andron: part of a Greek house reserved for men
Chiton: a form of tunic that fastens at the shoulder
Chlanis: blanket woven by a bride for the marriage bed
Damos: citizens
Epaulia: (Ancient Greek) post-wedding ceremony
Gamos: (Ancient Greek) wedding ceremony
Hetaera: (Ancient Greek) prostitute
Himation: a wrap usually worn over a chiton
Kore: (Ancient Greek) maiden
Krater: two-handled vase
Mesméri: (Greek) noon
Nýchta: (Greek) night
Philos/Philoi: (Ancient Greek) friend/friends
Polis: (Ancient Greek) city-state
Proaulia: (Ancient Greek) pre-wedding ceremony
Proí: (Greek) morning
Theios: (Greek) uncle
Wanax/Wanassa: (Ancient Greek) king/queen

COMING JULY 2024

THE DEATHLESS
GODS

BOOK 3

About the Author

MONICA BRILLHART grew up in Kentucky, relocated to Los Angeles where she worked as a healthcare administrator for 20 years, and now lives in Sedona, Arizona with her husband, daughter, and dog. She has a master's degree in metaphysical science and a doctorate in philosophy. Her first novel, *The Rape of Persephone*, received the 2023 IndieReader Discovery Award for historical fiction. *A Mother's Nature* is the second novel in *The Rape of Persephone* trilogy.